CATHLYST

To Jesse Von Weinsler

Thanks for reading

PAUL BYERS

Paul

VARIANCE

Variance Publishing
1610 South Pine St.
Cabot, Arkansas 72023
(P): (501) 843-BOOK; (F): (501) 843-2675

Published by Variance LLC (USA).
www.variancepublishing.com

ISBN: 0-9796929-3-8
ISBN-13: 978-0-9796929-3-2

Cover Illustration by Andy Wenner
Jacket Design by Stanley Tremblay
Interior layout by Stanley Tremblay

Visit Paul Byers on the World Wide Web at:
www.paulbyersonline.com

11 10 9 8 7 6 5 4 3 2

For my big bro, Mark

ACKNOWLEDGEMENTS

Like many authors, I have a myriad of people to thank for bringing my dream to reality. I need to start with my brother Mark. His constant encouragement, analysis and his just-keep-plugging-away-at-it attitude helped push me through the slow times.

Behind every great man is a great woman, I'm not sure about the great man part, but I am sure about the great woman part. My wife, Cheri, for the last three years has put up with me disappearing for hours at a time, going down into my hole, a laundry room converted into an office, to write. Without her support, Catalyst would not have gotten done.

Thanks to Charity Heller Hogge, my editor, for her editing skills that make me look like a better writer than I am. Also to John Frisby, Andy Wenner, Mike Williams, just to name a few of the many good friends that God has blessed me with.

And special thanks to Stan Tremblay and Shane Thomson for their hard work in producing the new, revised edition of Catalyst.

ONE

THE car drifted slowly to a stop with its engine and lights off.

The driver hesitated for a moment, his eyes darting back and forth, surveying the area for any hidden dangers that might be lurking in the shadows. He knew this had been planned out to the last detail, but even with the best-laid plans, things could go wrong. A cold shudder traveled the length of his spine because he knew what the deadly consequences would be if this plan went wrong. He took a deep breath to calm his fears, pushed his glasses up off the bridge of his nose, and opened the door. Even before his feet touched the ground, two figures emerged out of the darkness and moved toward him like specters.

Both men were dressed in military uniforms, but in the dim, pre-dawn darkness, he couldn't tell if they were American, British, or German. The taller of the two phantoms spoke as he held out his hand. "Good morning, Doctor Strovinski. If ya'll just step this way, we'll have you outta here and back in England in no time at all."

As soon as the soldier spoke, Strovinski knew: American. He hated the way the Americans had butchered the English language with their slang, but this American was even worse. He had a . . . what did they call it? A Southern drawl? He thought the man sounded like one of those cowboys from their shoot-'em-up western movies.

Doctor Nicoli Strovinski was on the high side of his fifties with thinning brown hair, and his large waistline reflected the fact that he was a man dedicated to science and little else. "Let's be quick about this," he said in Russian. Let the Cowboy try and figure that one out.

The Cowboy replied politely in perfect Russian, "Right this way, sir."

So what? Strovinski thought. The cowboy can understand and speak Russian.

He followed behind them in silence, clutching his worn leather briefcase. The night air was cool and clear, washed clean by heavy rains earlier in the day.

In the stillness of the night, their shoes crunched against the gravel, sounding like a column of marching soldiers rather than just three men walking. They rounded the corner of a small building that he guessed to be a barn because of the foul animal odors coming from inside. Strovinski stopped dead in his tracks. It was a peculiar sight to see two fighters and a bomber parked behind the barn. But it was an even stranger thing to see a cow grazing peacefully under the left wing of the bomber and a goat rubbing its head against the propeller of one of the smaller planes. These cowboys must be smarter than he gave them credit for, he thought, getting three Allied aircraft this deep behind enemy lines.

Strovinski was a little disappointed with the small two-engine plane that was taking him out of Germany. He had expected to be whisked away by one of their big B-17 bombers. Although he didn't know much about American aircraft, everyone in France and Germany knew what the Flying Fortress looked like. After nearly three years of seeing the big plane dominate the skies over France and Germany, it had become the symbol of the advancing Allied forces. To those in France, it represented their impending liberation; to the German Army, it represented impending defeat. For Strovinski, perhaps it would mean a new life.

He followed the two cowboys around to the back of the plane and watched the shorter one climb up a small ladder and disappear into the black abyss. The taller cowboy motioned for Strovinski to follow. Drawing a deep breath, he realized that this was no longer a dream but that it was really happening. There was no turning back now as his foot came to rest on the first rung of the ladder.

He froze in mid-step, a cry of terror on his lips, as another apparition appeared from the black void in the form of a disembodied hand that reached out to grab him. The phantom materialized into a round, baby-faced crewman who was reaching out to help him up the ladder. The blond young ghost looked to be only eighteen or nineteen years old, barely old enough to wear long pants, let alone fight in a war. He wondered if he had made the right decision.

The young man reached out to take his briefcase, but Strovinski refused to give it up. It contained the culmination of nearly twenty years of work and he wasn't about to trust it to a child who didn't know the meaning of life. Not even for a second while he boarded the plane. Grunting, and feeling a little foolish for letting his vivid imagination get the better of him, Strovinski managed to hoist himself up through the small hatchway with one hand. Once inside, he let the boy lead him through the bowels of the plane.

He thought that a bomber by its very nature should be big and spacious, but reality proved him wrong. He struck his head twice on the short trip from the hatch to his seat. He quickly sat down and nervously fastened his seat belt.

The plane had a dusty and oily smell to it. He could also smell the telltale odor of gunpowder, sweat, and something else . . . Was it the faintest trace of fear that mingled with the other aromas? But was it the plane crew's fear or his? His stomach answered his brain's question by rumbling and reminding him of just how much he hated flying.

"GOLDILOCKS, Papa Bear, Mama Bear, and Baby Bear are ready for takeoff."

Captain Jack Lofton of the Royal Air Force, or RAF, shook his head at the radio message from the bomber as he flipped on the ignition switch to his Supermarine Spitfire, waking up his sleeping warhorse. The bloody Yanks and their silly code words, he thought. When he'd been asked to volunteer for a joint U.S.-British mission, he immediately agreed; but he'd signed on to fight the Germans, not recite nursery rhymes. He was "Mama Bear," and his wingman, Lieutenant Reginald "Reggie" Smyth, was "Baby Bear." What next? he thought. If they got in trouble over the channel, were they to land on the Good Ship Lollypop?

At twenty-six, Lofton had a soft, youthful smile and bright blue eyes that were in contrast to the premature weariness which now fit him like his uniform. He had been barely more than a boy when he'd joined the RAF, but after nearly five years of fighting he appeared to be the age of a man ten years his senior.

He looked over to Reggie, whom he imagined wore a grin from ear to ear, eager for the adventure to begin. A sad smile crossed his lips as he shook his head. He wondered if he'd ever been that young. With one last good tug on his harness, he signaled Baby Bear to take off.

The fast, steady rhythm of the British Rolls-Royce Merlin fighter engines joined the loping sound of the twin Pratt & Whitney eighteen-cylinder radial engines of the American's Martin Marauder B-26. They combined for a mechanical harmony that reached a pitched crescendo when full throttle was applied.

"Papa Bear to Goldilocks, Papa Bear to Goldilocks: the package is in the basket and we are on our way home."

CAPTAIN Griffin Avery of the Office of Strategic Services, or OSS, took off his headset and dropped it on the table. He let out a sigh of relief and rubbed the back of his neck. He pushed himself away from the table that held a fifteen-hour collection of cigarette butts, empty coffee cups, and several stale, half-eaten sandwiches and doughnuts. It had been a very long day and night.

From his basement office in a nameless government building in London, he had monitored the flight of the Three Bears and their pick up of Dr. Nicoli Strovinski. He had watched them since they'd left England in the pre-dawn hours, followed them across the English Channel and over occupied France. Now at last, they were on their way home.

Avery stood and stretched. At forty-five, his hair was already turning gray, but he took comfort in the fact that he at least still had all his hair—unlike his father, who was bald on top with only a fringe of hair running around the side of his head. He preferred to think that his graying temples gave him the distinguished look of a gentleman and not that of an old man.

He heard sharp, fast-paced footsteps coming down the hall and wondered who could be coming here at this late hour. The door opened and Avery sprang to attention. "Good evening, General," he barked with as much enthusiasm as he could muster.

"At ease," came the reply. At sixty-two, Brigadier General Arthur Size-more carried himself like a man half his age. He was a short, barrel-chested man with the personality and face of a bulldog that liked to chase parked cars. Like his height, his demeanor was short and direct.

"Got a hot date, sir?" Avery asked, seeing his boss was wearing his dress uniform. Immediately Avery cringed, regretting his choice of words. *Got a date?* What was he thinking?

Sizemore ignored Avery's feeble attempt at humor and surveyed the messy desk. He scrutinized the room like a father visiting his son's college dorm room for the first time and not liking what he saw. "My 'date' is with the chiefs of staff at a late-running state dinner—a damn waste of time, if you ask me," Sizemore replied, plucking at his collar that vanity wouldn't allow him to admit was two sizes too small. "This is the fourth scientist this month we've nabbed. Who is this guy again?"

"Doctor Nicoli Strovinski, one of Germany's top nuclear physicists. It's been suspected that for the last year or so he's been working closely with Werner Heisenberg, head of the Nazi atomic program. He's also known in the academic community for his work in quantum mechanics and—"

"Right, he's some sort of hot-shot egghead. Didn't he also work with Von Braun at Peenemunde on the V-2s?"

"Yes sir, that's why we decided to grab him. If Germany could develop some sort of atomic weapon with the V-2 as the delivery system, then they could hold the world for ransom. We have no defense against a V-2."

"Man, I'd love to tell Ike that we bagged this boy." Sizemore paused then grunted, his face even more serious than usual. "If he's so damn important, you'd better not screw this up. And remember, Captain"—he pointed his stubby finger in Avery's face—"it may be my butt, but it's your neck on the line here." Sizemore turned to leave and stopped when he reached the door. "And clean this mess up." He tugged at his collar again and disappeared.

As the door slammed shut, Avery collapsed in his chair. He wasn't sure if he was more relieved that the mission was almost over or that Sizemore was gone. He grabbed a pack of cigarettes out of his front pocket and lit one with his Ronson. Avery leaned back, took a deep drag, and put his headset back on. He would continue to monitor the flight until they were halfway over the channel. Only then would he relax and go to the airfield to collect the doctor.

Avery began foraging through the scattered doughnuts on his desk, searching for one that wasn't stale enough to use as a doorstop. He found an edible morsel buried amongst the greasy rubble and held it up as if he had discovered a nugget of gold, a look of triumph filling his face. He took a bite and sighed. It wasn't the freshest he'd ever had; if only he had some fresh coffee. He was devouring the last bite when the radio crackled to life.

"Break left Baby Bear, Baby . . . oh, bloody hell, Reg! Break left!" the voice on the radio shouted. "You've got two bandits behind you!"

Avery sprang up and checked the channel on his radio.

"Bloody good, lad," the radio blared again. It was the voice of Captain Lofton, and it sounded like they were under attack. Avery heard the roar of the airplane engine and the unmistakable sound of machine guns firing. How can this be, Avery wondered. How could the Germans have known about Strovinski?

"Goldilocks, Goldilocks, this is Papa Bear. We are under fighter attack! I say again, we are under attack. Mama Bear and Baby Bear have engaged."

The sound of the bombers' distress call shook Avery out of his stupor and he grabbed the microphone. "Papa Bear, this is Goldilocks, do you copy? Where are you? Do you copy? *Answer me!* Papa Bear this is Goldilocks, do you read me? Mama Bear, do you read me, over?"

"Breaking left. I'm going to flip over and bring him back in front of you," Smyth replied. Avery could hear and almost feel the tension in the young British pilot's voice

"Roger, swinging around now to line up." By contrast, Avery could hear the calm voice of the seasoned Lofton over the drone of his engine.

"You've got two more coming down on you, Reg, eight o'clock high!"

"I can't see them. I can't see them!" Smyth shouted desperately in the radio.

"They're right above the bomber, swing back to your left, behind the bomber, NOW!"

His mission was falling apart, yet Avery could only listen with morbid fascination as the battle unfolded before him. He was reminded of Halloween night back in 1938. He was home on leave and had just come back from the corner grocer. His mom had wanted fresh corn on the cob to serve with their steak in celebration of the return of their long-gone son.

When he walked through the front door, he found his mother hysterical, glued to the radio. She kept shouting about being under attack. He dropped the bag of groceries on the table and rushed to the front room. On the radio, the reporter was saying something about people being killed and that the Army was on the scene but the enemy had some sort of new weapon, some sort of death ray. Avery could hear yelling and screaming in the background and something that sounded like gunfire. The reporter shouted that they were under attack, and then there was silence.

His mother was on the verge of crying, and his father just sat there and held her, not knowing what to do. Avery was reaching for the phone to call headquarters when the radio came back to life and the announcer said that he hoped they were enjoying the broadcast of Orson Welles and his Mercury Theater production of *War of the Worlds*. It took some convincing, but his mother finally realized that it was just a radio show and not the end of the world. Upon pain of death, she threatened him and his father against saying a word to anyone that she had believed the broadcast.

Now Avery sat and listened as his own radio played out its own scene. Only this time, the sound effects weren't made in a studio and those weren't actors. Real people were going to die.

"My left aileron's hit, I can hardly turn!"

Avery could hear the rising fear in Lieutenant Smyth's voice.

"Steady, lad," Lofton calmly responded over the radio. "I'm almost there."

Then silence.

Avery leaned forward in his chair as if that could help him hear better, but there was nothing to hear. The only sound was the pounding of his heart. *"This is Goldilocks! Does anybody read me?"* he yelled in frustration shaking the microphone as if he could bully it into working. Why won't this damn thing work? "Jack! Do you copy? He broke the rules by using Lofton's name, but he didn't care. "Jack, where are you?"

Silence.

Avery was resigning himself to the fact that the entire mission had failed and eight lives were lost, when the radio blared again.

"What the bloody hell! Is that a red star? *REGGIE!*" Even through the roar of the fighter's engine, Avery could hear a faint explosion and he knew that Smyth was gone. Sitting in his warm and comfortable office, it was hard for him to comprehend that he had just heard a man die.

Avery sat like a statue, his chest barely moving as he breathed, a thousand thoughts bounced around in his head.

"Papa Bear, this is Mama Bear. Do you copy? Papa Bear, this is Mama Bear. Do you read me? Over." Slowly, like the incoming tide, Avery felt hope creeping back into his soul as he heard Lofton's voice on the radio. Perhaps Lofton had fended off the attackers and Strovinski was safe.

But the incoming tide quickly turned into a tidal wave as the radio blasted another warning: "Break right, Mama Bear, break right!"

"Look out, Mama Bear, there's another one coming down on you! Break! Goldilocks, Goldilocks, this is Papa Bear. Mama and Baby Bear are both down, repeat, both fighters are down! Am under heavy fire. Wait . . . top gunner! Watch that one coming down, nine o'clock high! He's in behind us, swing it around *now*! Tail gunner report! Report! Goldilocks we have—"

Silence: total, deafening silence now invaded his office. It smothered the room like a thick heavy fog, driving everything else out, all thoughts of reason, any lingering feelings of hope and, oddly, even of despair. The silence was so consuming that Avery found it difficult to breathe.

What had gone wrong?

Avery placed his elbows on the table and buried his head in his hands, trying to think. After a moment he leaned back and ran his fingers through his hair and noticed a small mustard and mayonnaise stain on his sleeve. His desk that looked like a high school cafeteria. He shook his head and sighed. Given the way the room looked, his stupid date joke and stains on his uniform, it was no wonder General Sizemore didn't have much confidence in him.

But Sizemore was wrong! He'd planned everything, down to the last detail. It had taken him three weeks to go through each phase, step by step, and to finalize everything into a complete plan. He'd checked and rechecked it all at least a dozen times. Each of his two assistants had gone over it with a fine-tooth comb to see if they could find any flaws. And there had been none. He'd seen to the security precautions personally to prevent this very thing.

He didn't know how long he sat there, seconds, minutes, hours; it didn't matter. He fumbled mindlessly with a cigarette and burned his fingers before he realized that it was already lit. What had gone wrong? They should have been in and out before the Germans had even realized that Strovinski was missing, yet they had known and had been waiting . . . but was it the Germans? Something that Captain Lofton had said over the radio, something about a red star. The only aircraft he knew that carried a red star were Russian. In the dark of night and heat of battle had Lofton confused the swastika for a star? Not likely. He doubted that a man with his experience would make such a mistake.

Even though the Americans, British, and Russians were all allies, as they pushed further and further into Germany, it was becoming a race with the British and Americans against the Russians in an effort to capture German technology and resources. Did the Russians somehow find out about their plan and shoot Strovinski down themselves, Avery wondered, rather than let the Americans have him? Or was it just a case of blind luck? Had the Germans just been in the right place at the right time and stumbled across the three allied planes?

It didn't matter now. They were all dead and it was his fault.

Avery stood and tilted his head from side to side, trying to get the kinks out of his neck. His mind was as numb as his body. He couldn't think straight. He needed to get some fresh air. This was the first mission in which he'd been directly responsible for the deaths of those under him. He'd sent men and women into France before to help the resistance and he'd found out later that some had been captured and even killed, but this was different. The Three Bears and Strovinski were dead because *his* plan had failed!

He grabbed his coat and wandered down the hallway, ignoring the few early birds arriving to work, then climbed the stone staircase up two flights to the street above. Wearily, he leaned against the heavy wooden door and summoned all his remaining strength to push it open. Avery squinted his eyes as he stepped out into the street. It was one of those rare, bright sunny mornings in London.

Across the street was a small tailor shop with a bouquet of colorful flowers in the window, a splash of color that seemed so out of place in war-weary London. Half a block down there had been a little family-owned bakery. They made the best glazed doughnuts he had ever tasted. Each time he went in there, the sights and aromas took him back to his once-a-month family trips into the city when he was a boy. On the first Saturday of each month, providing his father didn't have to work, he and his brother would ride in the back of their old Ford Model T as it rambled and rumbled down the dirt road twelve miles into Portland, Oregon. His mother said that his eyes always grew to the size of the doughnuts themselves as he gazed upon row after row of the delectable delights. And the aroma . . . the warm, soft smells of the flour and butter baking made it an almost magical experience.

Sometimes when he felt homesick, he had gone into the British bakery just to remember; his own little personal escape from the war. Yesterday, before all this had started, he had stopped in and bought half a dozen.

Sometime during the night, he had heard the rumblings and felt the impact of what he guessed was a V-2 rocket that had slammed into the ground nearby, shaking his old building to its cornerstone. The V-2s were Hitler's *Vergeltungswaffen,* or Vengeance Weapons. It was a 46-foot-high, 3500-mile-per-hour monster designed for pure terror. They weren't extremely accurate, but by carrying over a ton of explosives, they didn't have to be.

Today, the bakery was a burned out crumpled ruin. It must have taken a direct hit last night. How ironic, he thought, that yesterday, like the bakery, he had been busy and full of life and hope for the future. Now, both the street and his spirit were a pile of broken dreams and rubble.

TWO

THE laughter was loud, drowning out conversation, music, and tonight, even the war. At the far corner of the bar sat an old man known to everyone simply as The Colonel. He was in good shape for a man of 81, too old to fight but not too old to proudly serve his country in the Home Guard, ready to rout the Huns if they dared to stick their noses across the channel. The Colonel had flaming white hair, a large handlebar mustache, and a passion for life still burned deep in his bright, clear eyes. His skin was a tough and leathery brown, reflecting decades of service for king and country.

Tonight, like most every night, he sat at the bar, reliving the glory days of his youth to whoever would listen. He often spoke fondly of the lads of the 24th Regiment of Foot and those fateful days in South Africa at Rorke's Drift in 1879—the time of the great Zulu uprising.

He reminisced about how he was just a lad, only fifteen at the time, and of how he had run away from home seeking adventure. He could think of nothing more exciting than camping out all the time, so he lied about his age and joined the army. He would describe the smashing old uniforms—how good they all looked in their bright red coats, white helmets, and bandoliers! He recounted how he and the lads had stood toe to toe with nearly four thousand Zulu savages and held them at bay.

One day, Avery remembered, a drunk British sailor had called The Colonel a liar and said he had never been in Africa or fought against the Zulu. The Colonel was silent for a moment then slowly stood and unbuttoned the top two buttons of his tunic. With great care and reverence he pulled out a Victoria Cross that hung from a tarnished chain around his neck.

"Twelve medals were awarded that day," The Colonel said slowly, "but only eleven officially. It was the most ever issued to a unit for a single engagement. When the army found out that I was really only fifteen, they couldn't acknowledge that they had let a boy fight, so they let me keep the medal but made me swear never to reveal my true age at the time."

After that, no one ever questioned The Colonel again.

SITTING at a table, Avery noticed, off to one side, was a group of women—girls, really—from RAF headquarters. They were with the Fighter Command. Some had helped direct the magnificent Spitfires and Hurricanes which had fended off the Luftwaffe in the dark days surrounding the Battle of Britain. They were young and pretty, but several, those who had been around since the beginning, had a few more worry lines and a few more gray hairs than the newer girls. They were seasoned veterans at the ages of twenty-three and twenty-four. Few people knew of the hard work they did or just how close the Germans had actually come to winning the battle and invading England.

There were several small groups of British and American soldiers scattered throughout the bar, telling tall tales and swapping lies in hopes of impressing the local girls. There were also a few civilians about doing their best to set aside the war for a moment. But most of the patrons that night were American airmen. It was easy to tell the bomber crews from the fighter pilots, Avery thought. The fighter pilots usually flocked in groups of three to four, while the bomber crews stuck together in packs of seven or eight.

At the far end of the bar were four flyboys, fighter pilots. One gestured with his hands, describing in great detail his latest aerial victory. In the back of the pub sat a group of eight flyers surrounding two empty chairs. They were much quieter than the rest of the patrons as they raised their glasses in a silent toast, a scene that was often repeated. They were a bomber crew who had lost two of their own and were now saying good-bye. Next to them was an empty table with ten chairs stacked on top of it. The crew that didn't come back must have been well known and liked, Avery thought, for the pub to hold a table in tribute to them on such a crowded night.

Captain Avery sat in the back of the pub taking it all in. It had been two days since his report on the loss of Dr. Strovinski, and General Sizemore had not been pleased. He'd had dreams of moving "upstairs" and working with the big boys on major planning projects. But with the war winding down in Europe, his chances of being transferred to the Pacific and being involved with the invasion of Japan were all but gone now with the loss of Strovinski.

His less-than-glamorous nine-to-five job involved working with the resistance cells in France, gathering information about German troop movements, and aiding the recovery of downed Allied pilots. With the rapidly advancing Allied forces, he'd also been assigned the task of locating top German scientists and grabbing them before the Russians did.

With certain technologies, the Germans held a slight edge. In some cases, however, their advantage was monumental. Though the British had a jet powered fighter in the Gloster Meteor, it was no match for the German Messerschmitt 262 . . . and the Allies had nothing to counter the dreaded V-2 rockets. While Russia was an ally, the United States and Britain still wanted to make sure that they were in control of these new technologies. It was Avery's job to get the scientists, a job he had now failed at miserably.

Avery took another sip of his beer—or his pint, as the Brits called it. It was his third, and he was nearing that place where he felt no pain, a place that suited him just fine.

The Three Bears had been his plan. His operation from start to finish. It was supposed to show General Sizemore that he could do more than just pass messages back and forth between headquarters and the resistance. It was to prove that he belonged upstairs with the big boys.

But none of that mattered now.

He'd gotten good men killed. In three large gulps, he downed the rest of his beer and waved his hand at the waitress for another.

"Griff, my boy, why the look of a man who's just found out his mother-in-law is coming to live with him?"

Avery looked up from his empty glass and watched The Colonel spin the chair around and sit backwards in it, holding his beer in one hand and leaning forward on the back of the chair with the other.

"Do you know what I had to do today, Colonel? I had to write letters to the families of the men I lost on a mission . . . a mission that I planned. I planned it down to the last detail, but somehow it went horribly wrong. I knew one of the men personally. I even ate with him and his family. He had a wife and two little girls, four and six. We don't even have a body to give back to her to lay to rest. She has no grave to cry over, only this lousy piece of paper saying her husband was a hero and is missing in action. For God's sake, I can't even tell her what happened to him or where he went down. They died for nothing."

The warmth and humor in the old man's eyes drained. "We were in France," The Colonel began, "in the early spring of 1916 during the war that was supposed to end all wars. The nights were still cold, as Mother Nature still hadn't taken off her winter coat yet, and the rains that April were unusually heavy, turning our trenches and the no-mans land into a sea of mud, muck, and mire."

A humorless smile slowly crossed The Colonel's lips. "It's funny what you remember, but what I remember most, other than my lads, was the smell. The rich, earthy smell of the soil was invaded by the musty stench of everything rotting and covered in mold from the continual rains.

"We'd been stalemated for most of the month, neither us nor the Huns taking more than a few yards of ground at a time, when some general back at headquarters decided that he wanted the stalemate broken.

"Our platoon was handed the nasty assignment of taking out a German machine-gun bunker on a slight rise that controlled nearly the entire line in our area. If we were to advance at all, those guns had to be destroyed." The Colonel paused and closed his eyes for a moment. Avery couldn't tell if he was trying to remember or trying to forget what happened that day.

"It was particularly cold that morning," he resumed, "and a thin layer of ice covered the mud. We were all cold so were stomping our feet to keep warm, and with each stomp of our boots, you could hear the crunching of the ice breaking. I think that the Germans must have heard the crunching and knew something was up because they were waiting for us.

"When the whistle blew, we all charged up over the top of the trench with our best war cries . . . straight into the teeth of hell. The war cries instantly turned in to screams of agony as the Kraut machine guns opened up on our boys.

"Johnny Biggelow was a scrawny mutt of a lad, but what he didn't have in size he made up for in heart. He was the first one over the top, and the first to die. His foot hadn't even cleared the top of the trench when he was hit. He was blown back and landed on top of me, and we both went tumbling down into the mud. He probably saved my life, because the whole first wave was wracked by machine-gun fire. I'll never forget the emptiness of his eyes as they stared back at me."

The Colonel paused.

"We eventually took those machine gun nests that day, but I lost three quarters of my squad. Three days later, we abandoned that field and the Germans moved right back in. It was my whistle that sent my lads over the top, my orders that got them killed. And just like you I had to write letters home to their loved ones. And to this day I remember each and every one of them. Did they die for nothing?" The old man silently shook his head. "No, they sacrificed themselves serving their country and serving their brothers; they died doing their duty and so did your lads. Don't take that away from them. If you forget that, then their deaths truly have no meaning."

"I guess you're right," Avery said. "I was feeling pretty sorry for myself and that's not what it's about."

"Good! Just remember the lads and their death won't be in vain." The Colonel raised his glass in a toast and Avery followed suit. "To our boys!" He said as their glasses came together. Both men drank, and Avery put his glass down, still distracted. The Colonel followed the gaze of his American friend until it stopped on a table across the room.

A smile reclaimed its rightful place on the old veteran's face as he saw that the center of his companion's attention was focused on a table with two girls sitting at it. "I see you have other things on your mind too." A spark of mischief ignited in his eyes. "Hm, is it the lassie with the short, dark hair? What is it with you American chaps and skinny women? She doesn't have enough ballast on her to hold her down in a stiff breeze. I prefer my women with a little more meat on their bones. When I put my arms around her to give her a hug, if my fingers can touch on the other side, then she's too skinny! Why, I remember this one lassie in Liverpool, she was—"

An American Army officer came walking up to the table and The Colonel stopped in mid-story. "Well, you have company here, lad, so I'll be talking with you later." He got up from the table and turned as he left. "Just remember what I said about your boys."

"Thanks," Avery replied with a small smile.

"There you are."

Avery looked up to see First Lieutenant Jason Peters. Peters was Avery's right-hand man and had come to work for him shortly after he'd arrived in England two years ago. He was a tall, lanky twenty-six-year-old drink of water from Alabama with curly blond hair and deep blue eyes. Jason had a bumbling country boy charm that the English girls found irresistible.

"I've been looking for you, sir," Peters said.

The waitress dropped off his fourth beer, and Avery downed half of it in a single gulp. He set it down and wiped the foam from his lips. In all the time he'd been in England, he still hadn't acquired a taste for English beer. He took another gulp and shook his head. What he wouldn't give right now for a hot dog and a *real* cold beer, like he used to get at the Dodgers games!

Peters sat down and put his hand on his boss's shoulder. "Still beating yourself up, Griff? You did everything you could to make sure things went right. Anna and I couldn't find any mistakes when we reviewed the plan."

"Anna," Avery said letting out a long, heavy sigh like a schoolboy with a crush on his first grade teacher. He looked around the room and his eyes stopped when they reached Anna's table. Anna . . . she was the love of his life, only she didn't know it. Anna Roshinko was a second lieutenant who also worked for Avery doing clerical duties. Over the last few months she had been helping him more and more, planning and assisting with her own French resistance cell.

"Look at her, Jay. She's beautiful, and she's as smart as she is good looking." Anna Roshinko was thirty-one with short, ebony hair that framed her heart-shaped face. She was a petite five-foot two inches tall and had a doll's figure that even the Army uniform couldn't hide. Her eyes had the piercing blue color of a northern glacier. Peters chuckled at his tipsy boss, glad for the distraction that took his mind off Strovinski and the failed mission. Roshinko was not bad looking, Peters thought, but not as beautiful as his boss was professing. Then again, he knew Avery was seeing her through a different set of eyes.

Anna sat at a table with her friend, another clerk from the office. The two of them had been there an hour and had been approached twice by American servicemen and three times by British officers, but had politely turned them away.

"Look," Peters said, "Anna's getting up. Looks like she's getting ready to leave. I think she lives somewhere around here. Why don't you go over and ask if you can walk her home? You know, be the gallant gentleman and all."

"I don't know," Avery hesitated. "She'd probably just say no."

"But she might just say yes."

"You think so?"

"Yup. And besides, this isn't the best part of town, you know. Look, there she goes. You'd better hurry."

THREE

ROSHINKO stepped into the night. A chill ran through her as a gust of wind swirled around her, embracing her into the darkness. Another blast cut in behind her, sweeping away the familiar sounds of the music and laughter. She felt alone and isolated, as if she'd just stepped onto another planet. Anna pulled her collar up walked swiftly to the corner of the building and turned down a side street toward her home. She'd walked home dozens of times before and felt completely safe, but for some reason the shadows of the poorly lit streets seemed darker and more menacing than before. She shivered again, this time as much as from her shaky nerves as from the coldness of the wind tugging at her coat.

Her heels clicked along the cobblestone streets, giving her the illusion that she had company.

A sudden noise in the alley just ahead startled her, and she fought back a small wave of panic. The streets were deserted except for a small black cat that lingered in the shadows. Why are they always *black* cats that wander the streets at night she wondered?

"Here, little kitty." She bent down and called him over. Nonchalantly the cat wandered over to her and stopped just out of reach. "Are you lost, little fella? Come here and we'll find your home together." As she reached for the cat, he arched his back and hissed, showing all his sharp teeth, and recoiled, bringing up its paw as if to strike, then suddenly turned and ran, disappearing into the shadows.

"Hey, what—"

A rough hand clamped itself tightly around her mouth while she felt a powerful arm engulf her waist and pull her up off the ground. She kicked her legs, swinging them widely, trying to find a target. But before she could connect, another set of hands grabbed her legs, and they started carrying her toward the alley.

She tried to bite the hand that was clamped against her mouth, but the man's grip was too tight. She could barely breathe, let alone open her mouth enough to scream or bite. Briefly she freed one leg, managed a small kick, and was rewarded by a groan from her abductor. But he recaptured her leg and she felt pain as he dug his fingers deeper into her leg, tightening his grip.

"She's a feisty one," the man holding her legs said. "We'll see how playful she is after we get through with her." He smiled a crooked smile, which grew bigger when he reached down and popped open his switchblade.

AVERY stepped out of the pub and lit up a cigarette. A sharp breeze sliced through his coat, but he didn't mind. The chill sobered him as he tried to decide which way Anna had gone.

It was a clear and beautiful night, with the sky covered by a carpet of sparkling stars. For once, there were no clouds to hide their beauty and no searchlights carving up the sky looking for phantoms. Only a simple, clear sky. It was the kind of night that was perfect for strolling hand-in-hand with someone. He sighed, threw his cigarette down, and crushed it under his heel. Fat chance of that ever happening, he thought.

Avery started walking. Even though the blackout ban had been lifted, there were not a lot of lights burning in this part of the city. Long, black shadows surrounded the buildings, silent sentinels, ready to engulf anyone who dared enter their domain. It would not be easy to find Anna in the dark and narrow streets.

After several minutes of walking and no sign of Roshinko, he was frustrated. Avery was just about to give up and go back to the pub to finish drowning his sorrows when he heard a cat screech. He walked a little faster now, a strange new sense of urgency gripping him by the collar and pulling him along.

Just as he rounded the corner of an old, gray building, he saw a shadow slip into the alleyway. Was it Anna? he wondered. Did she need help? He shook his head. It was probably just a street bum looking for a warm place to sleep. And yet . . . He quickened his pace.

Avery peered around the corner, and his eyes flew open. He has not expected to see the girl of his dreams being mugged. Panic grabbed him by his lapels and spun him around, pinning him up against the wall. This wasn't a Hollywood movie where he could just go charging in and save the day. He was forty-five years old, not some young twenty-year-old buck fresh out of boot camp! Besides, he thought he'd seen a knife in her attacker's hand, and he had no weapons. Maybe he could run and get help.

Anger mixed with shame welled up and pried panic's fingers off his coat. He knew he had to do something. He could not, would not, run away. He felt something brush up against his leg—the black cat, probably the one he'd heard earlier. This is a crazy idea, he thought as he bent down and picked up the cat, but at the moment I don't have a better one, and time is running out.

Avery took a deep breath, sprang around the corner, and ran straight at the attackers, carrying the cat like a football. At the last second, Avery let out his best war cry. His shriek echoed off the alley walls, surprising Anna's attackers.

The charging Army officer threw the cat at the head of the man holding Roshinko's feet. The man instinctively dropped her legs and threw up his hands to protect his head, but he was too slow. With a terrible howl, the cat clawed the man's face. Avery continued running and lowered his shoulder, ramming into the man's stomach, driving him into the wall. The mugger's head snapped back and smacked into the wall with a dull thud. He crumpled to the ground like a sack of old laundry.

Roshinko wasted no time once her legs were free. She slammed her heel down on the top of her attacker's foot. He let out a sharp cry of pain and relaxed his grip just enough for her to open her mouth and bite his hand.

The man released his grip, and Roshinko shot out of his arms. But instead of running, she turned and hit him with her purse.

Avery got up and turned around to face his other opponent and to help Anna, but he saw that she was in little need of his help. After taking three roundhouse hits from her purse, the man turned and ran down the alley.

"Come on!" Avery shouted, grabbing Roshinko by the arm. "Let's get out of here."

The two OSS officers ran for several blocks, slowing down only when they saw the lights of Roshinko's apartment building.

Gasping for breath, Roshinko turned to Avery. "Where did you come from? You saved me." She paused for a moment and stared into his eyes. "Are you my knight in shining armor?"

Avery tried to control his breathing. He didn't want her to think her Sir Galahad had been scared out of his wits and was out of shape to boot. "I was only protecting my lady's honor," he said, holding up her hand and kissing it.

She took his hand in both of hers and pulled them up to her chest, drawing him closer. They stared into each other's eyes. The moment was electrifying. Avery thought he saw a faint aurora surrounding her. He had never experienced anything like this before. The light grew more intense by the moment. He leaned forward to kiss her at the pinnacle of the light's brightness, when a car horn blared.

"Hey!" the driver of the car shouted. "You two get out of the middle of the road . . . and go find a room. Damn fool Yanks." He swerved and drove by.

They both laughed, embarrassed for being carried away by the moment. They awkwardly released each other and walked the short distance to her apartment.

They turned onto the path that led to her door.

"Wait right here," she said, then disappeared inside.

Avery stood, not quite knowing what to think. Why had she left him standing there? Suddenly, with all the wind knocked out of his sails, he was becalmed on the sea of love. With a heavy sigh, he sat down on the curb and was on his third cigarette when she came back out.

"Sorry about that," she said smiling, sitting down beside him on the curb. "I've got three roommates, and even though it's late, they'd be up in a flash. I'm not ready to share you yet. Here." She handed Avery a thermos of hot tea and threw a blanket around them. "We'll dine al fresco."

"This is nice," Avery said, feeling his sails begin to billow again. "Thanks." The two cuddled up under the blanket beneath the stars, sipping tea and talking. Avery had never talked so much in his life, but it felt good. He wondered if that was what love was like: talking for hours about absolutely nothing. Finally, at 3:00 a.m., he told her good night.

At 5:00 a.m., he was still telling her good night.

"I know you have to go," Roshinko finally said, "but just sit with me for a while longer and watch the sun come up." She squeezed his arm under the blanket and laid her head on his shoulder. Any thoughts of leaving slowly vanished like the darkness vanishing before the power of the rising sun.

They sat in silence, just watching the sky change colors. The heavens went from black to light gray, slowly changing to colors as the sun's rays began to infiltrate the bleakness. Pale yellow was the first to arrive, soon changing into orange hues, followed by passionate red.

"Isn't it beautiful?" Roshinko said softly. "Sunrises are my favorite part of the day. My grandmother use to say that a beautiful sunrise was God's gift to us, and since He started each day off right, it was up to us what we would do with the rest of it."

Avery smiled. "Your grandmother was a very wise, if sleepy, woman," he said, trying to suppress a yawn that was too powerful for his mouth to contain.

"I know." Roshinko sighed. "It's really late, or really early, depending on how you look at it." She smiled. "It's just that I don't want this night to end."

"Me neither, but I don't think General Sizemore would share our feelings." He reached over and kissed her tenderly. "I'll see you in the office." Avery stood and reluctantly went back to his apartment.

It was nearly six thirty before he finally got to bed. He wouldn't have thought it possible, but his life had just gotten even more complicated. He lay down, trying to put things in order, but sleep came too fast for him. The 8:00 o'clock alarm came even faster.

FOUR

THEY were four, yet moved as one. Riding effortlessly on the wind, their silver skins glistened against the dark, dull sky. They were fast, sleek, and deadly. And today, the four North American P-51 Mustangs were hunting.

"Estimated time to target: twenty-three minutes," Major Terrance Spencer announced. "You daydreaming over there, Mr. Lincoln?" he said, looking to his left. "Tuck it in a little; you're out of formation." There was a slight pause, then he continued. "I hope you're awake, because you're leading the strike today."

Fifteen feet off his wing, First Lieutenant Matthew Lincoln thought, and I'm out of formation? *Leading?* "Yes, sir!" Lincoln sat up a little straighter in his cockpit and adjusted his seat harnesses around his stocky frame because his chest had just swelled up two sizes with pride. His eyes were always smiling, reflecting the happy spirit that lived inside. Truth be known, he *had* been day-dreaming, but with the words *you'll be leading the strike today* the cobwebs of his daydream vanished in the daylight of reality.

Hot damn, the major is going to let me lead the strike! I just hope I don't screw it up. There was a short silence, then Lincoln heard the major clear his throat.

"Sir?"

"Your orders, Lieutenant?" Spencer said.

Lincoln rolled his eyes. How could he be so stupid? He was leading the group now and it was up to him to give the orders. "Leon, you and George—" He was interrupted again in mid-sentence by another throat clearing.

"'Leon'?" the major said.

Lincoln shook his head again. *Stupid, stupid, stupid!* He drew in a deep breath and let it out. He paused and organized his thoughts. "Lieutenant Davis and Lieutenant Johnson, you will remain at angel's twelve and provide top cover for us while the major and I attack the airfield. Upon the successful completion of our rocket attack and bombing runs, we will climb back to altitude and provide top cover for you while you dispose of your ordnance on the target."

He smiled. That sounded pretty official for his first real combat order. "The field runs in an east to west direction," he continued. "If there are no aircraft visible on the field, we will concentrate our rocket attack on the tree line at the east end and north side of the runway. That's where I believe the aircraft, if any, will be hidden. We'll come in hard and fast and walk the rockets along the tree line, drop one bomb on each hangar, and save the other two for any secondary explosions we may see. After that, strafe anything that moves. I will lead the first pass, followed by the major. Any questions?"

Lincoln held his breath, waiting for the major to amend his orders, but all he heard were three acknowledgments from his fellow pilots. He let out a little sigh of relief, then continued into his headset, "Sir, there's a POW camp near the field. I'd like to do a flyby after we drop. I think it would help boost their spirits when they see the hell we raise and let 'em know they're not forgotten."

"Good idea, Lieutenant."

Lincoln smiled so big he nearly had to take off his oxygen mask. Coming from the major, that was a big compliment. His heart pounded as hard as the twelve cylinders in his fighter. He sat upright and alert in his cockpit, surveying the skies like a hawk, searching for prey, looking for any sign of danger, any speck on the horizon that could turn into an enemy aircraft. It was a little strange, he reflected, to see empty skies without a flock of B-17s under his wing. Their usual mission was riding shotgun over the heavy bombers, protecting them from enemy fighters on their long flights deep into German territory.

And at that, there was no one better. The 332nd Fighter Group had the unmatched record and bragging rights of having never lost a bomber under their charge to an enemy fighter. But today there were no bombers to protect. Bad weather over their targets kept the big planes grounded . . . but not so their "little friends," as the bomber crews called them.

Today, instead of playing guardian angel, they would become Hells angels with their very own bombs, rockets, and guns. Each of the Mustangs carried two 500-pound general-purpose bombs, 6 five-inch, high-velocity aerial rockets, or HVAR, and 1800 rounds of fifty-caliber machine gun bullets.

Lincoln licked his dry lips as he saw their target coming into view, knowing that he was about to lead his first flight. "Commencing rocket run now," he said. "Arming rockets, turning gun camera on." Lincoln gently pushed the stick forward, sending his plane diving toward the earth. At the cruising level of twelve thousand feet, it took about fifteen seconds to drop down to the firing altitude for the rockets. The whoosh of the rockets could barely be heard over the roar of the plane's engine as they ignited from their launch rails and raced toward the ground, trailing streams of white smoke. Lincoln volleyed off his rockets, firing one every two seconds, walking them along the tree line in hope of hitting some unseen target.

He was down to five thousand feet and approaching four hundred and twenty-five miles per hour with one rocket left when he spotted a dark shadow among the trees. He couldn't tell if it was a building or a plane, perhaps a precious fuel storage tank. He envisioned his rocket hitting the five-thousand-gallon fuel tank, causing a huge mushroom cloud to erupt as the high-octane aviation fuel ignited. The fire would quickly engulf several nearby camouflaged tanker trucks, then spread to the four 190s that he just knew were hidden in the trees.

Smiling, he concentrated on lining up his sights. Closer, just a little bit closer, he told himself. He had only one shot left and he had to make it count. He could almost make out the shape now, just a few more seconds . . .

Screaming erupted over his headset: "Pull up Lincoln, *pull up!*"

As if waking from a dream, Lincoln realized he was dangerously close to the ground. He fired his last rocket and pulled back on the stick with both hands. His chest straps went slack as the pressure of the G-forces pressed him back against his seat. It was an odd sensation. He felt the blood drain from his brain and down into his feet. His legs became heavy, like they were made of lead, and he began to feel light-headed as the world started to turn a fuzzy gray.

Lincoln struggled to remain conscious as he watched the trees that only a moment ago had been so small now turn into five-hundred-foot giants, reaching up to swat his plane from the skies. If he blacked out, even for a second, it could spell disaster. He struggled to push the stick forward just enough to relive the pressure. Slowly, color crept back into his face as the blood began to flow again.

Lincoln snapped his head around and was disappointed not to see the huge mushroom cloud that he had hoped for, or towers of flames reaching toward the heavens. He saw only small patches of smoke where the rockets had landed in the forest, doing nothing more than scaring the animals.

"Lincoln! Are you all right?" Spencer asked.

"Yeah. I mean, yes, sir," Lincoln answered. He was disgusted with himself. Shaken, he continued to climb and looked over his shoulder as Major Spencer made his run. So much for my theory, Lincoln thought as he watched the major's rockets explode harmlessly in the trees.

"Okay," Spencer said, "I'll take lead for the bomb run. Let's see if we can drop the hangars in a single pass, and keep your eyes open. The hairs on the back of my neck are beginning to tingle," he added. Three months ago, every-one laughed at the major when he'd made that statement. Not now. He seemed to have a sixth sense about danger. The words at which his team had snickered behind his back were now taken as gospel. Lincoln slouched in his seat, relieved and disappointed. Disappointed at his own performance and that the major had taken over, but relieved that the major was back calling the shots. He thought about protesting to the major, but maybe he wasn't as ready to command as he thought he was. Lincoln formed back up on his commander's wing, a position he felt much more comfortable with.

Major Spencer dipped his wing down, angled for the target, and Lincoln peeled off after him. Their targets were two large hangars standing side by side on the north edge of the runway. Even from this height, Lincoln could see that they looked to be old and dilapidated, hardly worth a five-hundred-pound bomb . . . but a "real" target in the hand was worth more than two imaginary 190s in the trees.

A dozen clumps of hay dotted around the hangars and another dozen or more piles running along the length of the runway. The grass in the fields was still green and growing . . . it was too early in the season for there to be a first crop, Spencer thought, let alone a second.

The hairs on the back of his neck were now standing at attention. Before he could even shout a warning, the Germans sprung their trap. In unison, the haystacks were quickly thrown aside, revealing an array of antiaircraft batteries.

Spencer aborted his run and dropped his bomb prematurely in the forest. He continued his dive and shoved the throttle all the way to the stops. Speed and maneuverability were his only chances of survival. If he banked or pulled up, he would loose valuable air speed and become an easy target. He would have to blow by the gunners before they had a chance to load and aim their guns. It was now a race to see who was the fastest.

Halfway down the runway, the Germans' antiaircraft guns began to fire.

Spencer held the reins of his warhorse in both hands, steadying the stick, guiding his plane as it streaked over the runway, barely fifty feet off the ground and doing over 460 miles per hour. A trickle of sweat rolled off his eyebrow and ran into the corner of his eye. He didn't wipe it away; any mistake at this altitude and speed would mean instant death. He wouldn't even have time to realize that he'd made a mistake.

He screamed past the end of the runway, his plane shaking like a car running over deep potholes. The last four gun emplacements, two on each side of the field, had the most time to prepare; they were ready and waiting.

"Look out, Major!" Lincoln shouted when he saw the gun emplacements. But his concern for the major was quickly replaced by his own imminent danger. Six Bf 109s were dropping down on Davis and Johnson, who were still flying high cover.

In perfect formation, the German planes peeled off out of the sun, one after another, and dove onto the unsuspecting Allied fighters. The Americans didn't see their impending doom, concentrating instead on what was happening below them instead of what was going on around them. "Break left, Leon! Break left!" Lincoln shouted, but it was already too late.

The first 109 came in and fired a long burst, sending a large plume of black smoke billowing out of Davis' engine. The second 109 held his fire until he was right on top of the American fighter. Nearly every round from its 20mm cannon and twin machine guns found their mark as both wings collapsed. The plane exploded in a huge ball of fire.

Johnson panicked, forgetting he was still carrying his ordnance, and jerked back on the stick to avoid the incoming fighters. The sudden maneuver combined with the added weight of his bombs and rockets sent the Mustang into a tight spin. Two more of the 109s made sure of his fate by diving down on him, neatly slicing off one wing as if it were a slab of butter. There was no chute.

Lincoln realized that he was next in line as he saw the last pair of Messerschmitts line up on him. The Germans were in a perfect position: they had altitude, speed, and numbers on him. The way he saw it, he had one chance. If he could get past the first two, he might be able to drop the nose and see just how fast his thoroughbred could run.

He counted on the Germans having a lot of speed, so he pretended not to see them as he continued flying straight. They were coming to kill him yet he was setting them up, a thought in which he took little comfort. He twisted his head and looked back and up—it was sobering to watch the German fighters sweep down.

At the last possible moment, he dropped his bombs and threw the stick to the left, holding it for a moment, then shoved it back right. His Mustang responded by swinging like a pendulum. It swung out from in front of the Messerschmitts then slid in behind them. The trick worked; both planes were moving too fast to match his turns and sped by without firing a shot.

As the second German fighters sped past, Lincoln pulled his nose up and fired a long burst at the trailing plane. I don't have much hope of hitting it, he thought, but one can never discount luck.

Unfortunately, Lady Luck deserted him like a busted Vegas gambler. No bullets scored hits. Lincoln flipped his Mustang over on its back and pointed the nose straight down, trying to regain as much speed as possible. He'd underestimated the speed and maneuverability of the two 109s; they were already swinging around for another pass. The other four fighters were joining in the fight now, coming at him from all sides.

Pushing the rudder pedals over, he corkscrewed the plane down in an attempt to throw off their aim. His stomach churned as the plane spun downward in tight spirals. He ripped off his oxygen mask in case he threw up, but he knew that was the least of his worries.

He twisted and turned down to five hundred feet then pulled back on the stick with both hands to level out. His neck muscles were twisted from snapping his head back and forth in an attempt to find the German fighters. He didn't have long to wait: yellow tracers whizzed past his canopy. Several rounds hit his right wing tip and chewed up the wing as they moved toward the fuselage. Instinctively, he rolled the plane up and over the stream of bullets, but as he did so, cannon fire from one of the other fighters hit him on the underside of the fuselage. A seemingly insignificant puff of dark smoke announced that his engine had been hit, and a moment later all twelve cylinders seized up. His mighty stallion was dead.

Lincoln pulled up and opened his canopy. He had just crested twenty-eight hundred feet when the plane began to stall. He threw off all his harnesses, stood on the seat, then jumped over the left side. He yanked on the ripcord and was jerked as the white silk parachute blossomed and filled with air.

He was disoriented for a moment by the vastness of an empty sky until he heard the roar of an engine and looked back to see a 109 bearing down on him. The fighter was lining up on him, and there was nothing he could do but hang, helplessly, and wait to be strafed in his chute. The 20mm cannons looked like battleship guns pointed at him. Time froze, and his mind raced through the last twenty-one years of his life in a split second.

His thoughts settled on the last time his entire family had all been together: one year ago to the day since he had earned his wings and been commissioned as a second lieutenant in the Army Air Corp. Graduation day. He smiled warmly at the thought of his mother. All she could do at the reception was to put her hands over her mouth and say *my, my, my ooh my*, and then she'd cry. She'd stop for a few minutes and get distracted in a conversation, but when she looked at either one of her boys, she started to cry all over again.

His father had a grin that stretched across three counties. "I'm so proud of you, son. I know that it ain't been easy for you, but you made it, and there ain't a prouder man in this entire country than I am of my two boys."

That was the last time that any of them had heard from his older brother, David. David had joined the Marines, hoping for combat but was put in a support role because he was colored. In a couple of his letters he'd sent home, he spoke about how bad the fighting was and how their position was almost overrun by the Japs. He had grabbed a rifle and fought with the rest of his unit. Nobody minded what color he was then.

David was home on leave for Lincoln's graduation, but he shipped out again the following week. Two months later, his folks got a telegram reporting him as missing in action on some little island in the middle of the Pacific that none of them could pronounce, let alone find on a map.

Lincoln had tried to transfer to the Pacific, but there weren't any colored pilots flying there. He had been told that the best way he could get to Japan was to defeat the Germans, then the whole unit would transfer and carry the fight to the emperor.

The thunderous roar of the approaching Messerschmitt brought him back to reality. He watched the enemy warbird veer at the last second and fly underneath him. Suspended between heaven and earth, he looked straight down between his legs and saw the propeller emerge between his dangling feet. He'd missed a spot on his left shoe when he'd polished them last night.

The pilot wore a brown leather jacket and flight helmet, and he looked up and smiled as he flew by. The fuselage thinned out again, followed by the tail. The plane was gone in the blink of an eye, yet Lincoln could remember every detail of it. He bounced in his chute as the prop wash tossed him around like a cowboy atop an angry bull.

Not to be outdone, another plane charged in from the other side. He was coming straight at him and made no effort to veer off. The left wing of the German fighter sliced three shroud lines of his parachute. The chute fluttered at the loose ends but stayed full of air.

A third Messerschmitt made another pass, but he was not as brave or fool-hardy as the first two, and he swerved sooner than the others. They were playing with him and he couldn't do anything about it. Now he knew what the mouse felt like right before the cat ate him.

He heard a loud explosion and looked back to where his plane had crashed. It was on fire, and the red tail sticking up out of the flames. His heart sank. He was only about a mile from the POW camp, and all the prisoners were watching him. He'd put on quite a show for them, alright, but not the one he'd hoped for. He watched a large troop truck pull out from the main gate of the compound and guessed that they were coming for him.

Fortunately, he had drifted over an open field.

He landed hard because of the cut shroud lines and sprained his left ankle. He thought about trying to make a run for it, but there was nowhere to go. He couldn't run with an injured ankle and besides, he didn't think a black American pilot would blend in with the surrounding countryside.

When the truck pulled up, Lincoln was sitting on the ground smoking a cigarette. He figured it would probably be the last one he would have for quite a while. Nine soldiers piled out of the back of the truck and surrounded him with rifles raised. The officer in charge got out of the passenger's side door and slowly walked up to him. Lincoln smiled and offered him a cig- arette. The German studied the American flyer for a moment, then smiled back and took the whole pack. He offered each of his men a cigarette. The first six gladly accepted, happy to get American smokes. The next two politely refused, clearly not smokers.

The last man stared long and hard at the American then spit on the ground. Lincoln had seen that look before: it was the look of hatred. He didn't know if it was because he was an American and the enemy or because he was black. Only time would tell, and he seemed to have plenty of that. The officer took a cigarette himself and lit it. He enjoyed a couple of puffs then took two more cigarettes, put them in his pocket, and handed the pack back to Lincoln. After a few more long drags he nodded, and Lincoln climbed into the back of the truck for a short drive to his new home.

FIVE

SPENCER looked back to see what they had done to his girl, *Ellie*. It was common practice for pilots to name their planes and decorate them with nose art. Most fighter pilots named their planes after their wives or sweethearts, so no one ever questioned him about his choice of names. In fact, it was named after First Lady Eleanor Roosevelt. It was his way of thanking the lady responsible getting the Tuskegee airmen off the ground and showing America that blacks could do more for their country than cook and wash dishes.

When the war started, pressure was put on the War Department to utilize blacks as officers and pilots. The first lady came to the airfield in Tuskegee, Alabama, to evaluate it as one of two possible training fields. After looking around the base, she asked Charles "Chief" Anderson if Negroes could really fly. He smiled and said they could, then asked her if she would like to take a ride. When she accepted, it sent her Secret Service guards into a frenzy. They ordered Anderson not to fly and forbade her to go, but Mrs. Roosevelt overruled them all. They even called the president himself, but he knew his wife: once she made up her mind, there was no stopping her. After a thirty-minute ride, they landed and she turned to Anderson and smiled. "I guess Negroes can fly." A few months later, the training began.

Ellie was on a slow, gentle climb, and Spencer decided to leave her that way until he knew where he stood. He examined each of his gauges, looking for a sign that his engine had been hit. The P-51 Mustang was a magnificent aircraft, but a lucky strike by a single bullet in half a dozen places could kill the engine. *Ellie* had been his personal mount for over twenty-five missions, and his ears were well tuned to the way she sang to him. He listened intently, ears cocked to one side as if he were hearing music for the very first time. Her steady, unwavering drone was a symphony to his ears.

There were no holes in the left wing and the aileron was intact. On the right, the story was not so good. The wing had a few small holes in it; one jagged, six-inch hole was punched out toward the wing tip, but the real problem was his aileron. It was essentially shot away, and just a few strips of metal hung where the rest of it should have been. The plane would be less maneuverable with only one aileron, but it would fly.

Gently, he moved the stick to the left then to the right and the plane responded with the slow, sluggish rocking motion he expected.

He carefully applied pressure to the rudder pedals, alternating between left and right rudder. At the first sign of pressure from the pedals, the tail of the plane should sway back and forth, but it didn't. He pushed the right pedal all the way to the floorboard and nothing happened. The left responded by barely tilting the nose of his wounded bird just a few degrees. The German gunners had been more accurate than he first thought. That's okay, he tried to convince himself. A plane with no rudder can still fly.

Spencer nudged the stick forward to level the plane, and nothing happened. He tried to pull back on the stick to increase his climb and again, nothing. A wave of panic washed over him. Without the elevators, he had no way of making the plane go up or down. He could fly the plane without the rudder and with only one aileron but without the elevators, he couldn't land the plane.

He'd heard the fighting on the radio and wanted desperately to join his men in the battle, but even if he could turn the plane around, in his condition, he would only be target practice for the Luftwaffe fighters. The radio soon fell silent and the battle was over in a matter of moments. The silence from the radio was more deafening than the sounds of battle. If he was lucky, he could get into the cloud cover and limp back to England and bail out.

He was lucky to be alive and he knew it, yet something bothered him. The airfield had three times the normal amount of antiaircraft guns found at a strip that size . . . and was it just coincidence, he wondered, that there happened to be six 109s in the area?

His gun camera was still running. The camera had been recording the surrounding area as well as the close pass he'd made along the airstrip. If there was anything on the film that G2 could use, he would have to land in order to save it—something nearly impossible with no elevators. His life had just gotten a lot more complicated.

Major Terrance Spencer began working on the problem in that systematic way that had defined his life. He experimented with the throttle, chopping power to put the plane into a shallow dive, seeing how much altitude he lost. He timed how long it took to re-apply power and bring the nose back up again. Next, he analyzed his trim tab settings to see if he could get any additional lift from them and applied different fuel mixtures and power settings to see if the engine would be more or less responsive.

At last he had reached the coast of France and saw the choppy waters of the English Channel. Foul weather drew close, and he was flying in ever-growing swirls of dark, ominous storm clouds. His visibility was fast decreasing.

His shoulders ached, and his legs grew stiff from the many hours in the cockpit. In combat, adrenaline and fear kept fighters sharp; thoughts of death were pushed away by training and the sheer intensity of combat. There was no time to think about it.

But in this case, each new power setting, each new adjustment of the trim tabs, could mean a face to face meeting with the Grim Reaper. A cold shiver rippled down his spine. He felt like he was on a first name basis with Death.

The question he'd wrestled with, that had tormented him throughout the whole process was simple: was the possible information that might be on the gun camera worth risking his life for? Germany was on the brink of defeat and everyone knew it. It was just a matter of time before they surrendered. Some thought it might take place within the next couple of months.

But the Germans had something down there that they wanted kept secret, and that fact alone should be reason enough to attempt a landing. But most men don't die for logic, and neither would he. A man needed a reason to die, he thought, and sometimes king and country were not enough. In this case, he decided, he would risk his life not for the possible information on the film the G2 could use for the war effort, but for the fact that his men had died stumbling across it.

He glanced at his gauge. Fuel was getting low and he didn't think he had the maneuverability to find his own field; he would land at the first field he came across. That shouldn't be hard, he thought, as the entire English countryside is dotted with airfields. He only hoped it was a bomber field with a nice, long runway.

He kept one eye on the altimeter as he dropped his altitude down to five thousand feet and kept the other eye on the dark clouds that were devouring the English countryside. They covered the ground like a dark shroud, making the possibility of a landing difficult. Twice he'd been buffeted by strong winds that nearly sent his fragile plane into a spin. It was bad enough that the Germans had tried to kill him, now Mother Nature was getting into the act, too.

At last, Spencer spotted a runway off to his left. He was disappointed that it wasn't the long bomber runway he was hoping for, but he had no choice.

Timing would be everything. He knew he had to time the descent just right, then add full power to bring the plane's nose up enough to glide in on its belly. Normal landing speed was around one hundred and twenty miles per hour, but he figured he'd be going nearly two hundred miles per hour when he skidded in. He popped opened his canopy and cold air flooded his cockpit.

Even from a mile and a half out, he could see the emergency crews scrambling. The meat wagon with the big red cross raced toward the end of the runway, followed by two water-tanker fire trucks. Fortunately, he had a good line on the field as he made his final approach. He was down to less than a thousand feet, but his airspeed was dropping too fast and he realized he would never pull up in time. Spencer slammed the throttle all the way forward and made the fuel mixture as lean he could, coaxing every ounce of power out of his engine. It would burn up the cylinder heads and cause the engine to overheat, but he doubted if *Ellie* would ever fly again anyway.

He zoomed passed the end of the run, barely a hundred feet off the ground, and realized he was coming in too fast, too low, and at too steep an angle. With sudden clarity, Terrence Spencer knew he was going to die.

Inexplicable calm swept over him. He was proud of the fact that he was facing death like the man he'd hoped he'd be, and prouder still that he was dying trying to do something right by his men.

Spencer grabbed the stick, prepared to go down. Suddenly a blast of wind hit his plane, ripping the canopy off its tracks and shattering it into a dozen pieces against the tail. It felt like a giant hand had reached out and grabbed *Ellie* and set the plane down, rather than letting it plow headlong into the ground.

The Mustang landed on its belly and skidded down the runway, throwing up sparks as the metal skin scraped against the concrete strip. Spencer felt like he'd jarred a couple of teeth loose when he hit the ground, but at least he was still alive. He screeched past the emergency vehicles sitting at the end of the runway, waiting for him. It was almost comical to see the surprised look in the eyes of the ground crew as he sped by. They looked like Keystone cops as they scrambled to get back in their trucks and chase after the plane they were supposed to be saving. *Ellie* was still moving at over 150 miles per hour when she skidded off the paved runway and sent up an immense plume of dust, dirt, and grass. Spencer looked up and saw the trees at the end of the base property coming up fast. There was nothing he could do but ride it out.

Without warning, the jagged pieces of metal where the right aileron had once been caught on the ground, raising the left wing and causing the plane to cartwheel across the grassy field. It flipped twice, and on the third revolution, the right wing buckled and collapsed. *Ellie* landed hard and slid another fifty yards until she came to a silent stop, resting on her side like a wounded horse.

The chasing ambulance slammed on its brakes and skidded in the slick grass, nearly plowing into the broken plane before stopping. The medics jumped out of the back with their stretcher and raced to the pilot. They found him still strapped in his harness, arms dangling loose at his side, head tilted back at an impossible angle. They were sure he was dead.

The fire truck screeched up behind the ambulance with its siren blaring.

Three men dressed in hooded silver protection suits jumped out and started dragging a hose to the plane. "Hurry up!" one shouted. "I smell gas!"

The corpsmen quickly unbuckled Spencer's harness and lowered the limp body onto the waiting stretcher. They lifted the litter and took a step toward the ambulance when the Spencer shot his arm up, grabbing the medic's collar.

"Stop!" The startled medic shouted. "Put him down, put him down!" They lowered the wounded pilot to the ground and the medic followed, his collar still firmly in the grip of the wounded pilot. The medic got down on one knee and lowered his ear to hear what the pilot said. After a few whispered words, Spencer released his grip and the medic motioned for them to pick him up and place him in the ambulance.

"What'd he say?" an officer asked, walking up to the scene.

The medic stopped and shook his head. "It doesn't make any sense, Colonel. It sounded like he said 'gun camera.'"

"Very well, take care of him and keep me posted."

"Yes, sir."

"Lieutenant, get me the toolbox out of the Jeep."

"Right away, sir." A few moments later, the man returned with a small, olive drab metal box. The colonel grabbed it and headed for the plane. "Come on," he called after the lieutenant.

"Colonel, you should stay away, sir," one of the firefighters cautioned. "The plane's leaking gasoline like a sieve and it could blow any second."

"Well, you just make sure it doesn't until I'm finished."

"Yes, sir," he said aloud then turned and muttered a few choice words under his breath.

Colonel Wesley Adams climbed up the side of the broken, smoldering plane. At forty-seven, Adams was tall with wavy brown hair and just a touch of gray on his temples. He had an air of authority and looked every bit the dashing aviator.

Adams crawled onto the left wing and unscrewed the housing that held the gun camera while his wingman Lieutenant Luke Stevens stayed on the ground.

"Coming, Lieutenant?" Adams asked.

Stevens scrambled up and knelt beside the colonel. "Uh, sir, there's gas leaking from the wing tanks and it's flowing toward the engine, which is still mighty hot."

"Almost got it," Adams replied. "The housing's dented and pretty banged up, and the lens is shattered, too, but I think the film is okay." With a stout tug from Adams, the camera popped free. Stevens jumped down to walk away then stopped and turned around. Adams stepped down slowly and carefully, smiling as he walked past the nervous lieutenant. "What's the matter, Lieutenant? You look like a boy who's bringing his date home late and her daddy is waiting for you at the door."

"Yes, sir. It's just that I really don't want to be around when this thing blows. Besides, sir, what makes this film so important, anyway?"

"That's what we're going to find out."

"Sir?"

"There is something on this film the pilot thought valuable enough to risk his life for. He could've bailed out. I will not let his sacrifice be in vain. Besides"—Adams smiled—"we had plenty of time."

The plane exploded in a huge, red fireball.

SIX

GRIFF Avery stumbled past his office and headed straight for the small break area near the back of the offices. He had to have his coffee. If he could have picked up a cup on his way into work, he would have been fine. But even after all this time in England, he still hadn't found a local restaurant that served a good cup of morning coffee. The British and their damn tea!

Fortunately over half of his staff was American, so good coffee was readily available. He grabbed one of the mugs and poured the hot, steaming elixir of life out of a sterling silver carafe. If nothing else, the British did have class; it sure beat his tin coffeepot and hot plate he had at home.

Avery held the warm mug tightly in his hands as he savored the aroma. Normally he took cream and sugar with his coffee, but this was a straight-black morning. He felt tired and drained. He'd had a fair amount to drink last night, but it was more than just that. Maybe it was all the thinking he'd done about Anna, or maybe being a "hero" took more out of him than he thought. He smiled and wondered if Superman felt like he did the morning after he'd saved Lois Lane and beat up the bad guys.

Fortified with his mighty cup of joe, he walked back to his office and started his daily chores. An hour later, Peters knocked on his door.

"Morning, Jay, what's up?" Avery asked.

"Need to check the bomber routes for tomorrow's missions, weather permitting, and see who and what resources we have in the areas to recover any downed airmen." Peters stepped in and studied the large map hanging on the wall across from Avery's desk. It showed the southern and eastern half of England in the upper left-hand corner, while the largest portion of the map was devoted to Western Europe, France, and Germany. He studied it for a few minutes, made some notes, then turned and faced his boss. "So, how'd it go last night?"

"How'd what go?"

"Did you find Anna and walk her home?

"Yeah, I found her."

Roshinko walked by. "Good morning, sir," she said as she passed his door, her face beaming with a shy, broad smile.

"Okay, what happened?" Peters asked. "The look on her face was more than a just a 'thanks for the walk home.' Come on, boss, you're holding out on me. Spill the beans. I want details!"

"What?" Avery said, feeling his face becoming flush. "I found her, we ran into a little trouble, then I took her home."

"Yeah? What kind of trouble?" Peters kidded. "You couldn't get to first base?"

"No, actually she was attacked by a couple of thugs, and I chased them off, that's all."

Peters' expression changed. "She was attacked? And you rescued her?"

Avery frowned. "You don't have to say it like that. I'm not a crippled old man, you know."

Peters shook his head as he sat down on the corner of the desk. "No, no, I didn't mean it like that. I just can't believe she was attacked."

Avery retold the night's events.

"Okay, you saved her and got her back to her apartment. Did she let you in? What happened next?"

"Nothing. We sat on the curb and talked."

"Talked?"

"Yes, talked."

Peters looked disappointed. "You mean you didn't even kiss her?"

A smile curled onto Avery's lips. "I didn't say that."

"Now we're getting somewhere." Peters grinned, smacking his hands together and rubbing them like he was about to dig into a big turkey dinner. But before he could press for more detail, they heard a rap on the door and saw a colonel standing in the doorway. Peters excused himself and left.

Anna Roshinko was coming back down the hallway, her mind carrying as big a load as the bundle of papers she was carrying in her arms. Her thoughts were on work, well not *work*, just on her boss. Something had happened between her and Griff last night when he'd rescued her from the muggers, and she liked it.

She sensed a spark had been kindled, one that lay smoldering just below the surface, and all it needed was just the right circumstances to ignite. At first she thought it was a schoolgirl's infatuation on her part, like a student falling in puppy love with her teacher, but it was more than that. True, she did in a way look up to him as a father figure, but she also admired him for his wit, cleverness and charm. The fact that he was much older than her did bother her a little, but at 31 she was no spring chicken; almost an old maid as her mother liked to constantly remind her.

She was no beauty and she knew it. She was not a "real dish" as the boys would say, just your average plain Jane. She'd been asked out on dates before, mostly by younger men. They were boys really, but they weren't interested in her. They were just out for a good time. So the fact that Griff was not some young hot shot in heat appealed to her.

She felt silly, but she was already planning any little excuse she could think of to pop into his office just to say hi. She knew it wasn't very professional, but like that schoolgirl, she just couldn't help herself. Preoccupied with her thoughts, Anna didn't see Peters as he came out of Avery's office. The two collided and papers flew up in the air like a flak barrage.

"I'm so sorry!" Roshinko said. "I'm so embarrassed."

"It's all right," Peters replied as he stooped down to help pick up the scattered papers. "I should have been watching where I was going."

"No, it's my fault, really. I was the one who should have been paying attention. My mind was on other things."

Peters smiled. "I noticed."

Roshinko blushed and turned her head. "Is it that obvious?"

"To the normal passerby, no, but to a trained professional such as myself, yes," he said jokingly.

"I feel so foolish."

"There's no need to feel that way. If it helps, Griff is almost as bad."

"He is?" she asked in surprise.

"Yes." Peters chuckled. "He did seem a little distracted this morning, like his mind was away somewhere else. Yeah, I think he's got it bad, too."

Roshinko looked overwhelmed.

"If you don't mind, would you like a little advice?"

"Yes, please!" she almost shouted.

"Take an interest in what he does. Griff's work is very important to him so ask how his day is going or what he's working on. Show him that you care about him as a person, not just as a boss. Griff's a great guy, but he can be a little slow at times, if you know what I mean . . . so be persistent." He handed her the last folder off the floor and they stood together.

"Thanks for your help, Jay." She smiled sheepishly. "You know, helping me with the papers and the advice."

"Hey, we're a team here. We help each other out." He returned her smile and walked down the hall. Roshinko gathering her thoughts and courage, then headed for Griff's office. Head high, she threw her shoulders back and walked confidently down the hall towards the office.

With poise and grace she rounded the corner into Griff's office, where she promptly ran into a man coming out. Again, paper showered the room like scattering autumn leaves. Her eyes filled with horror as she looked up and saw a colonel.

Quickly she bent over to pick up the papers, then realized that she should stand and salute. As she started to stand, the colonel knelt down to help her. The top of her head struck the colonel's nose. Panic filled her eyes when she realized what she had done.

Roshinko reached out with her hand to help the colonel but accidentally scratched his hand with her fingernail, and he flinched. Roshinko became even more flustered and the only thing she could think to do was stand at attention. Her face lost expression, and a distant glaze replaced the usual brightness in her eyes, as if she had gone into a coma.

The statues at the local park held more life in them than she did, Avery thought. He had to look carefully to see if she was still breathing. He tried his best not to laugh, but it was such a comedy of errors, it was like watching a scene from a vaudeville act.

"At ease, Lieutenant," Avery said. Roshinko snapped to a parade-rest stance, but still remained stiff.

"Request permission to speak, sir!" Roshinko barked out as if she were in boot camp.

"Granted!" He shouted back with equal fervor. He knew he shouldn't be amused at her plight, knowing that she must feel terribly embarrassed, but he just couldn't help himself.

"Sir, the lieutenant didn't see the colonel as she came around the corner. She didn't mean to run into him and spill the contents of the file folders, nor did she intend to injure the colonel while attempting to render aid."

Avery couldn't hold it in any longer and burst out laughing. When she referred to herself in the third person as if she were filing a report, it was too much for him. And the part about "rendering aid," that put him over the top.

Roshinko remained expressionless through the laughter, even though she must have realized he was laughing at her.

"At *ease*, Lieutenant," Avery said again. Roshinko remained a statue, but her marble casting began to crumble and a little life and color returned to her face. Avery stood and came around the corner of the desk. "Colonel Wesley Adams, this is Lieutenant Anna Roshinko."

"Lieutenant," Adams said, nodding his head.

"Nice to meet you, sir," Roshinko replied stiffly.

Adams turned back to Avery. "I'll talk to you later, Griff. I've got a mission in the morning, so I'll see you tomorrow night." Adams turned, smiled at Roshinko, and gave her a wide berth as he walked out.

As Adams disappeared around the corner, Roshinko sighed in relief and collapsed on the corner of Avery's desk. "Well, I see that I'll never make it past lieutenant now," she said quietly.

Avery smiled as he bent down and started gathering up the papers. "It's not that bad, Anna. I know the colonel, and he's not the type to hold a grudge. Besides, he knows it was an accident."

"Well, I hope so," She replied, then her look of hurt and dismay became one of anger. "And what's the big idea back there? Why were you laughing at me? And don't you dare tell me you were laughing *with* me."

There was a biting tone in her voice, but Griff could also see playfulness in her eyes. He was glad. It meant that she felt comfortable enough around him to express her feelings yet joke about it. He felt good; it was a nice notion to think that a relationship might be blossoming.

"I'm sorry, Anna, but it *was* funny. Papers flying like a snowstorm, and then you two bumping heads. But when your report about 'rendering assistance' . . . well—"

"Okay," she said reluctantly. "But don't think you're getting off the hook that easily. You owe me dinner, and I don't mean fish and chips at the Dragon's Breath Pub, either. I want a real dinner at a real restaurant," she said and held her breath.

"It's a deal," Avery replied, hoping the answer didn't come out too quickly. In an awkward silence the two of them knelt together picking up the rest of the scattered papers.

"What'd you come in here for, anyway?" Avery asked, then added, "Not that you need a reason to come see me." He flinched inside. He was acting like a teenager again! He hated being a teenager the first time around, and yet here he was, living it all over again. Start acting like a grown man! But when he looked into her blue eyes, the horror of being sixteen again reared its ugly head.

"Oh, I almost forgot," Roshinko said. "While you were with Colonel Adams, FED called to remind you that you need to stop by and pick up your allotment."

"That's right. Have you ever been up to the Foreign Exchange Division before?"

Roshinko shook her head.

Avery smiled. "Don't ever let it be said that I'm a cheap date. I'm going to throw millions at your feet. Meet me back here in an hour."

"Okay." Roshinko walked out the door with a puzzled look on her face.

AVERY enjoyed the short, pleasant walk to the building where FED was housed. The day was overcast as usual, but the wind was still, not throwing itself at them like a restless sea pounding the shore. He and Anna traded small talk along the way, but mostly they were quiet. Avery fought the urge to hold her hand as they walked. On the outside, the FED building appeared to be like any other office building.

Avery pulled back the heavy wooden door and they stepped in. Just inside the foyer, a corporal sat behind a large, metal desk checking the ID of everyone who entered. Behind him, two armed guards with several more soldiers were scattered around the foyer. After showing their identification, they walked up the flight of stairs to the second floor, where they were met with another desk and more guards.

"As soon as we get inside, take your shoes off," Avery said.

Roshinko shrugged her shoulders. "Okay."

Avery opened the door and the pair walked in. A secretary at the front desk smiled and greeted them. "Good morning, Captain. Lieutenant. Your bundle is in the back, sir."

"Thank you."

"You can just put your shoes over there," the secretary said.

They nodded, removed their shoes, and walked into the office behind the secretary.

Roshinko stopped halfway through the door and froze. A young British lieutenant holding a stack of papers walked by with a smile. Several other people walked by nonchalantly, all in stocking feet, all walking on millions of dollars that were scattered on the floor.

"See?" Avery said with a smile. "Some men may promise you the moon, but who else is going to lay millions of dollars down at your feet?"

"I don't understand," Roshinko said. "Why is all this money just laying on the floor, and why is everybody *walking* on it?"

"Here you are, Captain." A young woman in her early twenties wearing a British Army officer's uniform walked up to Avery and handed him an envelope. He opened it, and Roshinko's eyes nearly popped out when she saw that it was full of French francs.

Avery quickly counted it, then signed the clipboard. "Come on," he said.

They quickly put their shoes back on and left. As soon as they were outside the office, she grabbed his arm.

"What was that all about?"

Avery smiled. "That was a million and a half francs we just walked on back there. And to answer your next question, there is ten thousand in here," he said, patting the inside of his coat pocket. "This money is for the French resistance. It's going over on a special drop, the one Jason's setting up tonight."

"Couldn't we keep just a little of it?" she said jokingly.

"Don't I wish."

"But why are they walking on it?"

"I tried to figure that one out on my own for weeks but couldn't, so I finally had to give up and ask. This money is brand new, and since France is occupied, they aren't making any new money. If someone showed up with crisp new bills, they'd be marked as an agent right away. Various methods had been tried to age the money, like rubbing it in dirt, or using chemicals, but walking on it in stocking feet was found to be the best aging process."

"You sure do know how to show a girl a good time." She smiled.

"It's the Ritz! I'm going to take this money to the courier. Why don't you go back to the office and get with Jay to prepare tonight's transmission. I'll pick you up at eight at your place."

SEVEN

AVERY sat in the car, wondering what he was doing. His feelings for Anna were growing much faster than he had anticipated, but logic told him to stay away, not to mix business with pleasure. They were a good working team, and he didn't want to jeopardize that. But she was so beautiful.

Glaring headlights and the blasting horn of an approaching car brought him back to the moment, and he swerved to get back into his lane. He'd been in England for over two years now and he still forgot, at times, to stay on the left. He just couldn't get use to driving on the wrong side of the road.

He'd borrowed the car from an elderly couple he'd met when he'd first arrived in England. They'd met in the train station. He was trying to find his way around London, and they were taking a short holiday in the country to see their grandchildren. Like many families in the city, they had moved their daughter and her two little girls out to the country to keep them safe from the bombings in London during the blitz.

They'd let him borrow the car once or twice before, and Mrs. Gentry was more than happy to let him borrow it tonight because he had a date. She'd cornered him at the kitchen table and was already asking him about Anna's family, if she could cook, and whether or not she liked children. The only thing Mr. Gentry had to say was that he had better be careful fishing in the company pond. Gentry smiled, then gave him a quick wink and sat down to read his paper. Avery knew he'd have to sit down with Mrs. Gentry when he got back and share all the evening's details with her, and he really didn't mind. But, he thought, smiling to himself, depending on how the evening went, he hoped he'd have to do a lot of editing for her.

One more swerve and blare of the horn followed by shouts from another mad Englishman and Avery pulled to a stop in front of the flat where Anna lived. He wasn't looking forward to this either, since Anna lived in an apartment with three other Women's Army Corp officers. There would be no keeping this office romance a secret from that gaggle of geese.

Avery took a deep breath and stopped the car, nervous as all get out. His stomach made him feel more like he was going on a mission behind enemy lines than on a date. He was halfway up the walk when the front door opened, and Anna came out to meet him.

"Hi," he said, smiling at her. He saw the two windows by the front door filled with the bobbing heads of her roommates, giggling as they watched.

"Thanks for meeting me out here and saving me from them."

She smiled and grabbed him by the arm. "I saved you for purely selfish reasons. Don't let their smiling faces fool you. If you'd gone in there, they'd have interrogated you relentlessly, far worse than any Gestapo officer could ever do. After ten minutes you'd be running for your life, and I'd never get my dinner."

"Well, thank you, I guess you can have dessert now, for that." He helped her into the car and they exchanged nervous small talk for a few short miles until he pulled into a driveway. The sign on the street said Wallaford Inn.

"A hotel? You're taking me to a hotel on our first date?" Roshinko batted her eyelids and pretended to fan herself, talked with the accent of a Southern belle. "My, my—are you planning to take advantage of me, sir? What ever shall I do? I do have my reputation to think of, you know. My daddy warned me of gentlemen callers such as you. I believe he called them 'scoundrels' and 'scalawags.'"

"Why, my dear woman," Avery replied in his own version of a Southern drawl, "I can assure you that my intentions are nothing but honorable, especially since I saw your daddy standing by the front door with his shotgun."

They laughed and the tension melted away.

"They have a wonderful prime rib here, in the *restaurant*. I've attended a couple of staff meetings here, and the food has always been excellent."

"Well . . . if you say so."

"Good, reservations are for eight and we're a little early. Lets go into the bar for a drink."

EIGHT

THE silver eagle hood ornament glistened. It reflected the sun's rays like a beacon from the front of the perfectly polished black 1938 Mercedes-Benz 770 Tourenwagen convertible. The Mercedes was a huge, stout touring car that looked at the world through two, dinner-plate size headlights mounted on either side of its massive chrome grill. It was supported by a stylish but no-nonsense bumper, giving the face of the car a bored, snobbish look.

Elegant running boards swept stylishly down either side of the car, nestled perfectly between graceful, flowing fenders. It was a spacious car built for the open road and equipped with a powerful 150-horsepower straight-8 engine. It seated six passengers comfortably, unlike its smaller cousins who could only accommodate four. The car's sole passenger smiled; only thirteen of the magnificent machines were manufactured in 1938, and he owed one of them.

The car turned off the main road and pulled up to a black wrought-iron gate that led down a tree-lined drive to a small compound. It was quiet, peaceful and picturesque, seemingly far removed from the horrors of war.

But nothing could have been farther from the truth. Before the war, the compound had housed a small trade school for domestic help, training them to serve the German aristocrats. Now, it was a housing facility and think-tank for some of Germany's greatest scientific minds, whose sole purpose was to come up with ways to defeat the Allies. It was a harmless place before the war, and the German High Command hoped that the Allied bombers would think it still was.

Two guards quickly opened the gate and the car entered, following the short, tree-lined driveway to the main compound. The Mercedes glided to a halt and the driver got out and went around to the rear passenger door and opened it.

Its occupant stepped out of the car, then pressed the travel wrinkles out of his black, immaculately tailored uniform. His deep-set eyes had a cold, indifferent stare that seemed to be a prerequisite for becoming an officer in the feared SS. He was clean-shaven, and his silvery-gray hair was short and neatly cropped. He stood at a fit six-foot even and managed to keep the usual belly roll off his belt, a good accomplishment for a man of sixty-one.

General Maximillian Jaeger drew in a large breath of country air, then meticulously folded his gloves and placed them in his belt. His boots clicked on the cobblestone walkway, pounding out a steady beat as he walked toward the main administration building. With long, purposeful strides, he stepped onto the wooden porch and opened the door. A corporal sat at a desk with a lieutenant standing directly behind him.

"Heil Hitler!" the lieutenant shouted out as he clicked his heels together and shot his arm out as if raised from a flagpole. Normally, Jaeger would simply have raised his hand in a token salute of Hitler, but Lieutenant Ackerman, knowing of Jaeger's dislike for the Führer, taunted him with his enthusiastic formality. Any sign of disloyalty these days was cause enough for a firing squad with few if any questions asked. Ackerman was just a lieutenant in the SS, but he had very powerful friends and connections that went nearly to the Führer himself.

He had to be careful with this one, Jaeger knew. It was said one should keep one's friends close and one's enemies even closer. He would keep Ackerman as close as possible. Jaeger stopped in mid-stride and clicked his heels so hard they vibrated throughout the room and shouted out with conviction a "Heil Hitler" that made Ackerman's decree sound like a whisper.

"Welcome, General Jaeger." Franz Ackerman could have been the poster child for the German Army with chiseled features and the patented Aryan blue eyes and blond hair.

"I have come to check on your progress," Jaeger said.

"But you were here only a week ago, General. Surely a man of your importance has better things to spend his time on than to check up on a few old scientists."

Jaeger ignored the jab and continued on. "Time is not on our side, Lieutenant, and a week is an eternity. Surely you understand the importance of their work." Jaeger reached over the desk, grabbed the logbook, and began thumbing through the pages.

"It says here that Doctor Strovinski did not report for work this morning, nor at noon. The day grows long. Why has he not reported for work? As I am sure you are keenly aware, his research is paramount to the Fatherland."

"If I may, sir," the corporal spoke up. "Dr. Strovinski called late last night and said he wouldn't be working today. He said he was tired and not feeling well."

"Why wasn't I informed?" Ackerman said angrily.

Before the corporal could answer, Jaeger unleashed his barrage. "I see; are you running a resort here where the 'guests' call in when they are not feeling well, or are you running a research facility, *Lieutenant?*" Jaeger asked. "Do you offer room service here in your little lodge? Perhaps I should spend my next holiday here if the accommodations and service are that good.

"If is not too much of an inconvenience for your guest," Jaeger continued, "could you please have the good doctor join us? Perhaps we could have some tea out on the veranda."

Ackerman practically threw the corporal out of his seat to go and find Strovinski. Jaeger couldn't hide the pleased look that crept across his face. He put his hands behind his back and paced slowly back and forth across the hardwood floors. Each click of his polished boots made the wonderful sound of another nail being pounded into Ackerman's coffin.

Five minutes had gone by and still no Strovinski. "I'm waiting, Lieutenant. Perhaps the doctor is on the tennis courts or is in the spa and cannot join us," Jaeger taunted as beads of perspiration were forming on Ackerman's brow.

"He will be here in a moment, General," Ackerman replied, trying his best to keep the frustration and irritation out of his voice. Footsteps sounded on the porch. "Ah, there he is now," Ackerman said.

The door opened and Ackerman's newfound self-assurance drained from his face as he saw Major Volker Reinard, his immediate senior officer, walk through the door instead of the corporal with Doctor Strovinski.

"Heil Hitler!" Reinard shouted, raising his right hand.

"Heil Hitler!" Jaeger roared.

"It's good to see you, General," Reinard said as he reached out his hand. "I've been away for a few days. Had I known you were coming, I would have returned sooner." Peering through round, wire-rimmed glasses perched on his small, hawkish nose, Reinard asked Ackerman, "Is everything all right here?"

The corporal rushed through the door. "He's not in his room, sir. We're searching the grounds now, but it appears he took his briefcase and most of his personal things."

"What is going on here?" Reinard demanded, looking at Ackerman.

"It seems in your absence, the lieutenant has instituted a new check-out policy for your guests. It appears that they can now come and go as they please," Jaeger said.

"They can't, Herr General," Ackerman replied weakly.

"Oh, but they can and seemed to have done so. You have let Doctor Nicoli Strovinski, one of Germany's top scientists in our Nuclear Research department, walk right out your front door! I will give you until tomorrow morning at 08:00 to bring him to me or else I shall have to report this indiscretion. To wait any longer would make me derelict in my duty."

"We will find him, General . . . and thank you, sir."

"I apologize for this, General," Reinard said. "Lieutenant Ackerman will find the missing doctor. You must be tired from your journey. Please, come into my office for some refreshments." Jaeger nodded and followed Reinard past the corporal's desk into the major's office. Before the door closed behind them, Ackerman was already halfway across the compound shouting instructions to find the missing scientist. Even with his connections, Ackerman knew that if he didn't find Strovinski by 08:00 tomorrow morning, at 08:01 he would be on his way to the Russian front.

Jaeger wore a huge grin, compliments of Lieutenant Ackerman, as he closed the door. Reinard pointed to a large leather chair, and Jaeger gratefully sank deep into the cushion. Reinard walked over to a small stand with a phonograph on it. He opened the cabinet door beneath it and thumbed through a dozen record albums.

"Ah, this one should do nicely; something light, Rimsky-Korsakov's 'Flight of the Bumble Bee,' in honor of our dear Lieutenant Ackerman as he scurries about the compound to and fro looking for the good doctor." Reinard smirked. He took the album out of its jacket and placed it on the turntable. With greatest care and reverence, he placed the stylus gently into the first grove.

The sound of dancing violins and flutes filled the office, and Reinard took a deep breath as if he had just had a religious experience. After a moment of letting the music fill his soul, he stepped to the other cabinet behind his large cherry wood desk and reached into the bottom drawer, producing a bottle of Courvoisier VSOP and two glasses.

"I see you have good taste in Cognac," Jaeger said. "I too prefer the Very Superior Old Pale with its rich, blended flavor. Ten-year-old?"

"Twelve."

Jaeger's smile grew even bigger.

Reinard poured each of them a glass and then sat down. "I take it things have gone well?"

Jaeger raised his glass. "Very well."

"Strovinski?"

"He has taken very well to his new assignment and has already contributed to the program."

"So no resistance, then? No moral or ethical dilemma?"

"No," Jaeger said taking a sip of his drink. The brown liquid burned slightly as it entered his throat but turned smooth as velvet as it reached his stomach. "This *is* good Cognac, Major, my compliments," he said, tipping his head and raising his glass. "Anyway, Strovinski is like most scientists, more interested in their work than in politics. He sees the value of our endeavors both to the Fatherland and to his own research . . . and he's actually made some interesting observations that could prove to be very useful."

Reinard smiled as he sipped his Cognac. "The American prisoners call the guards who look for tunnels and escape routes 'ferrets.' Ackerman has been like that for me here, poking his nose around where it isn't wanted, turning over stones that would be best left unturned. But it was a masterstroke to kill two birds with one stone, as they say—to have Strovinski disappear and blame it on Ackerman. By this time tomorrow, he will be on his way to the Russian front, and not even his friends in Berlin will be able to help him. With him out of the way, things should proceed smoothly."

"And our contact in London?" Jaeger asked

"The information has been invaluable, leading me to initiate phase two tomorrow. If all goes well, within two weeks the American will be dead, seemingly by his own hand, and there will be no doubt who his successor will be."

"Excellent!" Jaeger beamed. "And within a week after that, we will be ushering in the new era and the beginning of the Thousand Year Reign of the Third Reich."

NINE

"AFTERNOON, sir," Jason Peters said, sticking his head into his boss's office.

"Hi, Jay."

"While you were at lunch, a Colonel Adams called and said he wouldn't be able to make it tonight."

"Okay, thanks." Avery snapped his fingers. "Hey, that reminds me. Go get Anna and come back here. I want to show you two something."

Peters nodded and left. Moments later he returned with Roshinko. When they walked in, Avery had just finished setting up a movie projector.

"Come in and pull up a chair. Sorry there's no popcorn." He smiled.

"What's this?" Peters asked.

"It's gun-camera footage from a fighter that crashed a few days ago. Colonel Adams gave it to me."

"Why did he give it to you?" Roshinko asked.

"Adams said the pilot risked his life in order to bring his shot-up plane down in one piece to save the film. G2 has already looked at it and didn't find anything interesting, but the colonel knows how much I love a good mystery, so he gave it to me."

"Alright, let's have a look," Peters said, flicking off the lights.

Avery turned on the projector and the black and white film began. The film was grainy and jittery. It showed a fighter as it went into a dive and fired off its rockets. The camera continued to follow the plane, which looked like it was going to crash until it suddenly pulled up at the last moment. They watched as streams of smoke came from the filming plane as it fired its own rockets, then the ground disappeared and the screen was filled with sky and clouds. Roshinko tipped back in her chair as the plane pulled up and she grabbed the edge of her seat to steady herself. She glanced around, but neither Avery nor Peters seemed to notice her airsickness.

Roshinko tightened her grip as the plane swung up and around and started to dive on the airfield. "What are those flashes of light?" she asked.

"Those are anti-aircraft guns," Avery said, "and a lot of them." They watched as the plane swooped low over the field and raced away at an unbelievable speed. The film rocked and shook a little, then smoothed out. The rest of the film just showed countryside.

"Wow!" Avery said. "That was intense."

"Yeah it was, but I agree with G2, I didn't see anything remarkable about it," Peters said. "I've got some paperwork to do." He stood and gave Roshinko a quick wink. "Why don't you two watch it again and tell me if you see anything new."

Roshinko silently mouthed "Thank you" to Peters as he got up and left.

Avery rewound the film, and the two of them watched it a second time in silence. When it stopped, Avery got up and began rewinding it again.

"I enjoyed dinner last night," Roshinko said, leaning close to her boss. Avery didn't answer as he struggled with the film. Roshinko was a little disappointed when she didn't hear an immediate response. "Um." She cleared her throat. "I said I enjoyed our evening last night."

"Oh, I'm sorry, I did too. It's just that this film fascinates me. It's a mystery why the pilot landed his heavily damaged aircraft to preserve this film when he could have bailed out safely. What is on this film that's so important that he felt he had to risk his life for?"

"Why don't you just ask him?"

"I would, but he's in the hospital in a coma right now, and the doctors aren't sure if he'll ever come out of it."

"Why don't you just send another recon plane then?"

"That's part of the mystery: we don't know where this was taken. Major Spencer's group was on a fighter sweep hunting for targets of opportunity. This airfield could be nearly anywhere in France or Germany."

"Okay, well, if you don't mind, I need to finish those translations you gave me, the ones we intercepted from the Russians last night. I already translated a few of the communiqués, but so far everything looks routine."

"Yeah, okay," Avery replied absentmindedly, grabbing a pad and pencil to take notes. Roshinko got up and left the room.

Captivated by the mystery the film held, Avery watched it again and again, each time concentrating on a different aspect of the film. He focused on the gun emplacements, their type and number and how they were arranged, then he turned his attention to the hangars and then on the surrounding area as best he could. He tried desperately to see what the pilot saw to make him risk his life.

He watched the film eighteen times, carefully timing and marking portions of it that he wanted still photographs made from. After he got the stills, he would analyze it further. He had that little feeling in the back of his mind that there was something there, something that was just waiting to be discovered. A small part of him also wanted to find something to rub in the face of G2, since they'd had first crack at it. It was late afternoon by the time he made it to the photographers.

By 10:00 the next morning, Avery was back at the photo lab beating down the door.

"Do you realize how much work this was? Making a copy, finding your edit points, splicing and enlarging, not just one section but over a dozen!"

"I know Sam, I owe you."

"Oh, you owe me alright, and I intend to collect every bit of it. And then some!"

Avery smiled. He did realize the amount of work he had asked his friend, Captain Sam Lyons, to do in order to get the still shots he needed.

"I know you OSS guys don't have much of a life," Sam said, "skulking around in the dark and all, but some of us do. I've got a couple of pints with my name all over them down at the pub, and I may even get lucky and find a couple of girls that I haven't lied to yet."

"You know I wouldn't have asked if it weren't important."

Lyons just gave him a dirty look and kept on working. The two men were in the Photo Recon dark room. Avery watched in silent amazement as his friend performed his magic, taking blank pieces of seemingly ordinary paper, putting them under some machine, dipping them in water and making a picture appear.

"I suppose this is some sort of secret base or something mysterious like that." Lyons said sarcastically as he hung up one of the photographs to dry.

"Something like that." Avery smiled.

"You got a heck of a lot of AA guns there, 88s and 37mm and smaller stuff, but what I don't understand is why you have an American plane in the midst of all those German guns."

"What?" Avery said in shock.

"Sure, look right here." He pointed to the last picture he developed. "Here's a picture of the left hangar. It's kind of blurry because the guy taking the pictures was moving faster than a bat out of hell, but look right here." Lyons grabbed a pencil. "You've got these guys closing the hangar doors and right there . . . see the nose of that plane? That looks like a small to medium bomber, and you can see the nose wheel. Jerry doesn't have any bombers that have tricycle-landing gear like that, and the nose looks different than any Kraut plane I've ever seen before. No, my friend, that's an American B-26 bomber!"

A B-26? How did the Germans get a B-26? Suddenly a cold chill ran down Avery's spine as the realization hit him: this had to be the same bomber Dr. Strovinski had been on. But how did it get there? The photo was blurry, but it was clear enough to see that the plane was in one piece; and that meant it hadn't crashed.

It landed!

Could that mean that someone had tipped the Germans off about Strovinski? Was there a leak in his organization. A spy?"

"Are you okay?" Lyons asked.

"Ah, yeah, sure," Avery said, trying to keep his ever-growing facts straight.

"Something else, too, look at these tracks here at the end of the runway," Lyons continued. "They tried to cover them up, but they didn't do a very good job."

"What are they? I saw those too, but I thought they were just skid marks or something."

"They're burn marks on the pavement from jet engines. That's how we discovered where the first Me262s were coming from. But I don't understand why they would go to the trouble of trying to clean them up? It's not like jets are a big secret anymore, and this field is too small to be a major threat for a 262 jet base. If you look closely, you can see four sets of burn marks instead of the usual two. It could just be burn marks from two separate planes, or it could be a new type of jet."

A new type of jet? A four-engine plane . . . a bomber! This just keeps getting better and better, Avery thought, his mind becoming lost with all the implications.

"Am I boring you here?" Lyons asked again, seeing the far away look on Avery's face.

"No, I'm sorry. It's just that you've given me a lot to think about here, that's all." His mind was drowning in a whirlpool of information and thoughts. "Listen, Sam, I need you to forget you ever saw this stuff."

"Sure, as long as the heat doesn't get too hot. I can have a lapse in memory, but if for what ever reason the big brass come poking around, I'll have no choice but to tell what I know. If I can, I'll do my best not to hang you out to dry, but I gotta watch out for old number one."

"I understand and appreciate that. I owe you a big one."

"Like I said, I will collect." Lyons smiled.

Avery gathered all the photos and stuffed them into his brief case. What started out as one mystery had just turned into several, with more dangerous implications. Avery felt like he had just discovered the tip of the proverbial iceberg.

TEN

LIETENANT Matt Lincoln lay shivering on the wooden planks that were meant to be his bed, his knees tucked up to his chest, trying to stay warm. His mattress was stuffed with straw that any self-respecting farm animal wouldn't eat, and his so-called blanket had so many holes in it the moths couldn't find anything more to snack on. It was hard to believe that only a few short days earlier he'd been in England and had a warm, soft bed and plenty of food to eat. The stark reality of his new situation was only beginning to sink in.

When he'd first arrived in camp, they took him straight to an interrogation room before allowing the camp doctor to look at his ankle. He was helped into the room by two of the guards from the truck, then left alone. The room was small, and his fleeting hopes were as dim and meager as the single light bulb hanging from a frayed cord. High on the wall was a small, open window that did little to help the light bulb chase the shadows away, but seemed happy to let whatever warmth there was escape the room. It would probably be the only thing escaping, Lincoln thought as he shifted his weight off his wounded ankle and sat down in an old wooden chair that looked like it should have been broken up for firewood long ago.

He looked around at his austere new home and grew more and more apprehensive of what prison life was going to be like. He wasn't afraid to admit it; he was scared. As he sat, anger shoved its way in, joining his other emotions. He was angry for allowing himself to get caught off guard by the German fighters and for what he thought was letting the rest of his buddies down. He kept thinking that he somehow should have done more. But it was more than just anger gnawing at his insides. He also felt a slight twinge of guilt. He was grateful to be alive, but he couldn't help feeling a little guilty about the fact that he had survived while the rest of his flight hadn't.

He sat by himself, but he wasn't alone. He felt like a time bomb ticking away, ready to explode from all the emotions packed inside. Lincoln sat quietly with his thoughts for about a half-hour, guessing that it was all part of the interrogation process, when the door burst open and in walked the biggest, meanest looking man he had ever seen. The sergeant towered over him at six foot six inches and weighed a solid three hundred pounds, all muscle.

His faced seemed to be frozen in a permanent sneer that even a blow torch couldn't melt, and his eyes had such a coldness about them that the cool air in the room felt like a balmy July afternoon.

Lincoln felt like a little child when this monster walked straight in and kicked the chair out from under him, and he landed painfully on his ankle when he hit the floor. "You will stand at attention when Colonel Stein enters the room!" he shouted.

Lincoln heard the wooden floor creak and felt the planks bow under the immense weight. He looked up expecting to see two or three people walking in, but instead he saw a single man . . . and now he was now the fattest man he had ever seen.

Colonel Helmut Stein had walked into the room like he was being introduced to Hitler himself. His coat was fashionably draped over his shoulders, and he held his gloves in his right hand, slapping them into his left. The colonel was only two inches taller than Lincoln, but he was almost as big around as he was tall, tipping the scale at well over four hundred pounds, he guessed. Lincoln suddenly wondered if all three of them could fit into the tiny room.

Lincoln stood at attention while Stein took his time sitting down. As he sat, Lincoln was amazed that the chair didn't collapse under the colonel's massive weight. At last Stein was comfortable and motioned for Lincoln to sit down.

"I am Colonel Stein. This is my camp, and you will obey my rules. Do this and you will live; disobey, and you will have to deal with Sergeant Kohn here. No escape attempt has ever been successful, and none ever will be. Attempt to escape and you will be shot, no questions asked. Understand?" He slapped his gloves in his hands as he spoke.

"Yes," Lincoln replied.

Kohn struck out with the speed of a cobra and slapped Lincoln hard across the back of the head. Lincoln's head snapped back around and he stared at Kohn, anger flashing from his eyes. The man-mountain remained motionless, but there was a slight twinkle of amusement in his eyes, begging the American to respond.

"Yes, *sir!*" Lincoln shot back. He had just turned back to face Stein when Kohn struck him again on the head. Lincoln whirled around. "What was that that for?" he demanded.

"Because I can." Kohn smiled.

Stein placed his gloves down, opened up a file, and began asking Lincoln all the usual questions: What unit he was with, what base he had come from and what his mission was.

Lincoln tried to play it cool by refusing to answer any of their questions, giving only his name, rank, and serial number until Stein started to tell him about himself. The colonel knew his fighter group and what squadron he was in, which really didn't surprise him that much, since there was only one black fighter squadron in the whole Army Air Corp. He knew his father and mother's name, and really got his attention when he talked about his brother, even knowing the name of the island on which David was MIA and implying that he had information on his fate.

Stein seemed quite interested in Lincoln's mission and why they were attacking the nearby airfield. The bantering went on for about an hour until Stein finally decided that Lincoln knew no secrets and was nothing more than what he said he was: a fighter pilot in the wrong place at the wrong time.

He sighed.

That was three days ago.

Lincoln gathered his strength and lowered himself down from the top of his double bunk bed, gently touching down on the floor, favoring his sprained ankle. He was in one of the large center rooms of the barracks that he shared with nine other prisoners. Their barrack, or block, as it was called, was typical of all the others in the compound. It featured about sixteen rooms of various sizes, each housing four to eight men with a central kitchen, washroom and a two-man room at the end for the block commander and his aid.

They were part of the South Camp: twelve blocks arranged in three rows of four buildings each. An identical number of blocks made up the North Camp. A common, ten-foot-high fence topped with razor wire ran around the perimeter, joining the two compounds on the outside with a fifty-foot no-mans land running down the middle, dividing the camps in two.

Lincoln's room was blessed with a lovely view of the south wall of the next barracks. Their view to the outside world was a small window with four swing-out double panels to let the air in and wooden shutters on the outside that the guards closed and locked every night. The meager furnishings included a couple of small tables that they used for meals and card games along with ten stools, all of which were wobbly. A couple of cabinets for their gear and food were scattered about, and there was a coal-burning stove in the middle of the room used for heat and cooking. He would never complain about U.S. Army barracks again.

Lincoln hobbled out the door with a slight limp, deciding he would be more likely to get warm by moving around in the yard than from lying in his bunk. He milled around for a while, doing a whole lot of nothing, which he quickly found out was the norm. With boredom being as big an enemy as the

Germans sometimes, he decided to take a walk around the "neighborhood." He would walk down Main Street, as he called it, the main aisle between the barracks, take a left at Fourth, which was the forth barrack down, take another left on Elm, and then back to Main. He figured the whole trip covered about a quarter to half a mile.

When he was growing up, there has been a large field near his house where he used to play. As Lincoln grew older, he would just lie in the tall grass, stare at the clouds and think. It was there in that field that he made all his big decisions. In seventh grade it was the decision whether to play baseball or football. In high school, it was who he should take to the prom, Betty Garder or Georgina Whipple, or whether he should tell Dad that David snuck out of the house twice, once to go drinking and the other to see Sue Tanner. And it was also in that field that he had decided he would learn how to fly.

He could still remember the very instant he decided to become a pilot. He was a senior and had just gotten a "less than satisfactory" grade on one of his math tests, and he was lying in the field trying to figure how he was going to tell Mom and Dad about it and live. Suddenly, he heard a rumbling off in the distance and thought it was a freight train, but then he realized it had a different sound to it. He got up just in time to see a pair of Curtiss P-40 Warhawks zoom overhead. They were the most beautiful things he had ever seen. They circled like hawks searching for prey over the small airstrip at the edge of town, then landed. It was then and there that he knew he was destined to be a pilot.

It had not been an easy road, but he had earned his pilots wings.

He had no field now to lie down and think in, so his walks around his "home town" would have to do. He was just starting his second lap when he heard someone yell. "Hey, Kriegie!"

"What did you call me?" Lincoln asked the man walking up to him. At first he didn't recognize him. Then he took a closer look: it was Lieutenant Ben Taylor, a fighter pilot he'd met about six months ago while on a seventy-two-hour R&R pass to London.

Taylor walked with a slight limp, a warm smile, and an outstretched hand. He had thick, black hair that looked more like steel wool than hair, and his eyes were as dark as his hair. He was about the same height as Lincoln, but after six months in the prison camp, he was twenty-three pounds lighter.

"I wish I could say it was good to see you," Taylor said.

Lincoln shrugged his shoulders. "Yeah, I know what you mean. Still, it's good to see a familiar face. Say, what did you just call me, Kriegie?"

"Yup. Kriegie is short for *kriegsgefangenen*, it means 'war prisoner' in German."

Lincoln laughed. "Yeah, Kriegie is much easier on the tongue." Lincoln's stomach growled like a junkyard dog, protesting at not having been fed properly. "Man, I'm hungry," he said.

Taylor smiled again and shook his head. "Don't worry, it'll get worse before it gets better. Your stomach is still shrinking now, not used to the dramatic cut in food, but believe it or not, you will get somewhat used to it. The Germans don't feed us much, one because the weaker we are, the less able we'll be to carry out any escape attempt; and second, food has been getting scarcer all the time, a result of the larger and larger bombing raids we've seen flying overhead. We know we must be winning the war, but Stein and King Kong would never admit it. Often the Red Cross packages are all we get to live on."

"Who?"

"King Kong, Sergeant Karl Kohn."

Lincoln nodded his head. "Kohn, yeah, we met my first day here. Now that you mention it, I can see the family resemblance." Both men laughed.

"Neither one of them has skipped a meal, that's for sure," Lincoln continued. "I have never seen a man as fat as Stein."

"Some of the old timers here say that to curb his ferocious appetite he's been known to eat a prisoner or two."

Lincoln laughed. "Yeah, I can believe it." He quickly tapered off when he noticed Taylor wasn't laughing. He wasn't sure if he was kidding or not, but somehow he really didn't want to know.

They leaned up against the barracks, talking, watching several guys throwing an old football around that had come in a Red Cross package. The ball was coming apart at the seams and had more cuts and scrapes on it than a school-yard full of first graders, but it was one of the few forms of recreation they had and would be used until it literally fell apart. And then some.

Lincoln and Taylor watched as one of them kicked the ball. It sailed over the head of the intended receiver and rolled to a stop in front of Lincoln. Lincoln picked it up and held it in his hands for a moment, feeling the leather. "Boy, it's been a while since I held one of these babies." Like most kids, he had played football in high school, a middle linebacker. He had fun and did a decent job, but he wasn't destined to go into the Football Hall of Fame. Lincoln smiled at the memories that were a million years ago. He pulled back and threw a perfect spiral—ten feet over the head of his receiver.

"Now I know why you're a pilot." Taylor laughed.

"Very funny."

The ball landed in the dirt and flipped end over end until it finally came to a stop, resting on the edge of the outer fence. The intended receiver was a short staff sergeant who had lost so much weight his clothes hung on him like a clown in the circus. He looked at Lincoln, shook his head, and walked slowly over to where the ball lay in the dirt.

The sergeant placed one hand on the fence and then bent over to pick up the ball with the other. Suddenly a whistle blew and several of the guards started shouting, "Halt! Halt!"

Everyone froze.

Kohn came across the courtyard, charging at the sergeant like a raging bull charging a matador.

"You are trying to escape!" Kohn shouted.

"No I'm not!" the frightened sergeant shouted back. "I was just picking up the football. We were playing catch."

"You were testing the wire strength!" Kohn bellowed. Kohn grabbed him with one arm and picked him up and literally threw him ten feet into the compound.

"Hey!" Lincoln shouted. "He was just getting the football."

"Shut up," Taylor said, jabbing Lincoln in the ribs. "Stay out of it." But it was too late; the raging bull found a new target to charge.

"Did you say something?" Kohn challenged.

"Yeah, I threw the ball too hard, and the guy was just trying to pick it up, that's all."

"I say he was testing the wire strength. Are you calling me a liar?"

"No, all I'm saying is he just wanted the ball."

By now a crowd had gathered and Taylor had slipped away, leaving Lincoln alone with Kohn in the middle of the human ring. Kohn threw his big left fist, hitting Lincoln in the jaw, catching him off guard. He was slammed hard against the barracks, but Lincoln popped right back up in a fighting stance. His nostrils flared, and he could feel his heart pumping, pushing the blood through his veins faster and faster. He was ready for a fight.

The crowd cheered Lincoln on, urging him to knock Kohn's block off. Kohn threw another left jab that Lincoln easily side stepped. Lincoln began dancing around his bigger opponent and was just about to unload with a jab of his own when he heard someone shout, "At ease!"

He stopped and turned to see who it was, and that was the last thing he remembered.

When Lincoln opened his eyes, he had a hard time focusing, and his jaw felt like someone had hit it with a baseball bat. He lay there for a moment until his eyes cleared, then he slowly propped himself up on his elbows. Looking around, he saw that he was back in his own barracks. "What happened?" he muttered to no one in particular.

"You're lucky you aren't in solitary, or worse," Taylor said.

"Yeah, my jaw feels real lucky." Lincoln gently rubbed it, making sure it wasn't dislocated or broken. "What happened?"

"Simple, Colonel Presley saw the fight and came over to stop it before you got hurt. You turned to see who it was and Kohn didn't. It's just as well though, if you would have hit Kohn, you'd probably be dead now."

"But he hit me first," Lincoln protested.

"That doesn't matter. If a prisoner hits a guard for any reason, it's grounds to be shot."

"That's not right."

"There's a war going on, buddy. There are a lot of things that aren't right."

ELEVEN

CLAUBERT Merle nervously tapped his finger on the desk, then checked his watch for the seventh time in the last fifteen minutes. He looked out a window covered with five years of dirt and grime casting a dull, dim light about the room that had once been their favorite spot.

Theirs had been the first house in the countryside, and they had enjoyed the solitude. But most of all, Beka had enjoyed seeing the sunset from this very room as it slowly settled behind the low rising hills. For a few magical minutes they would watch together as the tree branches reached up and painted the last of the evening sky with yellows and reds and brilliant splashes of orange. But now, the green pastures that had once surrounded their peaceful home were covered with brick and mortar, and the horses that once roamed free drew carts behind them, bringing in their goods from the surrounding farms.

The rhythm of chugging motor cars and the clanging of trolleys replaced the melodies of the songbirds. But since she had died those many years ago, he had never bothered to clean the windows, never seeing the need to. Now, the dirt and grime served a purpose by keeping prying eyes out.

Claubert Merle ran his hand through hair that had thinned and was now more white than brown. His broad shoulders on his five-foot-eight-inch frame were stooped from years of hard work, yet his eyes were still as sharp and clear as they'd ever been. And at sixty-seven, they had seen a lot.

They'd seen machines replace the work of men and horses and seen the miracle of man soaring to the heights of the heavens like a bird. And they'd also seen the depths to which man could fall.

He'd seen first hand the carnage and death from the First World War; how the once beautiful green meadows and pasturelands of his country had been turned into killing fields where death was the only thing that flourished.

He'd also seen the folly of mankind. In less than a generation, the war to end all wars had reproduced itself, rearing its ugly head bigger and more destructive than before.

And yet, despite the monstrosity of war, he had found a new life, one worth living. Once Beka, his beloved wife and companion of forty-three years, had died, life held little meaning for him. One meaningless day dragged into another. He had watched with disinterest as the Germans rolled through his country, but soon that disinterest turned to hatred. And with that hatred came something totally unexpected, a reason for living: helping the Allies and the underground to defeat the Nazi tyrants and drive them from his country. After a long and dangerous journey he had become a key contact in the gathering and disseminating of information to and from the British and American armies.

Merle was proud of the fact that he had personally aided in the safe return to England of three British and twenty-one American airmen. He was also pleased to have helped lay the groundwork for a dozen successful sabotage raids against regular German Army units. The Gestapo had even placed a bounty of ten thousand francs on his head, something that thrilled and horrified him at the same time.

A tiny smile crept over Merle's face. Once again he could enjoy their favorite place together. Knowing she would have approved of his new life made his smile grow even bigger still.

Suddenly he heard the sound of boots shuffling on the cobblestones below. His tired heart started beating at the pace of a young man in love. He had no death wish, but he was thrilled by the danger and had never felt so alive as when he was facing death. He had been dead inside for so long after Beka's passing that it was good to feel alive again, no matter what the cost might be.

Holding his breath, he peered through a hole on the dirt-caked window and let out a long sigh of relief. The boots belonged to a group of railroad workers going to work and not a squad of SS soldiers ready to storm his house. He looked down and noticed that his casual tapping of his fingers had turned into a mad, frantic dance.

The second hand on his watch was trudged on from half past to the twelve mark with the slowness of a stubborn mule. At last, the second hand reached its goal at the top of his watch, announcing that it was time.

Merle was a skilled craftsman and had built their house with his own two hands. It had taken them nearly five years of blood, sweat and tears to finish, but it was a labor of love. The house centered around the kitchen, and for a year and a half they ate, slept and lived there until the other rooms were completed, one by one.

This was the last room to be completed, and he had built a secret compartment to hide their valuables from any would-be thieves who sometimes roamed the countryside. They were young and had dreams of wealth untold. But at the time, their sole earthly treasures were just a few old photographs, the family Bible that had been passed down for four generations, and a pressed flower that Beka had kept because it was the first thing he had ever given her.

It took him precisely thirty-four seconds to open the compartment and set up his radio in preparation for the day's broadcast. Over the years he had perfected his routine until it ran smoother than his Swiss pocket watch.

He looked out the window again. Was the day really that dull he wondered, or was it just because of the dirty window? Everything was laid out and ready. He poured himself a cup of tea, added a small amount of honey, and took a small sip. At first he had found that the tea helped calm his nerves and gave him a steadier hand when writing, but now it had become part of his ritual. Even though he'd been doing this for years, he still got a little nervous and excited at broadcast time, especially now in times like these.

He smiled as he put the cup down and looked at the teapot. Beka would have scolded him for using their good china; she said it was only for company. He would always counter with, Why have something if you never use it? They would go on and on, and in the end, she won most of the time. But after every "argument" he would say that he always got in the last word: "Yes, dear." He felt the familiar stabs at his heart, the pain of missing his Beka. The pain was so familiar now and has been with him for so long he could almost call it a friend.

He took another sip, picked up his pencil, and sent his on-air signal. The first segment of the messages was general and in code, sent out to those who could only receive and not transmit. He enjoyed listening to these "open-air" messages, the broadcasts that anyone could pick up, including the Germans. He wondered who came up with these codes and what they could possibly mean. Messages like "The cat and dogs will dine out tonight" or "The rain clouds look heavy today." He smiled and listened to them for the customary five minutes.

Then his ears perked up when he heard his code name called: Zeus. He thought it ironic that an old man would have the name of the mightiest of all the ancient gods, but he rather enjoyed it. He would love to have seen Beka's face when they called him Zeus!

Today it was all business, though. There were occasions that he would have a chance to talk to his controller, Hermes, the messenger of the gods, but not today. Hermes transmitted his instructions and the information he wanted gathered. Merle, in turn, transmitted the information that Hermes had asked for in the last broadcast and reported anything that he had thought useful.

Merle checked his watch. They were getting close to the cut-off time when he had to stop transmitting or risk the Germans getting a fix on his position. In the past, he'd seen several radio direction-finder trucks driving slowly through the neighborhood in hopes of catching any clandestine operators using the radios. He had almost finished his report when he heard the screeching of tires below. He peered out the window, expecting another bunch of railway workers gathering to go to the station.

Instead, he saw two trucks pull up and a flood of soldiers pour out. He quickly gave his emergency sign-off signal just as he heard shouting and the sound of his front door being kicked in.

He was near panic as he heard soldiers rummaging through the rooms downstairs. They sounded like a pack of wild animals as the sound of furniture being overturned and dishes being broken filled the air. His heart nearly stopped as he heard them running up the stairs, their heavy and clumsy boots scuffing and scratching the planks, they sounded like a muffled herd of charging elephants.

The soldiers broke open the door and rushed into the room like a surging tide, guns raised and at the ready. They found an empty room except for an old man who was about to pour himself a cup of tea. His eyes filled with horror as they aimed their weapons at him, their muzzles looking like huge artillery cannons pointed in his face. He was so frightened that the cup clattered loudly against the saucer as he put it down.

No one moved or said a word. The soldiers stared at him, Merle stared at the guns. Then, like the calm before the storm, two soldiers went on a rampage, tipping over furniture and throwing things around like a cyclone. They seemed to be enjoying the destruction they were causing more than the search for his transmitter.

Soon the storm abated as the soldiers tired and an awkward silence settled in. Then he heard a clop-clop, as another pair of boots climbed the stairs. Each step seemed to be measured in a slow and deliberate beat, drawing out the tension as they ascended the stairs. The footsteps stopped just outside the door, and a deafening silence filled the tiny room. Merle found himself peering around one of the soldiers to see who was there.

A solitary figure stood in the doorway, dressed all in black. He wore polished leather boots that came up almost to his knees. His pant legs were tucked neatly inside. His silver belt buckle was silver and engraved with the German eagle holding a wreath carrying the Nazi swastika. Numerous medals hung from his left breast pocket and a bright red armband with the swastika in it adorned his left arm.

He wore the rank of major on his left collar insignia. Merle's heartbeat paused when he saw the lighting bolts of the SS on his right lapel. He had the standard officer's peaked cap. It, too, had the German eagle with silver braid running across the brim above yet another emblem. Merle's mind filled with dread when he finally recognized the other emblem as a skull. The major belonged to the most feared and hated of the SS, the *Totenkopfverbände*, the infamous Death's Head unit.

The major looked around the ransacked room with disinterest. He slowly took off his gloves and carefully folded them into his belt. "Where is it, old man?" he finally asked.

"Where is what, Major?" Merle managed to stammer out.

"Don't play games with me, old man. Where is the radio transmitter?"

"Radio transmitter? What are you talking about? There is no transmitter here. I am an old man having my afternoon tea."

"What I see is a conspirator and an Allied spy with fear written all over his face."

"Fear? Yes, I am frightened. You break into my home and point guns at me and accuse me of things I know nothing about, yes, I am very frightened."

Nonchalantly, Major Volker Reinard took out his gloves and began mindlessly slapping his hands with them as he slowly surveyed the room. Suddenly he turned and slapped the old man hard across the face. Merle almost fell out of his chair, but managed to catch himself on the edge of the table. The major tilted his head, signaling for the soldiers to leave. He started to leave as well then stopped and turned around at the door. "I'll be watching you, old man," he said.

Claubert Merle didn't take another breath until he heard the last of the boots clomping down his front steps. He took in a deep breath, then hung his head in relief. He tried to take a sip of tea, but his hand was trembling so badly he quickly put it back down. Looking around, he saw they had destroyed everything. At least they hadn't found the radio, and he took great satisfaction in that. That had been the closest the Germans had ever come.

How had they known?

He peered out the window and was relieved to see the troops that had invaded his home were climbing into their trucks. Major Reinard was getting back into his staff car when he stopped and turned to look back. He pointed to his eyes, then at Merle and smiled, a warning that he would be watching him.

A cold shiver ran down Merle's spine. Maybe the major really would be watching him. Merle knew he had been extremely lucky up until now. He had always been cautious, but now he would have to redouble his efforts, not merely to be careful but to help bring an end to the Nazi reign. Tonight he would clean up the mess, and tomorrow he would do things as normal. He would not let them bully him, and he would not hide in fear.

AVERY sat there in disbelief as a sense of déjà vu washed over him. He had lost Strovinski; did he just lose Zeus? He double-checked his timer: they had been close, but well within the allotted time. Had the Germans come up with some new sort of radio detection equipment? He couldn't afford another loss, especially someone like Zeus. Since early 1943, Zeus had been one of his most trusted and valuable agents. Like his namesake, Zeus, if not truly a god, was in fact responsible for a number of Maquis resistance cells in the area, and it would be a major blow to him and the resistance movement if Zeus were compromised. He just couldn't lose him!

Avery took a gulp of coffee then lit a cigarette. He had taken several puffs when he realized he was doing it again: poor, poor *him*. He might get a reprimand or even lose his job and get reassigned if Zeus was compromised . . . but what would Zeus loose? Only his life. Avery swore at himself under his breath for being so selfish. He shoved himself back from the table and stood, tilting his head from side to side trying to get the kinks out. He could feel a headache coming on, and it was going to be a big one.

There was a slight tap on the door, and he turned to see Anna Roshinko. "I was walking by and noticed that you look upset. What's wrong, Griff?"

Avery shook his head. "I don't know, but I think we may have just lost Zeus."

"What?" Concern flashed across Roshinko's face

Avery took another drag and blew out the smoke in a long, steady stream. "Yeah, he was transmitting fine, when he tapped in his emergency sign-off signal, and that was it. We've got some big things going on around that area, and we need reliable intel."

"Don't we have any other agents operating in that area that we could send to check on Zeus to see if he's okay?" Roshinko asked. "With someone that important, we've got to know if he's been compromised and alert the other agents and resistance cells in the area."

"That's just it," Avery replied, lighting up another cigarette. "I've purposely kept the knowledge of other agents in the area secret from each other for just this very reason. In case one is captured, under torture they won't be able to reveal what they don't know."

"But shouldn't we at least let the other agents know they might be in danger?"

Avery shook his head. "They live with danger and suspicion every day. It's their way of life. No," he said, grinding out his cigarette out in the ash tray, "I'll wait until his next scheduled sign-on and see if he makes it before I start spreading around any unneeded panic."

"Okay, but we could be putting the other agents and cells in even greater danger by waiting," she said.

"We'll wait. Do we have any bombing missions going on in our sectors today? Do we need to alert anyone for possible downed pilots?"

Roshinko walked over to the oversized map on the wall. "I just got through talking with Jay. We've got two groups of heavies making runs in the south and a few fighter sweeps up north, but nothing in particular around our areas."

"Okay. I'm going up for some fresh air." Avery nodded and left. He needed time to sort everything out and the possible ramifications if Zeus had been captured. He did have a back-up plan, but it would take some time, and that was something he knew that neither he nor Zeus had.

TWELVE

"OKAY, everyone, I want a gun check. Top turret?" Captain Mike Perry called out from the pilot's seat of his B-17.

"Yes, sir," said Charlie. Technical Sergeant Charlie Tasker was a third generation farmer from Greenfield, Iowa, a small town about fifty miles southwest of Des Moines. He had finished out the last harvest in the summer of his nineteenth year, then went off to war. He spun the turret in a complete circle to check the motors and cocked the twin fifty-caliber machine guns. A light squeeze on the trigger sent several tracers arcing into open sky.

"Top turret check," Charlie said.

"Waist gunners?" Perry continued.

Staff Sergeants Jerry Idleman and Tony Ramos were the waist gunners. Ramos was from California and Idleman came from the hills of Kentucky. Both gunners pulled back the receivers and test fired their weapons.

"Right waist check."

"Left waist check."

Staff Sergeant Billy Jacobs was a country boy who hailed from near Shreveport, Louisiana. He was naïve and yet he had a strange country wisdom. Billy may have just fallen off the turnip truck, but had landed on his feet. He took aim on the B-17 that was following them, pretending it was a German twin engine ME 110 fighter-bomber. He made a few rat-tat-tat sounds then pointed the guns down and safely fired them.

"Tail gunner check," he said in his slight Southern twang.

A few moments passed and the captain spoke again. "Ball turret! Are you awake down there?"

No reply.

"Tiny Tim, you there?" Everyone laughed over the intercom.

"Ah, come on, Skipper, you know I hate to be called that!"

"Then answer me next time I call you."

"Yes, sir." Staff Sergeant Tim Hutton, or Timothy as he preferred to be called, obligingly test fired his twin .50s, tracking and shooting at an unseen enemy below. Hutton was from Columbus, Ohio, and topped the scale at 135 pounds soaking wet. Hutton had short, blond hair and a face covered with freckles, adding all the more to his troubles by making him look five years younger than he really was at nineteen.

He was the ball turret gunner, not so much by choice but by way of being born to it. The ball turret was one of the most important positions on the B-17 as well as one of the most dangerous. It was the only gun that could protect the underside of the airplane. The turret was a Plexiglas ball barely two feet in diameter and the gunner had to contort his body through the tiny hatch, sitting with his knees almost touching his chest. The triggers were between his legs, and the recoil of the guns was only inches from his face. The gunner was suspended beneath the aircraft with no protection except for a quarter inch of Plexiglas.

The *Red Light Lady* was a B-17G built by the Boeing aircraft company. When the first prototype rolled off the assembly line in July of 1935, a member of the press dubbed it "The Flying Fortress," and the nickname stuck. The big four-engine bomber carried twelve to thirteen .50-caliber machines guns with over six thousand rounds of ammunition for defense and could deliver over twelve thousand pounds of bombs.

The crew of ten and their plane had been together since their arrival in England four months ago. Like many planes in her squadron, the *Red light Lady* was adorned with nose art in the form of a scantily clad, red-haired beauty. The artwork was done by Ramos, who bragged that the inspiration for the picture came from his girlfriend back home. Everyone just laughed at him because they couldn't believe that a girl that good looking would go out with a guy like him.

The *Lady* really got her name not because of the picture on her nose, but because of what happened when they were flying across the Atlantic on their way to England. Halfway into the flight, the red warning light on the fuel gauge came on. Thinking they were running out of fuel, they frantically scrambled and prepared to ditch in the middle of the icy Atlantic. After flying for more than an hour with the red light still on, they relaxed a little and eventually landed safely.

Since then, the crew had logged eighteen missions together, and the ten individuals who had brought the plane over had now grown closer than brothers. They were relentless in their teasing of Tiny Tim. But like as with any family, if anyone else dared to make fun of his size, that person would incur the full wrath of the entire crew. On more than one occasion they had been reprimanded for brawls at the local pubs.

"What's going on down there, Ball Turret?" the pilot, Captain Mike Perry, asked. The *Red Light Lady's* skipper was a reservist who had worked for the railroad in the Minneapolis-St. Paul area. Perry had short black hair and brown eyes. At twenty-six, he was the "old man" of the crew and the only one who was married with a family back home.

"Nothing, sir," Hutton replied.

"Timothy?"

"Well," he answered sheepishly. "I've got the latest issue of *Captain America*. It's called 'Frozen Death' and he's fighting this guy called the Red Skull."

"You've barely got enough room to breathe down there, and you're looking at a comic book?" Perry just shook his head. "Okay, stow it now and keep your eyes peeled."

"Roger that, Skipper."

"We should be rendezvousing with our fighter escorts soon, so keep your eyes open. Pilot to navigator: are we on course?"

"Yes sir. We should be at the IP in about half an hour." The initial point was where the plane lined up for the start of its bomb run on the target.

Second Lieutenant Tommy Svensen was the navigator. He was a big blonde kid, also from a small town in Minnesota called Grand Falls, near the Canadian border.

"Roger that, stay sharp everyone," Perry continued. "I heard Ramos bragging that he's got a date with a cute little brunette he met at the USO last week in London, so I wouldn't want him to miss it." A few wolf whistles and catcalls echoed through the intercom, then all fell silent. Quiet filled the plane except for the steady drone of the four 1,200-horsepower Wright Cyclone radial engines. Each crewman was in his own world, deep in his duties and responsibilities, preparing for combat.

A few minutes later, Idleman spoke over the intercom. "Ah, Captain, we've got a big problem back here. Ramos is almost doubled over. He's in a bad way."

"What's wrong, cramps? Is his oxygen flow okay?"

"Well sir . . . he has to go to the bathroom sir, really bad."

"Just have him use the can." The Army Airforce asked the Boeing Company for a top-notch heavy bomber, but in their list of requirements, they forgot to ask for a bathroom. With necessity being the mother of invention and some flights lasting eight hours or more, the crew of the *Red Light Lady* had come up with an old one-gallon oilcan that was in the radio room.

"He has to go number two, sir." The entire crew now howled with laughter.

"He can't go up here," Svensen said, quickly joined by a strong "Amen" from Eric Blocker, the bombardier.

"Just have him sit over the ball turret. He can use Hutton's comic book,"

Tasker piped in.

"Hey! No way!" Hutton shouted.

Perry looked over at his co pilot, Jeff Gibbons. "You've got this one," he said. "I'm busy flying."

"Thanks a lot, sir," Gibbons replied. Perry just smiled. Gibbons was a first lieutenant and another member of the crew hailing from California.

"I know!" Jacobs said, joining the discussion. "Just open the bomb bay door and have Ramos drop a little extra present to the Germans."

"He can't do that, you idiot," Blocker retorted. "We're at 28,000 feet going one hundred and eighty miles per hour, and its forty-five degrees below zero out there. Ramos would literally freeze his butt off before he could even start to do his business."

"No, but Billy does have the right idea," Gibbons said. "I saw a cardboard box up front with some charts in it. Dump 'em out and he can use that. We can tie the box onto one of the bombs and give Jerry a little something extra from the crew of the *Red Light Lady!*"

The entire crew cheered the idea and the next several minutes was filled with chatter and jokes about "bombing the crap" out of the enemy, or visions of Hitler looking up and getting hit in the face with their special payload.

Technical Sergeant Joe Thomas, the radio operator, was not thrilled with the idea of his radio room being used as a restroom, but there was no choice. He went up to the cockpit while Ramos did his business. When he was done, Idleman picked up the box as gently as a newborn baby and took it to the bomb bay. There he sealed the box shut then tied it to one of the bombs they were carrying. Soon the plane quieted down as everyone prepared for the mission.

A few puffs of black smoke began dotting the air around the bomber formation. "Intel said we can expect light flak and little to no enemy fighter opposition," Perry said.

"Starting our IP now," Blocker announced.

"Roger that, you've got the plane," Perry replied. From his vantage point in the nose of the aircraft, the bombardier looked through the Norden bombsight and flew the plane, making any minor in-flight corrections needed in order to hit the target.

The Norden bombsight was developed by Carl Norden and was originally intended for the Navy. The bombsight was a system of gyros, motors, gears, mirrors, levels, and a telescope. With this, the bombardier would inpute the air speed, wind speed and direction, altitude, and angle of drift. Then the Norden calculated the trajectory of the bomb. A good bombardier could drop his bombs in a hundred-foot circle from nearly four miles up.

Carl Norden, its inventor, boasted that his bombsight could hit a pickle in a barrel from twenty thousand feet. At a press conference a reporter asked him if his claims were really true. Norden smiled and asked, "Which pickle?"

The Air Force considered the bombsight so top secret that it was guarded around the clock, and each bombardier had to swear an oath to protect it with his life to keep it safe and out of the reach of enemy hands.

"Opening bomb bay doors." There was a low whine as the motors opened the doors and then a solid *clunk* when they locked open.

"Ball turret, we've got no fighter contacts reported yet, so keep your eye on our special payload," Perry asked

"You got it, Skipper." Hutton spun his turret around so he could watch the bombs drop from the bay.

"Bombs away!" Blocker announced. Everyone could feel the *Lady* leap higher as she suddenly grew six thousand pounds lighter in a matter of moments. Hutton counted as the bombs fell. On the fifth one that came out, he saw the box tied to it. Suddenly they all heard Hutton howl with laughter. Moments later, Jacobs joined in.

"We got a problem, sir," Hutton said, trying to control his laughter. "Blocker, you've got to be the best damn bombardier in the whole 8th Air Force. You not only can hit a stationary target from twenty-eight thousand feet, but you can hit a moving one, too!"

"What are you talking about?" Blocker asked.

Perry's headphones were filled with yelling. "What the hell are you guys doing up there?" The voice of Captain Bingham of the *Baby Doll;* they were flying in the slot just below them.

"Hutton, what's going on down there?" Perry demanded.

"Our little present to Hitler didn't quite make it all the way. Seems that when the box hit the wind stream, it broke apart and scored a direct hit on the *Baby Doll.* It hit 'em square in the windshield, and it completely covered it," he said, still laughing. "And the lieutenant was right, it's so cold, it froze to the windshield instantly." The entire crew was rolling on the floor laughing.

Perry just shook his head. "This was your idea Jeff, you handle it." Suddenly Gibbons wasn't laughing any more as he spent the next ten minutes trying to calm the angry captain of the *Baby Doll.*

"I see dots up ahead," Tasker called.

"Look alive and stay alive people, playtime is over," Perry warned.

THIRTEEN

"LIEUTENANT Stevens, you want to stop daydreaming over there and tuck it in a little here, son?" Colonel Adams said.

"Ah, yes sir! Right away!" Stevens responded, shaking himself back to the present.

First Lieutenant Luke Stevens shook his head. He was flying wing for the commander of the entire fighter group, and he was day dreaming again. Stevens adjusted his oxygen mask and checked his fuel mixture, making sure it wasn't burning too rich or lean, then looked over and brought his plane a little closer to his lead.

He had just closed formation when he looked down over the left wing. His eyes flew open wide. "Colonel! Eight o'clock low. It looks like a flight of four 190s, Doras, sir, should we jump them?"

"What do you think?"

"Hell, yes . . . I mean yes, sir!"

"But what about our rendezvous with the bombers? We might be late."

"The way I see it sir, there are enemy fighters down there, and I don't think it matters much if we shoot them down here or wait until they're with the bombers."

"See those markings, the yellow nose and white S on the shield? That's *Jagdgeschwader (JG)* 26, The Abbeville Boys, down there. They're one of the most feared and respected of the German units. You want to take them on with even odds?"

Stevens thought for a moment. "We're with the 222nd Fighter Group, 33rd Squadron, the Full Houses, sir, and one of the most respected and feared units of the 8th Army Air Corp. But you're right, sir, we should wait for the odds to be better."

The colonel was a little surprised. He didn't expect to hear that from the lieutenant.

Stevens continued. "We should wait for a couple of more Doras to even up the odds, sir."

Colonel Wesley Adams smiled to himself. He liked this kid. "Very well then, you heard the lieutenant, drop your external tanks and follow me in. Major, I'll take the last one in line, you and Lieutenant Wiser get the next one up."

The four Focke Wulf 190Ds were flying in an echelon left formation, one plane behind the other, each to the left of the last, looking like a half V. They were dark green with noses painted a bright yellow. They looked very professional and very lethal.

The American fighters were in a standard four-ship formation. Adams was the flight leader with Stevens as his wing, flying on his left. Major Henry "Doc" Reins was the element lead with Second Lieutenant Andy Wiser as his wingman, both flying off the colonel's right side. The Focke Wulfs they were hunting were four thousand feet beneath them, flying in the opposite direction. Adams' heart began beating a little faster as he moved the stick to the left, applied left rudder, then gently pushed the stick forward and dropped the nose of his P-51D Mustang down toward its prey. His trusty steed galloped into battle with a Merlin-Packard V-12 that beat with the heart of 1697 horses.

Adams was a triple ace with eighteen kills to his credit, and yet his mouth still got dry every time he went into combat. Every single time he blamed it on the oxygen mask. The wind rushed past his canopy as he pushed past 400 miles per hour and gained quickly on his target. He brought the nose up slightly, keeping the 190 square in his sights. A quick glance over his shoulder assured him that all his planes were right where they should be. It was a perfect set up.

He had closed to an optimum range and was about to pull the trigger when the Germans broke formation. The lead aircraft split hard to the left with his wingman breaking to the right, while the two planes they were targeting both pulled straight up then crisscrossed each other.

"Extend on out!" Adams shouted over the radio. "These guys are good, I don't want to give up any of our speed and get into a turning match with them. Major, swing up and around to the right, you'll have lead now because you have a better angle."

"Roger!" Reins replied. Adams didn't like giving up the lead slot, but Reins did have the better angle and he had the utmost confidence in him.

Doc Reins was a bit on the plump side, but not plump enough to keep him out of the cockpit of his P-51 Mustang fighter. He had a round, pleasant face and bright blue eyes that lit up like a Christmas tree whenever he talked about one of his three favorite subjects: food, flying, and women.

Reins had been around for a long time and at twenty-five was one of the old timers in the squadron, a double ace himself with thirteen kills. Many of the younger pilots thought the major had gotten got his nickname of "Doc" because he was a real doctor or was in medical school when the war started, but it was the colonel who had really given him the name. He called him that because Reins was such a *smooth operator* with the ladies and never seemed to lack a date for Saturday night. Doc had a collection of scarves given to him by his lady friends. At this morning's briefing, he had worn a new, bright red one, and a big smile.

"They've broken into two groups," Reins reported. "I'll take the two on the left."

"Roger, Major," Adams replied. "I'm going to fly back over these two. They'll be forced to turn into me to keep their sixes from being exposed. At best, you'll have another tail shot at them; at worst, they'll turn to avoid you and then I can drop on them."

"Roger that."

Adams and Stevens turned slowly, keeping up as much speed as possible, not letting the gauge fall below three hundred miles per hour. The Doras were now about fifteen hundred feet below them and climbing. Just as predicted, when they were directly over the German fighters, they turned to keep their guns trained on the Americans. As they turned, Reins and Wiser flipped over and dove down onto the two 190s. A split second later, Adams dipped his right wing and dove down as well.

The Germans fighters immediately broke hard to the left. They flew in a tight circle, covering each other's six position and buying time until the other two planes in their flight could return. Reins and Wiser pulled up without firing a shot because their angle of attack had disappeared as soon as the Germans turned.

Adams dove down and tried to get on the inside of his opponent. His Mustang was straining at the high-speed, tight angle but obeyed. He needed just a little more angle to bring his nose up. He dropped a notch on his flaps and pulled back on the stick until heard the stall alarm go off. Adams pushed it for all it was worth. With agonizing slowness his sights crept up onto the fighter.

He fired a burst from his six .50-caliber machine guns. Each gun was capable of firing eight hundred rounds per minute. They responded by tearing up the 190's tail, shredding the rudder and vertical stabilizer and completely destroying its elevator.

In the split second before the man bailed out, Adams could clearly see the face of the 190s pilot. It wasn't a look of fear, but more of an expression of self-defeat at allowing himself to be shot down.

Instead of extending out and away from the remaining Dora, Adams continued his turn and headed right for the other two German planes. "I want to draw these guys back this way so the major and lieutenant can get the drop on them," Adams said to Stevens. "And stay low when we merge. You do not want to play chicken with these guys in a head-on pass. Their 20mm cannons will chew you up in a hurry. We'll slip under them and as soon as they pass. I want you to break right, and I'll break left. I want to split them up and isolate them even more."

The two silver Mustangs, with their red nose spinners and red rudders, turned gracefully together in a tight circle. As they leveled out, they saw the yellow dots of the other two fighters growing bigger and bigger. And in a blink of an eye, the four planes passed each other.

As the combatants flew past each other, the two American planes split up while the Germans stayed together and turned on Colonel Adams. Adams looked over his left shoulder and could see that the 190 was cutting on his inside. It would soon have a good firing angle. Stevens was coming back around, but he would be too late.

He dropped the flaps again just a notch and gained a little more in the turn, but the Focke Wulfs were closing. His heart was pounding in his chest as hard as it had been on the day he asked his wife to marry him.

Suddenly, Reins and Wiser dropped out of the sky, and Doc fired a long burst, catching the German pilots by surprise. His guns hit the lead plane right where the wing and fuselage met. The wing disintegrated, sending the plane into an awkward, headlong spin. The second fighter flipped over on its back and dove for the deck. Stevens was coming around and saw his chance and dove after him.

Stevens had the speed and soon closed to about two hundred and fifty yards then put the hammer down. He watched in amazement as bullets sparked and danced like a string of firecrackers on the 4th of July across the 190's wing. Bits and pieces of the wing were ripped away as the tracers moved along the outside of the wing toward the middle. They converged on the fuselage and a puff of gray smoke appeared as bullets hit the engine compartment. The trail of smoke quickly turned black as the engine ran out of oil and the propeller froze up.

Stevens watched as the pilot struggled to get the canopy back, then saw him pound with both hands against the glass out of frustration when it wouldn't budge. Stevens almost ran into the doomed fighter because he was so intent at watching the drama instead of paying attention. Quickly recovering, he pulled up and peered over his shoulder as the plane crashed outside a small village.

All of a sudden it hit him: he had just made his first kill! The thrill of combat was intoxicating, almost euphoric, and he could feel the adrenaline flowing through his bloodstream. But it was different, too. He was elated and yet somehow disappointed. It had all happened so fast. No great struggle, no heroics, just plain and simple.

"Thanks, Major," Adams said.

"Any time, boss."

"Where is the other 190?"

"He bugged out, sir," Wiser replied. "He kept on going after the major waxed his friend."

"Good work, gentlemen. Now let's form up and get to those bombers. We lost a little time here, but I think downing three out of four planes was worth it."

FOURTEEN

"STILL tracking the bogies, sir," Tasker reported from the top turret of the bomber.

"Pilot to radio. You picking up anything to our radio challenge?" Perry asked.

"Negative, Captain. I'm not getting anything on the IFF at all."

"They're dropping down!" Tasker shouted. "They're bandits alright, setting up for an head on pass!"

Suddenly the peaceful sky was filled with fire and fury. Four Focke Wulf 190s flying abreast in a perfect line attacked the formation from the front, which was the most vulnerable spot of the Flying Fortress. The Fw 190s were the fastest and most heavily armed of the German single-engine fighters.

Some versions of the Butcherbird had four 20mm cannons and two machine guns, designed specifically to bring down the big planes. They tore through the bomber formation in a matter of seconds and left in their deadly wake one bomber spinning out of control and another one with an engine on fire.

"Two of the 190s that just passed us are swinging around to hit our six," Jacob announced from the tail gunner's position. "The other two have flanked out, one on each side and it looks like they're going back up front for another head on pass."

Ramos caught a glimpse of the190 as it passed through the formation, then tracked it as it swung out wide and flew parallel to the group on the left side. Even though the German fighter was well out of range, he still fired a few rounds at him; he wanted the pilot to know that he was being watched.

"I've got another bandit at three o'clock high!" Tasker shouted.

"I see him," Idleman replied. "It's a 109." In order to line up the sights on the high intruder, Idleman had to crouch to one knee. "He's starting his run!"

"*Detroit Beauty* just got it," Gibbons said. The B-17 below and to their right was going down. Both engines on the left wing were on fire as the plane fell from the sky, leaving a twisted, spiraling trail of black smoke.

"I see three, no, four chutes," Hutton reported. No one said a word about the other six crewmen that didn't make it out, even though they knew everyone onboard. There would be time enough to grieve later, if they survived.

"That 190 is coming up on our tail fast," the tail gunner shouted. "Can you help me, Tiny?"

"Negative, he's too high on the tail for me. He's all yours, Billy."

"Pilot to bombardier. Two more 109s are setting up for a head on."

Lieutenant Blocker trained the guns of the chin turret on the approaching planes, preparing for the attack. As bombardier, his duties included operating the Bendix Chin Turret, which was remotely controlled from his seat behind the bombsight. The Germans had learned through trial and error that a head-on attack was one of the more successful strategies in hitting the Flying Fortress at its most vulnerable spot. The Chin turret was a stopgap measure that proved to have very favorable results.

"The 109 is nine o'clock low!" shouted Hutton. "There's another one trying to get underneath us.

KAPITÄN Ernst Keppler watched the sun rise that morning and couldn't remember a more perfect beginning to a day. He had thoughts of calling the infirmary and telling them he would not be in today, and as a captain, he would not be questioned. But he had obligations and his duty to perform. As was his custom, he ate a small breakfast, then kissed his wife, Helga, and their nine-year-old daughter, Greta, good-bye. He would make the short drive to the aerodrome, fly several missions, then come home again to this wife and daughter. It always seemed a little odd to him that this was the way he fought the war, while others were gone from home for months and even years.

The day was beautiful, perfect for flying. His usual plane was down for maintenance, so he was given one that had just arrived from the factory. He had flown it once upon arrival to test it, and even though it was the same model as his—a Messerschmitt 109G—it didn't feel right. He had flown seventy-three missions in his old aircraft, and he and the plane had grown accustomed to each other. The instruments in the new aircraft were in the same place, the controls all served the same function . . . and yet it was different. The best way he could describe it to someone who had never flown would be like trading a pair of old, worn, comfortable shoes in for a brand new pair. They did the same thing, but the fit just wasn't the same.

Their mission today, as it was most days, was to intercept a group of American bombers coming to destroy the Fatherland. He preferred the challenge of facing a quick and agile fighter in combat, a worthy opponent, not a lumbering four-engine giant. It didn't sit well with him to be shooting at a target so large that any first-month air cadet could hit it; there was little skill involved when the target filled one's entire gun sight. Bombers were a dangerous lot to be sure and not to be taken lightly, bristling with machine guns, but caution would serve one better than skill when fighting this opponent.

Flying was Keppler's joy, and he lived for his moments in the cockpit, but after nearly four years of war, the pleasure had been dulled. He had been there when Germany had rolled across Europe and was knocking on the threshold of England. He had flown against the British pilots and come to admire their tenacity and stubbornness. But those were the glory days when everything was in perspective and the objectives were as clear as this day was. Now things had changed for the Fatherland. The Americans and British were winning the war, Berlin had been bombed, and there was a growing sense of urgency in the air.

Yesterday he had noticed that the timing was a little off in his replacement aircraft and he hoped his ground crew had repaired it. A year ago he would have aborted the flight, but times had changed. Unless there was a major malfunction, a pilot was expected to fulfill his mission. That was their duty. So he stayed in the air to lead his men by example; that was *his* duty.

It was also increasingly frowned upon to for a pilot to return to base with even a few rounds left in his guns. They were expected to press the attack until the enemy was turned back or they were completely out of ammunition

So now he found himself in an untried aircraft, attacking a large flight of American bombers from underneath. His approach would be low and in from the side. He would coax as much speed as he could, pull up, fire all his ammo, then roll over and dive for the deck and hope his engine would get him back to base and home to his Helga.

His squadrons, along with two others, were already attacking the American formation. Several bombers had fallen as well as some of his comrades.

Looking up, Keppler saw what he was after. "There, that one," he said to himself.

"HERE he comes!" Tasker shouted, as the high Messerschmitt started its dive.

Almost in unison, Tasker and Idleman opened up on the 109. The sound of their machine guns firing could be heard as they rattled over the drone of the powerful engines. A small vapor trail appeared from the fighter as several bullets hit the plane.

"I hit his fuel tank," Idleman shouted.

"Bull, *I* hit his tank!" Tasker rebutted.

The big plane didn't flinch as the 109 dropped down firing its 20mm cannon and 13mm machine guns. The number three engine, the one closest to the co-pilot on the right wing, erupted in a large puff of black smoke as the Messerschmitts bullets found their mark.

"Number three is hit," Gibbons reported. "We're losing oil pressure fast."

"Okay, feather it before it catches on fire," Perry ordered.

The 109 continued its pass under the bomber, moving at more than four hundred miles per hour.

Then exploded.

"You hit a fuel line," Hutton shouted, "but I hit his tank." Hutton had his turret turned around and was waiting for the German fighter to pass by.

"Good shooting, all," Perry said. "Score a team kill for the *Red Light Lady*. Keep it up, gentlemen, there are plenty more where they came from, and we're still along ways from home."

"Yes, sir," Came their replies.

They had little time to celebrate as another fighter dropped down out of the sun, making a slashing, hit-and-run attack. The *Red Light Lady* shook from a string of bullets that ripped though the center of the fuselage, chewing up cables and twisting metal.

"I got a fire in here!" Thomas shouted from the radio room.

"Top turret, get down there and help him!"

Blocker sat at his station in the nose of the plane and stared at two fast-approaching dots that turned into a pair of 109s in this deadly game of chicken. The two were flying wing tip to wing tip and their yellow noses made them look like a pair of eyes suspended in the sky. Those eyes began winking with the firing of the machine guns and then started blinking when the cannons fired. Blocker answered back with a steady stream of tracer fire from his twin .50s.

Tasker slipped out of the top turret and made his way along the narrow catwalk in the bomb bay, between the cockpit and the radio room.

"Grab that extinguisher over there!" Thomas shouted as soon as he saw Tasker.

Technical Sergeant Joseph Thomas was from Seattle and had been in love with radios from the first moment he'd tied a string between two tin cans. He was short with a round, red face that made him look like he was in a constant state of embarrassment.

Tasker grabbed the extinguisher and started spraying at the flames. They had to get the fire out fast before it got to the oxygen system and blew up the entire plane. "Hey, you're bleeding!" Tasker shouted as he saw blood oozing from Thomas' right shoulder.

"It's nothing; a piece of shrapnel hit me when a 20mm round exploded. Come on, point that thing over here."

Right after Ramos fired his warning shots, the Fw 190 waggled his wings in response. "Did you see that?" he exclaimed to Idleman. "That SOB just challenged me, I think."

"Maybe he likes you," Idleman shot back, smiling under his oxygen mask. Ramos swore at him in Spanish until Perry stopped him.

"Cut the chatter, Ramos," Perry ordered. "Just shoot him, don't talk him to death."

"Yes, sir, sorry, Captain." He fired a longer burst at him out of spite. The 190 responded by pulling up and banking hard toward the bomber formation and the *Red Light Lady* in particular.

Blocker held the trigger down and held his breath as the 109s closed. At the last possible second, Blocker pointed the guns up. He had a split second to decide if they were going to go over or under the plane. He guessed right. A stream of bullets nicked the elevators of the fighter on the right as he passed overhead. The fighter lost control and rammed into *Trouble Coming*, a B-17 that was in the high formation behind them. Both planes exploded in a huge ball of fire, leaving only a black, dingy cloud of smoke as a gravestone marking where eleven brave men just died.

"One-o-nine low!" shouted Hutton. "He's trying to get underneath us."

ERNST Keppler dipped the nose of his Messerschmitt down for a little extra speed as he approached his target. It was a B-17 that seemed to be drawing a lot of attention and already had one engine out. He was hoping to make his run unnoticed, but all that changed when a fellow 109 dropped down in his attack, was hit by the belly gunner, and exploded when he went by.

The gunner was looking right at him.

Keppler wasn't overly concerned that he had been spotted. He had faced many bomber gunners before, but he had an uneasy feeling all day that he couldn't quite put a finger on. His mind flashed to Helga and Greta, but he quickly shook the image out of his head. It was not good for a fighter pilot to think of such things, especially when going into battle. He applied full throttle and brought the nose of his plane up, filling his gun sights with the massive bomber.

He started firing at six hundred yards out, sooner than he normally would have fired, but he wanted to get this mission over with. Still, even at that range, he saw a few tracers find their mark. They hit the belly of the fuselage and around the bottom turret and in the wings. With any luck, he would hit the gunner or at least disable the gun.

THE *Red Light Lady* vibrated as she was stung again. Bullets came up through the floor and ricocheted in the long tunnel between the tail and waist gunners. A few more 13mm bullets barely missed Ramos; the floor shook as a 20mm shell exploded near Hutton and the ball turret.

"Hutton! Are you okay? Tim?"

There was no answer.

SUDDENLY the Messerschmitt's Daimler Benz 12-cylinder engine coughed and sputtered like an old sway-backed nag instead of running smoothly like the thoroughbred that it was. Keppler cursed and swore at the plane, pounding his fist so hard against the instrument panel he broke several dials. Just when he needed power the most, his plane turned on him! He pushed the stick hard over and shoved his foot against the pedals, trying to get full rudder. But the plane just hung there, suspended in mid-air, and in time.

Keppler felt the plane being riddled with bullets. It felt as if the bullets weren't shooting him down so much as they were pushing him down to earth. He had had many close calls in his nearly five years of combat, but he knew that, save a miracle, he would not make it home to see his Helga again.

Smoke filled the cockpit and he had trouble breathing and seeing. He looked up—on the front of the bomber that he was trying to kill was a picture of his wife. In that split second before his plane blew up, Ernst Keppler saw the face of his beloved one last time.

TASKER sprayed the last of his extinguisher on the fire in the radio room, then beat the rest of the flames out using his leather flight jacket. With everything in hand, he put his singed jacket back on and returned to his gun position. Walking back along the catwalk in the bomb bay, Tasker looked down and saw daylight filtering in through the dozen or so bullet holes punched through the bomb bay doors. Some of the hydraulic lines had also been hit, leaving a musty, oily smell in the bay and leaking on the catwalk, making it extremely slippery. How lucky they were, he thought, that they had already dropped their bombs.

"The fire's out in the radio room, and we took some hits in the bomb bay," Tasker said, reaching the cockpit. "The walkway is slippery, and you can smell the leaking hydraulic fluid."

Perry held up his hand to stop Tasker. "Ball Turret? Tiny Tim, report!"

"Captain, I wish you wouldn't call me that, sir."

A collective sigh of relief came over the intercom. "Dammit, Hutton, you had us all worried here. Why didn't you answer?" Perry asked.

"Sorry, sir. I was concentrating on that 109 who hit us."

"Are you okay down there?"

"Yes, sir. The turret took some hits, but everything seems to be working fine."

"Top turret, I need some help back here!" Jacobs shouted. "My guns are jammed and that 190 on our six is about to have us for lunch."

Perry tapped Tasker on the shoulder and pointed for him to get up into his gun mounts. Tasker nodded, then stood back into his turret but stopped cold. The Plexiglas surrounding the guns was shattered and smashed by several direct hits from the 109s that had just made the head on pass. He now realized that if he'd been at his station instead of helping Thomas with the fire, he would be dead.

"I-I can't help, the turret's out," was all he could stammer.

"190 is coming in hard and fast at nine-o'clock!" Ramos shouted. "He's going to fire at any second!"

"Hutton?"

"Negative, Captain, they're both too high for me."

"The Dora on our six is firing!" Jacobs shouted. Each man of the *Red Light Lady* came to the realization that they wouldn't be going home this time. One by one they were relived the events of their all too short lives. They remembered being with friends, families, envisioning what their futures could have been. With no way to defend themselves, they knew they had minutes, to live.

"*Hot damn!*" Jacobs shouted. "Prettiest sight I ever did see. This P-51 just dropped out of nowhere like a hawk going after Mrs. Kimball's pet wiener dog back home. Man, he was moving! That 190 just disintegrated!"

"It must be raining Mustangs," Ramos added. "Another one just dropped down and cut the 190 over here in half."

"Bomber group, this is Colonel Adams of the 222nd. Sorry we're a little late."

"Colonel! Are we ever glad to see you," Perry replied. "It wasn't looking too good there for a while. When we get home, the crew of the *Red Light Lady* would like to buy you and your men a round of drinks."

"We'll do our best to see that you get home safe so we can collect."

"Thank you, sir. Much appreciated."

The attacking Germans soon lost interest when the American escort fighters showed up.

AN hour and a half-later, Perry announced he could see the white cliffs of Dover . . . and home. Jacobs crawled back through the tunnel out of the tail gunner's position and stood and stretched. The tail gunner's position was almost as cramped as the ball turret because he had to kneel in order to fire his guns.

Idleman walked over to help Hutton up out of the ball turret.

"Captain, we got a problem back here," Idleman said.

"Don't tell me Ramos has to use the can again?"

"No, sir. We can't get the hatch off the ball turret."

"Take over, Jeff," Perry said as he got up, stretched himself and went aft.

When he arrived, all three gunners were standing around the top of the turret.

"What have we got?" the captain asked.

"When that 109 hit us from below, several of the shells hit the brace supports and now the turret can't turn far enough to get the hatch open," Idleman explained. Perry walked around and examined the turret and pulled on the crosspieces a few times to see if they would move. He also saw that Hutton was almost lying on his side.

"How come you're laying like that?" Perry asked.

"A while back, I moved the turret around because the sun was in my eyes. It froze up, and I haven't been able to get it to move since."

"Sorry, Hutton, it looks like you are going to have to stay in there until we land and the ground crew can cut you out," Perry said.

Hutton shrugged his shoulders. "That's okay. I can finish reading my *Captain America* comic."

Perry returned to the cockpit and advised the tower that they were lining up for the final approach with one engine out and that they were shot up pretty bad.

"Throttling back number one and two to 50 percent," Perry said. "Keeping number four at 75 percent to help compensate with the torque for the loss of number three. Flaps. Lower that landing gear."

The gear motors strained at lowering the two huge tires and were supposed to make a solid *clunk* when they locked in place.

But it didn't happen.

Perry and Gibbons looked at each other. "Try it again," Perry ordered. Gibbons repeated the procedure with the same results. Nothing.

"There must be a short in the wiring somewhere," Gibbons said, and before Perry could even say it, Gibbons was out of his seat to manually lower the gear. The crank was located in the bomb bay behind the copilot seat and was a back up just in case this sort of thing happened. Neither man wanted to say it, but they both knew that they either had to get the gear down or Hutton out of the ball turret. If they couldn't do one or the other, Hutton would be crushed to death when the plane made a belly landing.

Gibbons grabbed the crank handle and started to turn. It took a great deal of effort to lower the massive landing gear. Each wheel was 56 inches in diameter and weighed 200 pounds.

The crank handle turned four times and a wave of relief washed over him. Gibbons paused and wiped the nervous perspiration off his forehead. Suddenly the wave of relief was replaced by a tidal wave of panic as the handle stopped turning. He fought the rush of panic and pulled the crank with all his strength, but it refused to move.

He tried again with no results. In anger and frustration, he tore off the sheet metal housing to get to the gears. If he had to, he would turn the gears one cog at a time. When he got the cover off he could see that machine-gun bullets had severed the main crankshaft. The gear assemblies were in shambles. It was beyond repair.

Gibbons return to the cockpit with a look of resignation on his face. "The gears are all shot to hell, there's no way the wheels are going to come down. How much fuel do we have left?"

"Not much. Maybe another half hour's worth of flying at best," Perry replied.

"Okay, if the gear won't come down, then Hutton has to come out. Here, take over the controls. I'm going back there." Perry went to the back and stood over the turret, looking down at Hutton lying in that strange and uncomfortable angle. He was lying on his side curled up in a ball, reading his comic book. Perry tapped on the top of the glass to get his attention.

"I'll give it to you straight, Tim, the gear's been all shot up and we can't lower it."

"Yeah, I figured something was up when we went around the field again and didn't land."

"Well, don't you worry, we'll get you out of there."

"I know you'll do your best, Skipper," Hutton said the words and he didn't doubt for a moment that they would do everything that they could. Yet he couldn't shake the nagging feeling that it wouldn't be enough. He was starting to feel sick to his stomach now. He wanted to throw up, it hurt so much. It was one thing to die in combat, where the end came quickly; it was another to have to wait for it, see it coming and have time to think about it.

For the next twenty minutes, each member of the crew offered his own suggestions on how to get their friend out. They pushed and pulled and pried and poked, but they couldn't budge the turret to get the hatch open. All the while, Hutton pretended to read his comic book. In reality, he was doing everything in his power not to scream. He didn't want the rest of the guys to think he was a coward.

Ten minutes earlier, he had reached the same conclusion that his crew-mates had only now come to accept: he was not getting out of the turret. He lowered his head in shame and finally broke down and started weeping. If he had looked up, he would have seen that Jacobs and Idleman and the tough street kid from LA were already crying.

Perry sat back down in the pilot seat in utter defeat. He wanted to be with Hutton at the moment that they landed, but he could not ask Gibbons to fly the plane and be responsible for Hutton's death. He was the captain. It was his responsibility.

"I've got the base chaplain standing by," Gibbons said quietly.

Perry nodded. "We've got the Chaplain. Tim, you want to talk to him?"

"I'm not Catholic, sir. My mom and dad raised me a Baptist, but I kind of fell away from the church as of late. You don't think God will hold that against me, do you? After all, I figure He's in the business of forgiveness."

"I guess He is," was all Perry could manage.

The plane was quiet. They had all seen death before and had lost friends, but they never expected to lose one of their own. Maybe by flak, by explosion, by bullets—but not being crushed to death in the belly of their own plane.

"Skipper, I know we've got to be running low on fuel, and you can't keep this crate in the air forever," Hutton said between sobs, not caring now if everyone knew he was scared spitless. "Just land it and get it over with. I know you and all the guys did your best. I don't want to sound all mushy or anything but you guys—"

"Ah, shut up, ya little runt," someone shouted.

"Hey, he's not a runt," someone else added. "He's Tiny Tim!"

The ground got closer now, and the chatter picked up the closer they got. Everyone was taking pot shots at Hutton and recalling stories. The *Red Light Lady* screamed in agony as she landed in the soft earth.

Anyone witnessing the landing would have said that the noise was just the scraping and twisting of cold hard metal against the ground as the plane hit. But anyone who'd ever flown in a B-17 and been part of her crew would know better. The *Red Light Lady* screamed in pain, for her own wounds and for loosing one of her own.

"Good-bye, Timothy," Perry said softly under his breath as the plane slid peacefully to a stop in the green grass of home.

FIFTEEN

THE rooster crowed in the distance, announcing the start of another day. But Claubert Merle was already ahead of the morning, sitting at the table with his breakfast half gone. Even being retired now for more than ten years, he found it hard to break habits, and getting up before the dawn to go to work was one of them.

Beka hated his early mornings and longed to sleep in; nonetheless, she would diligently get up and fix him his breakfast and pack his lunch before he would start his daily routine. A carpenter by trade, he would go out into the shed and carefully select the proper tools for the day's work, load them in the wagon, hitch up the horse and be on his way.

He had dreamed of giving her an easier life, one with servants to pamper her and in which she could sleep late and wake up to find breakfast waiting for her. The day he retired, they took a trip to Paris and stayed in a fancy hotel that had bellboys, monogrammed towels, even room service. They stayed for four days, then returned. She said she had a good time but that the fancy life was not for her. In reality, he was the one who couldn't stand it. She had realized this and had given it up for him.

He could never fool her, no matter how hard he tried. They'd had only a short five years together after his retirement before she became ill with pneumonia and died.

He could still see her sometimes, sitting across the table from him, telling him not to forget his tools or his lunch. He took a sip of tea, smiled, and finished his breakfast. It would take most of the day to repair the damage the soldiers had done to his front door when they broke it down. It had been unlocked.

THE door was not as badly damaged as he first thought. He finished it shortly after lunch and decided to take a walk. The air was cool, but the sun felt warm on his face. He walked a little slower than normal, an act for any prying eyes that might be spying on him. Merle made his way down by the river to find his favorite park bench.

There was a bakery just a block up from the park. As was his routine, he would buy a bag of day-old bread for a few francs and then sit on the bench and watch the children play and feed the pigeons and ducks.

Watching children play was always a bittersweet thing. He enjoyed their laughter and their play, but it was also a painful reminder than he and Beka had never been able to have children of their own.

From his favorite bench, the sun was at his back, and he watched the children in front of him with the water flowing peacefully behind them. It was also his favorite bench because from there, he had a perfect view of the only bridge for ten miles in either direction. He could watch any troop movements and count the number of armored vehicles that passed. Today, there was a large column of men and machines moving east, back toward Berlin. That was a good sign, he told himself, a very good sign.

After this, he would go home, fix a good meal, read a little, and go to bed early. It would be hard to miss his transmission that night. Over the months and years, he had grown to look forward to them, but tonight caution was called for. In the morning, before the SS Major even thought about getting out of bed, he would send a brief transmission to let Hermes know that he was still alive and well.

Merle enjoyed the day right up until the time when he felt a firm hand grasp his shoulder. "Good day, Herr Merle."

"Major." Merle feared his voice would reveal the terror that was screaming inside of him. The major walked slowly and deliberately around and sat down on the middle of the bench. "This is a lovely spot," he said, his voice smooth and friendly. "I can see why you like to come here. Although I don't have any children of my own, I, too, like to sit and watch the little ones play. They are so innocent, so oblivious to all that is going on around them.

Have you any children, Claubert? Oh, I'm sorry, no, of course you don't. You and Rebecca were never able to conceive." He shook his head sadly. "That's too bad, they can be such a blessing."

Rebecca? Children? How does he know all this? How long has he been watching me? Merle thought to himself. Was the major playing some perverse game with him?

Reinard continued, "And I see you enjoy feeding the birds, too." He reached over and tore off a chunk of bread, broke it into smaller pieces and threw it to the birds. "Now these birds, they have a different lot in life. Look at that one there, the fat one. He's happy as can be, thinking everything is just fine. Little does he realize that at any moment, someone could come along and snatch that away from him." The major reached out and grabbed at the air, pretending to grasp the duck in his hand.

Merle flinched as the major's hand sliced through the air. He could image his own throat in his clutches. Merle's lips were parched and his mouth dry. He hoped the major wouldn't ask him any questions, because he didn't think he could speak at that moment.

Reinard sat quietly on the bench, watching the children and the ducks; neither he nor Merle moved or spoke. Then Reinard sat back and crossed his legs.

"It is a fine day today. How many trucks have you counted going over the bridge?"

Merle's heart was about to give out, he was so frightened. Usually suspicion alone was enough to get one arrested and thrown in prison, especially with the SS and men like Reinard. Why haven't I been arrested yet? What is he up too? Merle calmed himself before he spoke. "Trucks?" was all he could manage to get out.

Three boys about eight years old were playing with a ball. One of them kicked it too hard, and it sailed past his playmate and rolled to a stop, landing at Reinard's feet. The major picked up the ball and tossed it back and forth in his hand as one of the boys walked up slowly to retrieve it. His mother saw him approaching the major and ran over and snatched him up in her arms as if she were rescuing him from a pack of wolves.

"Please excuse him, Major," she said. "He's only a child. I hope he didn't bother you."

"No, not at all," Reinard smiled and tossed the ball back.

Reinard turned back to Merle. "What do you suppose they teach the children in school these days? I'm sure it is much different than when you and I were boys. I wonder if they still teach the Classics like history and mythology. You know, the ancient Greek gods? Apollo, Poseidon . . . Hermes? I think my favorite has to be Zeus. After all, if you're going to be a god, why not be the king of the gods?"

Merle wanted to stand up and run. Instead, he remained as still and silent as one of the stone statues in the park. Zeus! He knows about my code name and that of my controller. But how?

"I don't know, Major, I have never really thought about it. If you don't mind, I'm feeling a bit tired now. I'll think I'll go home and rest."

"Can I offer you a lift, perhaps?" Reinard said. "You have such a long walk home."

"No, no, thank you. It's a nice day, and the sun will do me good." Merle started to stand but was stopped by Reinard's strong hand on his arm.

"You're tired, so I must insist. In fact, I'm enjoying our little conversation so much, I think we should continue it in the comfort of my office, don't you? But you're right, we should enjoy the warmth of the sun while we can.

The weather is supposed to turn ugly later.

Let's take my staff car and drive with the top down and enjoy the scenery. I do love your quaint neighborhood. I imagine you know all of your neighbors, and they know you. But do they know that you and I are such good friends?"

Merle was silent as he climbed in the back seat, and Reinard sat right next to him. Merle closed his eyes and wished he could crawl under his seat. Reinard was very clever, Merle thought. He would be ostracized in his own community. Guilty by association to be seen riding around with an SS major, no one in his neighborhood would ever talk to him again. Even though the day was cool, Reinard insisted on driving with the top down, parading Merle around for all to see as if he were a trophy. Merle tried his best to keep his head down, but there was very little he could do.

Twenty minutes later, the ride mercifully came to an end, but mercy was a stranger to their destination. It was the city hall before the German occupation and before the SS took it over for their headquarters. It was once a beautiful building with tall columns and steep gables, giving the building a false sense of authority and hope.

A huge banner with the German eagle hung down from the two center columns, flanked on either side by two larger red banners displaying the Nazi symbol. The Nazi flags crushed the spirit of the once proud eagle, bending its will, making it submit to their bidding.

With a heaviness he had never experienced, Merle got out of the car. He took a long look around, taking in as much as he could because he didn't know if he would ever see any of it again. He noticed the color of the sky, the details of the clouds, even heard the muffled sounds of the railway center a few kilometers away. Sights and sounds he had taken for granted now seemed to be very important. He knew that very few people who went into the SS Headquarters ever came out alive.

I've lived a good life, Claubert told himself as he walked up the stairs. Now he was glad Beka was gone. He could endure whatever torture they could inflict, but he couldn't stand the thought of anyone hurting his wife. He drew in a heavy breath. Never in a million years would he have thought he would ever be grateful she was dead.

Reinard left Merle with a guard who led him down to the lower levels of the basement. He was alone in a small, poorly lit room with nothing but a small wooden table and two chairs. One chair was a simple, uncomfortable-looking metal chair with a low back, and the other was a plush office chair, the kind one would find sitting behind the desk of a head of state.

The strangest thing of all was the classical music being played in the background. The cheerful melodies seemed so out of place, floating through the dark and barren corridors.

Merle stood in the center of the room, afraid to sit in either chair, fearing that if he did, it would somehow take his soul, that he would be doomed to stay down there forever. But soon his legs grew weary. He had no choice but to sit, so he chose the metal chair. He longed to sit in the other chair, to sink into the luxurious comfort of the deep cushions, but his fear of incurring Reinard's wrath for sitting in his chair overwhelmed his need for comfort.

The room was quiet, and it had been over an hour since the guard had left him. Merle struggled to keep his eyes open, but boredom, fatigue, and weariness overtook him. His head bobbed twice and he succumbed to sleep.

He sprang out of the chair as he heard the sound of someone screaming in agony. Had he been dreaming it? He listened intently, but the pounding of his own heart drowned out all other sounds. Surely the SS wouldn't torture people in a public building in the middle of town. Would they?

Wide awake, Merle looked around the room, then glanced down at the table in front of him. He hadn't noticed it before, but there were deep scratches in the top of the table. They started in the middle and drew outward toward the edge. There seemed to be a familiarity, a pattern to them.

He sat down and placed his hands on the table where the scratches started and slowly drew his fingers along the grooves. They were a perfect fit, like they were made to fit his hands. He yanked his hands off the table as if it were electrified. The scratches on the table were claw marks made by human hands. What kind of madness drove them to claw at the table like this?

Merle shot out of his seat and skirted around the table. He moved to the other side of the room, away from the table as if it were a snarling creature. There was something else now he hadn't noticed before, a stain on the floor next to the wall. It looked like something had dripped down from the ceiling, but there were no marks on the ceiling, only the puddle-shaped stain on the floor. It was a dark stain and looked like . . . blood.

Merle reeled away as if the stain were another wild animal, ready to devour him. His eyes darted around the room now. He was frantic, he had to get out, but there was no escape.

He took several more deep breaths then forced himself to return to the table and sit back down. He was not going to let his fears, real or imagined, rule him. Reinard may be in control, but he would not allow himself to lose control. He had just sat back down when again he heard screams followed by the sound of a single gunshot.

Merle bolted out of his chair again, not knowing what to do. He paced back and forth, trying to think, but his brain wouldn't work. Fear had just grabbed the keys to his mind, ready to reopen all the cages.

A moment later, Reinard walked in with a smile on his face and a pleasant greeting. "My dear Claubert, please sit down, you look pale. May I get you a glass of water?"

Merle shook his head and sat down without protest.

Reinard sat down in the leather chair, took off his hat and set it on the table, revealing a hairline that was receding faster than the Germans retreating back across the Rhine. "Now then," he said, folding his hands and placing them on the table in front of him, "we have much to discuss, you and I. To answer some of your questions, my dear friend, yes, I know who you are. You are working with the French Resistance and have been almost since the start of the war. I know you have a secret transmitter hidden somewhere, and that you've been talking with your controller in England on a regular basis. And to answer the next question that's formulating in your head: no, I'm not going to ask you to betray your contacts or to work for me as a double agent."

"Wha . . . what do you want, then?" Merle stammered.

The officer smiled. "I want you to do what you do best, I want you to relay a message for me."

SIXTEEN

"WAKE up, Tony," Idleman whispered. "Wake up," he said again as he shook Ramos by his shoulders.

Ramos swatted Idleman's hand away and swore in Spanish. "Man, I was having the best dream of my life, and you had to ruin it!"

"I had a dream, too! I dreamed that Tim was back. It was really weird, and now look, someone is in his bunk." They looked at each other then at Timothy Hutton's old bunk. All they could see was that someone was in the bed. They couldn't see a face on the apparition because it was facing the wall. They heard a low moan and the figured moved.

"Do you think it's his ghost?" Idleman asked.

Ramos looked at him and slapped him alongside the head. "No, I don't think it's his ghost." Still, they both just sat and stared at the mysterious figure for a moment. Then Ramos finally spoke. "Go wake up Billy, but do it quietly."

Idleman nodded and went and woke him up. Soon, the three friends were gathered around the bunk, staring down at the unsuspecting stranger. Without a care in the world, the mysterious figure rolled over and revealed his face.

"Look at him," Idleman said. "He's just a kid, a baby, really. He looks like he should still be in high school." To a twenty-two-year-old battle-hardened combat veteran, everyone fresh from the States looked young.

"Hey," Ramos said, "fresh meat for the poker game. I bet he's got plenty of dough too, just coming from the States. I'm get tired of taking you guys' money all the time."

Jacobs just shook his head. "Yeah, right, you still owe me a twenty from the last game."

Ramos quickly changed the subject. "I wonder where he's from."

"It doesn't matter where he comes from as long as his money is green," Jacobs replied. "And don't change the subject. You still owe me twenty bucks."

"Where's his duffel bag?" Ramos asked. "His orders have to be in there."

"I wonder if he's our new ball turret gunner?" Idleman asked.

"No, he's probably just some airman who wandered in off the streets looking for a place to sleep." Ramos reached over and slugged Idleman again. "Man, sometimes you are so dense. Of course he's Tiny Tim's replacement."

The sad reality of the statement caught everyone off guard. It had only been a few days since he'd died, but knowing that his replacement had already arrived made it painfully final—their friend really wasn't coming back.

The man in the bunk lazily stretched and yawned as he began to wake up. His eyes opened slowly to meet the new day. Then popped open to the size of silver dollars to find three strangers staring down at him. Nobody said a word. Then stranger sprang out of bed and shouted "Attention!"

The other men jumped up and snapped to attention.

Captain Perry and Lieutenant Gibbons smiled to each other as they walked in. "I like this guy," Perry said.

"Yeah, finally a little respect," Gibbons added. Perry let them stand there for a bit, then finally gave them the "at ease" order. He walked over to the new recruit and held out his hand. "Hi, I'm Captain Mike Perry, and this is my exec, First Lieutenant Jeff Gibbons."

"Staff Sergeant Hubert Mitchell reporting, sir!" Mitchell reached under his bed and pulled out his orders from his duffel bag.

Perry examined the orders. "Just get in?" he asked.

"Yes, sir. Touched down at 18:00 and then hitched a ride with some fighter pilots stationed nearby. They dropped me off at the gate, and the corporal in the guard shack told me to bunk here."

Perry handed him back his orders. "Welcome to the crew of the *Red Light Lady,* best damn bomber crew in the 415th Bomber Squadron, 819th Aerial Bombardment Group." Perry went around the room and introduced every-one.

Mitchell smiled and shook hands with everyone. "Good to meet you. Y'all can call me Mitch."

"Tony, you, Jerry, and Billy take Mitch to the chow hall, then show him around the base. We've got the day off today, so make the most of it. Just remember, we fly tomorrow," he quickly added. There were a few moans as they headed out the door to the mess hall.

Ramos and Idleman watched as Mitchell downed his second helping of powered eggs and his third piece of burnt toast. "Man, this guy can eat!" Ramos said to Idleman.

"It looks like he actually likes Army chow," Idleman added.

"Yeah, just give him time." They laughed.

"How long you fellas been over here?" Mitchell managed to say between mouthfuls.

"We've been here for a little less than five months," Idleman said.

"And we've flown 18 missions," Ramos added proudly. "Twice to the Big B."

"The Big B?"

"Berlin. Berlin, you know, where Hitler lives. Where've you been, boy? It's in Germany."

"Yeah, I know where it is."

"Mail call. Mail call for all squadrons." A staff sergeant walked in at the far end of the mess hall, dragging two huge canvas bags behind him like an overworked Santa's helper. The sergeant was besieged by nearly every man in the building waiting to get letters from home. At that moment, he was more popular than Betty Grable. Well, almost.

The noisy mess hall soon turned quiet as each man received his letters from parents, grandparents, wives, sweethearts . . . it really didn't matter. They were a connection to that faraway place that some hadn't seen in years and that some would never see again. Home.

Each member of the *Red Light Lady* jumped up from the table and waited in line to get their piece of home. They returned to the table, having forgotten all about eating.

"Hmm," Ramos said, waving his letters under everyone's nose so they could smell the perfume. He had frequently been in minor trouble with the law before the war. The last judge to see him gave him the choice of facing some serious hard time in prison or joining the military. He chose the Army. He would never admit it, but he was really getting use to Army life and was considering staying in after the war.

Ramos strutted around the table like a millionaire playboy. "This one is from my little Rosalita, and this one"—holding up another letter for all to see and smell—"is from my little Carmelita."

"Who's the third one from?" Billy asked.

He smiled again, with a less mischievous grin. "This one is from my *mamacita.*"

"Your mom?" They all laughed.

"What d'ya got there, Billy?" Tommy Svenson asked.

"I got me something better than Tony's perfumed letters." He unwrapped the box to reveal a tin full of homemade chocolate chip cookies. Most were broken and in pieces, but that didn't matter, not a crumb would go to waste from this precious package that had traveled halfway around the world. Without hesitation, Billy handed his priceless treasure around, sharing it with his extended family. He handed it to Tony who walked around to each crew member so they could have some. When he came to Mitchell, he kept on going, not offering him any.

"Hey, listen to this," Eric Blocker piped in. "My dad just made foreman at the paper mill, and he said that I have a job waiting for me when I get home."

And so it went around the table, each sharing their letters from home, things that had once seemed unimportant now held new meaning. All were sharing and joking except Jerry Idleman.

Idleman had finished high school, and one month after graduation, he and three other buddies joined up together. They chose the Army because the recruiter promised to keep the four of them together. He lied. Two of his buddies were in Italy and the third was dead. Killed in North Africa.

"Hey, Jerry, what gives? Why the long face?" Ramos said to his best friend.

"I-I don't believe it. I just don't believe it." Idleman was sitting on the bench clutching his letter.

"What is it, buddy?"

"She left me. Mary Jane left me. We've been going steady since we were sophomores in high school. We were going to get married when the war was over. She says she's really sorry, but she met someone at the factory where she works and they've fallen in love. She says she hopes I understand.

"She sent me back my picture and would like me to send hers back. I just can't believe she would do that to me."

"Hey, buddy, I know it's tough, but you'll get over her. In fact, I've got an idea. We'll go into town tonight and drown our sorrows. I'm sure the captain will spring for some twenty-four-hour passes for us. But first, you need to write her back."

"What? You want me to write her back? What am I supposed to say, 'it's okay for you to break my heart'?"

Ramos grinned his famous mischievous gin. "Not exactly. She sent you your picture back and she want hers back, right?" Idleman nodded his head.

"Okay, then, here, send it back." Ramos reached into his pocket and pulled out a handful of girl's pictures and laid them on the table.

"I don't understand."

"Simple. You just tell her that it's been awhile, and you don't remember which one was hers. Ask her to pick out hers and to send the rest back."

A smile slowly grew on Idleman's solemn face as he nodded his head. "I like it," he finally said.

"Good," Ramos said, slapping his friend on the back. "Come on, let's go bug the captain about those passes."

SEVENTEEN

"HI, Mike."

"Uncle Griff!" Mike Perry was sitting at the end of one of the long tables in the mess hall, drinking a cup of coffee and reading. He stood and threw his arms around his uncle. "It's good to see you."

"You too, Mike. I heard about Tiny Tim. I'm sorry."

Perry sighed. "Thanks, I appreciate the thought."

"A letter from Martha?"

"Yup, and from Alyssa, too." He beamed, holding up her latest master-piece.

"That's great. Hey, listen, is there a place where we can talk?"

"Right this way." Perry took a last swig of his coffee then led him through the doors. "Care to step into my office?" he said as they began walking down the tarmac past a row of parked B-17s.

"You and your father always had a flair for understatement," Avery said. "How is your mother? I haven't heard from her in a while."

"She's doing just fine. She's working in a factory that assembles instrument panels for the B-17s. For every panel she makes, she says a little prayer over it in hopes that it will help to bring it's crew home safe."

"Yeah, that sounds like my sister all right." Avery smiled. "Mike, I've got a question for you."

"Shoot."

"You and your crew have been together for a long time, right?"

"Over a year between the States and here."

"So you know them pretty well."

"I trust my life with them every time we go up."

"What about the new guy? What do you know about him?"

"He seems like an okay guy. Where is all this going, Griff?"

They walked past a silver-skinned B-17 that had a picture of a girl riding a bomb sidesaddle decorating the front of the plane. She was in a purple fairy-tale dress, complete with a tall pointed hat with a streamer coming off the top. The name of the plane was *Little Princess*. Next to it was another plane.

A truck with a large hoist on it had backed up on the left side, working on the number one engine. The ground crew had it pulled halfway out of its nacelle, suspended in mid-air, dangling like a giant charm on a bracelet. Two men were standing on the wing, shouting out instructions to the other crew-men on the ground.

"What do you know about what I do?" Avery asked.

"Just that you're in the OSS, and that's about it."

"Among other things, I have a network of agents that I control in France. Up until recently, everything has gone fine, but now I fear one of my most trusted agents may have been compromised."

"You mean spies? You're some kind of secret agent?"

"Something like that," Avery replied, trying to downplay it. Whenever anyone mentioned the word *spies*, they got a romantic image of people in foreign and exotic lands dressed up in tuxedos and evening gowns, playing with neat little gadgets and escaping danger and death as if it were a game.

"I'm sorry to hear about your agent, but what does that have to do with me and my crew?"

"I need someone I can trust," Avery said in a low voice, eyes darting back and forth. "Have you ever heard of anything called 'Joan-Eleanor'?"

Perry shook his head. "Sounds like a couple of local barmaids, if you ask me."

A smile failed to break across Avery's face. "It's a two-way radio system that allows someone on the ground to talk to someone in the air. It broadcasts on a frequency that the German can't monitor, making it virtually impossible for them to track it. The 'Eleanor' equipment will be mounted in your plane and the 'Joan' is a small handheld unit with a short range of about twenty miles or so, so the plane has to be pretty close.

"For this type of mission, we usually use the British Mosquito bomber. It can fly high and fast, usually leaving any interested German fighters in its dust. I guess I'm just being paranoid, it comes with the job, I reckon, but I need someone I know I can trust for this mission. You're the only bomber pilot I know personally."

"So you don't think you can go through your regular channels to make contact with your agent. You think you may have a spy among your group?" Perry asked.

"It looks that way. Too many things have happened for it all to be just coincidence."

Two B-17s flew low overhead. Avery watched as the pair flew by, then banked off to the left, circled the field, and peeled off one at a time to come in for a landing. Avery stared in amazement as the twenty-ton birds touched down with the grace of a ballerina, not the bulk of an ironworker like expected.

"This is strictly voluntary. I can't order you or your crew to participate, and it could prove to be dangerous, too. If you accept, I can get you and your crew temporarily assigned to the OSS under my command until I can get all this sorted out."

"Dangerous?" Perry laughed. "Like what we do now isn't dangerous."

"I didn't mean it like that; I just wanted you to know that it may not be a milk run either."

"Can we get credit for each mission we fly? Count it as a combat sortie?"

"I'm afraid not," Avery said, shaking his head. "I can't give you credit because these won't be sanctioned missions. But I can get you some fighter escorts. Colonel Wesley and a few of his pilots from the 222nd have agreed to ride shotgun for you."

"Hmm. You can pull a B-17 and its crew off the flight line, steal a few fighters to help escort it, and all for a mission that doesn't really exist." Perry shook his head. "What's taking you so long to win the war?"

Avery finally smiled.

The two Flying Fortresses that had just landed taxied off the main runway and turned onto the access strip. They trotted past with a steady gait, like a pair of tired workhorses headed for the barn. The first one rolled off the taxiway onto the grass. The pilot gunned his engines, creating a small tornado as he swung the big plane around gracefully and pointed the nose back out, ready to take off again. Not to be outdone, the second pilot turned his plane on a dime, lining up the two planes, wingtip to wingtip.

The sudden blast of prop wash grabbed Avery's hat and flung it a few yards off into the grass.

"When do you need us?" Perry asked.

"Tomorrow afternoon. That will give us plenty of time to install and test the equipment. I'll go back and cut the orders, releasing you from the 415th and assigning you for temporary duty. And by the way, I would appreciate it if you and your men didn't discuss this mission with anyone. The less they know as a whole, the better. However, we'll need your radioman at the radio shack at 0900 tomorrow for training. And after that, he can help install the equipment."

"Yes, sir. Everything will be taken care of," Perry answered.

"Okay, enough of business," Avery said. "Tell me about my niece."

Perry's face suddenly got brighter. "Well, for starters, Alyssa will be starting first grade in September, but she already knows her ABCs and can write a few words. Her printing is better than mine!"

"First grade? She's not really that old, is she?"

Perry laughed. "Yup, and that's not all." For the next hour, all thoughts and pressures of the war vanished for the two men as they talked of home and loved ones sorely missed.

EIGHTEEN

"I see how you are," Anna said. "Wine and dine me on the first date in a nice restaurant with steak and champagne so I'll say yes to a second date, then once you have me hooked, you bring me to a pub for a beer?"

"No, it's not like that," Avery stuttered "I was—"

Anna Roshinko smiled and put her hand on Avery's. "I'm kidding, Griff, this is just fine," she said, letting him off the hook. Before he could reply, a tall, good-looking woman came over and dropped off their pints, and as she walked away, she gave Griff a playful smile and a quick wink.

"Now *that* I don't like," Roshinko said, watching the waitress walk away.

"Oh, that's just Margaret."

"Oh, *Margaret?*"

"Yeah, her and her *husband* . . . Hey wait a minute, you aren't jealous are you?" Avery said with a growing smile.'

"What, me jealous? Of course not!"

Avery heard her words, but her face said otherwise. "You are too," he teased with a smile.

"I am not!" she said firmly. For added measure she reached out and hit him in the shoulder. Then slowly some of the sternness fell away as she looked down at the table, embarrassed. "Well, maybe just a little."

Avery's chest swelled with pride. "That's Margaret . . . and see the short guy she's standing next to at the bar? That's her husband, Cliff. They own the Dragon's Breath. She probably winked at me because this was the first time I've ever brought a date here."

Cliff Russet was a short, round man with rosy cheeks and a jovial disposition, which made him a great barkeep. In a red suit, he could pass for Santa Claus. His wife Margaret was the opposite: tall and slender with long flowing black hair, and a figure that would put an hourglass to shame. They said love was blind, but in this case it was deaf and dumb, too, as they were the most unlikely couple Avery had ever seen.

Yet they seemed truly in love. It secretly gave Avery hope to see a guy like Cliff with a woman like Margaret. It made him feel that if a guy like Cliff could do it, then he, too, still had a chance at love. And now here he was, getting his shot.

"What, you think she's good looking?" Avery said, not being able to resist the temptation of teasing Anna a little.

"What! Are you blind? She's gorgeous!"

"I never really stopped to think about it before, but I guess you're right, she is pretty good looking."

Roshinko shot him a dirty look and reached out to hit him again, but he caught her hand and held it in his.

"Yeah, she's good looking, alright, but not as good looking as the lady I'm sitting with."

Roshinko's anger melted away. She leaned across the table and kissed him lightly on the lips then slugged him again.

"Hey, what was that for?"

"That's for teasing me." She smirked as she took a sip of her ale.

"You hungry?" Avery asked after taking a gulp of his own beer.

"They serve food here? I haven't seen a menu."

"They don't. In fact most pubs don't, but I worked out a deal with Cliff. Twice a month, U-boats allowing, a friend of mine stateside sends me two fifths of Old Crow whiskey. Cliff has a particular fondness for it. He sells one bottle in shots to the homesick Americans, making a small fortune, and drinks the other bottle himself. In return, they keep me well fed. Margaret—uh, Mrs. Russet—makes the best deep-fried fish and chips you've ever tasted."

"Well, I was looking forward to another steak," she replied in mock disappointment, "but I guess it will have to do."

AT the far end of the bar was a group of twelve American airman who weren't scheduled to fly the next day, and their carefree drinking showed it. They were a couple of crews from B-24 Liberators and not afraid to let anyone know it. They were so proud of the fact that they started singing. However, their song wasn't about the virtues of their plane but of their dislike of their competition, the B-17.

The crew of the *Red Light Lady* sat hunched at the other end of the bar.

Each branch thought they were better than the other, and each unit knew they were better than anyone else, especially when it came to the crews of the B-17s and the B-24s. If you stacked up the two planes side by side, the Liberator would win in just about every category; yet it was the Flying

Fortress which had captured the hearts and imaginations of the American people—and it miffed a lot of the Liberator crews to no end.

A staff sergeant who looked too big to fly in a cramped bomber stepped in front of his fellow flyers and began singing to the crowd, leading them in the chorus, using his beer stein like a conductor's baton.

"The young pilot with his brand new wings hopes for a plane that's really tough;
But he feels like giving them back when he sees he's flying a B-17 buff."

"Oh how nice, a floor show," Roshinko said as she heard the men sing. "You think of everything Griff," she smiled.

Avery rolled his eyes. "And I thought it was supposed to be the dancers tonight. But I see how you are. I bring you to this icon of local history and have you serenaded, and you don't even appreciate it."

"Serenading is nice, but twelve drunk men singing a drinking song is not serenading."

Avery shrugged his shoulders. "I could start singing."

"No, no I'm not a fan of nails on a chalkboard, thank you very much."

Avery started to pout and then they both broke out in laughter.

"LISTEN to those jerks, will ya?" Idleman said.

"Take it easy, Jerry, they're just a bunch of drunk Liberator boys," Ramos said.

'MOST of the audience didn't seem to mind, and several were even whistling and applauding, but it was easy to see who the other B-17 air crews were by their scowls.

"Now they're making fun of the captain," Idleman slurred.

The Liberator crew continued.

"Oh the plane is big and they call it a flying fort
But all the crews who fly the thing just wish they could abort!

"They're making fun of the *Lady*. Nobody does that." Idleman shot out of his chair like a racehorse out of its gate and headed straight for the Liberator crew.

"Damn it, Jerry," was all Ramos could get out before he launched to his feet.

"OH boy, now the real floor show is about to start," Avery said as he saw the airman jump up from his table. Avery recognized Idleman. "Oh no, he's one of Mike's crew."

Roshinko turned just in time to see two more men rush forward. "Who's Mike?"

"He's my nephew, a B-17 pilot, and those three are part of his crew."

Jerry Idleman charged the group of B-24 crewmen like a linebacker going after the quarterback. He grabbed the song leader by the shoulder and spun him around.

"Damn Liberator losers!" he shouted, then unloaded his right fist and sent the man reeling back into his comrades.

"That did it!" Avery said. "All hell's about to break loose now." And break loose it did, like a spark hitting a fifty-gallon drum of gasoline. The room erupted into a fight rivaling that of any Saturday afternoon western bar-room brawl. "Quick, head for the bar," Avery shouted

"Aren't you coming?"

Avery shook his head, then ducked quickly as a beer mug went sailing by. "I've got to see if I can get Mike's boys out of there. I'll be right there, now go!"

"Be careful, Griff."

"Not to worry: I'm a lover, not a fighter." He gave her a confident wink, but as soon as he turned, his confidence fell a notch as he looked at the melee he was about to enter.

The Liberator crew caught their falling comrade and shoved him back to his feet, aiming him at Idleman. The big sergeant snorted like a raging bull seeing red and was in mid-stride as he charged Idleman. A blur sailed past the Flying Fortress gunner. And for the second time that night, the B-24 crew-man did a wheels-up land as Ramos hurled himself into his counterpart, sending him sprawling back into his crewmates like a bowling ball and scattering the crowd like a seven-ten split.

Ramos jumped up and landed hits on two more B-24'ers. It had been a long time since he had been in a fight, and it felt good to be busting somebody's chops. Ramos was about to land his third punch when he heard Avery shout above the crowd. When he turned to look, somebody sucker punched him from the left, sending him crashing into one of the tables. Before he could get back up, Jacobs grabbed him by the arm. "The captain's got Jerry, let's get out of here!"

Ramos looked disappointed but knew they were outnumbered, so he nodded his head, and they snaked their way through the mass of hurling fists and flying bodies to the back of the bar.

With no one to fight, a drunken Jerry Idleman stood in the middle of the room, confused.

"Come on!" Avery shouted. "Let's get out of here!"

Avery shoved Idleman and turned to go but ran into a roadblock in the shape of a short, stout corporal who looked like he ate B-17s for breakfast. Avery had the sinking feeling that his captain's bar wouldn't make the corporal think twice about hitting him. Avery's suspicions were confirmed when the man leered at him, revealing a smile that was missing two front teeth. Another quick glance to the corporal's shoulders also revealed hash marks where sergeant stripes had been added and taken off. The corporal's grin grew bigger as he pulled back his arm, ready to send Avery into next week.

Suddenly there was a crash, and the corporal teetered on his feet for a moment before toppling over like a felled tree.

"Waste of a good pint, if you ask me," The Colonel said, holding the remainder of the broken beer bottle in his hand. "Me and the lads used to go through quite a few of these in my day when we got leave. We were kicked out of more pubs than you could shake a stick at."

He smiled at Avery, his teeth as white as his hair, then he reached out and shoved Avery aside and threw a strong right cross, sending the man behind Avery reeling. He side-stepped a chair flying through the air, then turned back to Avery. "Now get your lads and your skinny lass out of here," he said with a wink and a quick glance to Roshinko at the bar. "I'll cover your back."

"Thanks."

"No. Thank you, Griff, my boy. I've been spoiling for a good fight for quite some time now."

Avery shook his head and smiled as he led Idleman through the crowd. Just as they reached the bar, the front door burst open and the sound of whistles could be heard about the shouts, the crashing furniture, and the moans and the groans, as the MPs came charging in. Avery turned and saw the white head of the Colonel bobbing among the sea of green Army uniforms like a whitecap on the ocean, still smiling, fists still flying.

"Hurry up, this way!" Cliff Russet yelled from behind the bar. A soldier crashed against the bar. He shook off the punch that sent him there, then spun around and grabbed Russet by his shirt, ready to take his anger out on the first person he could find. Suddenly a bottle came crashing down on his head, and the man dropped Russet like a bad habit and hit the floor, out cold.

"I'm putting that on your bill, too!"

Russet smiled. "That's my girl," he said affectionately, looking as Margaret stood over the man with a broken bottle in one hand.

"Come on, this way." Russet motioned with his hand as Avery, Roshinko, and the three crewmembers of the *Red Light Lady* followed him through the back room of the pub and out the back door into the alleyway.

"Thanks, Cliff, I appreciate it," Avery said, catching his breath. "I don't need to try and explain to General Sizemore what I was doing in the middle of a barroom brawl."

"Yeah, thanks, I don't think our captain would be too understanding, either," Ramos chimed in.

"You owe me *three* bottles of Old Crow next month," Russet said.

"Done!"

Russet smiled and went back inside to try and save what was left of the bar.

"Come on!" Avery grabbed Roshinko by the hand. "You fellas are on your own," he shouted over his shoulder. "But I suggest you get back to base ASAP!"

"Roger that, sir, and thank you!" Ramos shouted.

Avery and Roshinko raced around the corner and didn't stop running until they were halfway back to her apartment.

"You certainly know how to show a girl a good time," Roshinko said.

"Avery smiled. "You should see what I do for an encore."

"Yes, that's what scares me."

Avery smiled. "Now wasn't this more exciting than a boring old restaurant where the most exciting thing that happens is someone sending their soup back because it's too cold?"

"You're right, all this excitement has put me in the mood."

Avery raised his eyebrow in expectation. "In the mood, huh? I like the sound of that." He smiled shyly.

"Yeah, I'm in the mood to dance! Come on, the USO club is not too far from here. We can go there and dance all night, and then we can bring the sun up."

"Dance? Yeah right . . . dancing would be fun," Avery said.

She grabbed his hand and took the lead, pulling him up the street behind her. She looked back over her shoulder at him and smiled. "There's dancing and then there's *dancing*." She smiled and turned her head away. For being an intelligence officer, he sure was confused. Were they going dancing or *dancing*? And was his *dancing* the same as her *dancing*?

Avery just smiled to himself and shook his head. Then he realized that it really didn't matter if they were dancing or *dancing* as long as he was with her.

Fred Astaire, eat your heart out.

NINETEEN

AVERY grabbed a fresh cup of coffee, then went back to his office and began formulating the order of business to be accomplished that day. He was on his third page of scribbling, or "organization prioritizing" as he like to call it, when something wonderful caught his attention.

It was a welcome distraction, light, warm, and wonderfully buttery. It was the smell of fresh-baked bread. Croissants. When the aroma of his just-brewed coffee intertwined with that of the croissant, it was a marriage made in heaven. And the best part was that heaven had sent an angel to deliver the delicacy.

Anna Roshinko strolled in holding a plate that was covered with a white cloth napkin. The heavenly temptress walked around the desk and made several slow, seductive passes with the plate under Avery's nose. Twice he reached for the plate and twice she pulled it away.

She brought the plate to a stop right in front of him, then slowly removed the napkin as if about to reveal the meaning of life. The burst of escaping steam filled his nostrils with delight.

He looked at her, and suddenly all thoughts of coffee and croissants were gone in one defining moment. He didn't know how or when, but he was going to marry the woman standing before him. For a moment, time stood still. The entire universe had shrunk to the size of his office, and there were just two people in that universe.

They gazed into each other's eyes for a second, an hour. He didn't know and he didn't care. Then the angel spoke, the voice from heaven uttering but one word: "Butter."

"Butter," she said again slowly. "I forgot the butter."

With that simple word, the universe expanded back to reality. He smiled. "I'll survive. Care to join me?"

"Why do you think I brought two?" She grinned back.

For the next several minutes, the universe shrank again, and nothing existed outside of the four walls of his office as Griff Avery ate the best meal of his life. But all too soon the moment ended, and real life forced its way back in with the ringing of the phone.

Roshinko waited until he hung up the phone. He smiled and watched as the future Mrs. Griffin Avery vanished out the door.

He drew in a deep breath, then let out a long sigh as she disappeared. He sat there for another moment in his love-struck stupor, then shook his head and pushed his way back into his paperwork. He had a lot to do and very little time in which to do it.

IT was three o'clock in the afternoon when Avery passed through the airfield gates and made his way to the *Red Light Lady*. The sky was a dull, overcast gray, and sharp wind tugged at his flight jacket. The foul weather outside reflected his mood inside, a stark contrast to the way the day had started. He was apprehensive, not only for what he might find out about Zeus and his agents, but because he was not that fond of flying.

The driver stopped and let him out of the Jeep, then sped away. Avery felt strangely abandoned as he stood alone in front of the plane. He hadn't eaten anything since his breakfast croissant with Anna because he didn't want to embarrass himself if he got airsick. On the other hand, he must have smoked three packs of cigarettes already.

He had never been this close to a B-17 before, and he paused for a moment and marveled at its size. As he slowly circled the slumbering behemoth, he remembered talk he'd heard from bomber crews in the pubs and even a few stories from his nephew about their planes. They spoke as if they had a life of their own.

He wasn't a superstitious man, but still . . . He ran his hand slowly along the fuselage. If this were the case, if the plane really was "alive," he wanted the *Lady* to know this stranger was who was about to go up with her. He wanted her to know *him*.

Just as he was finishing up his introduction, a 6-by-6 truck pulled up with the crew in the back. They tossed their duffel bags to the ground and hopped out. The crew acknowledged him, then went about their business preparing for the mission, unpacking as if they had just arrived at a four-star hotel.

Avery watched in amazement as the crewmembers began laying out enough clothes for a week's stay. Each man pulled on a couple of pairs of long underwear, two to three pairs of socks, wool pants and shirt all covered over with a flight suit. And to top it all off, they carried heavy fleece-lined leather jackets and bright yellow Mae West life preservers.

"Here ya go, sir," Ramos said as he tossed one of the duffel bags at his feet. Avery watched the navigator open a small hatch on the left front side of the plane, right below the pilot's seat. The hatch was about five feet off the ground. He reached up, tucked his legs up, and pulled himself inside. With equal ease, the bombardier followed his crewmate inside.

Avery watched the young men disappear into the bowels of the aircraft. He suddenly felt very uneasy and lost. He doubted he could perform the same acrobatics at his age. There had to be another way in.

A Jeep pulled up with Perry and his copilot. Perry walked up with an outstretched hand and a smile.

"Captain Griff Avery, this is my friend and copilot, First Lieutenant Jeff Gibbons," Perry said.

"How do you do, sir?" Gibbons replied. "It's nice to meet you. Mike has told me a lot about you."

"Your technician completed installing the equipment around 1300," Perry said, "and he just finished training Joe on how to use it all. So to answer your question, yes, we're ready.

"And the crew?" Avery asked.

"I told them we're testing some new radio equipment, that's all."

"Excellent." Avery paused for a moment, then held up the duffel bag. "One of your crewmen gave me this bag. There's enough clothes in here to keep a Chinese laundry busy for a month. Is all this really necessary?"

Perry and Gibbons looked at each other and smiled. "Let's put it this way, Uncle Griff: there are no heaters up there, and the outside temperature will get to forty degrees below zero."

"Right. Give me a minute," Avery said as he began dressing. When done, he felt like a kid again, all bundled up by his mother in the winter to go outside and play. "Lets go."

He followed Perry and Gibbons as they walked under the plane and around to the far side. He was surprised and relieved to find a door hatch just in front of the tail section. Both pilots stepped up and through, and he followed them in.

If he was struck by how big the plane looked on the outside, Avery was just as stunned by how small it seemed on the inside. Stepping through the hatch, he looked toward the back of the plane and saw a long tunnel barely two feet in diameter leading to the tail gunner's position. The gunner had to crawl on his hands and knees ten or twelve feet to get to the back of the plane and his station.

He turned and took a step, bumping his head on the ceiling when he tried to straighten up. Looking toward the front of the plane, there was a single pair of machine guns, one on the left and one on the right, each covered with a Plexiglas window. Mounted on the wall next to each gun were two wooden boxes that held 250 rounds of .50-caliber ammunition for the guns.

"You know my crew, don't you?" Perry asked.

Avery nodded his head.

"Our bombardier and navigator are already up in the nose," Perry said. "So we're ready to roll. Mitchell, here, will show you where to sit during takeoff. After we get in the air, you can get up and talk to Joe or come up to the cockpit if you like."

"Let's do it," Avery said, giving a hearty thumbs-up, which looked more enthusiastic than he felt inside. Perry patted his uncle on the shoulder and disappeared into the front of the plane.

"You can sit here, sir," Avery heard the crewman say. Mitchell sat Griff down with his back against the radio room wall, facing the back of the plane. His right leg was against the outer fuselage and his left was leaning against the top of the ball turret.

The turret looked like a silver ball sticking halfway out of the floor. There was a metal shaft that ran from the top of the ball to the ceiling, and on top of the sphere were two metal ammo boxes. He got claustrophobic just thinking about how a man would contort himself to fit into such a tiny space.

Avery watched the other crewmen. They were so calm and matter-of-fact about going into combat. For the first time, Avery thought about dying. Up until now he had never been in any real danger. Sure, there were the occasional V-1 and V-2 rockets back in London, but they were scarce these days, so sporadic that they never seemed to pose any real danger. Now he was flying into true peril. How could these men be so calm in the face of that?

Yet he could feel the excitement growing inside. He was anxious to see what it was really like in combat and to see how he would react. He wanted to test his mettle. He'd always had respect for the real soldiers in the Army, those who did the fighting, but now that respect was growing deeper.

"Where you from, sir?" It was Mitchell again. He had seated himself in the same the same spot on the other side of the turret.

"I'm from Brooklyn, but grew up in a little town just outside of Portland, Oregon. And you?" Avery was grateful for the conversation. It helped derail the train his mind was traveling on.

"I'm from Twin Falls, Idaho."

"We're not too far apart. I hear it's nice up there."

"Yeah, lots of trees. But the winters get pretty cold."

Avery heard a dull roar as an engine started up. He reached out and felt the side of the plane to see if it was vibrating. It was, slightly, but nothing like what he had expected. Was the plane so well insulated that the sound and vibrations would be that muffled?

With an unmistakable thundering roar, the *Red Light Lady's* engine erupted to life. Sounding like a giant trying to clear his throat in the morning, the first engine sputtered once, then died. The starter motor whined, and the engine coughed again. Then the giant gargled for a moment until his voice steadied into a constant drone.

The other three engines started in much the same way, but each one had its own unique voice. As Perry adjusted the throttles, four different voices sang in unison, peaking in a great and steady roar. Sitting in the midst of the bass section, Avery couldn't imagine what the choir of a thousand-plane raid would sound like.

Looking back, Avery saw the shaft of the tail wheel jutting up out of the floor. Every time Perry gunned the engines, testing the power settings, the tail section would catch the prop wash and bounce up and down like a puppy anxious to play. The huge tail was now vibrating with the rumble of the engines, impatient to soar up to the heavens.

Now, with unexpected subtlety, the plane began to move. Looking out the rear gun windows, he could see the tail wing shaking like an old pickup truck driving over a washboard road. And his confidence waned in the sturdiness of the plane.

With surprising velocity, Avery was pushed forward in his seat as the bomber surged down the runway at full throttle. The plane continued to bounce and rattle as the tail lifted off the ground. A moment later, all the vibration and shaking stopped—they were airborne.

With the shackles of earth discarded, the *Red Light Lady* rejoiced in doing what she had been made to do. Avery had thought that the plane, being a bomber, should ride rough, like comparing the ride of a car to that of a work truck. But the *Lady* floated with great ease upon the winds, making her way ever skyward.

Mitchell gave him the thumbs-up signal, meaning he could now walk around the plane. With more enthusiasm than he'd expected, Avery got out of his seat and went back to look out one of the gun windows. The patch-work of fields, roads, and farmlands faded into the distance, and he felt like a kid with a pocket full of change in a candy store. He excitedly began explor-ing the plane, making his way into the radio room.

On the left hand side of the compartment was a small table with radio equipment on it. Even more was mounted on the wall above it. The room felt fairly spacious for its size, made more so by the fact that the ceiling was a Plexiglas hump with yet another machine gun sticking out the top. Behind the table, he recognized his Joan-Eleanor radio equipment. He smiled at Thomas, who was tinkering with the set.

Avery continued his journey forward as he opened the cabin door and stepped into the empty bomb bay. Balancing like a tight-rope artist, he walked across the narrow catwalk. Nervously he looked down at the doors and realized there was 5000 feet of nothing underneath him.

Curious, he noticed several holes in the solid bomb bay doors and wondered what . . . Bullet holes! Stepping a little quicker, he reached the other side and squeezed through the doorway into the cockpit. The top turret gunner was crouched behind the copilot, and Avery did his best to stuff himself between the supports of the gun turret and kneel behind Mike.

The pilot and copilot were seated next to each other in a cockpit that was so small they could almost stretch out their arms and touch both sides. Avery stared in awe at the array of gauges, switches, and knobs of every sort in front of them, on the ceiling, and to their sides. About the only thing he recognized were the four throttle levers that resting between the two pilots.

Avery reached up and patted Mike on the shoulder. Mike looked back, then pointed to a jack where he could plug in his headphones.

"What do you think?" Perry asked.

"Boy, this is something," Avery replied with a grin.

"I'd offer you a drink, but we gave the stewardess the day off to go shopping in Piccadilly Square."

"We're still over England, gaining altitude before we cross the channel and join up with our escorts, so you can go up front if you want to. But once we cross over into France, your station will be in the radio room with Joe. You'll stay there unless Jeff or I order you otherwise."

"Okay, gotcha. I think I will go up front, then."

"Roger. We'll be going above ten thousand feet soon, and then we'll need to go on oxygen."

"Understood."

"If you need to move about the plane after we go on oxygen, there are small portable bottles you can use to move from station to station. Oh, and be careful going past the nose hatch. It's an emergency escape hatch, and it'll pop open if you lean against it too hard."

Avery unplugged his headgear and began the slow process of stuffing himself down the small hatch located on the floor between the pilots. Now he knew what it felt like to be a sausage. He got down on his knees and had a hard time turning himself around in the cramped space, coming to the conclusion that flying in these planes was a job for the young.

He crawled on all fours the short distance to the front of the plane, eyeing the escape hatch as he went by. Reaching the light at the end of the tunnel, he finally immerged into the navigator/bombardier section in the nose of the plane.

There was a small table immediate to his left where the navigator sat, and he could see several charts unrolled on it. Their course was drawn out and plotted with hash marks and notations beside each mark. But the most impressive sight was the bombardier's station. The man was seated in front of a huge, round Plexiglas window that looked like a porthole to heaven.

With a "may I?" look on his face, Avery gestured toward the bombardier's chair. Blocker smiled and nodded his head. Slowly, almost reverently, Griff moved forward and inched his way into the seat.

It was an eerie feeling to sit in the chair, because when he leaned forward to look through the bombsight, there was no "solid floor" beneath him. He was literally hanging over the edge of the plane.

Avery sat in the bombardier's chair for a few minutes and took in the view of the world from a perspective only a very few had seen before. As the plane circled, climbing higher and higher into the sky, they began to pass through some clouds. The clouds brushed pass the canopy at first, like a car driving through the fog, then enveloped the entire plane, wrapping it in a blanket of impenetrable white.

Then, with the suddenness and urgency of a diver breaking up through the surface of the water, gasping for air, the *Red Light Lady* broke out of the clouds into the crystal blue of the sky. Avery sat in wonderment at the blue of the sky. It held a deep, intense brilliance he had never seen.

Below, the collage of greens, browns and blues that had stretched from horizon to horizon was replaced by the pristine white of the endless cloud cover. The clouds glistened in the sunlight, shimmering like crystallized snow on a cold winter's day. He couldn't wait to tell Anna what this was like.

Just then he saw something in the skies above them. There was one . . . no . . . two, three, four . . . there were four objects!

He watched for a moment as they seemed to dance on the wind. Then they turned and erupted into a blinding flash of light. He'd heard stories of what the air combat crews had called "foo fighters," unidentified objects. But he never thought they were real, let alone that he would ever see one.

Was he imagining it? Were they above ten thousand feet and was his mind playing tricks on him because he wasn't wearing his oxygen mask? Suddenly he felt foolish; he could see now that they were planes and that they were dropping down fast. The only question was: whose side were they on?

LIEUTENANT Luke Stevens looked down over the left wing of his P-51 Mustang. The sun's rays gleamed off the polished aluminum fuselage. A mischievous smile crept across his lips. "Colonel, request permission to attack the target?" Stevens asked.

Colonel Adams sat in his high perch, watching the lumbering giant below. Adams thought about it for a minute. They were still over England with more than enough fuel for the mission . . .

"School's in session," Adams announced. "We'll each make one pass at the bomber. Once we're back up into formation, we will critique each other's attack and see what we can learn.

"Lieutenant Wiser, you're up first; Major, you're on deck. By the way, Major, I noticed you have a green scarf on today."

"She's my little Irish leprechaun," Reins replied. "I met her two weeks ago at the Half Moon. Last night was the first chance we could talk."

"Talk? Boy, you sure can 'talk,' Doc," Wiser said.

"Yeah, you have such a way with words," Stevens added.

"Someday you're going to have to teach us all your amazing grasp of the English language," Adams said. "But in the mean time: Lieutenant Wiser, if you please?"

"Roger, Skipper, on my way."

"Captain Perry, this is Colonel Adams, we'd like to make a couple of practice passes at you if you don't mind. So please don't shoot us down," Adams called to the bomber down below.

PERRY smiled. "Roger that, sir. I'll tell the boys not to get too excited." He switched on the intercom. "Our little friends are going to use us for target practice. Buckle up and hang on tight. I'm going to show these fighter boys that they aren't the only ones who know how to fly a plane."

ANDY Wiser was about five thousand feet above his target when he started his dive. He had never made an attack on a plane that was this slow, or big. He came down so fast that he misjudged the speed of the bomber and realized that he was coming in too high on the plane for a good shot. Frustrated, he flipped the plane over and made an inverted snap-shot pass, making a fadeaway sweeping shot as he blew past the tail.

"Damn!" Wiser said as he pulled back up into formation.

"A little bit different than chasing a dancing 109," Adams said.

"Okay, Major, your turn."

"Roger." Reins remained level and pulled a little ahead of the B-17. When he was about half a mile ahead and a little to the left, he pushed the stick over and swung back around on his target. He came in fast from the high ten-o'clock position and made a slashing attack across the front of the big bomber. If his aim had been true, his fire would have raked the cockpit and taken out the number three engine.

"That, gentlemen, is the way to make a successful attack on a buff," Adams said. "The major came in high and fast, had good position on the target, and presented a minimal target for the defenders on his egress. Good run, Major."

"Thank you, sir."

"Okay, Lieutenant, your turn."

"Yes, sir!" Lieutenant Stevens applied full throttle and moved ahead of the bomber as the major had done. But instead of staying high on the target, he dropped down to the same altitude as the bomber before he started his approach. He came in fast from the left side, made his attack just behind the wing, then broke off, flying under the front of the plane.

"Lieutenant," Adams said, "I have the unfortunate task of writing home to your parents, telling them that their son was shot down by an enemy bomber. Your approach and angle were all wrong. You came in from the side, allowing the bomber to give you a broadside from the top and bottom turrets and the waist gun. They probably had a bead on you from the very start of your run. They would have shredded you into scrap metal."

"Well, sir, that would be correct if I'd been attacking a B-17, but I was attacking a He 111. They have one dorsal gun just behind the pilot that has no forward field of fire and a very limited arc to the sides, depending on the version.

"My line of attack would have exposed me to minimal fire from the dorsal gun and kept me ahead of and higher than the firing arc of the waist gun. My aim would have concentrated all six of my fifties onto the left wing, shearing it off in a matter of seconds. Sir!"

Adams smiled. "I see you've done your homework, Lieutenant. But I forgot to tell you that this was a captured bomber sent on a secret mission by Hitler himself to bomb the Allied Supreme Commander's Headquarters. By doing so, he hopes to throw our armies into chaos, thus slowing our advance, allowing them to mount a counteroffensive, setting us back weeks, even months."

There was a moment of silence.

"Point taken, Colonel."

"Well done," Adams said.

"Thank you, sir."

"Okay, I'll make my run now," Adams said. The colonel kept his Mustang high above the B-17 and pulled in front of it. His plan was to stay ahead of his target, drop almost straight down on it from the front, then zoom on past. It was a more difficult attack angle but would give him the best opportunity to hit the cockpit and present the least amount of exposure to of the enemy's guns.

Adams looked back over his right shoulder and pushed the stick over and began his run.

"THERE he is," Gibbons said, pointing to the bombers eleven-o'clock-high position.

"Roger. I got him," Perry answered. "Hang on, boys."

Avery was looking up at the fighters when Svenson tapped him on the shoulder. "You'd better sit here, sir," he said, setting the captain down beside the navigation table. "When the Skipper says hang on, you'd better hang on, sir."

Avery got an uneasy feeling that he wasn't going to enjoy this. He grabbed hold of the table with one hand and braced himself against the rib support of the fuselage with the other. He knew they weren't in any danger, but his stomach hadn't gotten the message. He leaned back and prayed he wouldn't get sick.

Perry carefully tracked the incoming fighter. Just before it was about to fire, Perry kicked the rudder over hard to the left, dropped a notch of flaps, pushed the yoke forward, and turned to the left. The tail of the plane swung out to the side. At the same time the big ailerons grabbed at the air, sending the plane into a tight circle, pointing his nose almost straight down.

Avery looked out the front of the plane, and the clear blue sky was replaced by the white of the clouds. He was very disoriented with no point of horizontal reference. His head began to spin as fast as the plane. He closed his eyes tight and held on for dear life.

The *Red Light Lady* seemed to enjoy playing with the fighters as she responded quickly to the controls. She snapped around in a tight dive out and reversed course as Perry pulled back on the yoke. The *Lady* leveled out, chasing the tail of its little friend.

"DAMN, did you see that?" Stevens said in amazement. "I didn't know a bomber could do that. He handled that thing like a fighter."

"My compliments, Captain," Adams radioed to Perry. "That was a very nice maneuver. Important lesson gentlemen," Adams continued, "things may not always be what they seem; never take any situation for granted.

"Okay, let's take our positions over the bomber. They'll be cruising at twenty-nine thousand feet, so we'll take up our stations around thirty-four, ready to pounce on anything that may come snooping our way."

Feeling his head and the plane stop spinning, Avery slowly opened his eyes and was happy to see the sky resting on the horizon where it belonged. He took a deep breath and started crawling back up to the cockpit. As he moved along, his pants caught on the handle of the lower door hatch. He froze in terror, envisioning the hatch opening and being sucked out of the plane, falling ten thousand feet to his death.

He carefully backed up and managed to squirm around the handle in his heavy flight gear just enough to reach down and unhook his pants. He succeeded in crawling the rest of the six feet without incident and emerged between the two pilots like a gopher popping out in someone's garden.

"You don't look so good," Perry said, seeing his uncle's pale face. "Why don't you settle in, go back and get things set up with Joe. He's bound to have a few questions, and you two can get it all worked out before we get on station. Besides, we're about ready to go on oxygen, so you'll need to stay put."

"Good idea," Avery replied weakly.

"Oh, and by the way, when you're working back there, try not to take off your gloves. When we get to altitude, the temperature will be around twenty degrees below zero. If you touch any metal with your bare skin, it'll rip your flesh right off."

"Okay, Mike, thanks."

Avery went back to the radio room and for the next hour and a half familiarized Thomas with the equipment and proper procedures. He sat in the makeshift chair that had been installed along with the extra radio equipment. The excitement quickly wore off, replaced by the tedium of working and waiting, followed by even more waiting.

He'd heard it said that air combat was hours of boredom followed by moments of sheer terror. He knew about the boredom first hand now; he wasn't looking forward to the moments of terror. He'd also discovered that his nephew was right: it was cold, very cold. All the bulky clothing he was complaining about earlier now didn't seem like he had nearly enough.

"Ball turret to pilot," Mitchell said. "I've got six bogies at four o'clock low." Avery's heart jumped into his throat upon hearing the ball turret gunner's report. He wanted to go to the back and look out the window at the approaching German fighters, but knew he couldn't. He had to stay at the position Mike had assigned him. He glanced up at the machine gun hanging from its mount in the roof.

"Who mans this gun?" Avery asked Thomas. "Shouldn't someone be manning this thing if enemy fighters are coming?"

"I'll man it when the time comes, but don't worry about it right now. For one thing, the fighters are below us, and for another, we have our own personal escort up there watching over us. You might call them our own guardian angels."

Avery looked up through the ceiling and took great comfort in the sight of the four silvery angels high above them.

"COLONEL, we've got six bogies on our four-o'clock low," Major Reins reported.

"Roger that. We've got a visual on them," Adams replied. He looked out his cockpit and found the six dots that would soon turn into German fighters. "All right, gentlemen, we do this one by the book. We've got altitude and speed on them, but they've got the numbers. So we'll make them work for every inch of altitude before we knock 'em down. If you make a pass and he dives for the deck, let him go. Remember, our job today is to protect this bomber, not to get kills. And stay *high!*"

HEARING the ball turret's report, Avery sat in the radio room, adjusting the equipment and trying to keep his mind occupied, but he simply couldn't. He looked out the tiny window again for the tenth time, straining to get a glimpse of the planes that were coming up to try and kill them.

"Ball turret to pilot. They look like Bf 109s, Captain."

"He's right, Skipper, confirmed," Jacobs added from the tail gun. "The bandits look like Emils or Gustavs. I can't tell from here."

"Roger. I'll pass it along to our escorts," Perry replied.

"Emil? Gustav?" Avery looked at Thomas with a puzzled look.

"*E* for Emil, *G* for Gustav . . . it's the letter variant for different models of Messerschmitt 109, like the Mustang, P-51D. But don't worry, sir, we still have the cavalry up there, and we ain't exactly defenseless ourselves."

"I know; it's just that this is my first time in combat, and you all seem so calm while I feel like a basket case. How do you do it? How can you not be scared?"

Thomas chuckled. "Oh, I'm scared, alright—we all are—and don't you let anyone ever tell you any different. Anyone who tells you he's not afraid is one of three things: a fool, a liar, or someone who's never been in combat before. And most of them are liars.

"You're handling your first mission a lot better than I did. First time I went up, I was scared spitless and froze. The captain had to yell at me three times before I finally snapped out of it.

"I used to think, like most everyone else, that if you were a 'real' man, you wouldn't be afraid. But I was wrong. After being with these guys so long, I came to realize that there's no shame in being scared. It's what you do with your fear that defines you. Courage is not being fearless, it's doing your job in the face of that fear."

Avery considered Thomas' words for a moment. "I never really thought about it before, but I guess you're right. Thanks."

TWENTY

ADAMS watched as the chess match unfolded below him.

"The German fighters are splitting up," Reins announced.

"I thought they might," Adams replied. "They've got the numbers on us and intend to use it to their best advantage."

"Just one question, sir, if I may," Stevens asked. "Are these real 109s, or are they other Mustangs just pretending to be the enemy?"

"They're the real thing," Adams replied dryly. "And by the way, Lieutenant, my plane needs to be waxed when we get back."

"Yes, sir," Stevens replied. There was no defiance in his tone, instead a respect that came from knowing his commanding officer could take it as well as dish it out.

The six Messerschmitts split up into two flights of three each, spreading out on either side of the bomber.

"Okay, let's see if we can break them up," Adams said. "Major, you and Lieutenant Wiser dive on the group on the right. Stevens and I will stay high. I want to see what they do."

"Yes, sir."

"And Major? Be careful. My gut tells me these guys are good."

"Roger that. Okay Lieutenant, like the Colonel says, by the book. I'll make one pass at Tail End Charlie and you stay on my wing. We don't turn to engage; we make our pass and then climb back upstairs. "

"Lead the way, sir."

Reins adjusted his harness, making sure all his straps were tight, then tucked his new green scarf in around the top of his flight suit. Even at thirty-four thousand feet, it still held the faint scent of her perfume.

Reins smiled as he looked over his wing to the approaching German planes below. He loved his job, if one could even call it that. He was living in a foreign land, guests of the queen, welcomed by the natives, and allowed to fly the hottest airplanes in the world.

"Stay tight on my wing, Lieutenant. Here we go."

The Mustang pointed down and seemed to leap with excitement. Escorting bombers was part of her job, and she did it with pride. But like her master, she yearned to run free in the fields of combat, for she was meant to attack, not defend.

Adams watched as Reins and Wiser started their first pass. At almost the same time, the last German plane in line started to dive as well. He didn't figure these guys to put their tail between their legs and run quite so easily. Of course, it was late in the war and everyone but Hitler knew that it was over. They probably just wanted to get home in one piece like everyone else.

But as he watched, he realized that the German planes weren't afraid or running away, they were setting up the American planes. One of the planes was already in a shallow dive, matching the speed of the descending plane. If the German plane timed it right, he could pull back up, match the American's speed, and set up a very good shot right before he pulled up. It wouldn't leave a very long window of opportunity, maybe four to five seconds, but to a fighter pilot in combat, that was an eternity.

"Major, Lieutenant, break off! Repeat. Break off!" Adams shouted into the radio.

Reins heard Adams' warning over the radio. Without hesitation, he pulled up hard and banked away. "Abort! Abort!" he yelled to Wiser.

The blood drained from Reins' head as he pulled back on the stick. He held the steep climb for about five seconds and eased up on the controls, then snapped his neck again searching for his wingman and for the danger that the colonel had warned him about.

The first two German planes had split in opposite directions, and the third plane, the one he thought was running away, had pulled up from its dive and gotten on Wiser's tail. Sparks came from the wings of the Messerschmitt as it opened fire, tracers streaking past his wingman's plane. With tormenting slowness, Wiser's momentum carried him out of range of the Messerschmitt guns before the 109 broke and reformed with the other two German planes as they resumed their steady climb toward the bomber.

"Andy, are you all right?" Reins shouted to Wiser.

"Yeah, I think so." There was a slight quiver of fear in Wiser's voice. "I took a couple of hits, but I think everything is okay. Where did he come from?"

"These guys are good," Adams interjected. "The moment you started your dive, the last plane in line also started to dive. His timing was impeccable."

"We're going to have to change our game plan a bit. You two, get back up here. I figure we have about ten minutes before they're in range of the buff."

After five full minutes of thought, Adams said, "Here's the plan. They have the numbers, and I know they're going to exploit it to their advantage because that's what I would do. So we will use that advantage against them and force their hand.

"We go in as before with the major and the lieutenant. I anticipate they will use the same tactics, so as soon as their shooter dives, Lieutenant Stevens will go after him. I also believe that, having the numbers, they will detach one unit from the other flight to go after Lieutenant Stevens. If so, I will drop on him.

"At that point, it will be four on four, and we'll see if their loyalties lie in the mission or to their squad mates. I expect the fifth plane to join the fray. Then, if worse comes to worst, we have taken five fighters away from the bomber, leaving them better–than–even odds for them to defend themselves against just one aircraft.

"Remember: to win, we don't have to shoot these guys down, only make them dive for the deck. It'll take them too long to get back into the hunt for the bomber before their fuel's spent, and they'll be forced to return to base. Either way, we win.

"Lieutenant Stevens, you and I have the best shot at getting a kill, but stay sharp! Major, Lieutenant Wiser, keep your tails clear and watch for the other high German; he may drop at anytime if he thinks he can get a quick kill and then pop back up."

Adams took a deep breath. They had to give the bomber time to complete her mission. "Okay, Major, let's take it to them."

"Roger that." Reins pointed the nose of this trusted warhorse toward the enemy below. "Stay with me, Andy, we may be turning on a dime here."

"I'm on you like glue, sir."

The two Mustangs were picking up speed like rockets on rails. "Last time, the lead Hun broke right. I'm betting he'll go left this time. Be ready to get a snap shot at him as we go by. We'll swing left, too. It'll set up a better shot for Stevens as he comes down on the shooter."

"I'm with you, boss."

"High Tail End Charlie is diving again!" Adams shouted. "Go, Stevens!"

"Roger."

Lieutenant Stevens snapped his Mustang over and disappeared off Adams' wing. Just as Adams had predicted, the Charlie from the second flight was watching and broke off to engage Stevens. "Be advised, Stevens, Charlie two is in the hunt."

Four of the six German planes were engaged and distracted from the bomber. Time to make it five.

"I'm in," Adams announced. He watched the last two Messerschmitts carefully as he nudged over the stick and started his dive. The second plane in line start to break off—but then it stopped, as if he were being ordered back into formation.

Adams swore under his breath. Why didn't they attack? Were their orders to get the bomber at any cost? If so, that brought a whole new meaning to the importance of this mission. A sense of urgency swept through Adams, and something deep down inside told him that the clock had just started ticking.

Reins and Wiser made their pass, and once again Tail End Charlie had perfect timing. But now the American fighters were moving too fast for him to take even a quick snap shot. This time around, the German plane was the hunted, not the hunter.

Stevens sliced through the heavens and hit Charlie with perfect timing, just as the German was pulling up to catch Wiser. At the last moment, the German tried to break left and drop down under the approaching fighter. It was too little too late. Stevens caught him with a long burst, shredding the tail and the rear fuselage of the doomed fighter.

There was no explosion or fire and very little smoke as the back half of the plane disintegrated, as though caught in a giant meat grinder. The 109 went into a tight spin, but the pilot managed to get out before the plane tore itself apart.

Adams smiled and turned his attention back to his prey. This new pilot must have been more alert than the one Stevens had shot down, for just as he was lining up on him, the pilot flipped his plane over on its back and dove for the deck. Under normal circumstances, Adams would have followed him down; however, doing so would violate his own orders to stay with the bomber. The German must know as well as he did that it was unlikely that Adam would follow him down to the deck.

"Andy," Reins yelled. "I'm going up and over, take a short cut!"

"Roger."

Reins pulled back on the stick. At the top of the loop, blood rushed back in to his head like an incoming tide. His head felt like it might explode, and his eyes pop out of their sockets from the pressure. Looking directly out the top of his canopy, he was now looking straight down as he went over the top of his loop. He saw his target and the other Messerschmitt as they split out from each other then turned back in.

In a well-choreographed move, the first Messerschmitt rolled, came back to his right, and pulled his nose up to meet his assailant while the other plane cut back to the left, covering his tail. It was a good maneuver that provided protection for the first plane, but what the second German pilot didn't see was Lieutenant Stevens coming back around.

As the 109 banked around to cover his wingman, Stevens, unseen, hit him on his underside. A long burst drilled into the center of the plane, and in a split second, it exploded in a huge red ball of fire that quickly vanished, leaving a dark smudge against the blue sky. It was the only sign left that showed a plane had just been there.

Stevens let out a shout that could be heard in the others planes without using the radio. Two kills in one mission! He was now just two victories away from joining that elite group of fighter pilots known as Aces.

Reins continued his high loop and was coming almost straight down while the other German plane was coming straight up.

Wiser cut his loop tighter than his wing lead and came over the top in about half the distance. At the top of his loop, he leveled out instead of going back down and caught the German fighter on its side as it was going straight up to attack Reins.

Wiser opened up with his six .50-caliber guns at 275 yards. It was a thin silhouette to hit—just the narrow side of the fuselage to target—but because it was moving in a straight line, Wiser had little trouble. The bullets hit the 109 in its engine compartment and raked the entire length of the fuselage as the plane flew up through his bullets.

The pilot was killed instantly, and the plane flipped over on its back before going into a tight spiral spin towards the ground. The plane gathered so much speed in its dive that the wing ripped off at fifteen thousand feet. At ten thousand, the tail section tore free and the 109 became a flaming missile that disintegrated upon impact.

Three fighters were destroyed and a fourth was out of the fight. The odds were now two to one in the American's favor, but that still left two. Adams looked back up to the bomber and to the remaining two German fighters… but saw only one fighter trailing the bomber.

He twisted and turned in his cockpit, frantically searching for the missing enemy. "Check your sixes!" Adams shouted. "I only see one of the German fighters!"

When Adams turned to look, his hand dragged the stick over and the plane turned slightly. He caught a flash of movement on his right side, just under his horizontal stabilizer. It was just enough for him to see the flash of the camouflaged green Messerschmitt as it swept up underneath him.

Adams yanked back on the stick for all it was worth. Like the stallion she was named after, his plane reared up as he pulled on the reins. The maneuver worked. He saw a volley of deadly cannon fire go streaking by, just inches from his canopy. The maneuver got his plane out of harm's way, but also threw it into a dizzying, tight flat spin. He was caught in a whirlpool spin that was sucking him out of the sky.

"Stick with the bomber. That's an order!" were the last words his crew heard from Colonel Adams.

TWENTY-ONE

"COLONEL!" Stevens shouted, watching the colonel's spinning plane disappear from sight into the clouds.

As soon as the plane vanished, something snapped inside of the young fighter pilot with an almost audible sound, as if all hope had been swallowed up in the clouds.

The colonel had been more than a commanding officer to him—he had been a surrogate father, helping him to adjust not only to Army life being so far from home, but also coping with the roller coasters of emotions of dealing with the loss of friends with whom he might have breakfast in the morning, only to stare at their empty place at the dinner table that night.

And now Colonel Adams himself was gone.

Stevens was mad. Not just mad, but howling, screaming mad. It was an out-of-control forest fire consuming him from the inside out. Yet his thoughts were clear and focused, no smoky haze from his burning wrath blurred his vision. His rage was channeled into a single purpose: destroy the German Messerschmitt that had attacked his colonel.

It wouldn't have mattered if there had been a hundred Messerschmitts or Focke Wulfs between him and this particular plane. He would not be denied.

"My God . . . he got the colonel," Wiser said in stunned shock.

"Do you see a chute?" Reins asked.

"He's not dead!" Stevens shouted. "He'll pull it out!"

"Where's the other fighter?" Wiser asked, eyes darting nervously across the sky.

"To hell with the other plane," Stevens said. "This one is mine.'"

"That fighter is still climbing after the bomber," Reins said, "but the other fighter is swinging back toward us."

"Keep his attention while I get in behind him," Stevens ordered.

"Careful," Reins cautioned. "This guys flies like a demon."

"Yeah, well, that's okay," Stevens said coldly. "He may be a demon, but today I am the devil himself."

Stevens banked hard to get in behind the German fighter. The Messerschmitt had been angling back up toward Reins and Wiser but quickly reversed when he saw Stevens turn after him.

Stevens was still turning on his side when the German shot under him and pulled up and over to drop down from above.

Stevens snap rolled the rest of the way over and brought his Mustang back up and under the 109. The German pilot matched his American opponent move for move as the two planes chased each other, like a dog chasing its own tail, neither gaining advantage over the other.

"Shouldn't we go and help him?" Wiser asked.

"Negative, there's still another fighter up there, and we've got our orders," Reins answered.

"But, sir . . ."

"Negative, Lieutenant, our job is to protect that bomber," Reins replied, his shaky voice betraying his order.

"Roger." Wiser looked down at his friend as he followed the major, pulling up toward their charge and leaving their comrade to battle the German and his own demons.

TIME and again, Stevens fought the effects of blacking out because of the high G-forces to which he subjected himself and his plane. He didn't care that he was pushing himself and his aircraft past their limits. And despite all the abuse, his Mustang kept on flying, doing her job as if she, too, were eager to avenge the loss of her sister.

Both planes were locked in a circle, each trying desperately to get just enough angle on the nose to bring her gun sight to bear on the other.

Stevens looked out the top of his canopy and straight into his opponent's cockpit. The eyes of death were cold and fixed, filled with a bloodlust yearning to be fulfilled. The eyes were so close that Stevens felt he could reach out and touch them. He realized that he wasn't staring into the face of his opponent but at his own reflection off his canopy. Today the devil would get his due.

Both planes were on their left sides, locked in a mortal turn that would end in death when one of them broke the circle.

Suddenly the German plane flipped over on its back and started to dive. Normally, such an action signaled that the pilot had had enough and was diving for the deck and home, but Stevens knew better. He knew this pilot was not running from the fight. Rather, he was trying to dive down, then roll up and over and get in behind him.

Stevens knew there would be nothing gained by matching his opponent's move and playing follow the leader. Instead, he threw his stick in the opposite direction, leveling the wings, then pulling back on the reins, urging his steed into a steep climb to the right and held it there.

When the German pilot saw his trick wasn't working and that his adversary wasn't following, he continued to roll the plane over and swung up behind the American fighter, trailing behind him at about eight hundred yards. Stevens knew it was crazy to let the German get in behind, but he was crazy like a fox and was betting his life that his Mustang would out climb its Messerschmitt counterpart.

Stevens decreased his climb and eased back on the throttle a little, allowing the German to gain altitude . . . and confidence. Every fighter pilot needed confidence, for without it he could never climb into the cockpit, realizing every mission was the one he might not come back from. Confidence in one's own abilities was essential, but underestimating one's opponent, pride, would precede his fall.

Stevens looked back and watched the green plane with the bright yellow nose spinner bring death closer and closer. Stevens saw the Grim Reaper riding on the wing, his black hood and cape sailing in the wind, a grin stretching across his lipless mouth. He was readying his scythe and bringing it up from his side, pointing its sharp, merciless blade at him.

But Stevens wore a smile of his own. He knew the Reaper didn't care if he took an American or German life. That was one thing about Death: he was just as happy with one as with the other. He knew the silver scythe that was pointed at him and ready to slash at his plane would soon be swinging down to take off the wings of the German plane.

The Me 109 was close now—only about four hundred yards away—and Stevens could see the dark, empty, hollow eye sockets of the Reaper as he rode on the wing. He could see the dark, hollow hole of the 20mm nose cannon. It was time to make the Reaper happy.

Stevens shoved the throttle all the way to the stops and pulled the nose almost straight up. The altimeter climbed rapidly, and the airspeed fell just as fast. The Messerschmitt continued to gain for a moment, then fell slowly back. Stevens imagined the confident smile fading from the German's face as he realized that he couldn't overtake the American in the climb. The Reaper's smile never dimmed, knowing he would surely get his pound of flesh.

The Mustang clawed at the air, straining to gain every inch of altitude that Mother Nature would give until she imposed the law of gravity. Just before the gavel came down, Stevens kicked the rudder over and lowered the nose of his fighter. Pointing straight down, he was held snug by his seat harness and stared at the German pilot and the Reaper face to face.

Though he couldn't see the face of his opponent, Stevens imagined the German kicking himself, not for being out flown but for being outwitted, not for being beaten by an opponent but by his own hand. Stevens wished the German could see what he was seeing.

The Grim Reaper smiled at Stevens as he shifted his attention away from him and to the German plane he was riding on.

Maybe the German pilot could see, because out of desperation, the Messerschmitt maintained its climb, perhaps in hopes of getting a lucky shot rather than turning while he still had power to maneuver. Sparks flew as the cannon, and machine guns opened fire, but the deadly shells flew wide as the 109 went into a stall, sliding backwards, tail-first, down through the sky.

Colonel Adams would have been proud, Stevens thought; his timing was perfect. The nose of his war bird was pointed straight at his opponent as it slid backwards, then flipped over on is back. It was falling out of control and spinning, just as Colonel Adams' plane had.

Because of the low speed, Stevens knew the German pilot would regain control of his aircraft shortly, but he meant to see that his adversary would never get the chance.

Stevens' air speed was slow as well, but he was in control of his warhorse. The cross hairs of his gun sight fell down across the Messerschmitt, and he pulled back a little on the stick to keep them there. As soon as they held steady, he opened fire.

The Reaper took his scythe and began his deadly harvest, slicing off the rudder and left elevator as the American bullets found their mark.

Stevens held the trigger down.

Next, the Reaper surgically removed the left aileron. Then in a sweeping windmill motion, he brought the scythe up and over his head, the 109 starting to spin in an awkward motion as the Reaper neatly severed the left wing.

The Messerschmitt was fatally wounded.

Still he held the trigger down.

The Mustang picked up speed as she chased her own bullets down after her target. Stevens was so close now that nearly every round found its mark, shredding the aircraft. The Reaper stood on the fuselage, right behind the cockpit, his boney hands working the scythe as fast as a sewing machine needle, punching holes in the 109. He looked at Stevens with cold, empty eyes, void of all compassion. His jawbone formed a slight, knowing smile: he saw the same expression simmering in the eyes of his American benefactor.

Stevens kept the trigger down.

The Mustang was so close now that she threatened to trample the Messerschmitt under her hooves if the bullets failed. The Reaper turned back to his work and with one mighty swing buried his blade deep into the center of the German plane. In one blinding, explosive moment, the Messerschmitt and the Grim Reaper disappeared.

Victory held no glory today. There was no sweet aroma of success, nothing to savor. Stevens shivered in his cockpit, then leveled out his wings and headed back toward the bomber.

"PILOT to tail gunner," Perry's voice crackled over the bomber's intercom. "What's going on back there, Billy?"

"Man, this is better than a Saturday afternoon matinee back home," Jacobs replied in a slight country-boy twang. "You should see this. Those fighter jocks are really something else." Jacobs gave a blow by blow description of the aerial combat as if he were a sportscaster calling the big football game on a Friday night. It was exciting right up until the part where Adams' fighter went spinning out of sight.

Listening to the commentary, Avery imagined Mike sitting up in the cockpit. What if the German fighters got through and something happened to Mike? How could he live with himself knowing that his orders killed his nephew? And what would he tell Martha, Mike's wife? How could he ever tell her that she had lost her husband, because of him?

Already he could feel guilt clearing out a little corner of his heart in which to dwell. Was this something that he could live with for the rest of his life? What other choice did he really have? He didn't know what to do; he wasn't a combat officer, he didn't have training for this sort of thing. Panic churned his stomach faster than the four propellers turning on the plane.

Do what you know how to do, he told himself, and worry about the rest later. He got out all his supplies and readied the equipment for the umpteenth time.

"Pilot to tail gunner," Perry said. "Billy, what about that last fighter? Is he still on our six?"

Billy Jacobs peered between the barrels of his machine guns. "Yes, sir, he's on our low six, about a thousand yards out."

"What about our escorts?"

"One of them is tangling with a 109, and the other two Mustangs are on their way back here."

"Do you have a shot on the one trailing us?" Perry asked.

"Yes sir, my guns will train that low," Billy said.

"How about you, Mitch? Do you have a shot at him too?"

"Roger that, Captain," Mitchell reported from the ball turret.

"Okay, since we don't have any bombs on this trip, we were able to carry a couple extra boxes of ammo. So feel free to take a few pot shots at this guy," Perry said. "I know he's out of effective range right now, but who knows? You might get lucky."

"Okay, Skipper," Jacobs said.

"Yes, sir," Mitchell agreed.

Each gunner took a different approach to shooting at their pursuer. Mitchell took advantage of the extra ammunition, fired several long bursts, trying to "walk" the rounds into the German plane. Jacobs, more experienced and disciplined, fired shorter bursts, taking care to aim and to correct with each shot. Both men had the same results, however: no visible damage.

The German plane did weave once as several rounds from Mitchell's long bursts hit. After that, the Messerschmitt pulled out wider from the bomber, gaining altitude at a safer distance.

"Navigator to pilot," Svenson called, looking up from his chart. "We're at the designated coordinates, Skipper. You can orbit here and tell Captain Avery he can start transmitting anytime."

"Roger. Captain, it's your show now," Perry said.

"But what about the enemy fighter?" Avery replied.

"Don't worry about him; you've got your job to do, and we've got ours."

"Roger, Captain, and thanks." Avery turned to Thomas and gave him a short nod. "Okay, Sergeant, let's fire this thing up." Avery adjusted his headset and grabbed his notebook and pencil.

"This is Hermes calling. Repeat, this is Hermes."

There was no reply, only static filling his headphones. Avery's heart sank. After all that, Zeus had to be alive and be here to transmit. He had to be!

"I repeat, this is Hermes calling."

Again, he was greeted with nothing but static.

"Switch to alternate frequency," Avery said. Thomas nodded and adjusted the equipment. "This is Hermes, do you copy?" Had Zeus been captured after he gave his emergency sign off? The static seemed to grow louder, confirming his fears that Zeus really was gone.

"This is H-E-R-M-E-S, D-O Y-O-U C-O-P-Y?" Avery droned as if spelling it out would get the message across better. Suddenly the static gave way to a loud click.

"I know you're five miles up, Hermes, but there is no need to shout. This is Zeus."

Avery sank down on the small wooden stool, a rush of relief washing over him. At least the mission and Colonel Adams' death would not be in vain. His mind flashed back to his conversation with the Colonel in the pub; Adams died doing his duty, and he would be remembered.

"Zeus, this is Hermes. Nice to hear your voice. Please go ahead and relay your message."

"Thank you, Hermes. I will get straight to the point. I've been approached by a Major Volker Reinard of the SS. He knows both our identities and wants to make a deal. He wants me to tell you that he is ready to negotiate a surrender of the troops under his command, which he numbered to be seven thousand.

"He also says he has knowledge of German battle plans and other top-secret information he is willing to trade for safe passage and other considerations. Reinard also says he doesn't expect you to believe him and that I should mention the name 'Dr. Nicoli Strovinski' to you. He says you would know the name.

"I do not trust the man. I need instructions on how to proceed. I will not transmit on my normal WT until I have conformation of how to proceed with Reinard. I will also suspend my normal operations unless instructed otherwise. Over."

"Understood, Zeus. I agree. Do you wish to be extracted?"

Merle sat comfortably among the bales of hay in a barn loft that was used by the resistance to help smuggle downed Allied airman out of the country. It was the secondary transmission location to use if he had been compromised. He had never considered being pulled out. The thought of leaving had never entered his mind.

If he left, would he be running from danger or escaping from the enemy? He wasn't a soldier and wasn't expected to act like one. But he also knew that they didn't run from danger, and when it came right down to it, he didn't much like the idea of running either.

But what if Reinard's offer was genuine? How many lives could be saved if he surrendered seven thousand SS troops without a fight! And what of the other "secret" information he claimed to have? Could that shorten the war, saving even more lives? Logic told him to get out and get out fast, but as Beka had often told him, he was a man, and men weren't logical.

"I would like to stay and see this one through, Hermes."

"Roger, Zeus, understood. I will continue to transmit information over normal means. I will broadcast on this same frequency again in two days, same time."

"Understood. Zeus over and out."

AVERY was taken by surprise by the SS major's involvement and offer of surrender. Was the surrender gambit genuine, or just part of his game? Zeus, now identified as a resistance fighter, might indicate that he had a leak in his organization. Reinard could have discovered him through other means, though Avery didn't think so. Reinard's knowledge of Strovinski all but sealed the fact that he not only had a leak, but a spy in his organization!

Avery's head swam. The ramifications of a spy were unimaginable. Was his entire network in jeopardy? Was all of his hard work for the past two years about to go up in smoke? Should he shut down operations and warn his people, or hope that Zeus was an isolated incident, that Reinard's offer genuine? Now more that ever was he glad that he had stepped outside the bounds of normal operations and enlisted the help of his nephew in making contact with his informant.

Then again, how secretive was that decision? Avery's team had a reception committee of six German fighters waiting for them. A case of being in the wrong place at the wrong time, he wondered, or the work of the spy?

Even though he was in the spy business himself, the very thought that he might have one in his own organization repulsed him. Whom could he trust? He dare not tell anyone at all.

He had two days to do all the research on Reinard himself, reschedule another flight, then try and figure out who was betraying him.

Betraying *him?* As if it were a personal vendetta against him! What if the failure to capture Strovinski was really a set up to make him look bad so he would lose his job and get reassigned?

Avery shook his head. He'd been in this business too long. Paranoia was making him think he was so important that the German war machine had it in personally for Captain Griffin J. Avery. Avery didn't know how long he had been sitting there, not moving a muscle, trying to arrange all the information he had just been overwhelmed with. His joints and muscles had given up protesting the extreme cold and being forced to sit still for so long. His mind was now in control, processing, filing, manipulating this new information.

He felt a hand on his shoulder, startling him. It was Joe Thomas. "Sir, are you alright?"

"Yeah, sorry, I was just thinking. Is everything okay?"

"Yes, sir, we're almost home. I just thought you might want to look out the window. We're also below ten thousand feet, so you can take off your oxygen mask now."

Avery nodded. He felt terribly weary, physically and mentally, beyond anything he had ever known before. He stood, released the strap from his mask, and took a deep breath. The air he had been breathing for the past five hours had had a canned, rubbery smell and taste from the mask. It felt good to taste clean, fresh air again.

It was dark now, and he couldn't imagine what might be interesting to see at night, but he needed the distraction. The sky had cleared, and stars dotted the black velvet night like the New York City skyline. But what he saw was not in the sky, but on the ground. The moon had already started her journey across the heavens, and a trail of light draped across the water and washed up on the white cliffs of Dover.

He had always heard of their beauty and had even driven to the coast once to see them, but they had never looked like this. He'd heard the aircrews talk about the cliffs, about how seeing them meant one had made it home in one piece.

At that moment, they were the most beautiful sight he'd ever seen. They seemed to glow in the moonlight like a beacon guiding the flyers home.

He hung his head low. He just wished everyone could have seen this. How was he going to tell Wes' wife about his death? He knew it was his responsibility as mission commander to inform the next of kin about the death of their loved one. He'd just finished writing the letter to Captain Lofton's widow. Already he had to write another?

He would trade his very soul not to have to write that letter.

TWENTY-TWO

HIS head, like his plane, was spinning out of control. Adams' vision was blurry and his head was pinned against the side of the cockpit, held tightly in place by the weighty hand of centrifugal force. Twice his hand was dragged off the stick by the spinning and twice he fought back and managed to regain his grip on his controls. He got weaker by the moment and knew that if his hand slipped off a third time, he wouldn't have the strength to grab it again.

With great effort, Colonel Wesley Adams raised his left arm and reached over to pull the throttle back to idle. That helped slow the spin and relieved the pressure a little, but his plane was still twisting out of control. He knew he wouldn't be able to pull the canopy back and unbuckle himself to bail out.

Through the blurry haze, Adams found the altimeter spinning around faster than the plane. It seemed like only moments since he had dodged the German fighter, but he had already lost five thousand feet. At this rate, he had about two minutes to live. He lowered the landing gear, trying to change the center of gravity to help him regain control.

With both hands, he "stirred" his flight stick as if churning butter, rotating it in the opposite direction of the spin, trying to break Death's hold on his plane. At ten thousand feet he hit the clouds. Despite their soft, fluffy appearance, they did nothing to slow him down as he punched through them like a bowling ball through a newspaper.

He plummeted out the bottom of the cloudbank, trailing pieces of broken clouds behind him like streamers. Adams didn't need the altimeter to tell him the ground was closing in. The swirling greens and browns of countryside reminded him that time was not his ally. His head pounded like a piston with each revolution of the plane, and he had already lost most of the sensation in his arms and legs. It was a contest to see who would claim him first, the ground that seemed to be reaching up for him or the air working hard to drain away his consciousness.

Adams refused to give in and quit. The only image he held onto was that of his wife, daughter, and two sons. With renewed strength and motivation he worked his controls and did every trick he knew to regain control. Slowly the revolutions abated and twice they almost stopped, but Death was tenacious and would not let go freely.

At two thousand feet, he gunned the engine and threw the stick in the opposite direction that the plane was spinning. It was just enough to slip through Death's tight grip. He leveled out at five hundred feet. The plane stopped spinning, but it was two minutes before his head cleared, and another five before he could reach over and turn on his radio.

"CAPTAIN, Captain!" Thomas shouted.

Avery turned back around. "Yes?"

"I just heard from our escorts, sir: Colonel Adams is okay! He's just crossing the channel now!"

Avery collapsed onto his stool. He felt like bawling like a baby, but that wouldn't do for an officer in the United States Army. Instead he simply turned and said thank you.

Even though the hour was late, he couldn't wait to get back to his office and start reviewing the material he'd just received. But was the office a safe place to go? No; he needed time to think. Perhaps home would be the best place to go right now and sort everything out. Or better yet, go to sleep, if he could, and get a fresh perspective on it all in the morning.

The *Red Light Lady* descended slowly and met the ground that rose up to meet her. The tires screeched and the smooth ride of being airborne was replaced with the roughness of being earth bound. The plane rolled to a stop in the grass in the exact spot from where it had taken off.

Avery thanked the crew and admonished them not to mention a word of what had happened or what they had done tonight. Their job was over, but his was just beginning.

TWENTY-THREE

THE aroma was tremendous. The crackling and sizzling sounds were almost as appetizing as the smell that drew Matt Lincoln to the kitchen like a moth to the flame. He felt like he hadn't eaten in a week, and his stomach growled in anticipation. He walked in the kitchen and stared at the bacon cooking in the fry pan. Smiling, he looked up to see his dad at the counter cutting up onions and slicing cheese. His mouth watered in anticipation.

Whenever his mom was away for the night, which wasn't very often, the only thing his dad ever fixed was what he called his world-famous "Out Of This World Sandwiches." His father returned the smile as he put the sliced onions into the pan with the bacon and stirred them together. There really was no secret to his world famous sandwich. It was bacon and onions mixed together and fried with scrambled eggs, topped with melted cheese and served on buttered toast like a sandwich.

It was a rare delicacy he seldom got to enjoy, but the fact that his dad had cooked it made truly it special. What really mattered now, though, was how hungry he was. He could eat a dozen eggs, a loaf of bread, a pound of bacon! He licked his lips as his dad set the steaming treat in front of him. He closed his eyes as he slowly brought it up to his eager and waiting lips when all of a sudden he heard two loud bangs.

NO! NO! Lincoln moaned to himself as the vision of his dream faded into nothingness faster than the steam rising off his fantasy sandwich. He wasn't sure which was worse, waking up and still finding he was in the prison camp, or not being able to eat the sandwich in his dream. He was still a little groggy; if he could only get back to sleep, he might be able to finish his dream.

The door burst open and three guards rushed in shouting for everyone to get up and out for roll call. Any thoughts of recapturing his vision were trampled to death by the boots of the German soldiers.

Lincoln had already lost five pounds and tried not to think about food—difficult when it was one of the major topics of conversation. Still, talking about the food they didn't have was better than eating what they did.

Among their meager rations, prisoners received one loaf of black bread to every seven prisoners. It was said to be 50 percent sawdust, a fact that he didn't doubt after tasting it. But spread a little jam from the Red Cross packages on it, he thought, and it would do. In their Red Cross packages, when they could get them, was a variety of foods such as the versatile Spam, chocolate bars, and a one-pound can of margarine . . . though Lincoln liked the British packages better because they contained real butter. Almost as important as food were the five packs of cigarettes each prisoner would receive. Cigarettes were the gold standard and were used like money for buying anything and everything in the camp. For the rare prisoner who didn't smoke, they had great bargaining power. Lincoln was one of those.

So why were they doing a roll call in the middle of the night? The Germans randomly did roll calls to disrupt any escape plans, but it was still unusual for them to call one at this time of night. Then it dawned on him: he had been awakened by loud bangs. Were they gunshots? Had someone tried to escape and been shot by the Germans?

Lincoln jumped down from his bunk and had just slipped on one boot when one of the guards shoved him, yelling at him to hurry up. He started to stand up and protest but when he turned around, he saw that the guard had his rifle up, just looking for an excuse to pull the trigger. He stumbled out the door, hopping though the courtyard, pulling his boot on as he went.

The night air was cold. Several men attempted to get warm by stomping their feet or rubbing their hands together but were stopped with the butt of a rifle planted in the middle of the back. After half an hour, the yelling of the guards died down and an eerie silence descended over the camp. The Germans seemed satisfied with their prisoner count, but they still kept them standing at attention out in the cold.

Lincoln's feet were freezing. He hadn't had time to put socks on when they'd been rushed out of the barracks. Rifle butts or not, he would have to do something soon or his feet would freeze. A few more minutes passed, and he had lost all feeling in his left big toe. The sun's rays shot out over the hill. Then, as if waiting for the sun to announce his presence, the door to the camp administrative office opened.

Colonel Stein stepped out of the office door, the creaking planks moaning under his immense weight. He stood like a statue at the top of the stairs, wanting all the prisoners to see that he was the one in charge.

He stepped down and walked slowly through the open gate into the prisoner's courtyard, gloves smacking as he went, keeping time with his strides. Halfway across the compound, he stopped and waved for the senior prisoners of war officers to come to him. The three Allied officers walked up and briskly saluted. He returned the salute and spoke to them for a few minutes then motioned with his gloves for them to fall back in line. He turned and, with another wave of his gloves, three men approached from the left. Two of them dragged bodies.

Kohn marched behind Stein, did two sharp ninety-degree turns, faced his commanding officer, saluted smartly, then took two steps back and to the left. Kohn stepped back and grabbed the body of the dead American and walked over to the Allied senior officers. He tossed the body of the airman on the ground in front of them like a bag of mail.

Stein's voice boomed over the prisoners. "This man was caught trying to escape. As you can see, he did not get very far. I will not tolerate any escape attempts in my camp. He ignored my orders and has paid the ultimate price for his disobedience, and now you will pay yours for your complicity in his escape attempt. All yard privileges will be cancelled for the next four days. Dismissed."

As the prisoners broke formation, their grumbles echoed through the yard like a roll of distant thunder as they herded back to their barracks. Stein turned to go to his office, when someone caught his eye. "Sergeant Kohn, bring me that man there. The black one. Lincoln, I think, is his name."

Kohn nodded and went into the crowd. He pushed and shoved his way through, parting the sea of prisoners like the prow of a mighty warship.

Lincoln was almost to his barracks door when he felt a huge and powerful hand grab him by the shoulder. He spun around and found himself staring into the chest of Kohn. Kohn didn't say a word as he guided Lincoln back toward the commandant.

"Why am I here, Colonel? Have I done something?"

"Silence!" Kohn ordered. "Do not speak unless spoken to!"

Lincoln stood a little straighter, keeping his eyes forward. His last encounter with Kohn had left him with a bruised jaw.

Stein circled Lincoln, looking him up and down like he was buying a plow horse. Satisfied, he turned back to Kohn. "The prisoner who was killed was part of my kitchen staff and I need to replace him. This man will do fine. Have him cleaned up and brought to my compound this afternoon at 1400 hours."

TWENTY-FOUR

SLEEP came to Griff Avery more easily than he had thought possible, especially considering the revelation that he'd just had about Zeus and the SS major. The alarm clock sounded with an unusual harshness, as if it held a personal vendetta against him. He slowly sat up and rubbed his eyes.

The day would be filled with excitement and dread. He loved a mystery and looked forward to unraveling this one concerning Zeus, Reinard, and Strovinski, and how their lives had become intertwined.

Avery opened the window and sat on the sill of his third story flat, lighting up a cigarette, his morning ritual before plunging into the day. He took a deep drag then blew it out, watching the people scurrying about their business below. Looking at the tattered landscape of crater holes, burned-out buildings, and piles of rubble, he wondered how the Londoners managed it.

The city and its people had taken quite a beating from the Luftwaffe during the Battle of Britain, and later from Hitler's vengeance weapons, the V-1 and V-2 rockets. They'd been battered and bruised, but their spirit was never broken and they never gave up hope, not even in the darkest days of 1940 and 1941 when they faced Hitler's tyranny alone.

He blew out another long stream of smoke. He felt rather like that now, alone and unsure who was a friend and who was an enemy. How can I act normal in the office today knowing that someone there might be a spy? he wondered. The leak could have come from another department, but he didn't think so. He tried to be methodical in his reasoning, but as hard as he tried, he kept coming up with the same answers, and his list kept coming down to the same two people, the two people he trusted most: Jason Peters and Anna Roshinko. *Hi Jay, talk to the Fuhrer today? Good morning Anna, I enjoyed our date the other night; will you take me back to Berlin with you?* It made his stomach hurt to think that it could be either one of them.

He crushed the cigarette out and finished getting dressed. He couldn't find anything to eat in his kitchen so he decided he'd grab a doughnut and wash it down with some coffee at work. Half way down the stairs, he remembered the doughnut shop had been destroyed. He shook his head: life just wasn't fair.

The morning air was brisk. It felt good, helping him focus and think as he walked to work. However, it couldn't keep his stomach in check, as the closer he got to the office the more nervous he became. He reached the front door and stood outside, lighting another cigarette to calm his anxious nerves. He didn't want to tip his hand to the spy, if there really was one.

Avery walked in to see Corporal Christopher Blankenship seated at his throne behind the ID desk, personally protecting the interests of the United States government and the OSS. Avery had made the mistake once of calling him "Chris," which was quickly corrected. Blankenship's uniform was always neatly pressed, and he was clean-shaven with never a hair out of place. He examined the ID of each person who entered his kingdom as if he were reading a great book. If there was even the smallest smudge on their ID, he would issue them a guest pass and order them to get a new identification card before entering his realm again.

Avery had always secretly laughed at the corporal's strict adherence to regulations, but under the present circumstances, he appreciated it.

Blankenship examined his ID with all due thoroughness, then handed it back. "Thank you, sir," he said.

Avery descended the stone staircase to the basement. At times he felt like he was entering the dungeon of a castle rather than an office, since there were no windows.

"Good morning, sir," said Vivian, one of the girls from the typing pool. "Have a good evening?"

Did I have a good evening? Is she really just being friendly and polite or does she have an ulterior motive? Is she trying to get information out of me, to see if I really did learn anything last night? Stop being so paranoid! Avery shouted to himself. "Good morning, Vivian." He smiled back. "Have you seen Lieutenants Peters or Roshinko this morning?"

"No, sir, you're the first to arrive," she said. Of course they're not here yet, Avery thought. They can afford to sleep in; after all, they already know what's going on. I am the one playing catch-up.

She returned his smile and kept walking.

He grabbed his coffee, went straight to his office, and sat down to organize his thoughts. How would he proceed? The first thing to find was information on Major Reinard. Reinard was a new player in the game, and Avery needed to know as much as possible about the man. He glanced up at the map of Europe on his wall and considered how similar it looked to the one the navigator used for their flight last night. Something clicked.

He had a hunch. He might not be the sharpest tool in the shed, but over the years he'd learned to trust his instincts. He dug through his desk drawers and found the photos from the gun camera film. He opened the folder and shifted through the photos until he found the one he was looking for. It was one of the last photos Lyons had made for him. It was taken after Major Spencer's plane had escaped the airfield and showed nothing of interest except for a group of buildings in the bottom corner of the photograph. The photo was a little blurry, so he couldn't tell if the buildings were part of a POW camp or some sort of factory complex.

Avery got up and took a closer look at his map. He found the town where Zeus lived. The map did indicate there was a POW camp next to it, but showed no airstrip. How long had Spencer been flying when he took this photograph? The airfield had to be close, but why wasn't it shown on the map?

He sipped his coffee and automatically grabbed a cigarette, then opened his top desk drawer and rummaged through it, looking for a book of matches.

"Good morning, sir."

Avery slammed his fingers in the drawer. Startled, he looked up to see Peters and Roshinko standing in the doorway. He felt a twinge of jealousy surge through him, seeing the two of them together.

Peters was tall and charming and nearly twenty years his junior. Avery and Anna hadn't been dating long, and he still felt insecure with their relationship. He could interpret German cipher code, direct a dozen operatives in the field, but was still unsure of himself when it came to dealing with the opposite sex.

"Geez, you scared me," Avery said. "Don't sneak up on me like that."

"Sorry, boss," Peters said. "What're you doing?"

Wouldn't you like to know, you Nazi spy! "Nothing, just looking for some matches."

"What've you got there?" Peters asked, nodding at the pictures on his desk.

Should I lie and say it is nothing? Avery wondered. No, hide the truth in the light and see what happens. "It's photos from the gun camera film we looked at the other day."

"Did they turn up anything new?"

"No, nothing unusual. Would you like to take a look?"

"No thanks, I'll pass, then."

Liar! I bet you can't wait to get your hands on these! "How about you, Lieutenant?" he said, turning to Roshinko.

"Not unless you want me to. I've got to prepare today's messages for broadcast."

No! Not you too! Aren't you even the least bit curious? he wondered. Not unless you already know what's on them! "Okay, you two sound pretty busy so I won't keep you," Avery said. "I'll be in and out all morning, but we'll sit down after lunch to go over a few things."

They both nodded and turned to leave. He held his gaze on Anna just a moment longer and was rewarded with a very personal smile as she left. He felt a little better, but the green-eyed monster of jealousy living in his heart now had a new roommate that threatened to take over, and its name was "mistrust."

First order of business: find out who this Major Reinard was. Avery walked five blocks to the G2, or Military Intelligence building, and went to the personnel section.

ONE full pack of cigarettes and five cups of coffee later, Avery felt he had a pretty good idea who Major Volker Reinard was and he didn't like it. Reinard had joined the SS in 1933, right after Hitler took power. There was nothing outstanding in his file until the night of June 29, 1934. It was called the "Night of the Long Knives," or the "Blood Purge," in which Hitler rounded up all of his political enemies, real and imagined, and had them killed.

It was during this purge that Reinard made a name for himself, especially with the man Hitler saw as a threat: Ernst Roehm. Hitler considered Roehm and the two million members of his *Sturmabtrilung* (SA), or "brown shirts," too powerful and dangerous. Though part of the Nazi party, the SA was too radical, challenging the German Army itself for the military control of Germany, and Reinard had been instrumental in Roehm's capture. His quick thinking impressed Heinrich Himmler, head of the SS, earned him a promotion, a high profile position, and time in the spotlight.

It was here, too, that Reinard was introduced to Reinhard Heydrich. Heydrich was appointed by Himmler and had a gift for organization. He was the perfect Aryan: tall, dashing, and blond. Reinard looked up to and admired him and later patterned his command upon Heydrich's template. Heydrich was an accomplished violinist—his father was a composer—and Avery imagined that was where Reinard's love of classical music had blossomed.

In September of '42, Reinard went with Heydrich to Prague, where Heydrich was named as the acting Reich Protector of Bohemia and Moravia. Heydrich earned the name "Butcher of Prague" when he promptly began killing thousands of men, women, and children in an attempt to Germanize the Czechs. It was there that Reinard honed the skills of his wicked craft.

But the true monster was not unleashed until May 23, 1942, when two British-trained Czech agents attacked Heydrich in his car. He soon died and Reinard lashed out like a madman, searching for those responsible for the death of his mentor and hero. It was reported that he killed and tortured hundreds of innocent people in his quest to find the assassins, and that he was instrumental in the razing of the entire village of Lidice. There, he had every male in the village shot and sent all the women to concentration camps.

Seeing his devotion to duty and fervor for his work, Himmler sent Heydrich's protégée to France to help crush the Maquis and the underground resistance movement. Reinard's reputation for cruelty quickly grew, bordering on the sadistic, as he approached his job as though it were a religious calling. He was personally involved in the torture and execution of dozens of agents and civilians.

In his professional life, Reinard had no real friendships with other officers, either in or out of the SS, with the possible exception of a Luftwaffe general named Jaeger. In his personal life, he was a loner, having no close contacts, preferring instead, the quiet solitude of his home and the comfort of his music.

Could Reinard see the writing on the wall, that the Third Reich was doomed? Was he now trying to negotiate his way out of war criminal charges? Or was he laying some sort of trap? And what, if any, connection did he have to the airfield where Strovinski's plane was photographed . . . and how did he know about Strovinski in the first place?

Reinard could have found out about Zeus through his own means, his own counterintelligence network. But Strovinski was different. There were only three people on the European continent that knew about the operation and only a handful more in England.

It was well past noon and Avery's head was starting to hurt. If he didn't eat soon, he would get a splitting headache, and then he'd be worthless for the rest of the day. He didn't feel like going back to the office, so he returned the files and caught a bus back home.

Avery got off a couple of blocks from his flat and was heading to the Dragon's Breath to have some of Margaret's famous deep fried fish when he passed a small, family-owned deli on the corner. He'd eaten there once or twice, but he really wasn't that much of a sandwich man. He preferred more than a hunk of meat flanked by two pieces of bread. But now that he had a love interest in his life, he knew he should lose a little weight. He should go into the deli and have half a sandwich, and some soup, perhaps . . . but Anna was probably the spy and, within a week or two, he would never see her again, so why not have the fish?

He marched past the deli and turned to the pub to console himself with a large order of Margaret's fish and chips. He wondered why the English called potatoes "chips." It especially escaped him why they would put vinegar on their fish—that's what tartar sauce was for—after all, it was meat, not a salad. The plaque of the Dragon's Breath Pub hung out over the sidewalk. His pace quickened.

TWENTY-FIVE

"NO trouble today, love, okay?" Margaret said as she set down the glass of bitter ale. Avery raised his hands in surrender.

"You'll get none from me," he said smiling. Margaret shook her head as she walked away. Avery took a sip of his beer and looked around. It was much quieter this time of day, mostly locals, but there were still a few military personal scattered around, and the bar didn't look too worse for wear after the brawl. One table was missing and several chairs were gone, but all in all, no major damage.

Even though it was early in the day, it was comforting to see the Colonel sitting at his usual spot, bending the ears of a couple of wide-eyed American GIs who looked fresh off the boat. Avery caught his eye and raised his glass. The Colonel gave him a quick wink and smile, then continued on with his tale. Seeing the Colonel sitting at his favorite stool seemed to give some sort of stability to the universe.

Most people needed peace and quiet to think, but Avery had always found that too much quiet was distracting. He did his best thinking when there was noise around. It seemed to help him focus on the task at hand—and he'd never had a bigger task than the one before him now. While waiting for his food, Avery took out a notebook and began writing. Another one of his habits was to write everything down, no matter how small the detail, for it helped him organize his thoughts. A dangerous habit in his line of work, he knew, but his mind was overflowing with facts and suspicions.

He started scribbling. Some people spoke out loud, he wrote out loud. What precisely did he know? Reinard was a wild card, but after this morning's visit to G2, Avery had a better idea of who Reinard was. He was a very dangerous man, not to be taken lightly. Reinard knew exactly who Zeus was since he had mentioned Strovinski . . . which pointed the finger right back to him and his staff, since retrieving Strovinski was their project.

He took another sip of beer, then wiped the foam off his upper lip with his napkin. He had to watch how much he drank, since the English beer was much more potent than its American counterpart. He had found this out the hard way when he'd arrived in England. His first night out had not left a good first impression with his new boss, General Sizemore. The general was a strict teetotaler and didn't understand this common mistake that took many American GIs by surprise.

The general found it inexcusable that an officer in the American Army would let himself get falling-down drunk. From that point on, the general had labeled him a drunkard and misfit, and Griff had worked very hard for nearly two years to erase that image.

At last Margaret came back with his order. The aroma was heavenly. She placed the steaming dish in front of him and he inhaled deeply, satisfying his nostrils before he satisfied his stomach. For a moment, he felt guilty about not having the deli sandwich, but only for a moment. He devoured the fish like a hungry shark.

Wiping the grease off his hands, he grabbed his pencil and tablet and started writing again. He figured he had three problems to solve, and they seemed to all be intertwined. First, someone on his staff had leaked information either intentionally or unknowingly about the Strovinski operation; one would be easy to fix, the other would not. He hoped it was just sloppiness on someone's part and not a deliberate attempt at espionage. He had to come up with a way to find out; some sort of test to ferret out the cause.

Number two: Strovinski, Reinard, and Zeus. How were these three related? He had an idea: he would create a fictitious file with "Tom," "Dick," and "Harry," code words for Strovinski, Reinard and Zeus. In this business everyone loved code names, so this would fit right in without causing any suspicion. He would craft three separate mission objectives for these covert operatives. If any one of their names or information from the fictitious files surfaced, the spy would be narrowed down to his office and his group. He smiled as he sipped his beer, then shoved the piece of paper in his pocket and grabbed another

The third and maybe the most important: had he discovered a new four-engine jet aircraft? Four engines suggested that the plane would be a bomber. Assuming that Lyons had interpreted the photos right . . . he decided to let his mind run with this one for a bit.

Okay, he thought, if the Germans had a jet fighter, it would stand to reason that they might develop a jet bomber. And like its little friend, the bomber could probably fly faster than any interceptor we have, making it immune from anything other than flak, and even there, its great speed would protect it.

But what would they bomb? The Germans had tried bombing London into submission before and it didn't work—and that was when they had a lot more planes. What purpose would it serve now to attack with only one or two planes, even if they couldn't be touched?

Avery glanced over and watched the Colonel on his stool, motioning vividly with his hands, no doubt enacting some great battle scene to his audience of two young Americans. It hit him.

America?

That notion gave him reason to pause.

One or two planes wouldn't cause any significant damage . . . ridiculous. Or was it? He sketched out a rough outline of the Eastern Seaboard of the United States on one side of the paper and Europe on the other. He marked all the major cites on his map. The only two targets that made any sense were New York and Washington D.C. But it was over three thousand miles from Germany to New York.

Why bomb New York? Were the Germans planning their own Doolittle-style raid? When Japan had attacked Pearl Harbor back in '41 things looked pretty bleak, and Roosevelt ordered Colonel Jimmy Doolittle to attack Japan. The sixteen planes that made up Doolittle's attack force did very little damage to the Japanese war machine, but psychologically it was a tremendous victory for the United States. It began sowing seeds of doubt in the minds of the Japanese people. But that was at the beginning of the war, not at the end, and a morale boosting shot in the arm wouldn't do much good for the German people now. There was nothing just one plane could do.

Avery froze, feeling the icy fingers of fear wrapping its claws around his body. What if the Germans only needed one plane and one bomb? Though he didn't know much, he did know that the United States, and possibly Britain, was working on some sort of a nuclear bomb. He had a friend at the State Department who had told him it was possible to split atoms. If it were done in the proper way, a bomb of unimaginable power could be created. Strovinski was a nuclear physicist; what if he had discovered how to do this? And if the Germans had a secret jet that was all but impossible to shoot down to deliver such a bomb? That would put them back in the driver's seat of this war.

Had Major Spencer's flight of Mustangs stumbled across the airfield where the bomber was stored? The idea of having a spy in his organization didn't seem to matter that much anymore. And he still didn't know where the airfield was. Now he almost wished it was an intentional act of espionage and not simple carelessness. Then he could catch whoever the spy was, beat the truth out of them, and order a bombing raid to destroy the base.

The problems he had tried to divide up into three smaller bite-size chunks became a choking mouthful, as all three were now intertwined together. Find the spy, and he leads me to the base. Find the base, and it leads me to the bomb or plane. Figure out what Reinard wants and his connection to Zeus, and he leads me to the spy.

Should he go to General Sizemore with his information? Sizemore was a cautious man who liked his facts, like his ducks, all lined in a row before he would make a decision. Avery didn't have any hard facts to bring to the general.

He shook his head. He knew that Sizemore wouldn't listen to him, but he couldn't just stand by idly and do nothing while he felt sure the Germans had new technologies and weapons that could be pointed at America itself. No, he had to try. He had to show the general what he had, even though he knew it could be nothing!

Damn, he wished he knew where that airfield was.

He slammed his fist down on the table out of frustration, knocking his beer over. The dark amber liquid splattered on his shirt and spilled onto his pants before he could get up.

He was more upset that all his notes had gotten wet than the fact that his shirt and pants were soaked. He grabbed his napkin and cleaned up the mess as best he could. He would walk back to the office to see the general and let the air dry his clothes. He only hoped the general was in a mood to listen.

AVERY paused outside General Sizemore's office and drew in a heavy breath. He was anxious to show the general what he'd found but didn't want to sound like a babbling idiot. He organized his thoughts, straightened his tie, pulled down at the hem of his jacket, then grabbed the door handle and stepped in.

The lieutenant behind the desk paused from her typing as Avery walked in, peering at him suspiciously with hazel green eyes over dark rimmed glasses.

"I'm Captain Griff Avery of the OSS and I need to see the General right away," Avery said. "It's a matter of national security."

She obliged and rang the intercom.

"Sir, I have a Captain Avery here from the OSS that would like to speak to you. He says it's urgent."

"Very well, send him in."

"Thank you for seeing me, General Sizemore," Avery said as he walked briskly across the room holding out his hand. "I've got some very important information on a new German jet aircraft."

Sizemore stood up from behind his desk and reached out and shook Avery's hand. "Have you been drinking, Captain?" Sizemore asked, the frown on his face growing longer and longer.

"No, sir . . . well, yes, sir," he replied nervously. "I had a beer with my lunch—"

Sizemore cut Avery's words off at the roots. "Good lord, man, it's not even five in the afternoon and you're already drunk. You smell like a brewery."

"I'm not drunk, sir! I accidentally spilled—"

"I don't want to hear any excuses, Captain. You're a disgrace to that uniform."

"But, General, I have important information about a new German jet bomber—"

"And speaking of bombers, I heard about your little adventure the other day and your appropriations of government property by commandeering an Eighth Air Corp bomber and several fighters."

"But, sir, that was for contact with one of my most important agents. I needed a secure radio transmission and in the past—"

"Out, Captain! I don't want to hear about any drunken hallucinations you've had. I have neither the time nor the inclination to listen to anything from rabble like you. If you ever come into my presence drunk or take one of the Army's planes for a little joy ride again, I'll have you court-martialed. Do I make myself clear? Now go!" he shouted, pointing his finger at the door as if ordering a dog out of the room for chewing up his favorite slippers.

Like that bad dog, Avery turned and left the general's office with his tail dragging between his legs. Possibly one of the greatest discoveries of the war, and Sizemore wouldn't even listen to him because he smelled of spilled beer.

And how did Sizemore know about the radio flight? That only confirmed in his mind that there was a spy in his section.

One thing was for certain: the general would be of no help. Avery was in this one alone. He had to find out where that airfield was! He had an idea, but he would need to move quickly before the general changed his mind and decided to relieve him of his duties altogether.

He needed the help of an old friend.

TWENTY-SIX

THAT afternoon, Avery pulled through the gates of the airfield of 222nd Fighter Group. The base was about and hour and a half northeast of London, and it had been raining as usual for most of the trip, but it had been a nice drive in the country nonetheless.

One of the first things he had sworn to do when he arrived in England was to get out of the city and explore the countryside. He wanted to see the dark and dangerous moors from Sherlock Holmes fame in *Hounds of the Baskervilles,* and he especially wanted to see the great castles and the vast estates of the wealthy English lords.

As a kid, he had spent endless hours in the woods behind his house slaying dragons and winning tournaments. When he was ten, he and his friend Bobby Abbot held their own jousting tournament to win the affections of the fair damsel, Suzie Buckmeier. They cut the heads off their mother's brooms and used the sticks as lances, garbage can lids for shields, and their Schwinn bikes as trusty steeds.

The tournament lasted exactly one pass. Avery's lance slipped and got caught in Bobby's front spokes. Bobby did a flip and broke his arm, and Avery was grounded nearly the whole summer. Avery smiled. The worst part was that even though he had beaten Bobby, Suzie had felt sorry for him and they ended up going steady.

And so far, the only castles he had seen in England were those on the post cards he'd sent home to his folks.

Avery drove past the hangars, hoping to see some fighters buzzing the field, but none were flying today because of the weather. Most of the P-51 Mustangs were lined up in neat rows along the tarmac, their polished silver skin glistening in the falling rain. Still more of the war birds sat inside the hangars in various states of maintenance and repair. Off to the side, away from the hangars, was an odd sight, one he'd never seen before. Several planes had their tails propped up, looking like they were flying on the ground . . . except that they were about to "crash" since they were pointed at a heavy dirt embankment several hundred yards ahead of them.

Avery pulled the car over for a moment to see what they were doing. He rolled down the window and watched as several men worked on each wing, a couple more on the ground. Avery was just about to leave when the plane exploded. Or so he thought.

Smoke and fire belched from each wing, and the side of the dirt embankment disintegrated into dust. Just as suddenly as it had started, it stopped. He heard several of the ground crew shouting to the men on the wings. They did some adjusting and the whole process started all over again.

It took Avery a minute to figure out what they were doing: adjusting the convergence on the plane's guns. Each of the six guns had to be aimed separately so they would all hit at the same point, doing the greatest damage to the enemy aircraft. It was interesting to watch: each time they fired, the pattern on the embankment got closer and closer together until it looked like they were digging a tunnel.

Avery left and pulled into the base headquarters, which were housed in a typical Quonset hut brought over by the Americans and covered the English countryside like locusts.

Inside, Avery found Colonel Adams' office clerk much more pleasant than General Sizemore's secretary. They exchanged pleasantries, and the clerk told Avery that the colonel was out for a moment but would return shortly and that he could wait in his office. Avery thanked him and went in.

It was a simple office, that of a working man. An American flag was in the right corner behind the desk, with the English banner on the left. The desk was a large, wooden piece of furniture with its share of nicks and dings. Across from the desk was a worn leather couch that Avery imagined had seen better days. A blanket was stuffed behind one side; clearly the colonel had spent more than one night burning the midnight oil in his office. To the side of the couch stood a coffee table covered with maps and charts.

Avery had just sat down when Adams walked in.

"Hi, Griff," he said, reaching out his hand. "What brings you all the way out here?"

"Do you believe in hunches, Wes?"

"I sure do. You know us pilots, we're a superstitious lot."

Avery smiled. "Well, I got a big one. I tried to go to General Sizemore this morning with what I have, but he wouldn't listen. So I need concrete proof before I go to him again."

"How can I help?"

For nearly an hour, Avery laid out everything to his friend. The reconnaissance photographs, Zeus, Reinard, his failed extraction of Strovinski, and how he thought he had a spy in his own organization. He ended up unloading more of his burdens than he wanted to, but Adams was one of the few people he knew he could trust.

"So after dumping all that on you, I need to know if you and your boys can do a photo recon flight for me. I need to know where that airfield is."

Adams nodded his head and went over to the table, sorted through several maps, selected one of the larger ones, and unrolled it on his desk. It was a detailed map of Western Europe. "Show me where to start."

Avery looked at it. The map was very similar to the one he had hanging in his office, but he noticed it was more detailed, showing things on it that weren't on his. "How old is this?" he asked.

"It was updated about two weeks ago."

His map was only a month old, so the battle lines wouldn't have changed that much in two weeks, he told himself. Griff scanned it and quickly found where Zeus lived. His heart began pounding as if he'd just seen a ghost. "Do these two symbols here mean what I think they do?" he said, pointing on the map.

Adams leaned over and took a look. "Well, if you think that this one's a Stalag POW camp and the other a small airstrip, then I guess they do."

"How long have they been there?"

Adams shrugged his shoulders. "I'd have to do a little checking, but they weren't built overnight."

What better way to keep me in the dark than to hide a lie in broad daylight! Avery thought. All this time he'd been looking at an old map, while the truth was hiding right in front of him.

Another, more chilling thought filled his mind: Anna was responsible for keeping the maps updated. She went to G2 at least twice a month and was supposed to bring back the most recent copies. It would have been easy for her to alter the maps before she brought them back. His heart ached as he considered that the woman he was falling in love with could be a German spy. He'd been holding out for the hope that it had just been carelessness that had leaked the information, but now he knew it was deliberate.

Avery felt like the heavy weight champion of the world had just punched him in the stomach. He breathed out a heavy sigh. "There, start looking there," he said, pointing on the map. "I need photos of the camp and the airfield. And be careful, I think this is the field where Major Spencer was hit. The anti-aircraft could be substantial."

"We're on it."

"Thanks, Wes, I owe you one. I'll need those photos as soon as it's possible for you. I gotta go now," Avery said quietly. He was going to go get drunk, and this time it wouldn't be an accident.

TWENTY-SEVEN

THE truck pulled up at exactly 13:50, and Lincoln, along with three other prisoners, sat in the back along with two guards. He was still fuming at the idea that just because he was black, Stein automatically thought he was destined to work in the kitchen.

Kohn stood by the back of the truck and smiled as Lincoln got in. "Bring us back some leftovers . . . Cookie," he snickered.

Lincoln considered a retort, but decided that discretion was the better part of valor, or in this case, the least painful.

Growing up as one of the few black people just outside Fort Dodge, Iowa, he was always outnumbered by bullies, so he had to be quick on his feet, had to out think his opponents. This was especially true, since he was just average size. His brother, David, however, was just the opposite. David had fought more because he was big enough to take on the world. Hardly a week went by that David didn't come home with bruises or a fat lip from a fight. Their folks had chastised him for fighting and getting into so much trouble, but their father had always had a proud look in his eyes. His boy was standing up for himself, which only seemed right, even as he was telling David not to do it again.

Lincoln, however, was always the "good boy" for not getting into fights. That had always bothered him a little. It wasn't because he didn't want to fight; he wanted Dad to be proud of him, too. But it was more of a matter of self-preservation, being smaller than David as he was.

Come to think of it, that's why he'd joined the Army Air Corps. David joined the Marines to fight with his hands, but Lincoln joined the Air Corp to even out the odds and fight with a plane that weighed eight thousand pounds and could fly over four hundred miles per hour.

So here he was again, a little boy being pushed around by bigger, stronger kids. He had to do what he did best: use his head.

The real irony was that he really could cook. His mother was a great cook and Dad's waistline proved it. She'd taught Lincoln and David at an early age how to cook and take care of themselves. She said she didn't want any boys of hers wasting away because they didn't know how to flip a burger or boil an egg.

He had a knack for it and she had encouraged him to pursue it. She said he could make a good living at being a chef, but he wanted to do more. He didn't want to cook for people, he wanted them to cook for him. His mother worked for a doctor in town, cooking and cleaning four days a week. He didn't like his mother cleaning other people's houses because he thought it degraded her. But she scolded him and told him to take pride in whatever job he did, that there was shame in it only if she didn't do her best.

Lincoln smiled and shook his head. There he was, a half a world away, staring at a man with a gun who would be more than happy to shoot him, and he was thinking about his mother's advice.

The bumpy ride came to an end a lot sooner than he'd expected. They'd driven only about two to three miles from the camp. The four prisoners got out and took a look around, it was strange to see the countryside without having the view marred by barbed-wire fencing.

The house was set atop a small hill. Lincoln could see the tops of the hangars below and the last few hundred feet of the airstrip's runway between the trees. Back to his right, he could barely make out the top of one of the guard towers from camp. Off in the distance were the green flat lands. In the middle of one of the fields was a black, burned-out crater where his plane had crashed. He shuddered and said a silent prayer for Major Spencer and his two friends, Leon Davis and George Johnson, who hadn't made it.

Lincoln turned around and marveled at the house: it was an image right out of a storybook. It was a masterpiece of stone masonry, accented by wrought iron with towering peaked gables, complete with their own set of guardian gargoyles. The only things spoiling the picturesque setting were the armed guards parading back and forth.

Lincoln and the three other prisoners were ushered toward the house through an impressive brick archway that led from the drive through a small receiving garden in front of the house. It had several strategically placed fountains, each flowing with sparkling water. Myriad plants and shrubs were all held together by neatly trimmed hedges. They were met at the door by a civilian dressed in a tuxedo who spoke to the prisoners in English with a heavy German accent.

"My name is Diederick Vogel. You have been brought here to assist in the household tasks associated with the running of this compound. Just as the camp belongs to Colonel Stein, this house belongs to me. Nothing is done in this house without my approval or permission. You will be transported here on a daily basis and on a few rare occasions, you will spend the night. You will have an assigned set of duties to perform and a specific amount of time in which to complete them. Any deviation from these plans will result in disciplinary action. And remember, you are no longer within the confines of the prison camp, so the rules of the Geneva Convention do not apply to you here. Do I make myself perfectly clear?"

The four prisoners lined up and he gave each of them a long, hard stare. When Vogel locked eyes with him, Lincoln felt very uncomfortable. Vogel's eyes felt like they were burrowing into him, drilling deep into his soul as if he could see what kind of man he was. He grunted at Lincoln then moved onto the last man in line. Vogel paused with this man even longer than he had with Lincoln, starring at him like he had gone into a trance. After an uncomfortably long period of silence, he said, "Take this man back to the camp, he won't do." The guards grabbed the man and put him back in the truck.

As the truck pulled away, Vogel signaled and another servant came to the door. "Mr. Mueller, take these gentlemen to their work stations, if you please." Mueller clicked his heels together and nodded.

Alben Mueller was shorter than Vogel, with thinning brown hair that he combed over the top to cover his growing baldness. His dark eyes seemed out of proportion to his small face, and he spoke with a high, irritating voice. Mueller reminded Lincoln of a small, high-strung nervous dog, the kind that rich old ladies carried, tucked under their arms like a living handbag.

Stepping through the door, Lincoln stood in awe at the interior of the house—its beauty and opulence matched in every way the splendor of the outside. The main entry salon alone was larger than his folks' entire living room back home. Several paintings hung in the foyer, and there were more on the wall leading up the curved staircase. He didn't know much about art, but he had a feeling that they were all originals and that they were very expensive.

Mueller gave them a brief tour, pointing out the various rooms and places where each of them would be working. Vogel lingered in the background, like a shadow hiding from the light. At the end of the tour, the other two prisoners went to their assigned stations, leaving Lincoln the last to be assigned.

"You will be working in the kitchen," Mueller screeched. "You will assist the cook in preparing the meals, be chief wine steward, serve the master his meals, and clean the table when he is finished."

"Yessa, massa," Lincoln replied.

Vogel slapped Lincoln across the face. "Do not patronize me or my staff," he growled. "That is the only warning you will receive."

Lincoln stared back, holding the side of his face. It was all he could do not to lash out at Vogel. He would rather be punched or kicked than slapped in the face. It showed no respect to him as a man to be slapped like an errant schoolchild.

"The kitchen is in here," Mueller continued as they turned the corner at the end of the hall. A short man, round as a barrel, stood at the sink washing potatoes. He wore a classic white chef's uniform, complete with the tall, white, puffy hat. The kitchen was huge, and every kind of pot and pan hung from the ceiling. There were two ovens and lots of flat counter space; his mother would be in heaven here, Lincoln thought.

"This is Armin Faust," Mueller announced. "He is the head chef here."

Faust, wearing a slight smile, looked up from the potatoes he was peeling and nodded in acknowledgment. Vogel and Mueller departed, leaving him alone with the chef.

"Colonel Stein takes dinner at 1800 hours promptly; that give us just a little over three hours to prepare."

"Your English is very good," Lincoln commented.

Faust smiled. "When I was younger, I studied the culinary arts at several of your American universities. It was a wonderful time. I was much younger and much thinner back then. Do you know wines, Mr. Lincoln?"

Lincoln nodded his head. "A little."

"Good. Can you read?"

Normally Lincoln would have flown off the handle at a question like that. But Faust asked in such a matter-of-fact way, it was apparent that he simply wanted to know.

"Yes, I can."

"Good. The wine cellar is through that door to your left and down the stairs. We are having beef tonight, so a Merlot would go nicely. Pick any of the bottles on the last rack to your left from the top two rows, preferably a vintage before 1925."

Lincoln nodded and started down the hall and found the staircase. He descended seventeen steps down the narrow staircase and came to a heavy wooden door that looked more like it belonged in a medieval castle than in the mansion of a German officer. He pushed hard against the door and the hinges moaned as they struggled to keep the door upright. As it opened, he half expected to see a torture chamber complete with the rack and an iron maiden.

It was dark and the air was cool and dry. Taking a step forward, he ran into a pull chain hanging from the ceiling. He pulled on it and two light bulbs, dangling down from the ceiling on single cords, flickered on. They did a poor job of chasing away the deep shadows. At least he wouldn't have to find the oil and light a torch, he thought.

It was a large cellar with six freestanding rows of wine racks, each about five feet high and fifteen feet long. The back wall was lined with large kegs burrowed into the wall, and several smaller kegs sat on the ground in front of them. Thankfully, he found no torture devices. Lincoln walked up and down each row, stopping and looking at bottles as he went. He was amazed: some of the bottles were over a hundred years old!

He went to the rack where Faust had told him to go, grabbed a bottle, and blew off the dust. It was a 1921 Bordeaux from the Château Lafite Rothschild winery, somewhere, he assumed, in France, because of the fancy writing on the label. He turned out the light and headed back to the kitchen.

He was halfway down the hall heading back to the kitchen when one of the side doors burst open and a man spilled out, ramming Lincoln into the wall, sending both men tumbling to the floor. Terror filled the stranger's eyes as he grabbed Lincoln by his lapels and pulled him closer.

"You're an American, aren't you?" he asked.

"What?" Lincoln stammered.

"You're an American! You're an American!"

"Yeah."

"Good." His eye darting back and forth as if searching for some unseen force about to grab him. "I've got to trust you."

"Trust me?"

"Wine cellar, last keg on the left, metal band."

Lincoln heard shouting in the background and the sound of rushing boots. The man's head snapped toward the doorway then he jumped up off the floor like a Fourth of July rocket and raced toward the kitchen.

A moment later, four German soldiers came charging through the open door. One tripped over Lincoln in his haste as the other three rushed after the man. The soldier ignored Lincoln as he scrambled to get back up and followed the rest of his squad. An officer trailed, holding a pistol in his hand. He stopped to examine Lincoln lying on the floor.

"What did that man say to you?" he demanded.

"He asked if I was an American."

"And what did you tell him?"

"Nothing," Lincoln said. "I didn't have time to say anything before he got up and ran off."

The German scrutinized Lincoln then ran off toward the sound of shouting and gunfire. Lincoln jumped to his feet and followed him through the kitchen and out to the front of the house.

Lincoln arrived at the front door just in time to see the officer grab a soldier's rifle and drop the man with a single shot. The runner had almost made it to the tree line about eighty yards away. Ten more feet and he might have had a chance.

Vogel stepped onto the porch and ordered everyone back inside. Lincoln was beginning to get a real dislike for the man. He was more concerned that dinner be served on time than the fact that a man had just been killed.

A huge black car came up the drive, circled around in front of the villa, and stopped. A Luftwaffe general stepped out and slapped the dust off his coat with his gloves. Colonel Stein walked up, snapped to attention in front of the general, and saluted. The general returned the salute and extended his hand. "Helmut, it's good to see you."

"And you, General Jaeger," Stein replied.

"I see you are having a little trouble with the hired help." Jaeger smiled.

"Yes, yes, good help is so hard to find these days." Stein laughed.

Lincoln stared in disbelief. "Why, you son of a—" Lincoln heard himself saying out loud. He quickly shut up, but it was too late. One of the guards had heard him and was about to introduce Lincoln to the butt plate of his Mauser rifle, but a raised hand from the general stopped him. Jaeger walked over to the American airman and slowly circled him.

"Something you would like to say?" Jaeger asked.

"No sir!" Lincoln barked, standing at full attention.

"I'm curious, Lieutenant, why do you call me 'sir' and stand at attention?"

"I show respect to the rank of general, not the man."

"Ah, I see. You don't approve of my comments, then?"

"It's not my place to approve or disapprove, sir!"

"Lets stop fencing shall we, Lieutenant? You'd like to hit me, wouldn't you?"

Lincoln looked at him briefly. "Very much so, sir!"

"Then what is stopping you?"

Lincoln relaxed his stance a little. "My dad always said I could do whatever I wanted, if I thought it was worth it. I would take a great deal of satisfaction of knocking you on your butt; however, I don't think it would be worth the amount of pain in the long run for the beating I'd get from your soldiers, sir!"

Jaeger looked around the compound then shouted, "Everyone, everyone listen to me, you will take no action against this man. Is that understood?" Jaeger walked over to Colonel Stein, took off his coat and handed it to him, then walked back over and stood in front of Lincoln. The American stood, puzzled.

"Here is your chance, Lieutenant, to knock me on my butt, as you so eloquently put it."

"You're going to let me hit you, and your troops aren't going to do anything about it?"

"Yes. Even a simple farm boy such as yourself can understand that, can't you?"

Lincoln could feel his anger coming to a boil. If this Kraut general was stupid enough to let him hit him, then he was more than willing to oblige. Lincoln cocked back his right arm and fired his fist at the German general like a howitzer. True to his aim, his fist landed square on the German's jaw, just a little left of his chin. Lincoln recoiled in pain as his knuckles made contact with the jawbone.

The general staggered back a few steps from the force of the blow. His knees started to buckle but held, much to Lincoln's dismay. He had put everything he had into that punch, and the German still remained on his feet.

Jaeger straightened up and rubbed his jaw. "Not bad, for a farm boy." He smiled. "Now it is my turn."

Lincoln put on his best poker face. He stood a little taller as he faced his opponent and tilted his head slightly, giving the German a better shot at his chin. An act of defiance. Jaeger stared into the eyes of his adversary. Then in a lighting fast move, he shot his left arm out like a giant piston, burying it deep into Lincoln's stomach.

Lincoln doubled over like a jackknife. His eyes bulged out from the pressure of the blow. He opened his mouth and gasped for air, but none entered his lungs. Lincoln staggered back a step but remained on his feet. Sheer willpower kept him on his feet. Lincoln began to feel a little light-headed from the lack of oxygen, and he could almost see a galaxy of stars floating around his head.

At last, a small trickle of air made its way into his lungs and he began gulping air like a thirsty camel gulping water at an oasis. Placing both hands on his knees, he pushed himself up and stared at the German officer. "That wasn't fair," he managed.

"There's a war going on, Lieutenant, a lot of things aren't fair." Jaeger walked over and grabbed his coat from Colonel Stein. "What time is dinner? I seemed to have worked up quite an appetite." Both officers laughed, and Jaeger stopped and spoke briefly with Vogel before he followed Stein into the house.

Lincoln slowly straightened up and staggered a step, still a little dizzy. He sluggishly began moving towards the house when a dark shadow crossed his path.

"And just where do you think you're going?" Vogel said.

"Back to work."

"Oh, I think you've done quite enough 'work' already. You are going back to camp now. If it were up to me, you would not return at all, but General Jaeger says you need your rest now, and for you to return tomorrow."

Lincoln felt his anger rising again like a thermometer in the desert sun. Who did the general think he was, just because he landed a good punch didn't mean he'd beaten him and needed to rest! He was about to say something about the general he knew he would regret, again, when he looked in Vogel's eyes and saw the contempt swirling in them. At first he thought it was contempt for him, then he realized it was contempt for having to obey the general's orders.

"Well, then I guess it's a good thing that the general likes me, huh?" Lincoln smirked. He turned and walked over to the truck and climbed in the back. It was worth letting the general think he'd won just to irritate Vogel.

TWENTY-EIGHT

COLONEL Adams checked his map again then looked out his cockpit: Lieutenant Stevens was just off his left wing, and Major Reins and Lieutenant Wiser on his right, a perfect finger-four formation.

"Okay, remember, we stick to the plan," Adams began. "Lieutenant Wiser, you'll go first, followed by Major Reins and then Lieutenant Stevens. I'll be Tail End Charlie. The hard deck is five thousand, so any one goes below that and there'll be hell to pay."

"Begging your pardon, sir," Stevens said. "But isn't five thousand a little high if they want detailed photos?"

"No," Adams said, shaking his head inside the cockpit of his Mustang. "We don't need detailed photographs, just ones good enough to give the intelligence boys an idea of what's down there and to compare them with earlier photos. And besides, word has it that the place is lousy with AA. Push her over hard, make one high-speed pass over the field, then up and out . . . and keep the camera running. Nothing fancy here, just a simple day in the country taking pictures and then home. Copy?"

"Roger that," the three pilots replied in unison.

"Lining up now," Wiser said, putting his plane into a steep dive from twelve thousand feet.

At ten thousand feet, Wiser expected to see the black puffs of flak exploding around his plane, but there were none. The heavens remained empty.

He hated low-level flying. Flak and tracer whizzing passed his canopy always made him nervous, but his confidence was growing in the ever clear skies. At 5600 feet, he throttled back to keep his speed under 420 miles per hour and pulled back on the stick. His plane was a little heavy and slow to respond because of the compression of the airflow over his controls.

The faster a plane's speed, the faster air flowed over control surfaces. This caused pressure to build up on the ailerons and elevators, making them slower to respond and in some cases lock up, causing the aircraft to crash. The nose slowly came up, and he leveled out at 5010 feet.

Still no flak.

With his camera on, Wiser flew straight over the field and pulled up a little harder than he had to, anxious to climb back into the safety of the skies. He fought the urge to tip his wing over during his pass to take a look and see what all this fuss was about. If he did, it would throw the camera angle off and he didn't want to have to come back for a second run.

Reins adjusted the blue scarf he was wearing today and tucked it inside his flight suit. Today's scarf was not a reflection of the good doctor's renowned "bedside manner," but it was for a woman he loved nonetheless. He'd bought the scarf for his mother and was going to give it to her for her birthday. She had never ventured more than fifty miles from home in her fifty-three years of life. When he was ten, the circus came to town, and he remembered how excited she was at seeing all the exotic animals. She talked for days about the mysteries of the Dark Continent and vowed right then and there that she would go there some day—but that was not to happen.

His father died that summer and, with his death, her hopes of ever traveling outside the borders of Tennessee died, too. Reins smiled to himself. He knew she would get a kick out of having a genuine silk scarf bought in a foreign country, and he hoped that knowing that it had flown all over Europe with him would give her a little sense of adventure.

Reins lined up and made a clean pass over the airfield, then pulled up beside his wingman at ten thousand feet, again with no flak to mar this cloudy but dry day.

Stevens followed Major Reins and joined the other two planes waiting for their leader to make his run.

"Colonel?" Stevens asked, "I thought you said there was a lot of AA around this place."

"Don't look a gift horse in the mouth, Lieutenant," Adams said. "If you want flak, I can send you to Berlin." Adams knew that Stevens may be right. He, too, had expected heavy flak. Maybe the Germans had abandoned the field. Abandoned or not, he knew his friend still needed the photographs so he lined up and started his pass. Adams had just dropped below eight thousand feet when the radio came to life.

"Three, no, four bandits dropping out of the sun!" Stevens shouted.

"Make that two more," Reins added. "Total of six bandits coming down hard. Stevens, peel off and join the Colonel; Andy on the count of three, break left. Three, two, one . . . BREAK!" Reins and Wiser did a flat turn to the left while Stevens rolled right and dropped down towards his commanding officer. As he dove, he heard the colonel shout, "Go, Red Flight!"

Red Flight? Who were they? Stevens thought. That wasn't their call sign, they were Bronco flight.

Two of the green camouflaged flight of Messerschmitt 109s descended on Reins and Wiser in an attempt to break them up, while the other four stayed high, ready to pounce on the plane that broke formation. The odds were six to four in the German's favor. At least now he knew why there wasn't any flak.

Steven's worry turned into outright fear as he saw eight more high dots, circling above the 109s. Fourteen to four was going to be nearly impossible. He was just about to call out another warning when he noticed that the angles on the high dots were all wrong. The new planes weren't setting up cover for their buddies; they were setting up attack angles.

Stevens had caught up with Colonel Adams on his high right side and they quickly turned to chase the pair of Messerschmitts that had flown past Reins and Wiser. Above them, Stevens watched six planes of the eight high dots peel off and dive down on the four remaining German fighters. Concentrating on their prey, the Germans hadn't noticed the reversal of fortunes.

Stevens flew with one eye on Adams and the other eye on what was happening above them. He watched the mysterious six planes of "Red Flight" turn into silver Mustangs with fiery red tails. They streaked down from the heavens like flaming arrows shot by the gods on Mount Olympus.

The pilot in the first Mustang took his time and set up his attack well. He came in on the unsuspecting German high and out of the sun. He came down fast and opened up at near point blank range giving the German pilot no time to think or pray. The six .50-caliber machine guns were aimed with deadly accuracy as they hit the 109 just a few feet behind the canopy and tore up the fuselage, cockpit, and engine like a lawn mower chewing through tall grass. The Messerschmitt disintegrated in a ball of fire. The second attack by the next two planes was timed so perfectly that the German pilot suffered the same fate as his wingman, dying before he even knew what happened or before he could warn the others.

"Get ready!" Adams said to Stevens, his voice calm and steady. "We got two Red Tails diving on the pair we're chasing. If the Krauts don't see them coming, they're finished. If they do, then they'll be forced to turn. They'll loose their speed and energy and we've got a shot at them."

"Roger that," Stevens replied, his voice showing more emotion than that of his leader. Stevens looked straight up through his canopy and watched as the mystery fighters streaked downward toward their quarry. Only moments ago, things hadn't looked so good, the odds stacked against them. But it was a whole different story now that the cavalry had arrived.

Stevens understood now what the bomber crews felt like when his

Mustangs showed up to escort them. He had secretly looked at the big lumbering bombers as bait, luring the German fighters in so he could have his fun and shoot them down. Now that the shoe was on the other foot, he didn't care too much for it. He would definitely look at his role as an escort differently the next time they were assigned to cover the buffs.

The Germans didn't get a good shot at Reins and Wiser, so they continued on their dive when the Red Tails dropped on them. The second German plane saw the Americans first and yanked hard on his stick, turning his plane sharply, nearly putting his plane into a stall but avoiding the fury of the diving Mustangs. The lead plane wasn't as lucky. He didn't see the approach of the Grim Reaper as he rode in on the wings of the Mustangs.

The first American plane's angle was a little steep and he could only fire a quick burst before he had to pull up. Bullets ripped through the rear of the fuselage, but no lethal damage was done.

The second plane was in a trail formation and was about two hundred yards behind the lead. His angle was somewhat flatter, and his burst literally sawed the tail off the 109. There was no fire or explosion as the plane flew straight and level for a moment like a wounded beast who'd been shot and didn't know he was dying. Then aerodynamics took over and the Messerschmitt began flailing in the air like a fish flopping on the dock. The pilot tried to bail but as he jumped from the cockpit, the wing swung around and hit him in the head, killing him instantly.

Just as Adams had predicted, the first 109 was an easy target, and when the second plane maneuvered out of the way, it drained away all his speed and altitude advantage. Adams pulled his fighter up to come underneath the German plane but it quickly angled off, banking down and to the left. The 109 had managed to reverse its course and was heading directly at him.

Stevens was behind Adams and had more time to react. He continued to climb, then swung up and around, getting behind the slower moving German fighter. He, too, almost stalled until his nose dropped down in a perfect firing position. He pulled the trigger and watched as the line of tracers fall right on top of the German. The bullets swept through the left side of the plane and a black puff of smoke came from the engine cowling, followed by a flash of flame. The German pilot knew he was in trouble and scrambled to get the canopy back and bail out. He had just cleared the plane when it exploded. Moments later, his chute opened.

"Nice shot, Lieutenant," Adams said. "Form back up on me and we'll find the others."

"Roger that, sir. And thank you, sir," Stevens replied.

The last two German fighters were smothered by the remaining Red Tails and met the same fate as their countrymen. Soon, the four members of the 222nd were back in formation high above the enemy airstrip. "Colonel? Who were those guys and where did they come from?" Stevens asked.

"That was Major Ryan and a few of the boys from the 332nd, Tuskegee Airmen."

"Yes, sir, I could tell by their red tails, but I don't get it. You knew they were here all along . . . and you even seemed to know that we'd be jumped."

"Remember a couple of weeks ago when that Mustang crash landed at our field and we salvaged his gun camera film? Well, I had reason to believe that this was the same airfield that he got shot up at, and that the Germans would try and do the same thing to us. With that in mind, I contacted Major Ryan and asked him if he and his boys would be interested in a little payback."

"But why didn't you tell us we had top cover?" Stevens asked.

"Because I wanted you guys to stay sharp and alert. I didn't want you to get lazy because you knew you had help. And it worked. The Germans were careless and overconfident, so they didn't see it coming."

"Understood." Stevens reflected for a moment and knew the colonel was right. If he'd known there was top cover, he wouldn't have been so vigilant and Jerry might have gotten the drop on them before the Tuskegee boys could intervene.

Stevens looked over his left wing and saw a prison camp a few miles away. "Colonel, there's a POW camp down there to our nine o'clock. Request permission to do a flyby over the camp."

"Negative, Lieutenant. We've got to get these photos back to be developed; a lot is riding on these shots. Besides, Major Ryan has already claimed that honor. He wants the Germans to know who just shot up their Luftwaffe."

"Roger that, sir." Stevens watched as the eight red-tailed mustangs peeled off and flew low over the POW camp one by one, each doing a victory roll as they went by. He hoped the prisoners had seen the battle, for this would give them a big morale booster shot in the arm.

THE cheers from the prisoners were a deafening roar, louder than a thousand-plane raid, increasing in intensity as each of the red-tailed planes streaked by. The guards tried to quiet the prisoners down, but they gave up trying after the third plane flew over.

Matt Lincoln viewed the air battle from the corner of 7th and Main. He saw the red tails and watched with special pride, knowing it was planes from his own squadron that were tearing the Germans apart. He also took great pleasure from that fact that Kohn was fit to be tied. Stein had had heard the cheers and came out of his office to see what the commotion was. When he saw the futility of trying to rein the prisoners in, he ordered Kohn to stand down or face a possible all-out riot. Stein simply turned and went back into his office while Kohn, steaming like a locomotive puffing up a steep hill, paced back and forth on his side of the fence. A soldier walked up and tried to talk to him, but Kohn backhanded the man, sending him sprawling to the ground. After that, no one dared approach him.

The last plane in line came in lower than the others, and Lincoln recognized it as Major Ryan's plane. In a split second, as the plane streaked by less than one hundred feet above the barracks, he caught Ryan's eye. Time stopped. Lincoln seemed to hear the *swoosh* of each of the four blades of the propeller as the warplane floated by like a cloud. In that frozen moment, Ryan looked over and saw him and recognized him. In that glance that lasted barely longer than a heartbeat, a wealth of information was passed: acknowledgement, encouragement, and for the first time in a long while, hope.

Ryan cleared the back fence, waggled his wings, and pulled straight up, lifting the spirits of each and every prisoner with him. The cheering and yelling lasted another two minutes after Ryan had disappeared. Slowly the camp returned to normal and routine took over again. Yet each man heart was a little lighter for the rest of the day.

Lincoln looked over at Kohn, who was still fuming and smiled at him. Kohn reached out and hit the nearest soldier to him. Lincoln knew there'd be hell to pay for that, but he didn't care. He knew as well as Kohn did that it was only a matter of time before the Allies would come and liberate them, and the two of them would have their own final showdown.

TWENTY-NINE

GRIFF Avery's head still hurt as he walked down the hall. After leaving Colonel Adams yesterday afternoon and realizing Anna had not been posting the right maps, he stopped at a little pub on the outskirts of London.

He thought about going to the Dragon's Breath, but he wanted to get falling-down drunk—and he wanted to do in a place where nobody knew him. He succeeded, and now he was paying for it. Maybe it would help him hide the way he felt. Today, the coffee's aroma did little to excite him. He felt like taking the whole pot and chugging it down on the spot. It was another day to skip his usual cream and sugar and drink it black. It seemed fitting that his coffee was as dark as his mood.

He'd been in his office about an hour, trying to get motivated, when Roshinko walked by. She saw him sitting at his desk and went in. The smile quickly vanished from her face.

"Are you okay?" Roshinko asked. "You don't look so good, Griff." She placed her hand on his arm as she spoke. It felt so good to have her touch him in that kind and gentle way, yet he didn't know what to do. What was he going to do? Yank his arm back and tell the Nazi spy to keep her hands to herself? Ignore all the mounting evidence and continue merrily along with life?

"Yeah, I'm okay," he lied, not very convincingly. "I'm just feeling a little under the weather." The phone rang. Avery was grateful for the distraction, for he didn't really feel like talking to her. He spoke on the phone for a few moments then hung up.

"I've got to go," he said curtly. "I don't know what time I'll be back."

"Where are you going?" she asked cheerfully.

"I have an appointment."

He could see the hurt and disappointment from his short reply filling her face, but he would have time to apologize later, if he had to. He grabbed his coat and headed out the door. He thought he heard a feeble "good-bye" as he left, but he didn't turn around to see.

"THIS is twice you owe me . . . and even more than before." Captain Sam Lyons' face was smiling. His tone was light, but it was clear that he meant it. "Colonel Adams gave me these and said you needed them no later than 1400 today. I gathered from his tone that it wasn't a request." Lyons took a sip of his coffee, then set a file folder on his desk.

"That looks pretty good," Avery said pointing at the coffee. He was starting to feel a little better. "Got another cup?"

Lyons sighed, grabbed a cup near the pot, and started pouring. Avery couldn't tell if the mug was really brown or simply coffee stained to death, and he really didn't care.

"Would you like a doughnut to go with it too?" Lyons said sarcastically. "Judging from the photographs, nothing significant has changed on the field or at the hangars since the first pictures were taken."

"First pictures?"

Lyons gave him a quizzical look. "You did know this was the same air field, didn't you? And you call yourself an intelligence officer!"

Avery smiled. He didn't mind the jab from Lyons, as this was the first piece of good news he'd had in a long time. Now he knew for sure that this was the right airfield, the one with the secret jets, and where Strovinski's plane was.

"Thanks, Sam," Avery said as he started to get up. "That's all I really needed to know, that this was the same airfield."

"Oh, okay. Then I guess you don't want to know what else I found."

"Something else?"

"Oh, now you're interested in all my hard work?"

"Okay, Sam, what else do you have? And yes, I know I owe you big time."

"As long as we understand each other." Smiling, Lyons shuffled through about ten photographs until he stopped and said, "Bingo," and pulled one out of the pile. "This may be something, but then again it may not. It was taken from the number three plane."

"Number three plane?"

"You didn't know? Your friend brought me not one, not two or even three films to edit and analyze—he brought me four! This plane flew at a lesser angle than the others, providing a better view of the area at the end of the strip, look here." Lions handed Avery the photo.

Avery studied it but didn't see anything out of the ordinary. "What am I looking at?" he finally asked.

"Right there on the hill." He pointed.

Avery examined it again. "You mean these stumps?"

"Those, my friend, aren't stumps, they're ventilators. They're laid out too geometrically to be naturally occurring. See how they form a line down this way, and then cross back over, forming a grid pattern? Something is buried under that hill there, something big."

Of course! It made perfect sense! Avery thought. If the Germans were working on some sort of experimental aircraft, they'd need to keep it hidden or risk it being bombed. Thoughts popped into his head faster than kernels of popcorn at a movie concession stand.

What kind of treasures were buried beneath that hillside? Did the Germans really have a new *Wunderwaffe,* a wonder weapon jet plane? Was this where Strovinski was hiding, building a nuclear bomb for the jet to carry? He thought about going back to General Sizemore, but he knew he'd have to have a lot more proof than a few photographs of what looked like tree stumps to request a bombing mission. He needed proof positive before he confronted Sizemore again.

"Are you OSS guys always this spacey?" Lyons asked, seeing the detached look on Avery's face.

"Sorry, Sam, it's just that you've given me more here than I expected. I guess my mind was going into overdrive."

"Yeah, well, tell Colonel Adams that I had the information you needed, when you needed it. And if you don't have another dozen or so films to be developed, edited, and copied, I'm going to go into my darkroom and saw some logs."

Avery looked at his friend. "So you mean to tell me that when you go in your dark room and the 'Do Not Enter' light is on, you're really sleeping?"

"Hey, I need a lot of sleep to stay this good looking." He smiled.

Avery just shook his head. "Thanks, Sam. I hope one day I can tell you just how valuable the information is that you've given me."

Lyons grunted as he disappeared into the darkroom and shut the door. A moment later, the "Do Not Enter" sign flashed on.

Avery felt better, but he still didn't want to go back to the office and have to face Anna. Instead, he chose to go home and work there, all the while desperately hoping that she would not be the one to fall into the trap he was laying.

THIRTY

"THE war had better be over soon," Volker Reinard said, pushing himself away from the table, "because if I keep coming here and eating like this, I'll be as fat as Goering." He chuckled.

Colonel Stein smiled. "It is because of this war that you eat so well. The negro standing by the kitchen door who served us also created this dinner."

General Jaeger raised his glass with one hand and rubbed his jaw with the other. "You are a man of many talents, Lieutenant."

Matt Lincoln nodded his head and smiled slightly, wishing he'd hit the SOB harder and broken his jaw.

"Is everything still on schedule?" Reinard asked.

Stein put down his glass, concern flashing across his face. "Should we be talking about this openly with the American here?"

"It's not as if he has a radio and can run out and file a report, is it, Colonel? Your camp is secure is it not?"

Lincoln was standing in the kitchen doorway when he stiffened like a corpse upon hearing Jaeger's comment. His mind flashed back to when he had been knocked down by the stranger in the hallway. His mind's eye replayed the look of sheer terror that gripped the man's face. Such odd words he spoke: something about the wine cellar, something was hidden there. In the excitement and horror of seeing him killed, Lincoln had blocked it out of his mind until now.

"What is it, Mr. Lincoln? You look white as a ghost, a considerable feat for a man such as yourself."

Lincoln blinked as if he'd been slapped in the face. "Sorry, I-I am negligent in my duties. Your glasses are almost empty." Lincoln cursed himself and walked slowly into the kitchen as if he were a zombie. His mind struggled to catch up to the present reality.

Lincoln felt Reinard studying him as he slipped into the kitchen, and knew
the SS officer didn't believe his half-baked excuse. He only hoped Reinard
didn't push it; he had never been a very good liar.

"And as to your question, Major, the answer is yes," Jaeger continued.
"Doctor Strovinski has been most useful in offering some helpful ideas on
the configuration of the bomb and its design."

"How so?"

Jaeger frowned, as if something he had eaten was now eating at him. "The
Führer and his worthless henchmen have ruined the destiny of the Fatherland. They have prostituted it for their own use and, through their own
stupidity, destroyed nearly all chances for victory. Did you know that it was a
German, Otto Hahn, who, in 1938, was the first man to split the atom? And
that some of the most of the brilliant scientists in the field were Austrian?

"The real trouble started early in the '30s, when the fanatics were just
coming into power. They polluted everyone and everything with their poison.
Instead of looking out for the best interests of Germany as a whole, they
used their power to promote their own ideals. They became so arrogant they
thought that only the mind of a German could conceive brilliant ideas. They
considered Einstein's theories to be 'Jewish Physics,' dismissing them because
of his ethnic background rather than on scientific merit. Their smug, ego-
tistical self-righteousness has doomed Germany and given the Americans
time to complete their nuclear weapon first."

Stein frowned but continued picking at the remains of the turkey carcass
like a vulture that hadn't eaten in days. "Then all is lost?" he said, pausing to
sample the new wine his American servant had poured.

"Forgive my ranting," Jaeger said, swirling the wine around in his glass.
"On the contrary, all is not lost. In fact, we are in a far better position than I
had earlier thought, all thanks to Dr. Strovinski. As you know, we were
hoping for the large, full-scale chain reaction of an atomic detonation, but
alas, Germany does not have the capability to produce that. However, as
pointed out by Dr. Strovinski, we can still utilize some of its deadly effects
without overcoming the technical difficulties the Americans have had to deal
with."

Lincoln returned to his post next to the kitchen door, looking as impas-
sive and disinterested as he could. This wasn't hard, because he really had no
idea what they were talking about. Instead, he tried to pick up any key words
or phrases he might be familiar with.

"At Strovinski's suggestion, instead of trying to build an atomic bomb, we
now have what is called a 'dirty bomb.'"

"A dirty bomb?" Reinard asked.

"Yes, basically an atomic bomb without the big bang. The benefit to this
is that it is still very deadly, owing to the radioactivity it produces. If we take a
five hundred kilogram bomb packed full of radioactive material and disperse

it at the proper altitude over a large American metropolis, New York in this case, the results would be devastating. At first, no one would probably even notice the bomb exploding, especially if we detonate at night. Within a few days, hundreds of people will begin getting sick, as if stricken by some unknown virus. Soon the numbers of afflicted will climb into the thousands and the deaths will start to accumulate after just one week.

"At the end of the third week, we will announce to the world that the might of the German Luftwaffe is responsible for their deaths. We will demand their immediate surrender. Of course the American government will deny all of this and, to prove our point, we will bomb London. This will prove to the American and British people that their governments are powerless to defend them. We will sue for a negotiated surrender, providing the catalyst to propel Germany to the forefront of world powers."

Stein stopped in mid chew as if the food in his mouth had suddenly turned sour. "Is such a thing possible? I didn't even know that our V-2s had that kind of range and accuracy."

"They don't. We have come up with an entirely new delivery system."

"Well?" Stein said, sufficiently recovered from his surprise to ask between bites as he devoured the last roll.

"Right here in our own little grotto, we have created a new long-range bomber, inspired by the flying wing fighter, the Ho229, designed and developed by Captains Walter and Reimar Horten. With the modifications we've made, it will have the range to reach New York. Halfway back across the Atlantic, the pilot will ditch and be picked up by a waiting U-boat. Dr. Strovinski should be finished with the final modifications to the bomb in a day or so, and we will launch by the end of the week. "

"Most impressive, General," Stein said as he reached for his wineglass. "Lincoln, we need more wine. Something sweet, I think, for after dinner."

Lincoln remained at the door, quietly talking to Faust. Even though he was stricken by everything he had just heard, he was still trying to play the disinterested POW-turned-cook.

"Lincoln!" Stein shouted.

"Yes, sir?"

"More wine, something sweeter for after dinner," Stein grunted.

"Right away, sir," Lincoln replied then turned and walked down the hallway as fast as he could without appearing to be in a hurry.

"And what of your efforts, Major?" Jaeger asked.

"All the groundwork has been laid and everything is in place. As soon as the trap is sprung, my operative will be able to take over the reins of the OSS, and none will be the wiser," Reinard replied.

"Excellent!" Jaeger raised his glass. "To our success."

Lincoln reached the bottom of the staircase, his hand resting on the door. His heart was beating fast in anticipation. He took a deep breath as if he were about to jump off the high dive, then stepped into the wine cellar.

What was it the man had said? Wine cellar, last keg on the left. Something about a metal band? Lincoln went straight to the back wall and started looking, even though he wasn't quite sure what he was looking for. He carefully inspected the keg on the left. It was a large wooden barrel about two feet in diameter and three feet long, set back halfway into the wall. It had a faint smell of oak, mingled with the aroma of alcohol. He ran his hands down the front and sides of the keg, trying to find some sort of indentation or catch to release a hidden door that he imagined would be there, but there was none.

With time running out and frustration overtaking him, he sat down on the front of the keg. The keg started to give way. Lincoln sprang back to his feet—he could just see the barrel breaking and gallons and gallons of alcohol spilling on the floor. He turned and looked at the barrel. The metal band around the end had moved a quarter of an inch, exposing clean wood, but the end of the barrel was also angled down. It shouldn't do that, since the barrel planks were one solid piece . . . or were they?

Lincoln was on his knees and pulling on the band, slowly inching his way around the front, when unexpectedly the whole front of the barrel came off where the band held it together. The front half of the barrel was sealed and quite heavy, still full of whiskey, giving the illusion that the barrel was full. The back half was empty and dry with a small package inside.

Very clever, Lincoln thought as he reached in and grabbed the package. He carefully unwrapped it, finding a radio transmitter/receiver inside. He'd been nervous before, but now the butterflies turned into a stampeding heard of cattle as he stared at the radio.

Was this thing real? Was the man he'd known for only ten seconds a real honest to goodness spy? Whom was he working for? The Americans, the British, the French resistance, perhaps? What should he do now? Just shove everything back in the case and forget he ever saw it, pretend that none of this ever happened? Suddenly the face of the man whose name he didn't even know came rushing back and the memory of it hit him as hard as his body had hit in the hall that day. At least he had to try.

He reached down and turned it on, then grabbed the small headset and microphone and began talking.

THIRTY-ONE

IT was late and Avery was reaching the end of his mental rope. He'd been working by himself since right after lunch, putting together a plan to tip the hand of the spy in his organization. Around eight, he decided to get out of his apartment and get some fresh air before he went stir crazy. He grabbed all the files and the photographs and headed down to the Dragon's Breath Pub for a break. He fancied having a beer and a quick bite to eat.

Margaret served him with a big smile and a cold stein of ale, plus a new treat. Instead of her trademark fish, she had tried something new: cornbread from a recipe she'd gotten from one of the American GIs. The aroma was heavenly. He layered on the butter like mortar on bricks and watched with great satisfaction as the butter melted deep within the bread. He devoured the piece that Margaret had given him.

It felt good to be in a crowd. The food and noise nourished him the same way a summer's rain brought relief to a drought-weary plant. He hated the thought of going back to his silent, empty apartment, so he decided to return to the office. Even though it was late, it was comforting to see Corporal Blankenship on duty. After exchanging pleasantries—little more than a "Good evening, sir" and "Thank you, sir,"—Avery settled into his chair and turned on the radio used to broadcast to the Maquis units. The static background noise masked the silence of his empty office and helped him concentrate.

After a couple more hours of diligent work, the file was finished at last. He shoved himself away from his desk and rubbed his eyes. It was past his bedtime, and he felt like he could sleep for a week. Maybe when he woke up in the morning, he would discover that all this had been a bad dream, that things were the way they had been.

He planted the Tom, Dick, and Harry file in his safe, then gathered up the volumes of scribbling he had piled in front of him. They'd been designed to help him think but resembled Chinese at this time of night. He shoved them in his briefcase and was just reaching to turn off the radio when it made a clicking noise, like someone was playing with the microphone.

His fingers had barely touched the knob when he heard a faint "Hello?" In the silence of his mind, the voice echoed like thunder. He shook his head. Was he hearing things? He really must be more tired than he had thought.

Now the voice spoke again and reality slapped him in the face.

"Hello," he replied, "who is this?"

MATT Lincoln nearly jumped out of his skin when the voice on the other end of the radio answered him. In the silence of the wine cellar, the reply filled the room like thunder, sounding like the voice of God. He crouched, down waiting for the door to burst open and guards to come pouring through with machine guns blazing. He was thrilled and terrified all at the same time to think that this thing actually worked! But what should he do now? Answer it, he guessed. After all, he was the one who started the conversation.

"Who is this?" he asked cautiously.

"This is Hermes."

Lincoln frowned, *Hermes?* Who the hell was Hermes? Was this guy kidding? A Greek god? "This is Hades," he snickered. Well, he was living in hell now, wasn't he?

Griff Avery's mind raced. *Hades?* Who the hell was Hades? He didn't have any agents named Hades. Was this guy kidding? "Who are you, how did you get this radio frequency, and where is the agent whom this belongs to?"

Agent? Suddenly the light clicked on: agent . . . code name . . . Hermes! Why hadn't he thought of that sooner? Still, he had to be careful since he really didn't know who was on the other side of the conversation.

"My name is Lincoln," was all he dared say.

Lincoln, Lincoln? Avery rolled that name over in his mind like a cement mixer. The name sounded familiar. Then it hit him: Lincoln was one of the pilots from Major Spencer's flight who was MIA, presumed killed.

"Lieutenant Matt Lincoln?" he asked, almost not wanting to know if he were wrong.

Lincoln was stunned and scared. Who was this guy, and how did he know who he was? Lincoln's heart was beating so hard he thought Stein and the others could hear it upstairs. A guarded "yes" was all he could muster.

Avery was about to break every rule in the book by using his real name, but he felt he had no other choice. "My name is Captain Griffin Avery of the OSS, and I assume you are the same Lieutenant Lincoln who flew with Major Terrance Spencer?"

"Did the major make it?" Lincoln asked.

"Yes, he managed to bring his plane back to England and crash-land. He's pretty banged up but alive. Where are you? I can have the underground pick you up and arrange safe transport back to England."

"Negative. Believe it or not, I'm a POW and right now I'm at our camp commandant's house, Colonel Stein. I just got through serving him, an SS major named Reinard, and General Jaeger dinner. Right now I'm in his wine cellar, supposedly picking out a nice after dinner wine."

Reinard! Avery's mind shouted. Reinard is there? "Did you overhear anything tonight? Any little detail could prove to be valuable," Avery spoke into the transmitter.

"It was a really weird conversation. The general kept talking about some new bomb, a dirty bomb, whatever the hell that is, and they were going to bomb New York with it in some newfangled plane. After that I didn't hear any more, 'cause I had to come down here."

"Anything else? Names, places, times. Anything like that?"

"Yeah, now that you mention it. They talked about some Russian who was helping them. But I thought the Russkies were supposed to be on our side. They also mentioned a timetable, they could launch by the end of the week."

"Strovinski, was that the Russian's name, Strovinski?"

"Yeah, I think it was. Listen, Captain, I gotta go."

"Wait, Lieutenant, just one more question: did they say anything about an underground base? This is very important."

"No, nothing about any secret base or anything." Lincoln was just reaching to turn it off when he remembered something. "Wait a minute, Captain. The general did say something about 'my little grotto here.' That's all I can remember. I gotta go."

LINCOLN quickly packed everything away then put the front of the barrel back on, making sure that the metal band covered the crack.

Stepping back, everything looked normal. He turned and he grabbed a bottle Gewürztraminer off the top rack, a 1903 vintage, hoping this would do since he didn't have time to look. He turned out the light and opened the door only to be surprised by a figure silhouetted in the light from the hallway.

"You took so long to get the wine, I was afraid something had happened to you," Reinard said with a pleasant smile.

"You startled me, Major. I didn't expect to see you."

"Yes, that's obvious. May I ask what was taking you so long?"

Lincoln held up the bottle. "I don't know about you, Major, but I don't read French, so it makes it kind of hard to tell what I'm getting. I was looking to see if any of the labels were in English. Since very few were, I made my best guess and chose this one." He handed the bottle to the SS major.

Reinard took it and held it up to the light. "Good choice. The general should be pleased."

"Thank you, sir." Lincoln slipped past the major and headed up the stairs, not daring to look back.

AVERY sat motionless in his chair, wrapped up in his own thoughts like a mummy. So Strovinski was helping the Germans—that definitely means that the loss of Strovinski was a set up, an inside job. On the one hand he was relieved, knowing that he didn't screw up somewhere along the line, getting Lofton and the other airmen killed. But on the other hand, it infuriated him to know that beyond a shadow of a doubt that there really was a spy in his organization, just when he'd almost talked himself out of the notion.

Since Reinard was involved in all this, he now knew that his request for terms of surrender was phony and that the German was using Zeus . . . and if Reinard was using Zeus, then Reinard was using him! But why? Why was Reinard trying to manipulate them?

More important, Lincoln had mentioned that the Germans had a dirty bomb and that they would be able to launch it by the end of the week. He had to convince Sizemore to order a bombing raid against the hidden base now, while they still had time. But how? This was all just hearsay and, even though it was convincing, he knew Sizemore wouldn't budge without real, hard evidence. He had to come up with something and come up with it fast. Tomorrow he would try to contact Zeus to see if he could poke around the airfield and get some photographs, anything solid to put into Sizemore's hands.

THIRTY-TWO

CLAUBERT Merle had just gotten out of the shower and was tidying up a bit before he went out for the day. The bedroom, the whole house, for that matter, needed little attention since Beka had died—but it was another habit that was hard to ignore, one that his wife had beaten into him over the years. No, perhaps "impressed" upon him was a better way to put it. He smiled. No, beaten *was* the right word.

It promised to be a busy day. After the conversation with Hermes, he had decided to "lay low," as the Americans put it. He hoped that out of sight would be out of mind for the Germans, and for Reinard especially, but he had many decisions to make and couldn't remain cooped up forever.

He had just folded his towel and was just coming down the stairs when he heard a knock on the door. Odd, he thought. It is still early in the day and I'm not expecting anyone. He opened the door and to his great surprise and horror, Major Reinard stood there with a big smile on his face as if he were an old friend. Behind him were two soldiers who didn't look so friendly.

"Good morning, my dear Claubert!" Reinard said in an unusually loud but friendly voice. "I hope we are not too early."

Merle was stunned. All he could think of was how happy he was that they didn't break down the door again—although the two troopers standing behind the major like stone gargoyle bookends looked like they were disappointed that they'd missed their chance.

"I'm not too late for breakfast, am I?" Reinard said pleasantly, walking in before Merle could even think to protest, followed by the two soldiers. The last trooper through closed the door, then stood in front of it like a human gate.

"Come, my friend," Reinard said, placing a firm hand on Merle's shoulder. "Why don't we go up stairs, have some tea and talk, just you and I, shall we?"

Knowing he had no choice, Merle led the way up the stairs, each step a chore, feeling like a condemned man.

"Please, have a seat." Reinard gestured when they reached the top. One of the soldiers followed with the teapot, pouring them both a cup. The door sounded like a prison cell slamming shut as the guard departed, leaving Merle alone with his jailer.

"What do you want?" Merle asked with less fear in his voice than he'd imagined.

"Quite simple. I need you to send a message to Hermes for me. Come now, Claubert, we both know that *I* know who and what you are. Let's make this easy on the both of us, shall we?"

Reinard still needed him. That was probably the only reason he was still alive; once he sent the message all that would change. He had to stall, he had to have time to think. "But it isn't the scheduled time to broadcast," he replied weakly.

Reinard reached back and snapped his glove against Merle's face, unleashing it like a tightly coiled spring. The impact stung the Frenchman's face. Reinard calmly stood over Merle. "Now, we will try this one more time. Will you send the message?"

Merle looked up at his tormentor with fire in his eyes. "I told you it's not time to broad—" Merle saw a slight smile on the major's face, right before the fist struck his face. This time the force of the blow propelled Merle out of his chair, sending him into the side table. The two teacups flew up in the air like clay pigeons at a trap range, and he watched in horror as the picture of his beloved Beka teetered on the table and fell to the floor. He let out an audible sigh of relief as the frame landed flat on the floor and the frame and glass all remained in one piece.

But the half-full teapot rolled around on the table top like a fat, drunken ballerina about to fall off the stage. Just as the pot was about to do a swan dive to the floor, Reinard reached out and caught it.

Merle was taken aback by the unexpected act of kindness, and it must have shown on his face, because Reinard looked at him with a genuine smile. The smile stayed on his face as he delivered a kick to the Frenchman's ribs. When the boot collided with his ribs, Merle was lifted off his hands and knees and sprawled on the floor a few feet away from his chair.

Reinard lifted his boot and brought the heel down like a hammer on an anvil, shattering the picture frame and destroying the photograph of Beka.

Merle felt a stabbing pain shoot through in his heart as surely as the shards of glass sliced into the picture of his beloved Beka. It had been his most cherished photograph of his wife, taken on the day of their trip to Paris. It had survived the German Blitzkrieg at the beginning of the war and the constant air raids of the Allied bombers at the end.

Merle lay there, not wanting to get up. But he had no choice. A strong hand grasped him by the back of the collar, lifting him into the air like cat lifting up her kitten by the nape of the neck. Reinard held him up just long enough to deliver another fist to his jaw, sending Merle sprawling back into his chair. Merle's lip split open from Reinard's handiwork, blood splattering on the floor and the chair, several drops landing on the exposed picture of Beka.

The old Frenchman collapsed deep in the chair, barely able to breathe.

"You are a hard man, my dear Claubert," Reinard said, putting his gloves back on. "You know that I could beat you into submission, but where is the challenge in beating an old man? Perhaps you're right. I have never been able to discover your radio, I will give you that much. No matter, maybe I'll be able to find it in the ashes after the fire."

Reinard reached into his left breast pocket and pulled out a sterling silver cigarette case engraved with the German eagle and swastika. He took out a cigarette and began playing with it as he spoke. "A pity, too, I always believed that a man should leave something behind when he dies. For most people their children are their legacy, but then I forgot"—he smiled—"that you and Rebecca never had any. And you never created any great works of art or penned any masterpieces. I must conclude the only thing you have left for anyone to remember you or your wife by is this house that the two of you built with your own hands and in which you spent so much time together."

Merle looked up, pain etched deep across his face. Reinard was right. The house that he and Beka had built together was the only tangible thing he had left of her.

After her death, the house had seemed so huge, so empty without her. But then he began to see not the walls of wood, glass windows, or stone fireplace—he began to see the little things that she had done to the house to make it a home, their home. The curtains she had sewn by hand and he had hung, the colors she had chosen for each room. The little knickknacks she had collected over the years . . . all of it had combined to make this her home. And in her absence, it had come to comfort him. A small part of her was still with him.

Merle watched as Reinard slipped the cigarette between his lips, then put the case back in his pocket. He reached down into his outside coat pocket and produced a book of matches. With the hands of a magician, he opened the book and lit his cigarette.

Reinard drew a deep breath, then blew the smoke out into the room. He held the match up and studied the burning flame as if it were a beautiful piece of art. To Merle it was a monstrosity.

"No. I'll get the transmitter and send the message now," Merle pleaded.

Reinard looked at Merle, smiled, then tossed it at the base of the curtains. Merle tried to leap out of the chair but a sharp pain from his three cracked ribs made him collapse in sheer agony.

The match landed under the corner of the red linen curtains, ones that Beka had sewn mostly by hand because the material was too thick for her old sewing machine. Quickly the dry cloth turned brown, then black as it began to smolder. Ignoring the pain, Merle gripped his ribs with one arm, dropped to the floor on one knee and began crawling toward the window. Halfway across the floor, his hand slipped and he fell on his side, knocking the wind out of him. He nearly passed out from the excruciating pain, by with sheer willpower, he managed to drag himself the rest of the way. He swatted at the smoldering curtain tip just as it burst into flame. The smoke made him cough, adding to his agony.

Reinard looked at his watch. "We are wasting time here, Claubert. I'm almost through with this cigarette and I feel like having another." Merle lay on the floor in quiet celebration. Celebrating first, that he had put out the fire in time and second, that he hadn't passed out from the pain.

Merle slowly forced himself to his feet, then propped himself against the chair. He rested there as long as he dared, catching his breath, each inhalation causing him pain. He took two more shallow breaths, then steadied his mind against the pain, grabbed the back of the chair, and dragged it over to the center of the room.

Reinard watched Merle step shakily onto the chair and push on the huge beam that ran the length of the room. The beam was eight inches wide and tongue-and-grooved together in two-foot sections. Merle pushed on one of the joints, and a whole two-foot section swung out neatly, revealing an empty compartment hidden within the false beam.

Reinard ground his cigarette butt into the hardwood floor next to Beka's picture and clapped. "My dearest Claubert! I have seen some ingenious hiding placs in my time, but I have to take my hat off to you. Yours is the best-crafted, most well concealed transmitter that I have ever seen."

With trembling hands Merle pulled out his small radio set and began setting up to transmit.

"Please, let me do that," Reinard said walking up behind Merle. "You look tired, please sit down and let me help you."

Merle was so tired and in such great pain that he would have taken a glass of water from the devil himself. He slowly made his way back to the chair, and Reinard eased him down gently. Pain shot through every part of his body until he finally settled down and came to rest in the deep cushions.

The SS major took the radio in his hands and studied it for a moment, looked at Merle, then dropped it on the ground. Merle watched in dismay as Reinard proceeded to smash the radio under the heel of his boot.

"I-I don't understand," Merle stammered. "I thought you wanted me to send a message for you."

Reinard dragged the other chair over, sat down next Merle, and took his hand. "Do you think you were the only spy in this war, my dear friend?"

Reinard smiled and patted Merle's hand. "Dear Claubert, I have had my own spies in place in the middle of your little organization for three years now. I know your broadcast times, the frequencies you use, and the meanings of most of your prearranged signals."

Merle was stunned. He looked at the broken radio on the floor then at his broken body in the chair. "Why, why do all this, if you already have all the information you need?"

Reinard looked down at Merle. "Any thug can beat a confession out of someone, but it takes a true professional to get the subject to voluntarily give up information. I pride myself on finding out what's important to that person and use their own fears and insecurities against them. For you, it was the fear of losing what you perceived as your last tangible contact with your dead wife—in this case, the house you two built together. The beating was to inflict physical distress to go along with your mental distress. It is a combination that works very well together."

Reinard turned to leave. "Don't worry, I will send the message myself this evening and at one of your regular broadcast times. I shouldn't let you live— call it a weakness—but I like you, Claubert, I really do. Perhaps when all this nasty business of war is over you and I can become good friends.

"Besides, I like this house. It's very well crafted, and I might just take it as my summer home." He paused, looking around the room like he was rearranging the furniture in his head, then clicked his heels, nodded his head and left.

Merle knew he had to get out, to warn Hermes before Reinard changed his mind and decided to kill him. The spirit was willing but the body was weak. He finally succumbed to the pain and drifted off to sleep, his last waking thought was that he would sooner burn his house down himself than let Reinard have it.

THIRTY-THREE

AVERY arrived at his office the next morning after a very short night of fitful sleep. He knew it was going to be a long day. Part of him wanted to leave, to give the would-be spy access to his office and to the planted files, but the other part knew he needed to be there so as not to tip his hand. He made several trips to the coffeepot, being seen by all, but he avoided Anna and Jason, giving them as wide a berth as possible.

He'd seen Anna twice and twice he'd managed to avoid her. He'd seen the hurt and confusion in her eyes. It was killing him not to talk to her, but he just couldn't take the chance.

Finally at two in the afternoon, he couldn't take it any longer. He knew he couldn't go home; the words that had been echoing in his head all day would be magnified by the silence of his empty apartment. So, he went to the only other place he could go, his home away from home.

"AH, there you are," Jason Peters said as he sat down at the table in the Dragon's Breath next to Avery. "It's three-thirty in the afternoon, a bit early to be drinking, isn't it?"

"This is coffee. And how did you find me here?"

"I saw Anna. She told me you looked pretty upset yesterday, and you haven't been yourself today, either. I know you like going to crowded places to think, and I also know you own stock in this place, so I figured this is where you'd be."

Avery smiled weakly. "I'm that predictable, huh?"

"Is there anything that I can do to help?" Peters asked.

"No, not really." He sighed, needing someone to talk to but not sure if Peters was a wise choice. "Just some things I have to work out on my own."

"Okay." Peters hesitated for a moment then continued. "I don't know if this is the best time or not, but I've come across some information that you might be interested in."

Avery's ears perked up. "Shoot," he said, trying to stem the anticipation growing in his stomach.

"I started doing a little digging on my own after the Strovinski deal fell through. I know that because of the way things went down you might suspect a leak on the inside, so I thought I would try to see what I could find out from my end."

"So you think that I suspect you or Anna? What would make you think that?"

Peters shrugged his shoulders. "Because that's what I would think if I were in your shoes. Either the Germans were very, very lucky, or else some-one tipped them off. There were very few people who knew about the mission from the start, so it would stand to reason that Anna and I would be your prime suspects."

Avery took a sip of his coffee, trying not to let on that he did in fact suspect the two of them. "Makes sense, I suppose," he replied.

"So, in an effort to get to the truth, and hopefully clear my name, I started going over everything I could find out about Strovinski, and a very interesting name popped up."

"And . . . ?"

"And the name I found in not one but several instances was 'Anna Roshinko.'"

"What!" The word was almost a shout and conveyed far more emotion that he wished to reveal. Suddenly his stomach was twisting itself into more knots than a group of Boy Scouts trying for their merit badges.

"Yeah, I was pretty shocked, too. Has Anna ever mentioned her past to you?"

Stunned, Avery thought for a moment. "No, now that you mention it, no, she hasn't."

"It seems that she is some sort of aristocrat in Mother Russia."

"Aristocrat? Really? We talked a little about her parents. She mentioned that her father was a baron, but I was thinking of 'cattle baron' or 'land baron,' not real royalty."

Peters nodded. "Yup. Her parents are some sort of blue bloods from way back, having survived all the political unrest through the different Czars. Before the war, she and her family spent a lot of time in Europe. Because of her father's academic connections in the field of engineering, she traveled with him to the University of Hamburg, where her father met several times with a physics teacher there named Nicoli Strovinski."

"Strovinski? Are you sure about all this?"

"I swear, boss." Peters raised his right hand. "Here, look for yourself." He handed Avery the file folder he had with him.

Avery was too dumbfounded to speak. He stared into the folder, unable to concentrate. He felt like his heart had just been ripped out and served to him on a platter. How could she do this to him? "Does anyone else know about this?" he stammered.

Peters shook his head. "I didn't see any reason to say anything. I mean after all, she hasn't really done anything wrong . . . that we know of."

"Yes, of course. Well, just keep it quiet for the moment, at least until I can talk to her and see what she says. I'm sure she has a perfectly good reason for not telling us any of this."

"Yeah, sure, boss, you're right. It's all just a big misunderstanding. Anyway, I've got to get back to the office. I'll talk to you later."

Avery barely acknowledged his assistant as he got up and left, as his face was buried in the file.

THIRTY-FOUR

IN high school, Avery had enjoyed acting in the school plays and, for awhile, he'd even been bitten by the acting bug. He envisioned himself as a rich and famous movie star with a starlet hanging off each arm, but he never made it to Hollywood. Griff Avery was about to give an Academy Award-winning performance by pretending to the woman he loved that nothing was wrong and that he didn't suspect she was a spy.

At first, all things considered, he was going to cancel their date, but after his conversation with Jason he figured it would be the perfect time to talk to her. Her guard would be down; he'd learn if any of it was true.

The Gentrys had loaned him their car again. Mrs. Gentry could tell that things weren't right, but she didn't press the matter, for which he was very grateful. Hopefully, the night would have a happy ending and he could tell Mrs. Gentry that everything was fine, that it all had been a big misunderstanding.

He picked her up at her flat and evaded all the questions thrown at him by her roommates like a flight of B-17s going through flak. Thankfully, that gave them something to talk about on their way to the restaurant. That and the fact that he only got honked at once for driving on the wrong side of the road.

Arriving at the restaurant, they were seated at a small corner table just off the dance floor at the Fitzgerald, an American-style dinner and dance club. He had called in a lot of favors to get a table, since they were booked up solid a couple of weeks in advance. On top of that, it cost him a ten-pound note to the maitre d' not to seat them by the kitchen.

The meal was delicious and, for a British restaurant, the coffee wasn't half-bad. They were listening to the twelve-piece band playing all the popular songs from Glenn Miller, Tommy Dorsey, and Benny Goodman. They had even danced once or twice, but the evening was strained. He was afraid he wasn't going to win that golden statue after all.

Roshinko finally leaned over the table and took Avery's hands in hers. "Griff, what's wrong? You haven't been yourself tonight. Have I done something wrong? Do you wish we hadn't gone out?"

Avery smiled softly. "We haven't been married for fifty years and you can already tell that something's up." He'd already decided that the straight-forward approach would be the best—get it out in the open and see what her reaction was, follow it to wherever it led.

"Okay," he sighed. "I came across some information about you today and I need you to clarify it for me."

"Sure, go ahead."

Inwardly he took a deep breath. "I know you are Russian in origin, but just how Russian are you?"

"I'm sorry, Griff, I don't understand."

"Are you the daughter of a poor Siberian farmer, a factory worker, a princess and heir to the throne? And what brought you into the service of the United States government?"

"It's really no secret. I already told you my father was a baron."

"Real royalty? So that makes you some sort of princess or something?"

"No, just his daughter."

"Why didn't you tell anyone that you were royalty?"

"Several reasons." She shrugged. "As a child, I got anything I wanted because of who my parents were. As an adult, I wanted to make it on my own, to make something for myself without getting special privileges or breaks because my father was a baron. People treat you differently when they know you're royalty. Some people are nicer to you just because of that, and some people are not so nice just because of that. I wanted people to like or dislike me because of me, Anna Roshinko, not Anna Roshinko, a member of the royal family.

"Also, it's not too healthy to be associated with any royalty right now in Russia. Stalin has purged a lot of royal families from Mother Russia, all in the name of reform—another word for eliminating political opposition." Roshinko turned sad and quiet. "I haven't had any word from my parents since right after the war started. I fear they've been sent to Siberia to one of the 're-education camps,' or worse."

She paused for a moment and took a sip of her wine regaining her shaky composure. "I've never hidden the fact that I'm Russian; in fact you have used my language skills several times in deciphering intercepted messages."

Avery nodded, his heart picking up a small trace of hope. "That all makes sense. Did you do a lot of traveling before the war?"

"Oh, my, yes. Being a baron's daughter wasn't all bad. During the sum-mers we would travel extensively all over Europe . . . France, Germany,

Austria, and all along the Mediterranean. I loved swimming in the ocean. As you can image, one hasn't a lot of chances to go swimming in Russia."

"I understand your father held several degrees in engineering?"

"Yes, he did a lot of civil engineering in the province where we lived. He designed and built several bridges and main highways throughout the region. He really was a brilliant man."

"On one of your trips, did you ever have occasion to go with him to the University of Hamburg?"

The smile was swept off her face. "Did I have occasion? *Did I have occasion?*" Her anger grew. "What is this, Griff? Are we on a date here or in an interrogation? Or should I say 'Captain Avery'? Just what are you getting at? If you have a question you want to ask me, then go ahead and ask it."

"Alright." Avery mentally crossed his fingers. This was the moment of truth. "When you went to the University of Hamburg with your father, did you met with Professor Nicoli Strovinski?"

Roshinko had a puzzled look on her face. "Strovinski . . . Strovinski?" Her expression changed. "Now I understand, you think that I had something to do with the failed attempt to retrieve Dr. Strovinski. Because I'm Russian and my father met him years earlier, I must be some kind of spy. Is that it?"

"I'm sorry, Anna; it's just that I have to consider every possibility." Avery tried not to sound apologetic, especially if she really *was* the spy, but he just couldn't help it.

"Haven't you been listening to anything I've said? I told you that Stalin and his thugs have kidnapped or killed my parents. Why on earth would I want to help anyone like that after what they've done to me?"

"Perhaps that's the very reason you would help them, your cooperation in exchange for their safety."

Roshinko glared at Avery with an intensity he could feel down into his soul. Her gaze couldn't have been more penetrating if he had been standing before God Himself on Judgment Day. He just wanted to reach out and hold her, but he could not.

"I thought you were interested in me, but I guess I was wrong. Thanks for the date, *Captain*. You certainly know how to show a girl a good time." Roshinko got up from the table, threw her napkin down, and rushed for the door.

He followed her out and put a hand on her shoulder.

"You came after me. Why?" she managed to get out between sobs. "I thought I was the enemy."

Avery pulled Anna into his arms and gazed into her eyes. She stiffened a bit, but she didn't resist.

"I came after you because I don't want anything to happen to you." He wanted to tell her that he loved her, but he couldn't. He was getting himself into big trouble, and he knew it. He felt like he was standing on the high-wire tower at the circus big top, about to step off onto the tightrope of love. There was no safety net below. He knew he shouldn't be doing this, he still didn't know if he could fully trust her, but he just couldn't help himself. Against his better judgment he kissed her, and to his shock, surprise, and delight, she kissed him back.

THIRTY-FIVE

JASON Peters walked down the hall with long, purposeful strides, carrying a manila folder. His stride was broken as he passed by Anna Roshinko's office and saw that she was crying. He quickly changed gears and knocked on her door.

"What's wrong, Anna?" he asked.

She looked up, wiping her eyes with a tissue. "I'm sorry, Jason. I know I shouldn't be bringing my problems to work."

". . . but part of your problem is work, or at least someone at work?"

Roshinko nodded. "Griff and I went out last night and we had a really good time, right up until the part where he all but accused me of being a Nazi spy. Somehow he found out that I had met Dr. Strovinski once. I must have been perhaps ten or eleven years old, and I don't remember it. But in his mind, since I had met him that automatically ties me to him, to the Germans, and to the fact that we lost him."

Peters hung his head. "I'm sorry, Anna. I was the one who told Griff about your past."

"What? But how did you find out about all that? So now you think I'm a spy, too?"

"No, not anymore."

"What do you mean?" Confusion filled her red, tear-stained eyes.

"I was looking for answers, too, and I knew that you and I were on the top of Griff's spy list. I knew it wasn't me, so the next step was to look at you. The evidence against you was pretty strong, but I don't believe any of it now."

"Why?"

Peters held up the file. "You didn't check with the night desk when you came in this morning, did you?"

"No, I was too upset."

"This proves that you're not a spy. One of your agents sent an urgent message last night saying he was contacted by Zeus and that he has positive proof of a new German aircraft and of a secret underground base. I checked the confirmation codes, and they match. It really was Zeus who contacted your agent."

Roshinko looked hopeful but still confused.

"Don't you see?" he continued. "If you were the spy, your agent wouldn't be reporting this, especially if Zeus contacted him. This message proves you're not a spy!"

Suddenly she understood. "Thank you, thank you, thank you!" she said as she leaped up and gave Peters a hug.

"And don't blame Griff," Peters said. "He was just trying to do his job."

"Speaking of Griff, let's get this to him right now!" Roshinko grabbed the file and took Peters by the arm. Peters was a good eight inches taller that Roshinko, but he had trouble keeping up with her as she flew down the hallway.

Roshinko walked into Avery's office to find her boss sitting behind his desk. She waited until Peters came in, then closed the door. "So you think I'm a spy, do you? Working for Hitler instead of Uncle Sam?"

Avery's eyes flew open wide but before he could get in a word, Roshinko plowed ahead. "All because I was born into a wealthy family and had a brief meeting with one of our targets when I was a child?" She paced in front of Avery's desk like a defense attorney working the jury. She turned and gave Peters a quick wink, then continued the assault on her boss, picking up speed and fury like an approaching hurricane.

She moved slowly toward Avery letting the tension build. "And you believed this information, coming from Jason, one of you own aides, someone who was a suspect, too? You chose to believe him instead of me? Did it ever occur to you that he might be covering *his* tracks?" The hurricane was at full force now, threatening to destroy everything in its path.

In the middle of its path was one man sitting behind a desk which he knew would offer him no cover.

She was now leaning over him, about to unleash her full fury. "And you took what he said as gospel, trying and convicting me on such flimsy evidence?" She was only inches from his face and could see the doubt and worry in his eyes, then she abruptly stood up and threw a file folder on his desk.

"What's this?" Avery asked in surprise.

"It's proof that I'm not your spy!" She meant for the words to be harsh and sarcastic, but she just couldn't put the sting in them. "That's okay," she said, her voice becoming a soft, gentle breeze. "I forgive you." She gave him a quick peck on the cheek then retreated to the other side of the desk.

The sound of laughter began to filter through Avery's dazed mind and he noticed that Peters was seated in the chair across from the desk, doubled over in laughter. He looked back up at Roshinko, who stood with her arms crossed, wearing a sadistic smile and a smug look on her face.

Avery began to realize that he'd been set up, and a sheepish grin cracked the stone features of his solemn face. "What is this?" He said as he reached for the file.

"It's a report from one of my agents, confirmed by Zeus, informing us that he has evidence of a new type of German aircraft and of the secret base where it's being developed."

"What?" Avery shouted. He grabbed the file and tore it open like a kid opening up his first present on Christmas morning. His heart was racing as he scanned the report, which briefly described the new aircraft, and what the agent suspected was going on at the base. It was near a POW camp, and the agent suspected that some of the prisoners were being used as slave labor. He had managed to take nearly a dozen photographs.

Avery was beside himself. This was just the break he'd been looking for! With physical evidence, Sizemore would have to believe him and would be forced to order an air strike. He'd have to work fast; Lincoln had said that the Germans were ready to make their move by the end of the week. Suddenly his heart stopped when he read in the report that the agent couldn't smuggle the film out for another two weeks.

"We can't wait another two weeks," Avery said to himself out loud.

"Sir?" Peters said.

"Sorry. This information is extremely valuable, and we can't wait two weeks to get it."

"Begging your pardon, sir, but having read the message myself, I took the liberty of informing the agent that we would meet him tonight and retrieve the film ourselves."

"What?"

"Look, the timing is perfect," Peters said as he walked over to the big map. "Weather forecast is for low lying clouds for the entire trip, making it ideal for me to get in there in a Lysander, grab the film, and get out. I can leave late this afternoon and be back early tomorrow morning—just in time for you to buy me breakfast."

"You?" Roshinko said with a flare in her voice. "I should be the one to go, since it was my operative who brought us the information in the first place."

Avery shook his head and looked at Roshinko. "No, I should be the one to go. It's my operation, my neck."

Peters shook his head. "You're both wrong." Both faces suddenly snapped in unison and stared at him. "Griff, you can't go just because you are the head of operations. Just think how much information and knowledge you have. The Germans would have a field day if they got hold of you, and we both know there wouldn't be much left after they got finished. And you can't go," he said turning to Roshinko, "because of this whole spy business. The info came from one of your agents. Even though this should clear you, some people might question the authenticity of this information if *you* were the one to bring it back. I, however, have nothing to gain or lose from the information or by being captured."

Avery looked over at Roshinko and could tell she was about to say something. He held up his hand. He let out a heavy sigh. "He's right. Sending Jason is the only way we can make the information he brings back be credible."

"But, Griff—"

"Jason goes. Please don't fight me on this. We haven't got much time. I'll get the Lysander. You two make the rest of the necessary arrangements."

THIRTY-SIX

THE sky was dull and flat, and the steady drone of the small engine made conditions ideal for sleeping. But sleep was not on Jason Peters' agenda. The air was rough, and the small aircraft bounced around the sky like a shuttlecock in a badminton tournament, making the immediate task at hand one of keeping his dinner down.

The Westland Lysander he flew was a rather ugly plane, originally built as an artillery spotter for the British Army. Though it sported the same insignia and camouflage paint as its more famous cousins, the Spitfire and Hurricane, the similarities ended there. It was slow, with a top speed of only 217 miles per hour, and the lack of maneuverability made it an easy target for the Luftwaffe and antiaircraft guns. However, the ugly duckling found a new role in the war, one it was much better suited for. With a stall speed of only 60 miles per hour and needing only 300 feet to take off or land, it became the plane of choice for smuggling men and material in and out of enemy-occupied territory, the Spitfire of clandestine aircraft.

Peters stared out the window, trying to take his mind off the fact that he didn't think this was such a good idea anymore, and the fact that the idea had been his. The plane flew low over open fields and forests and over countless little villages scattered about the countryside like rice after a wedding. Several times they had to change course to avoid larger towns and cities where the Germans still might have a garrison.

Though the landscape and scenery kept changing, there was one constant throughout his journey: the color gray. He felt trapped inside a vast living painting and the only color in the artist's palette was charcoal gray. The winding rivers and streams they crossed were the lightest shades of gray, light shimmering off their glassy surfaces, while the forests and mountains were of the deepest and darkest shades. Even the sky was a flat gray, blanketed by clouds. The occasional tear in the canopy allowed whatever color there was to escape into the blackness of space.

Peters gazed off into the distance and saw bright flashes of light popping all over the dark carpet below like a summer's rain bouncing off hot pavement. Shafts of light stabbing into the night sky, trying to scrape away the darkness.

Peters had never seen a bombing raid at night before, and the sight was both intriguing and horrifying. The brilliant flashes of each bomb burst were beautiful against the night sky. Each of the individual flashes gathered together into a river of light as the fires they had started quickly overflowed into a flood of flame that engulfed their target.

He watched in fascination as one of the searching lights found a British bomber. In quick succession, other searchlights latched onto the bomber like the tentacles of a giant octopus straining to bring its prey down. Even from this great distance he could see the puffs of exploding flak converging on the plane. Soon a red glow appeared as the wing of the big plane took a direct hit and sheared off in flames. And as quickly as it had begun, it was over as each tentacle went its own way again, searching the skies for more victims.

Turning from the destruction, Peters tried to carry on a conversation with the pilot, but it was just too hard to talk and listen over the drone of the engine.

Peters had just dozed off when an elbow to his ribs woke him up. "We should be near the drop zone, sir," Lieutenant Rudy Cline, the pilot, shouted. Cline was a mirror image of his plane, only in human form. He was stout and durable, not good looking but a very capable pilot. His curly blond hair and freckles gave him a boyish charm, but it wasn't enough to carry him very far with the opposite sex, so he concentrated his skills on flying and had become the "go-to" pilot whenever the Americans or British had a dangerous mission to fly behind enemy lines.

"Keep a sharp eye out for the signal." Peters nodded and sat up and began scanning the jumbled gray shadows below. Within minutes he spotted a blinking light on the ground. He reached over, hit Cline on the arm, and pointed off to their right. The pilot nodded, and the small plane banked over as they circled to confirm the landing codes. In the darkness, Peters searched for a runway but all he saw was a tiny island of light gray floating in a sea of ebony. It looked like a grass field, too small for them to land in, way too small.

Cline flew over the field once, sized it up, then banked hard to the left, standing the plane on its side. Even though he was buckled in, Peters frantically grabbed for his door handle to hold himself up. Then the steady drone of the engine that had been annoying up until now suddenly fell silent as Cline cut the power.

The plane began to lose speed and altitude as it slid almost sideways down the sky toward the trees. At the last possible moment, Cline leveled the wings and pulled back on the yoke, making the plane flare just inches above the ground. It then settled down gently on the grassy field, rolling to a stop and using only three-quarters of the length of the field.

Cline's devilish smile was visible even in the darkness. Peters ignored him and opened the door to get out.

Three men approached from the edge of the field. Cline swung the machine gun off his shoulder and pointed it at the intruders. Peters stepped forward and exchanged some quick words in French, then motioned for Cline to come over.

"It's okay, Lieutenant," Peters said. "They're waiting for us over there by the edge of the woods." Cline nodded and lowered his carbine, then followed the small group toward the tree line.

They were just at the edge of the forest when they heard shouts and the sound of rushing feet. Cline brought his gun up to fire, but Peters quickly put his hand on the barrel and pushed it down as twenty soldiers surrounded them, each with their gun trained on them.

"Don't," Peters warned. "We don't have a chance; live to fight another day."

Peters slid his gun off his shoulder and let it fall to the ground. In a show of defiance, Cline threw his own gun to the ground. At once, they were swarmed by German soldiers, who blindfolded them and tied their hands. They were led a short distance through the woods and put into the back of a troop truck.

Peters and Cline sat in the back of the truck, wedged between two soldiers, as they bounced along the rough road. Cline leaned over and tried to whisper to Peters but was stopped in mid-sentence by a sharp slap to the head and an order to keep quiet.

After about half an hour of driving, the truck stopped and a pair of strong hands lifted Peters up and guided him toward the tailgate. The guards threw Cline out the back of the truck with his hands still tied behind his back. Peters' heart raced as he braced himself, knowing he was next.

Peters was led to the end of the truck. With the blindfold on it felt like he was on the edge of the Grand Canyon. He felt a hand from one of the soldiers on the ground grab his pant leg. He tensed, but the hand guided his leg to a step and he was lead safely to the ground.

"Are you alright?" Peters whispered to Cline.

Cline moaned softly and finally replied, "Yeah, I think so. Watch that first step, it's a doozy."

Peters smiled at the Brit's dry attempt at humor.

"Silence!"

The faint sound of machinery and what sounded like a rail yard could be heard in the distance. The noise of a car driving by indicated to the men that they were in a city.

They stepped over a threshold in a seemingly big room, the only sounds being the rushing of breath and the clopping of boots against the tile floor.

They descended lower and lower into the bowels of the building. The air was damp and musty, but there was also a very faint odor of something that had not so much hung in the air but had sunk its talons into the atmosphere and refused to let go.

Peters was led into a room where he was shoved into a chair, his hands untied, and his blindfold removed. The guard smiled as he closed the door and left the American alone.

It was a plain, simple room with a concrete floor, the walls covered in a dull institutional green. He sat in a black, metal folding chair across from a large chair of rich brown leather positioned behind a desk.

The silence was abruptly broken as light classical music came spilling out of the speakers.

After a few minutes, the door opened and an SS major came in. The major walked over and sat down. "Sorry to keep you waiting," he said as he sat sank into his chair. "But we were having a little trouble with your pilot. He doesn't seem to like our hospitality too much.

"Listen to this. This is one of Schubert's earlier works. I believe he is relying too much on the woodwinds. Had I written it, I would have used violins and cellos as a foundation for the woodwinds." The two sat silently for a moment as they listened to the music play.

"Where's my pilot?" Peters finally asked.

"We took him to another facility not too far from here." The major smiled then opened the drawer of the desk and brought out a large flask and two glasses.

"Care to join me in a drink, Lieutenant Peters of the OSS?"

THIRTY-SEVEN

"HAVE you heard anything from Jason yet?"

Avery shook his head, looking up from his radio at Roshinko. "No, not yet." He tried to hide his growing frustration and uncertainty, but he wasn't doing a very good job of it. "He should have checked in three hours ago."

Neither one wanted to say it, but they both knew something was wrong. Avery felt the teeth of regret gnawing away at him. Even though he knew Jason was right, he still shouldn't have let himself be talked into it. He should have been the one to go.

Probably getting all worked up over nothing, he tried to convince himself. Most likely Jason just had radio trouble. He looked at his watch again. Even with no radio contact, the plane should be returning home in another hour.

"It must be his radio," he said. "Come on, we'll go meet him at the airfield. Then I'll buy us all breakfast, steak and eggs." He smiled weakly, in an attempt to build Roshinko's confidence as well as his own.

Avery stood and grabbed his coat. He was almost to the door when he heard foots steps coming down the hall at a steady, purposeful pace. Then they stopped at his door.

"General Sizemore," Avery said as the general strode into the room. "What are you doing here at this late hour, sir?"

"I hear you have a man missing."

How does he know? It is nearly one in the morning! What is he doing up so late, and how did he know about the mission . . . let alone that fact that Jason was missing? "No, sir. We have a man who is overdue reporting in. Probably just radio trouble, but he is not listed as missing. Yet."

Sizemore frowned. "When is his aircraft due to land?"

"In just a little over an hour, sir," Avery answered

"Very well, then, I'll want to see a full report on my desk by 0900 hours."

"Yes, sir," Avery replied, then snapped to attention and saluted.

Sizemore returned the salute and disappeared. Avery collapsed against the corner of his desk. "What was that all about?" he said, looking at Roshinko. "Did you tell anyone about this mission?"

"No."

"You didn't tell any of your section people, say anything to your room-mates, mention to anyone in passing that Jason would be gone?"

"No," Roshinko replied. "I didn't tell anyone."

Avery could hear the frustration and anger building in her voice. "Sorry, Anna."

He grabbed his coat again. "Okay, lets get out of here and to the airfield before Eisenhower shows up and wait for Jason's plane to land. Once he's down, we'll show the evidence to Sizemore and get this all sorted out." Roshinko nodded and followed him out the door.

THE first rays of light broke over the horizon to push back the night, which was being held in place by the ever-present clouds. They had been sitting at the airfield now for three hours, and Anna had fallen asleep on his shoulder. He had dozed off himself a couple of time, his arm was wrapped around her. He was awake now, watching the sun come up.

A beautiful sunrise, a beautiful woman at his side . . . the whole scene could have been very romantic had it not been for the fact that they were waiting for a missing friend to return, and that his boss was breathing down his neck. He thought about waking Anna up because she loved to greet the new day, but she looked so calm and at peace, he just didn't have the heart. He gently laid her down on the seat, then slipped out of the car. The morning air was surprisingly cool. An occasional gust of wind would tug at his coat like a playful dog pulling at his pant leg.

He lit up a cigarette and gazed to the east, straining to hear the sound of the little Lysander that had spirited his friend away just a few hours before. As the sun rose, the brilliant reds and oranges of its first rays faded to the dull gray of the clouds. The vanishing colors reflected his fleeting hopes. His friend wasn't coming back.

Jason was more than eight hours overdue. In desperation he stared in the skies as if he could will the small plane into existence, but the skies were empty. He flicked his cigarette to the ground and crushed it out as he turned back to the car.

There was going to be hell to pay.

Just as his hand was reaching for the door, he thought he heard the faint drone of an airplane engine. He scanned the horizon and found a small dot just above the rolling hills to the east. The sound of the engine and the size of the dot grew, carrying back his lost hopes.

Jason would come back home safe and sound with the photographs, and the general would be satisfied, and all would be forgiven and forgotten. But that the dot was moving too fast. He was no airplane expert, but he knew the Lysander couldn't move that fast. Within seconds the dot took shape, and the plane roared overhead. It was a British Spitfire, fast, sleek, and beautiful . . . and not the plane he wanted to see. The fighter waggled his wings as he went by. A moment later, he was gone.

He turned and was surprised to find Anna standing next to him.

"I heard the plane and thought it might be Jason," she said in a soft, quiet voice. Avery looked into her lovely face. Even after a three hour nap in a car, she still looked beautiful.

"You missed the sunrise, although you didn't miss much. A quick splash of color followed by the same old dull, boring gray."

"Jason's—"

Avery put his hand to her lips. He reached out and wrapped her in his arms, as much to comfort himself as her. "I haven't given up all hope yet," he lied. "Maybe when we get back to the office he'll have reported in through another agent in the area."

"You're right. I'm sure he's just fine," Roshinko said, preferring to believe the lie instead of the truth that they both all ready knew. Avery opened the car door for her. Neither spoke much on the way back to the office, neither wanted to be the first to admit it, to say out loud: Jason wasn't coming back.

THIRTY-EIGHT

"AND what are we drinking to?" Peters asked.

"Why, to the end of the war, of course."

"A victory by the Allied Forces?"

"No." Reinard smiled. "I was thinking more along the lines of a glorious victory for the Third Reich." He poured two glasses and offered one to Peters.

Peters reached over and took it and raised it up in a toast. "I'll drink to that!"

"It's good to see you again, my friend," the German said.

"And you. I must say that I was a little concerned tonight, as I didn't recognize any of the soldiers who picked us up. I was afraid we had run into a regular army patrol, and that they would shoot first and asked questions later."

Reinard smiled. "You were never in any danger . . . unless your pilot had crashed."

Peters took another sip and paused to savor the flavor. "This really is excellent brandy. And speaking of my pilot, I hope Lieutenant Cline didn't give you much trouble."

"No, he's in a cell not too far from here. We'll interrogate him, threaten him with the appropriate amount of force, then get him ready for the 'escape' when the time comes."

"Good, good. This little charade should be the last nail in the coffin of Captain Griffin Avery. When I return after my miraculous escape and tell them it was all a set up, that the information from Roshinko's agent and Zeus is counterfeit, it will look bad for Roshinko, but even more so for Avery, who approved it. It will be more damaging still because he's sleeping with her. And all this will make the brave hero, me, the perfect choice to take over his position. But tell me, Volker," Peters said as he put his drink down on the table. "I can appreciate the fact of having a mole in the government intelligence agency, but what good will it do us now? The war really is all but lost."

"Patience, my friend. Patience." Reinard smiled back. "There was just a little over twenty years between the first war to end all wars and this one. Is twenty years such a long time to wait to take vengeance upon our enemies? Your position will not only provide us information on what the United States is doing, but her allies as well. We have had our spies in this war, but none could give us the information that you'll be able to provide once you're in place."

Reinard poured himself another drink. "But there's more going on here than you can possibly imagine. Tomorrow I will show you something wonderful, something that will give you new hope and inspiration. But tonight you will rest and refresh yourself. Tomorrow promises to be a big day. Come, I will take you to where you will spend the night. The accommodations there are a bit more appealing than these." Reinard smiled.

THE dining room that welcomed Peters and his countrymen was a work of art itself, but the truly captivating thing was the aroma from the kitchen.

"We have a special treat," their host, Colonel Stein, said. "Our very own Lieutenant Lincoln, formerly of the U.S. Eighth Air Force, has made one of his traditional American dinners tonight."

Peters was disappointed. He'd been away from Germany so long he was hoping for a traditional German meal.

Stein continued. "On the eve of conquering our enemies, I think it's only appropriate that we celebrate by dining on food that will soon become a thing of the past. To paraphrase our dear adversary, who said this is not the beginning of the end, but the end of the beginning . . . I say to you Mr. Churchill, this *is* the end of yours!"

Stein raised his glass in a toast and was joined by Major Reinard, General Jaeger, and Peters. They took large drinks and smiled at one another. "This is very good wine, Colonel, my compliments on your choice," Peters said.

"Again," Stein replied, "compliments of our Mr. Lincoln."

Lincoln was standing by the kitchen door waiting for Stein to signal for the meal. When he heard Peters speak, he knew he was an American. But what, he wondered, would an American be doing in the middle of Germany as the guest, and not a prisoner of a POW commandant? He didn't have the look of a prisoner who had turned. A spy perhaps?

Stein snapped his fingers. Lincoln nodded his head in acknowledgment, then went into the kitchen, reappearing moments later laden with a large platter of steaming fried chicken. Lincoln served each officer, starting with the general and working his way down according to rank. When he came to Peters, Lincoln stopped for a moment.

"You're a long ways from the States, Mr. . . ."

"As are you, Lieutenant."

"I can't quiet place the accent," Lincoln continued. "The mid to Deep South, perhaps?"

"Not only can you cook and choose a good wine, but you're also very observant." Peters took another sip of wine. "But I thought that here in Germany, it is the Germans who should be asking the questions and not the prisoners."

"My apologies," Lincoln said quickly before Stein could dismiss him. "I was just curious. Besides," he said as he placed the chicken on the table, "who am I going to tell? At the end of the meal, I will clean up and go back to the prison camp."

"True," Peters said. "But let's just say I'm visiting and leave it at that, shall we?"

"As you wish." Lincoln went back to the kitchen and brought out the mashed potatoes. He began serving the potatoes, again starting with the general. Jaeger grabbed the salt shaker and poured a blizzard of salt on the potatoes. Lincoln cringed.

"Mr. Lincoln, twice I have eaten here, and twice you have impressed me."

"Thank you, sir," he answered. "After Germany looses the war, you can come to Fort Dodge in Iowa, and I'll cook you up a bunch of other American specials."

Jaeger smiled. "Perhaps after *we* win the war, you can come and work for me as my cook. You'll need a new job and since you are already here . . ."

Everyone laughed while Lincoln smiled politely through his teeth.

THIRTY-NINE

PETERS crept into the room, pausing every few steps, watching and listening to see if he'd been detected. Satisfied that he hadn't been discovered, he slipped his hand over the mouth of the man lying asleep on the ragged cot. He had expected the man to be startled, but not to throw a right cross in his sleep.

The fist swung wildly and hit the intruder on the top of the head, knocking him to the floor. The man sprang up from his bed, ready for round two.

"Hold on, hold on," Peters whispered, rubbing the top of his head. "It's me!"

Lieutenant Rudy Cline shook the last remnants of sleep out of his eyes as he stared at Peters sitting on the floor. "Sorry, sir, I didn't mean to hit you. How did you get out?"

"Long story. I'll tell you later. Can you fly?"

"You bet. They didn't work me over too bad. But where are we going to get a plane?"

"We're at a small airfield. Believe it or not, our plane is just outside. They must have brought it here sometime yesterday. It's parked about a hundred yards away, but I think we can get to it without being seen. Come on!"

The two men slipped out of the room and crept down the short hallway, hugging the wall like a new coat of paint as they went. They rounded the corner and came to a door. Peters opened it slowly and peered outside.

"Come on." Peters stepped through the door, followed by Cline. Once outside, they ran down the length of the building, then hid in some bushes close to the corner.

Right on schedule, a guard came walking around the corner and Peters leapt out of the bushes. In a few well-rehearsed moves, he knocked the guard out and took his gun. It was loaded with blanks to protect the Germans soldiers in case the American pilot got a hold of it.

"It won't take long for them to miss him," Peters said. "Let's get to the plane." They sprinted across the open field and collapsed breathless next to the aircraft. "How long will it take you to get this thing ready?" Peters said between gasps.

"Start strapping in, Lieutenant, 'cause we're already out of here." Cline threw open the door and climbed in. True to his word, before Peters could even crawl over to the other side of the plane and open his door, Cline had the engine running.

They heard shouting and the sound of gunfire as five soldiers came running after them. Peters jumped out of the plane and returned fire. He fired two shots and three soldiers went down. He fired another shot, hoping Cline hadn't noticed.

"Get in!" Cline shouted as he revved up the engine and the small plane began moving. Peters threw down the rifle and jumped in. With the guard's weapons blazing away, the small plane lifted into the air, heading for home.

"We did it!" Cline shouted. "We actually did it! Man, you were something back there! Taking out that guard with your bare hands and then *bam*! Three shots and three Germans go down. They're not going to believe this when we get back home."

Peters just smiled.

THE phone rang with its annoyingly loud British ring, and Griff Avery woke from a fitful sleep. Not that he would have been any happier to have been woken up with an American-style ring. No, it was just one more thing to remind him that he was in a place where he didn't want to be. He grabbed the clock: 2:30 a.m. Why did people always look at the clock first instead of answering the phone? As if it would be okay to be awakened at 3:00, but not before. He shook the illogical, not-yet-conscious thought out of his head and picked up the phone.

"Yeah." It wasn't the politest way to answer the phone. Then again, he didn't have to be polite for another half-hour.

"Griff! Griff!" The voice on the other end yelled. It was a woman's voice.

"Who is this, and what do you want?"

"He's alive, he's alive and back here!"

"Who is? Who's back where?"

"Jason! Jason's back!"

"Anna?"

"Jason landed an hour ago and wants to meet with us right away. He said he'd meet us both at your place. Oh, Griff, isn't it wonderful?"

Sleep released its last hold on his thoughts, and he realized what Anna was saying. "That's great! Okay, yeah I'll see you soon."

Avery hung up the phone. He could hardly believe that Jason was back safe and sound. Maybe now he could get some answers. He only hoped that Jason had gotten his hands on the film and brought it back. He threw on a pot of coffee and jumped in the shower, his mind racing like a runaway freight train. The next few hours could prove pivotal for the entire war effort.

FORTY

AVERY heard a knock and tripped over a kitchen chair to get the door. He opened the door and was plainly disappointed to see that it was Anna and not Peters.

"Well, you sure know how to make a girl feel welcome," she said.

"I'm sorry, Anna, it's just—"

"Yes, I know. Are you going to invite me in, or shall I wait out here until Jason arrives?"

Avery hung his head in mock submission, threw open the door, and invited her in with a sweeping motion of his arm. Roshinko walked in and threw her coat on the couch, shaking her head as she looked around. There was a small writing desk against the wall near the window with a hot plate and a tin coffeepot on it. The coffeepot was surrounded by three badly stained coffee mugs and an overflowing ashtray. Avery's uniform jacket was draped across the chair and his shoes rested on the seat of the chair.

Suddenly feeling self-conscious about Anna's inspection of his lackluster apartment, he hurried to his bedroom door and shut it. She didn't need to see that most of the dirty clothes never made it into the clothes hamper, or that the clean ones sometimes didn't find the dresser.

"You know, this is the first time I've been in your apartment," Roshinko said, enjoying Avery's embarrassment. "They say you can tell a lot about a man by the way he keeps his apartment. It could use a woman's touch, that's for sure."

Avery smiled. "Know anybody who might want the job? Long hours and little pay, but the fringe benefits are pretty good. Great view of the city street below, running water. Its even hot sometimes. Oh, and all the coffee you can drink." He walked over and poured some coffee into one of the stained cups.

With a sly, seductive smile on her face, Roshinko sauntered over to Avery, drew herself close and put her hand on his as he was about to pour her a cup. "I just might know someone who's interested in the job. But before we start negotiating," she said, her lips just inches away from Avery's, "do you know what I *really* want right now?"

Avery's stomach did somersaults, and his heart beat like a marching band. He knew what *he* wanted right now; he only hoped she wanted the same thing.

"I'd really like some of that coffee, in a clean cup." She gave Avery a quick wink, spun around, and sat on the couch. Avery stood for a second with a deer-in-the-headlights look, then a smile crept over his face as he walked into the kitchen for a clean cup.

Avery had just sat down and handed her the coffee when they heard a knock at the door. He sprang up and threw it open. As soon as he saw it was Peters, he threw his arms around him, Roshinko quickly following suit.

After a few moments of celebration, Peters' face turned grim as he asked them to sit down.

"It was a set-up, Griff. The Germans knew I was coming and were waiting for me. I hadn't even been on the ground for two minutes when the Gestapo, lead by a Major Reinard, swarmed all over us."

"*What!*" Avery shouted.

Peters glared at Roshinko. "It was *your* agent who made the contact with us. It was *your* agent that set this all up."

"I thought we were past this."

"Your people were the only ones who knew the exact time and place. The raid was too well organized for it to be just bad luck. The Germans were tipped off."

"Now wait a minute here, Jay, do you really think she's the spy?" Avery asked.

"I've worked with the two of you long enough to see lots of little discrepancies that all add up to big trouble."

Peters walked over to the door, Roshinko and Avery still seated on the couch in front of him. "The message was from her agent, but the original message was from Zeus, *your* agent," he said, looking at Avery

"Jason, what are you talking about? Now you think that *I'm* a double agent?"

Peters shook his head with a light smile. "No, Griff, I don't think you're a double agent, but General Sizemore will think Anna is. And so will everyone else by the time they get through reading my report. And they'll know that you knew all about it and did nothing to stop her."

Avery looked at him with a blank stare. "Have you lost your mind? What's the matter with you?"

"For some time now, you've known that Anna has been selling secrets to the Germans. She's the one who betrayed Strovinski, she set me up, and she's the one who compromised Zeus, one of the most reliable agents of the war. You see, Griff, you knew all about it, but once she became your lover, you turned a blind eye to it all." Peters looked at Roshinko and gave her a wicked little smile. Roshinko turned away.

"After I escaped, you knew there'd be no hiding the truth, that you'd have to admit that you knowingly let a German spy continue working by your side. You realized that your career would be over and there was only one thing left that you could do."

Peters revealed a gun he had hidden under his coat and pointed it at Roshinko. "Filled with guilt and remorse, in a moment of anguish, you killed her, then turned the gun on yourself."

"So, Jason . . ." Avery said as he took out a cigarette and lit it, stalling for time as his mind raced, trying to figure a way out, "how long have you been working for the Germans?"

"Since day one."

"So all of this is, what, just to get my job? The war is practically over, what information could you possible hope to gain?"

Peters laughed. "Don't flatter yourself, Griff, it's not just about your job. That's another one of your American faults, you don't look at the big picture and plan for the future. You see, you were right—the geniuses of the Third Reich have developed a plane that will fly higher, faster, and further than anything you Americans have come up with. Now, on American soil you once thought of as immune from the devastation of war, your people will finally get a taste of their own medicine. We'll take the fight to your own doorstep and unleash the kind of destruction that you've been so quick to ravage my home-land with. We will let your people, so smug and safe in their homes, know what it is like to see everything they've have worked hard for all their lives go up in flames. We will let them see first hand what war is really like, then we'll find out if they still have the stomach to fight on as the brave people of Germany have. We will bring America to her knees!"

"You really think the United States will surrender? You underestimate our resolve."

Peters smiled and shook his head. "That's the beauty of this entire plan. If the United States continues to fight, I'll be in the perfect position to pass on valuable information to the Fatherland. You Americans do love a hero. And as a hero, they will reward me with a promotion that will open up new avenues that I couldn't dream of.

"Oh, and by the way, my credentials not only include 'master spy,' but 'matchmaker' as well. I set up the little encounter Anna had with those thugs, as you called them, outside the Dragon's Breath. Nothing like rescuing a damsel in distress to bring out the knight in shining armor. Just think, if it weren't for me, you two probably wouldn't have gotten together."

"At least you did something right," Avery said, smiling at Roshinko.

Peters rolled his eyes, pointed the gun at Roshinko, and pulled the trigger.

The gun had a silencer on it, and a single bullet struck Roshinko in the center of her forehead. Her head snapped back, hit the back of the couch, then tilted forward and to the side, coming to rest as if she were looking at Avery and about to say something.

"A shame," Peters said. "I really did like her, too."

"You son of a—" Avery made a motion for Peters.

He shook his head and trained the gun on Avery. "Good-bye, Griff."

An explosion louder than anything Avery thought possible was followed by a blinding flash of light that stunned his senses. He was thrown against the wall, he presumed from the impact of the bullet, and lay on the floor in a crumpled heap, unable to breathe.

He'd always thought that death by a bullet would be quick and simple. What an odd sensation, to feel his head getting lighter. He knew it wouldn't be long now. Would his next breath be his last? And if so, would it find him standing in front of the glistening white pearly gates and St. Peter or staring into the eyes of Cerberus, the three-headed dog that guarded the gates of hell?

He closed his eyes to take one last gasp of air. He could breathe again! He inhaled deeply. The air was neither sweet smelling nor furnace-blast hot. Instead, it tasted like dust. *Dust?*

He coughed, breathed, then coughed again. Slowly he began to realize that he really wasn't dead.

His ears rang like the bells of Notre Dame. He looked over at Anna lying on the floor. Her face still held that blank, emotionless stare. This wasn't a dream. Anna was truly dead.

The outside wall behind the couch was completely gone. Timbers and wires hung from the ceiling like vines in a jungle. Dust, plaster, and debris filled his apartment.

One of the last V-2 rockets had exploded in the building next to his, destroying it and damaging his building.

Avery tried to stand, but his legs were too shaky to support his weight. He grabbed one of the chairs that had been in the kitchen and pulled himself up. He had to find Peters, and the gun. Avery staggered to his feet and climbed over a large beam that only moments ago had held up his ceiling.

As he climbed over the rubble and reached the front door, he saw Peters lying under a pile of debris. Peters lifted his head. "Going somewhere?" Peters' face was covered with blood from a deep cut above his left eye, but he still managed a sadistic smile as he raised the gun. He coughed and let out a cry of pain.

The shot went wide, and Avery bolted out the door. He had miraculously escaped death twice, and he wasn't about to push his luck by trying to wrestle the gun away. Avery stumbled onto the street and disappeared into the crowd of spectators and rescue workers. He slipped down a deserted alleyway, then collapsed out of sight in the shadow of a doorway and cried. All he could see was Anna's lifeless eyes staring back at him. The thought of never holding her again was almost more than he could bear.

What should I do now? he wondered. Peters still holds the upper hand. Now I will not only be wanted as a spy, but a murderer, too! Sizemore will be more than happy to throw the switch.

If he went back to the office to use any of the radio equipment, he would be arrested on the spot.

An idea began forming in his head. Was it an idea forged out of desperation or inspiration? It was crazy, to be sure, but he felt he had no other options. He would have to work fast to have even the slightest chance for success. He got up and ran down the alley.

FORTY-ONE

"YES, Lieutenant, I know it's very unusual," Avery said, trying not to let his impatience show. "I have important business with the colonel and it can't wait until morning." The lieutenant on guard duty at the side gate of the 222nd Fighter Group's Airfield shuffled nervously back and forth on his feet. He looked at Avery, down at his ID and then back to Avery again.

Avery could see the wheels turning in the lieutenant's head, so he decided to help him make the right decision. "I know is late, Lieutenant, but I really don't think you want to wake up your captain just so he can ask you why the hell you didn't let me see the colonel in the first place? You can make the decisions yourself right here, right now, or wake up your captain and let him make it for you. But, hey, it's not my funeral." Avery shrugged his shoulders, then leaned back in the seat of his Jeep and lit a cigarette. He looked down and hoped the lieutenant didn't notice his trembling hands.

The lieutenant hesitated but signaled for the sergeant to raise the gate. "Does the captain know where the colonel's quarters are?"

"Yes, Lieutenant, carry on!" Avery returned the salute and drove off toward Colonel Adams' quarters. He let out a sigh of relief. So far so good, he thought. At least everyone in the Army doesn't know that I am a wanted criminal. Not yet. Three minutes later, the Jeep rolled to a stop in front of the small Quonset hut.

Going up the short walkway, he wished there was another way, one that didn't involve using any of his friends. Reluctantly he knocked on the door. The night was quiet and still, and the simple knock sounded like he was beating the door down with a sledgehammer.

After a moment, a very groggy Adams opened the door. "Griff? What are you doing here, and at this hour?"

"It's a long story, Wes," Avery answered. "Can I come in?"

Adams stepped back. After a quick look around, Avery entered. He explained the entire situation to Adams. About the bomb, the secret base and aircraft, the plan to bomb New York, how Peters had killed Anna and framed him for everything. As he spoke, at times he felt like he was giving a report, at others, he felt like he was in a court of law defending himself. Still at other times he felt he was in a confessional, especially when talking about Anna and her death.

When he'd finished, he just sat, waiting for the colonel to say something. He felt like a kid, explaining to his father something he'd done and waiting to see if he was going to be angry or not.

Adams was silent, and the longer he sat the more nervous Avery became. *Did I do the right thing by coming to Adams? Is he going to turn me in? Will he even believe me?*

"Do you have a safe place to stay while I make the arrangements for transportation?"

"Transportation?" Avery asked.

"You need transportation to France, right?"

"Well, yeah."

"I think I know just the man for the job . . . and if he's going to get court-martialed for it, I think he should be asked face-to-face and not over the phone. He's going to need help flying the plane. Besides, if I'm going to be an accomplice to this whole thing and get court-martialed as well, then I should at least have the pleasure of the plane ride."

"Just like that, you're ready to throw your career away and maybe even your life?"

Colonel Adams smiled. "I got curious and did a little checking on my own. I went to Captain Lyons to see for myself what was so important about that airfield we buzzed and why the Krauts had so many fighters there. At first Lyons was pretty tight lipped, but after I reminded him of the fact that he was a captain and I was a colonel, and how I knew the Air Force had a photographer's position open in the Aleutian Islands, he suddenly became very talkative. I agree that there's probably some sort of underground base there and, though I don't know General Sizemore personally, I've heard he can be a real stickler for regulations and an overall pain in the butt. He probably wouldn't move even if New York got hit today, so he won't be of any help.

"It's too late tonight to do anything. Do you know where Kensington is?"

"The bomber base?"

Adams nodded his head. "Yeah, meet me there at 1900 hours tomorrow. I'll leave instructions at the gate, and the guard will bring you to us."

"Wes, I—"

"Shut up before I change my mind. We've got a lot to do and not much time. Now go find yourself a hole to hide in until tomorrow night."

FORTY-TWO

GRIFF Avery turned off the paved road and onto the rough gravel access road leading to the air base. The reality of the entire situation came crashing down on him. He felt like Atlas, bearing the weight of the world on his shoulders. Doubts swept into his soul like a surging tide driven by a powerful hurricane. Avery could feel fear rising up from the depths of despair and wrapping itself around him like a mythical sea monster, squeezing the breath out of his lungs. He started hyperventilating and became lightheaded. He didn't want to go to prison or be shot as a spy! Who was he kidding—he couldn't do this, this was insanity. The reality of the situation was that he was a mediocre intelligence officer, outclassed and outmaneuvered by Peters and the German war machine. Peters had duped him, then killed Anna.

Anna.

She had believed in him. Not so much in his ability to do things, but a simple faith in him. Suddenly he felt ashamed of himself for betraying that trust with his little wallow in self-pity. But she wasn't the only one who believed. Adams had said yes to his pleas for help without reservation, and Avery knew if the storm troopers were waiting for him at the gate, it wasn't Adams' doing. Zeus also trusted him with his life on a daily basis. If that many people had faith in him, then, by God, he would honor their faith by showing a little more faith in himself!

The heavens didn't open up, nor did he hear a choir of angels singing at his new revelation. He was still scared spitless, and the odds were still stacked against him, but with his newly planted mustard seed of faith, he could go on.

Avery pulled his Jeep up to the small guard shack and tried not to look as nervous as he was. A single guard stood outside as he drove up. Avery gave a small sigh of relief at the sight of only one guard. But the relief vanished as another guard appeared out of the shack as he stopped. The second soldier walked slowly behind the Jeep and halted.

At least he isn't going for his gun, Avery thought.

"I'm Captain Griffin Avery," he said, trying to sound nonchalant. "I believe you have some instructions for me from Colonel Wesley Adams."

"Yes sir, it will be just a moment. May I see your ID, please?" the corporal said as he checked his clipboard, then looked at several wooden boxes stacked in the back seat of the Jeep. "I need to know what's in the crates, sir, before I can let you pass."

Avery wasn't afraid anymore. He was angry. Angry that his best friend had turned out to be a spy and had been playing him for a fool all this time. That that very same best friend had killed the woman he loved. And that he now had to "escape" and run on a fool's errand to stop a secret weapon that could change the course of the war.

Now he was even angrier that this little snot-nosed corporal, who didn't have a damn clue about anything, would try and stop him!

"Take a look at my ID again, Corporal. What branch of the Army does it say I'm with?"

The young corporal held it up to the light again. "It says you're with the OSS."

"And do you know what the OSS is, Corporal?" Avery continued. "'OSS' stands for the 'Office of Strategic Services.' Do you have any idea what the OSS does?" Avery turned at looked at the other soldier standing behind him. Avery was on a roll, and it felt good. "How about you, son? Do *you* know what the OSS is?

"No, of course not," Avery said, shaking his head. "Among other things, I work with the French underground, the Maquis. I'm sure you've heard of them," he said, making no attempt to hide his sarcasm. "All I can tell you is that I have equipment vital to the war effort. Now if that's not good enough for you, Corporal, then you can call the duty officer and get him over here to look at my ID, and he'll see what my clearance is, and he'll wave me on through. At that point, I go on happily about my business while you and your friend here spend the next ten minutes getting your butts chewed for making me wait. The choice is yours."

"Just one moment, sir," the guard said nervously. "Please wait here." He vanished back into the shack. Avery was down to his proverbial last good nerve; the others had frayed and split away. If that last thread broke and he fell into the pit, he didn't know if he would be able to climb back out again. He knew this was not the time or place to light up, but he needed a cigarette more than he ever had in his life.

With hands shaking like a drunk trying to go cold turkey, he lit up his cigarette and nearly burned through half of it with one draw. He looked behind him and saw that the guards looked almost as nervous and confused as he was. It was clear neither was accustomed to being challenged. He only hoped he could continue his bluff.

The guard emerged from the shack. "Captain, if you'll follow me, I'll take you to Colonel Adams."

Avery blinked his eyes. He had pulled it off! The corporal gave him an odd look, then got in another Jeep and signaled for Avery to follow. Avery was in such a hurry to follow that he spun his tires out in the gravel before falling in line behind the corporal's Jeep.

Dusk had fallen and the base was quiet; things were winding down for the night. Most of the B-17s were corralled together according to squadron. It reminded Avery of a large herd of cattle being bedded down for the night. Near the hangars, lights cast huge shadows as crew chiefs stood roughshod over their crews as they worked diligently into the night to get their planes ready for tomorrow's mission.

Half a dozen of the big planes sat idly by, being groomed like racehorses after the big race, having their battle wounds soothed. Some of the planes' engines were being replaced, others had new turrets installed. Nearly all of them had men swarming all over patching the countless bullet holes.

Avery followed the corporal as they drove around the outside perimeter of the base. It was a large base and the going was slow; the service road hadn't seen any service for quite a while.

Avery expected to see a lone plane hiding in the dark, waiting to whisk them away on their secret and desperate mission. Instead, he found a beehive of activity. A B-17 surrounded by two trucks with their headlights on was sitting at the end of the field. Men scurried back and forth between the trucks and the plane, feeding crates through the open bomb bay doors.

The corporal got halfway out of his Jeep and pointed at the plane, then quickly got back in and turned the Jeep around. Even in the dark, Avery could almost see the relief and the good-bye-and-good-riddance look on the guard's face as the man sped back to his post.

Avery pulled off into the grass behind the bomber. He grabbed one of the crates out of the back of his Jeep and started carrying it toward the plane. Colonel Adams saw him coming and waved. Avery set the box down. It was whisked away by one of the ground crew and soon disappeared into the belly of the plane.

Avery shook Adams' hand. "Who are all these people?"

"Three of them are my pilots," Adams said, "and the rest are the crew of the *Red Light Lady*."

Avery spun around to find his nephew standing behind him. "Mike! What are you doing here?" The joy of seeing his nephew was replaced by worry. "You shouldn't be here, Mike. Take your crew and leave. I don't want you involved in this."

"I'm sorry, Griff," Adams said. "But like it or not, they are involved. We need someone we can trust, and all things considered, Mike and his crew are our only choice."

"I appreciate your concern, Uncle—Captain Avery—but the crew of the *Red Light Lady* flies for Uncle Sam, and we go where the fight is, sir!"

Avery nodded. "I understand." He took a deep breath. "Okay, so what are in all these crates?"

"Probably the same thing that's in yours, only a lot more of it. You can't start a war without a few guns and ammunition," Adams said.

Avery stood in amazement. "A few? It looks like you have enough arms here to invade Japan! Where did you get all this?"

"You've got your sources, I've got mine." Adams smiled. "You'd be surprised what a bully the colonel can be when no one wants to rock the boat and get their butts chewed out."

A major wearing a bright cavalry yellow silk scarf came walking up. "She's all loaded, Colonel."

"Thank you, Major."

"Hang on a second. I'll get my map and we'll coordinate the rendezvous point."

Adams reached out and put his hand on the major's shoulder. "Sorry, Henry, you and the boys aren't going on this one."

Major Reins looked dejected, hurt, then angry. "What do you mean, we aren't going? Of course we are. If you don't need us in the air as escorts, then you're going to need us as gunners on the plane or to help with all this stuff once we're back on the ground."

Adams shook his head. "Captain Perry and I are the only ones going. He's not taking any of his crew, either. What we're doing is not exactly sanctioned by High Command. So besides being killed, you could be court-martialed."

Reins shook his head. "Do you think that really matters to us, sir? We're a team."

"I know." Adams smiled. "I'm willing to take this risk, but I'm not willing to let you or the boys take it with me." Reins started to protest but was stopped by Adams' raised hand. "No, Henry, it's a done deal. I appreciate it, and to tell you the truth, I'd have been a little disappointed if you hadn't protested. But you guys are just going to have to sit this one out."

"Yes, sir, but don't expect us to like it," Reins reluctantly agreed.

"Thanks, Doc. Now get the fellas out of here before someone from the real Army shows up." They shook hands, and Reins went back and gathered his men. Adams turned back to Avery. "Are you sure about all this, Griff?"

"Yeah, I am. We've got to stop them." Avery heard his own words and was surprised at how much confidence his voice had. For the first time in his life, he knew he had made the right decision.

Adams nodded. "Then your chariot awaits," he said, making a sweeping gesture toward the Flying Fortress. Avery walked up to the nose of plane and patted it as if greeting the family pet. "Hello, Lady," Avery said under his breath as he reintroduced himself to the plane. "I know you've been through a lot, but this could be the most important mission that you've ever flown." He patted the side one more time, then hollered, "Let's get this show on the road!"

Avery climbed in the side hatch and made his way forward to the cockpit. Ignoring his nephew's recommendation to sit down, Avery crouched behind Perry and Adams as they prepared to take off, wanting to see what it was like from the pilot's point of view.

Perry shoved the throttles forward. At the sudden unleashing of the powerful engines, Avery had to grab hold of the seats to keep from being thrown backwards. With tremendous acceleration, free from her normal heavy bomb load, the plane raced down the runway. In an instant, the blackness of the ground merged with the darkness of the sky. They were suspended in murky darkness. The only thing keeping them from being completely devoured by blackness was the dull glow of the instrument lights.

Avery had sent men on missions like this before, flying low into enemy territory, but now he was going. His stomach was churning, his heart pounding, and his mouth was so dry he couldn't even whistle. He was petrified, excited, and scared to death, all at the same time. Had those men felt the same things he was feeling now? It so easy to sit behind his desk and send people off into occupied territory, all in the name of helping the war effort. Had he known what it was like, would he have been so quick to send these men into action?

But he supposed that, like them, he would manage to push it all away and concentrate on the mission ahead. He liked to plan things down to the last details, to know what was going to happen, and have a plan to take care of it. But this was so different. He was taking an idea that hadn't even grown up into a full-fledged plan and running with it.

He was feeling like a new man, and he liked it. He only hoped those around him wouldn't pay the ultimate price for leaving the old Avery behind.

The excitement of the journey wore off, and boredom took its place. Avery sat on the floor with his back against the door that led to the bomb bay. He tried to go over the plans in his head but had trouble concentrating. The rocking of the plan and the steady drone of the engine made it hard to think and keep things straight. The next thing he knew, a hand was shaking his shoulder.

"Wake up, Griff, we're about an hour from the rendezvous point. Thought you might want to be awake," Adams said.

Avery shook his head, trying to cast off the last remnants of sleep. "I can't believe I fell asleep."

"It's good to see our Daniel so calm before we go into the lions den." Adams smiled.

"Thanks for waking me. We still have the Joan-Eleanor equipment on board. I'm going to try and raise Lincoln, the POW I was telling you about. If we can get his help when we break into the camp, then we've got a ready-made Army all set to go."

Adams nodded his head. "Good idea. You intel guys are always thinking"

"Yeah, well it's only a good idea if I can raise him on the radio," Avery said as he patted his friend on the shoulder, then went back to the radio room.

FORTY-THREE

MATT Lincoln was tired, bone tired. He'd been at Stein's house since early afternoon, and it was well past midnight. Stein had thrown a large dinner party with ten guests: five officers and their wives. Lincoln had to laugh at some of Stein's guests. For members of the superior Aryan race, they sure were ignorant. One older lady, the wife of a lieutenant colonel, could have been their spokesperson. She was in her late fifties and had the classic Hollywood look of a duchess or some other royal title that she draped around her neck like her fur boa.

She wore a light purple formal evening gown with a matching purple feather hat. Her diamond and pearl necklace and matching earrings looked real, but Lincoln would have bet they were fake.

At dinner, she stared at him and had actually touched his hand when he poured the wine. He thought it amusing and pathetic at the same time, that this woman of obvious wealth had never met a black man. She had wanted to touch his skin just to see if it felt like hers. A few others treated him more like a pet than a human being, not out of disrespect or to antagonize him, but out of ignorance. The only colored person most of them had ever seen was at the 1936 Olympics in Berlin, where a black man named Jesse Owens had stood their Aryan ideal on its ear by winning four gold medals.

Several times he wanted to just to say "yessa, massa or nossa, massa," but pride, self-respect, and the fact that he was a United States Army Air Corps officer made him carry his head high. The guests had long since gone, but he was still there cleaning up their mess. He had finished with the kitchen and was now down in the wine cellar, putting away a dozen or so bottles that Stein had left scattered about in his search for the perfect bottle to impress his guests.

Before he had started cleaning, he had set up the radio in hopes of hearing from Avery. He had finished sweeping and had stalled as long as he could and reluctantly placed the last bottle on the shelf. Just as he was reaching to disconnect the radio, it crackled with the sound of life.

"Hermes to Hades. Come in Hades."

"Hello? Hello?" Lincoln said softly. "Hermes?"

"Is that you, Lincoln?"

"Roger that, sir. Boy, a lot has happened since we talked last."

Avery shook his head. If he only knew the half of it!

"Listen, time is short. We're going to be breaking into the camp and need the soldiers organized into fighting units."

Breaking in? This guy must be nuts! Lincoln thought. "Copy. When?"

"Tonight."

"Tonight!" Lincoln almost shouted. "Nothing like giving a guy short notice."

"I understand. A lot has happened here on this end, too. Can you do it?"

"Yes, sir, consider it done."

"Thanks, Lieutenant, you have no idea how important this is."

"Lincoln?"

Lincoln whirled around to see a man standing behind him: Diederick Vogel. "What are you doing here, Vogel?" Lincoln asked in surprise.

"No. The real question is, what are *you* doing here?" Vogel walked closer to examine what the American was huddling over. "Well, well. A radio? I think Colonel Stein will be very interested to see this."

Lincoln knew what he had to do.

With nothing to lose, he shot up at the German like a cat on a hot tin roof. Lincoln's sudden move caught the German off guard. His fist sank deep into Vogel's midsection, sending him crashing into one of the wine racks. Several bottles fell and crashed to the floor. So much for doing this quietly, Lincoln thought.

Vogel reached down, picked up one of the shattered bottles by the neck, and pointed the jagged end at Lincoln. He sneered at the young black pilot. "I've always been curious to see if your blood was red as well." Vogel lunged forward, using the broken bottle like a knife. Lincoln side-stepped the charge, grabbed Vogel's wrist with his left hand, pulled the arm forward, then brought his right elbow crashing down onto it. Vogel howled in pain and dropped the bottle. Lincoln snapped his right arm back, breaking Vogel's nose.

The big German staggered back, holding his nose, blood streaming out. "Well, what do you know?" Lincoln said. "At least we know *your* blood is red."

Vogel charged, grabbing Lincoln up in his long arms, wrapping them around him in a deadly bear hug. Vogel tightened his arms, crushing the American like a giant vise.

Lincoln struggled to free his arms, wiggling like a fish in the grip of a proud fisherman, but the vise too tight. He could feel his head beginning to grow light; it wouldn't be long until he would pass out. Out of desperation, he swung the only part of his body that could move: his head. He cocked it back and fired it forward like the hammer on a gun, smashing into Vogel's chin with enough impact to loosen his grip. Lincoln managed to squirm one arm free. He reached out desperately to gasp something, anything, to hit Vogel with. His hand landed on a bottleneck. His fingers wrapped around it and he brought it up full force against his attacker's head.

The bottom rim of the heavy bottle smashed into Vogel's temple, and his grip relaxed as he died. They crashed to the floor, and Lincoln lay there for a moment, gasping for breath and thinking. If he hurried, he could clean up this mess, stash Vogel's body, and be back at camp and warn the others before Stein or anyone else was the wiser.

He had just started to roll the dead bulk off when he heard foots steps running down the stairs.

"What is going on in here?" Stein shouted, bursting into the room with a Luger in his hand. Stein's eyes darted about the room, first to Lincoln, then to his chief steward lying on the floor, then to the radio. Lincoln summoned his strength and finished rolling Vogel off him.

"I'll tell you what's going on here," Lincoln said as he slowly stood and brushed himself off. "Vogel here tried to kill me."

Stein frowned. "He tried to kill you? Why?"

"I was beat after the dinner party so I came down here to clean up. I was so tired that I crawled behind one of the wine racks to take a quick snooze. Vogel came down here to use the radio and must not have seen me. His talking woke me up and, when he saw me he tried to kill me so I couldn't reveal that he was a spy."

"A spy! It's more like you are the spy and he discovered *you*."

Lincoln laughed. "Come on, Colonel. I've been here for a couple of weeks, and in that amount of time I've been able to set up a spy network and smuggle in a radio? And in that same two weeks, what information of any possible value could I have gotten to pass on? But look how long has Vogel been around General Jaeger and Major Reinard? How much valuable information could *he* have accumulated and passed on?"

Lincoln paused for a moment, hoping Stein would buy it all. "Pardon the expression, but I'm dead tired, sir. So either shoot me now, or let me go back to camp." Lincoln held his breath.

AVERY leaned forward and turned the volume up. He had heard another voice and then the sound of something breaking. He pushed his headphones tight against his ears, trying to trap every decibel of sound coming out.

He heard the crashing and breaking of glass, the sound of two men struggling, a dull thud, then silence. He knew one of the two men must be dead, but which one? The seconds ticked by, then with great relief he heard the voice of Lincoln. He listened intently as Lincoln twisted the truth of what had just happened.

Good man, Avery thought, pin it on the dead guy.

Avery heard a voice so loud it startled him. "Hello, hello, who is this?" Stein demanded on the other end.

"Vogel, is that you? What the hell is going on? Do you have the rest of the information about Reinard?" Avery said.

"Who is this?" Stein demanded again.

"Where is, Vogel?" Avery shot back. "This transmission is terminated."

Stein held the headphones, then turned back to Lincoln with a shrug. "Your story is confirmed."

"Can I go back to the camp now? I need some sleep."

Stein waved him toward the door with his gun and Lincoln obliged, never having thought he would be happy to return to the camp. As he trudged up the stairs, he knew sleep would not be coming soon. His real work would start *after* he got back to camp.

FORTY-FOUR

"WE'RE near to the rendezvous point, but I don't know what to look for," Perry shouted to Avery, who was crouched behind the pilot's seat again. "I've never been this close to the ground behind enemy lines before, let alone tried to land."

Avery patted his nephew on the shoulder. "As soon as they hear the plane, they'll flash a light three times in rapid succession. When you see that signal, circle once and land. They should have both ends of the landing strip marked for you."

Perry nodded his head. "Roger." Perry slowly pulled back on the stick and brought the big plane up to five hundred feet.

Adams shouted, "Over there!" and pointed to a flashing light just off the right wing tip. Perry banked the *Red Light Lady* over and circled the light. It flashed three more times. Avery took his flashlight and signaled back, flashing twice to the ground. Moments later, four dull lights glowed in the dark, marking both ends of the runway.

"I'm no expert," Avery said, "but that looks like an awful short runway."

"Yeah," Perry replied. "And I bet it isn't paved, either."

Adams smiled, but Avery failed to see the humor in it.

"Hang on." Perry banked the plane around hard and lined up in the middle of the two lights. The roar of the giant engines turned to a whisper as Perry pulled back on the throttles, bringing the engines to a near idle.

The heavy bomber settled fast, as if the angels that were flying with them had gotten tired and jumped on the wings to take a rest. A loud buzz sounded in the cockpit. "What's that?" Avery asked, not really sure if he really wanted to know or not.

"Oh, that's annoying, isn't it? That's just the stall warning."

Great! Avery thought. Now the plane is about to stop flying like a bird and start falling like a rock, and my nephew has decided to quit his day job and become a comedian. Avery sat down on the floor and braced himself against the back of the copilot's seat. The engines roar to life again. The angels finished their coffee break, and the nose of the plane flared up and jolted twice as it touched down.

The makeshift runway was rough. They bounced up and down like mad, but Avery didn't mind. They were on the ground. Avery popped his head back up and watched as they rolled down the narrow, dark runway. He felt like they were in a giant box, with high forest on all sides. Even before the plane came to a stop, two men came running up along either side of the plane with flashlights, guiding them until they came to rest at the edge of the trees. The propellers hadn't even finished their last revolutions when a group of men descended upon them like a nest of ants swarming over a picnic basket. Perry opened the bomb bay doors and the ants wasted no time carrying off their treasures of wooden crates as fast as they could.

The three officers got out and watched their crates being whisked away. Avery spotted a lone figure approach from the woods.

"Hermes?" the man asked.

Avery smiled. "That's me. I'm Captain Griffin Avery. And you must be Zeus?"

"I am Claubert Merle. Zeus, if you will. I am so happy to finally meet you face to face." Merle shook Avery's hand, pulled him close, then kissed him on each cheek and hugged him like he was being reunited with a long lost son.

When Avery pulled back from Merle's kiss, he noticed the bruises and cuts on the Frenchman's face. "What happened?"

"A gift from the SS."

"Reinard?"

Merle nodded his head.

"How many men do we have?"

"I have eighteen able-bodied men at your disposal," Merle said with pride in his voice. "I would have had more, but the notice was so short."

"I understand. I would like to have had more time myself, but we'll make do with what we have." Avery watched one of Merle's men walk by, struggling with a large wooden crate. Even in the dark, he could see that he looked young, very young.

Merle spoke, reading Avery's mind. "Do not worry about him. He is young, but he fights for France and will not let us down."

"Is eighteen enough to take the camp?" Adams asked.

"It'll have to be," Avery replied flatly. "And I don't know if Lincoln was able to organize any of the prisoners. If not, then we'll just have to go with plan B."

"Plan B? I didn't know we had a plan B," Adams said.

"We don't."

"KEEP it down," Avery said as loudly as he dared. "Remember, you're supposed to be POW's so you can't talk . . . and don't walk so fast, you're suppose to be tired and worn out." Avery's voice was laden with irritation and frustration, but he couldn't help it. He was trained to look at maps, decipher codes, and, in the intelligence business, take two plus two and come up with five. He was not trained to lead men into battle, and he didn't know how to handle all the emotions that were running rampant through him.

Second thoughts chipped away at the pillars of his confidence. He was beginning to doubt the sanity of the mission and his capability to lead it. They had only twenty-one men to capture the camp, and he prayed it would be enough. He had no idea how many guards there were, but his men were heavily armed with pistols, rifles, and grenades hidden under their coats.

Their plan was simple. They would walk right in the front door. After all, how many people tried to break *into* a prison camp? Once in, his people would disperse and mingle with the camp population, distribute the guns, then overthrow the camp. After they had secured the camp, they would find Lincoln, who would take them to the hidden base. Then all they had to do was to capture the secret aircraft and the bomb.

Avery tugged at the collar of his ill-fitting German uniform. He was grateful that it was dark, so the gate guards couldn't see just how badly it fit.

Unlike Sizemore's clean and pressed uniform, this one had a couple of dark stains on the back. He didn't want to know what they were or how they got there—he only hoped that he would fare better with it than its previous owner. If he got killed, would they bury him in the German uniform or in an American one? He felt an overwhelming urge to dash back to the plane and fly home. He wasn't ready for this, he needed to do more planning, he needed to get more resources. What was he thinking? He felt like screaming at the top of his lungs.

Perry was on the left. Two more Maquis members dressed as German soldiers were on either side of the column as they led their Trojan horse up to the prison gates. Adams was on his right side and moved over to talk to him.

"Platypus," Adams said.

"What?" Avery asked, sure that his nerves had affected his hearing.

"Platypus," Adams said, like it was an everyday topic of conversation. "Have you ever looked at a platypus, I mean really looked at it? Ugliest thing I've ever seen. And they say God doesn't have a sense of humor."

Avery stared at the colonel, not sure whether Adams had gone crazy or he had.

"It's got the tail of a beaver, the bill of a duck, webbed feet, covered in fur, and has poisonous barbs. It lays eggs and yet suckles its young. And it has no external ears."

"What the hell are you talking about?" Avery asked in complete astonishment, amazed that his friend could even be thinking something like this before going into battle.

"And what do you call more than one? Platypus? Platypuses? Platypi? No, platypode is the correct term."

"Wes, have you been drinking? Snap out of it. We've got a mission to complete, a very important mission, and I need you to be thinking straight, not about some furry reptile."

"It's a mammal," Adams corrected.

"Mammal, reptile, I don't care. I need you to stay focused on the task at hand, not let your mind wander all over the place." Avery stopped. *Stay focused.* The snowplow of doubt ran into the ditch. *He* had to stay focused. *He* had to stay on task, or they all would be in trouble. Avery turned to his friend. "Thanks, Wes. I guess I was getting a little overwhelmed there, with so much to think about."

Adams shrugged. "It's easy to do."

"Do you mean to tell me that when you're about to tangle with a German fighter at twenty thousand feet, you think about the duckbilled platypus?"

"Me? No, as a pilot my life is simple. Only two bad things could happen to me, and that's all I have to worry about. One: one day I'll walk out to my aircraft knowing that it'll be my last flight in an airplane, and two: that one day, I will walk out to the airplane not knowing that it will be my last flight in an airplane. And besides, I don't think about the platypus; I think about naked women."

Avery laughed aloud. The sound of laughter was so out of place, yet it broke the chains that bound him and set his mind free to do what he needed to. Avery patted his friend on the back as they continued.

The small troop marched down the road, their numbers doubled by the shadows cast from the dull, soft light of the full moon. They were a mile away when they saw the tops of the guard towers looming out of the darkness. The towers looked huge and undefined in the dark shadows, something out of a nightmare. Rising up, they stabbed at the sky, threatening to puncture the moon.

The glowing searchlights atop each tower stood out like spires on a dark crown, their beams crisscrossing the compound, looking to expose the brave or the foolish who might try to escape.

As they drew nearer, light from the closest tower broke its pattern and moved its beam outside the confines of the barbed wire, sweeping the darkness from them. Avery shielded his eyes from the scrutinizing light, then swore in German at the guard and told him to turn the light off.

With a grunt, the guard shifted the light away and let it flood the crowd of prisoners. Soon another beam captured the group in its light as Avery walked up to the main gate and handed his papers to the guard.

Once again Avery was glad for the cover of darkness so the guard couldn't see just how nervous he was. They exchanged small talk and the guard, satisfied with the forged papers, opened the main gate. Avery drew a deep breath as he took a stepped across the threshold of freedom and entered into the confines of the prison camp. He and the others were now fully committed. There was no turning back.

The group passed through the main gate and entered into a holding area separating the two compounds by a ten-foot-high barbed-wire fence. The Trojan horse was now in Troy. They were in no man's land without cover. If they were discovered, there was no hope of escape. Playing the part of war weary soldiers, they all shuffled passed the guards.

With a deafening clunk, the gate closed and latched behind them. Avery fought down a wave of panic as he concentrated on the next gate and Adams' platypus.

Two guards approached from the other side. One fumbled with a set of keys while the other stared at the prisoners. With the searchlights bathing him in the limelight, he felt like an actor on the stage. Everyone was watching his every move; he prayed that this wouldn't be his final performance.

At last the key slid into the lock, and the gate opened. Avery, Adams, and Perry walked through first, followed by the first group of prisoners. As they filed in by pairs, one of the guards shoved the new "prisoners" in an attempt to hurry them along. He maliciously pushed one of the prisoners so hard the man ended up in a heap on the ground.

A revolver he had hidden under his coat fell out. Both men stared at each other. The guard recovered his wits first and shouted, then grabbed his whistle and started blowing.

Adams was closest to the guard and silenced him with the butt of his rifle, but it was too late.

Every spotlight in the camp cut across the darkness, eager to expose the intruders in the grip of their man-made daylight. The docile prisoners of war became soldiers at war as they threw off their coats, took out their hidden weapons, and began firing at the Germans. Bullets flew in every direction and fell like rain; soon men fell, too.

"Get the lights!" Avery shouted. The closest spotlight went black, but there was little time to celebrate as the guards in the towers sprayed the men with machine-gun fire. Three or four of the Maquis fighters on the outside of the group dropped without a chance to get out their weapons.

A big Frenchman threw off his coat and pulled the pin on a hand grenade. Before he could release it, he was hit by a hail of bullets from guards rushing in from the other side of the compound. The grenade rolled out of his fingers and exploded at his feet, killing him and four other resistance fighters.

Several prisoners rushed out of the barracks to see what was going on; they too were quickly cut down. The guards shot at anything that moved. The Maquis fighters spread out, seeking whatever cover they could find from the hailstorm of bullets.

"Come on!" Adams shouted, grabbing Avery by the arm and racing toward the barracks. Avery felt bullets chasing him like a swarm of angry bees. He dove the last few feet and hit the ground hard, sliding behind the barrack wall.

As he landed, he felt his right foot snap hard to the side. Had he been hit? He felt no pain but was afraid to look, afraid of what he might find. The side of his pant leg was covered with something dark and gooey. He was so scared he felt like throwing up.

Time stood still as he slowly reached down to see what was left of his foot. He realized that it wasn't blood that covered his pant leg, but mud. His trembling hand continued to examine his leg and ankle, and much to his relief he didn't find any holes or missing parts.

All those around him must have thought he'd lost his mind as he started laughing out loud. A large piece of leather was hanging off the heel of his boot where a bullet had ripped it off. Suddenly he felt foolish for letting his imagination run wild, but at the moment no one noticed.

"We're pinned down. We've got to knock out those towers or we're through," Adams shouted

One of the Maquis fighters, a tall, thin man who reminded Avery of a giraffe, leaned around the corner to shoot but was killed by cross fire from the towers and guards who were gathering at the gate. Before they had scattered, one of the Maquis had managed to close and lock the gate as the shooting started. By doing so it had locked them in, but it had also locked the German reinforcements out.

For the moment, it was a stand off.

Adams stuck his gun around the corner of the building and fired blindly in the general direction of the gate. "Anybody got any ideas?" he shouted. "It won't be long before they get that gate open and, when they do, we're finished."

"Can we work our way into the camp, away from the main gate, and get some guns to the prisoners to help us?" Avery asked.

"Negative!" Perry shouted over his shoulder between bursts of gunfire. "The way they have the towers set up, we're stuck in this row of buildings. We might be able to get one or two of us to the next row before they'd cut us down, but it wouldn't do much good. Those guns in the towers have all the entrances to the barracks covered, so even if we could get across, we couldn't get the guns to the prisoners."

"We've got to get out of here," Avery said. "There's too much at stake."

"I know," Adams replied. "But getting killed isn't going to solve anything, either."

Avery leaned against the building, shaking his head in despair.

The side of the building began to vibrate and the ground shook. An earthquake? Avery thought he was losing his mind now, too, but he looked around and everyone else had the same puzzled look on their faces.

Avery did a double take as he looked down between the long rows of barracks. One of the buildings was moving toward them. Now he was certain he had lost all his marbles. A deep rumbling settled into the pit of his stomach. It felt like his entire body was vibrating. Then, above the roar of gunfire, the explosions of hand grenades, and the screams of dying men came the unmistakable sound of clanging metal against metal.

"My God, it's a tank!" someone shouted.

Avery was no quitter, but what could they do against a tank? Despair and hopelessness weighed heavily on his heart. He didn't care if he lived or died. Any second, the tank would surely open up with its machine gun and cannon and finish them all off. His only regret was that he had dragged his friends into this maelstrom.

Staring death in the face, Avery thought he would see flashbacks of his life. Time spent growing up, his parents . . . Anna, but no. His mind was in the present. The only thing he saw was the tank and for a fleeting moment in his minds eye—a platypus swimming.

He watched in morbid fascination as the huge metal beast drew closer. He'd seen tanks before, but never in battle. They were awe inspiring and dreadful at the same time. Moving slowly through the shadows, their exhaust swirled between the buildings like a shroud of fog, adding to their mystic impression of power and terror.

The steel brute was close now. He could hear the engine rumbling. The clanging of the steel tread sounded like a leviathan's stomach growling for fresh meat and grinding its teeth in anticipation. It was just one row of buildings away now; the machine gun would lash out at any second, ending their desperate gambit. He could see in the shadows that the monster wasn't alone. No, two more were right behind it!

Why didn't they fire? They were close enough to hit them, even in the dark. New terror gripped his heart. In their cruelty were they going to run them over instead of shoot them? Crush them beneath thirty tons of steel?

The tanks surged out of the shadow of the last building and roared past them. Avery pressed himself against the side of the building and felt the hot breath of the exhaust as it rolled by him, missing him by less than two feet.

Within seconds, all three had passed and pulled into the middle of the compound. The first one stopped, flanked on either side by its companions. It raised its gun barrel and let loose with a clap of thunder so loud it nearly burst his eardrums.

It was the sweetest thunder Avery had ever heard. The three tanks were not their demise but their saviors: American Sherman tanks!

The first guard tower vanished, exploding in a white-orange ball of fire. The second tank pulled up and slammed on his brakes and fired its big gun. The tank rocked back and forth as the brake caught, throwing its aim off. The roof of the second tower disappeared as if a great wind had just scooped it off, leaving just the base. The guards manning the tower had just enough time to jump before the tank corrected its aim and fired again, leaving nothing but the four legs of the guard tower standing, giving it the appearance of a decapitated spider.

The third tank fired a round from its 76mm gun at the crowd of troops by the gate. The tank shell exploded in a white plume, then smothered the area with its machine gun.

Avery was dumbfounded. Infused with new power, he dashed out of the shadows and scrambled up the side of the first tank until he reached the machine gun on top of the turret. He swung the big .50-caliber machine gun around and began firing. He laid down a steady rat-tat-tat rhythm of fire in harmony with the small arms fire that was accented by the thundering boom of the tank's main guns. His fire kept the German soldiers pinned down behind their barracks, just as he and his men had been pinned only moments earlier.

Prisoners poured out of their barracks and picked up the guns of the fallen Maquis, as well as those of the dead Germans. Guard towers three and four were quickly destroyed, and two of the tanks went off through the compound followed by a growing army of prisoners. Many who followed the tanks weren't armed, but even in the dark Avery saw the pride in their eyes. They were happy to be back in the war and fighting for their freedom.

The first tank stayed in the compound and guarded the main gate, its engine at an idle like the low growl of a vigilant watchdog. The hatch opened and a captain popped his head out, took a quick look around, and climbed out. He jumped down and was met by Perry and Adams.

"Captain Brian Stokes, 5th Armored Division. Sorry to crash your party, but we heard there were Army nurses here. Who's in charge?"

"I am." Avery jumped down off the back of the tank and shook the captain's hand. "Captain Griff Avery, OSS, and are we ever glad to see you and your men! We don't have any nurses, but we'll sure find you some later. Listen, Captain, can you and your tanks stay and assist us? A couple of miles east of here is a small airfield and a secret underground German factory. We don't know what kind of resistance we'll run in to, but we could sure use your help."

"Secret base huh? Not a problem, Captain, but we'd better hurry. The Russians are in this sector and coming this way too. I'd sure like to get there before they do."

"Understood. We just have to find the prisoner who knows where the complex is, and we'll be on our way."

FORTY-FIVE

LINCOLN awoke with a start. Gun shot. Had some one else just tried to escape? The single shot was followed by muffled yelling, then by a volley of gunfire. He sprang out of his bed and rushed to the window. Their barrack was in the middle of the compound, so he couldn't see much. The gunfire was followed by the camp alarm signal, warning all the prisoners to stay inside their barracks or they'd be shot on sight.

The beam of a searchlight blanketed their row of buildings, and Lincoln heard more shouts.

"Hey, the guards are barricading the doors shut on the huts behind us," someone shouted.

Ben Taylor stood in front of Lincoln and cracked the door open to peer out. "Can you see anything?" Lincoln asked. Taylor stuck his head out, then turned back to Lincoln to speak. He was hit by a burst of fire from one of the towers.

Taylor was propelled backwards by the impact of the bullets onto Lincoln, knocking him to the ground. A moment later, the entire side of the building was raked again by machine-gun fire. The bullets had no trouble penetrating the thin wooden sides of the building. Bits of wood, mattresses, dishes, clothing, and human flesh were sent flying around the room as if in a giant blender.

Someone shouted, "Tank!"

The room grew quiet. Even the moans of the wounded diminished, and the gunfire turned to dull thuds as they listened intently to the advancing thunder. Now the stillness was shattered by a shout.

"That rumbling is the sweet music of an 1100-cubic-inch, 500-horse-power, V-8 Ford dual overhead cams and dual carbs. That's a Sherman tank! It's one of ours!"

A cheer erupted that did more than raise the roof of the barracks, it raised the spirits of desperate men and gave them a hope they had not known for months, even years.

The building rattled and shook, and dust drifted down from the rafters as the mechanical stampede rolled by. They heard the blast as the tanks opened up with their main guns. Soon the spotlights that had been shining down on their barracks went out.

"Come on!" shouted Lincoln. He threw the door open and rushed head-long into the yard.

The guards who had been locking the doors on the other huts were gone and, for the moment, they were the only ones out. Soon, more prisoners poured out of their barracks like a raging river, flooding the yard with a sea of men. Some milled around, trying to figure out what was going on. Most rushed to the front of the camp to where the shooting was, eager to get back into the fight.

Lincoln ran to the other barracks to free his fellow prisoners. The first barracks had only a bar across the door and was easily removed. The next barrack was padlocked. He started to yank on it, hoping the Germans in their haste hadn't locked it all the way. He gave it one good yank when someone inside shouted for him to look out.

Lincoln felt and heard the thunder of footsteps behind him. He had just managed to step to the side when a blur ran past him and slammed into the door, hitting it with such force that the board across the door in snapped like a twig, and the top hinge was pulled from the doorframe. The man shoved himself off the broken door and spun around, throwing a huge fist with such speed that Lincoln tumbled to the ground, scrambling to get away.

Off balance from the missed blow, the man caught himself and rose to his full monstrous height. Sergeant Karl King Kong Kohn smiled.

Lincoln sprang to his feet, ready to take on the challenge that had finally arrived. Kohn had made his life miserable from day one, and now was the last chance either man would have to face the other. Lincoln knew it wouldn't be easy, that he would have hell to pay for it, but he wouldn't turn down this fight for all the world.

He looked back at Kohn and returned the smile.

The men in the barracks ripped down what was left of the door and surrounded the pair slowly circling each other, sizing one another up for the final time.

Several men started to step in, but Lincoln called them off. Lincoln knew that Kohn outweighed him by at least eighty pounds and had a good six inches of reach on him, but it was something that he had to do. He didn't like to fight but had all his life, sometimes for pride, sometimes to prove a point, and sometimes because he had no choice. This was one of the few times he could remember that he really wanted to fight. He had to fight not only for himself, but for the entire camp now, too.

The only advantage he had over the man-mountain was speed. He would have to use hit and run tactics and wear the big man down. Lincoln began dancing around his opponent like Joe Louis, the heavyweight champion of the world. He stepped in and got in a few quick jabs that snapped back the German's head, but it only seemed to make his hands sore. Lincoln jabbed a few more times with his left. Confidant, he overextended a little with a hard right that missed.

Kohn seized the opportunity and delivered a thundering left to Lincoln's head that drove the American fighter to the ground. Before Lincoln could move, he felt two massive hands reach down and pick him up like a rag doll. With his left hand, Kohn held him up, pummeling him with his right.

So much for hit and run tactics, Lincoln thought, as he hit the ground again like a newspaper thrown by the paperboy. Kohn taunted Lincoln with racial slurs as he reached down and yanked him up by his arms.

Lincoln wobbled for a moment, then swung his head back and head butted Kohn. A sharp pain shot through his head. His head hadn't hurt so bad since the going-away party his brother had before being shipped out with the Marines.

The German staggered back but never lost his grip. Kohn shook off the effects of Lincoln's head butt, then smiled and head butted Lincoln back, sending the American sprawling back to the ground. He almost passed out from the pain but managed to retain a slender hold on his senses.

Kohn roared with laughter at the crowd, taunting them as much as he was Lincoln. A big British sergeant started to step in, but Lincoln shouted no through his gasps for air and waved him off. He dragged himself up to one knee, then with even greater effort, managed to push himself up and stand on both feet.

Kohn laughed. "You must be really stupid, black man. You were stupid enough to believe your government when they told you you could fly a plane, and stupid enough to believe them when they told you you were an officer." He reached over and ripped Lincoln's pilot wings off his shirt. "You do not deserve to wear these. You didn't earn them. You are nothing more than a cook." Kohn placed his massive hand over Lincoln's face and shoved him back down on the ground.

Something inside of Lincoln snapped. He had worked harder for those silver wings than anything else in his life, and he wasn't about to let him or anyone else take them away from him.

Kohn had his back to Lincoln, taunting the crowd again. When he turned back around, he was surprised to find his opponent standing. The smile faded from his face.

Kohn grunted and, with powerful, deliberate steps, he moved toward Lincoln, drawing back his right arm like he was cocking a giant crossbow.

Lincoln lunged forward, dropped to his left knee, and thrust out his right hand with all his might.

The body blow caught Kohn unprepared as Lincoln's fist drove deep into his midsection. Lincoln hit him with such force that the German doubled over in pain, gasping for air as he dropped to both knees. Lincoln staggered back up to his feet and looked down at his opponent. Kohn's mouth was open wide, gulping for air.

If it was one thing Lincoln had learned in all his fights, it was never gloat over one's opponent. Just finish him off. There would be plenty of time to celebrate later.

Kohn looked up at Lincoln. Lincoln unleashed all his fury, frustration, and vengeance into one pile driving blow that hit the German square in the jaw.

The big man dropped to the ground.

The crowd of prisoners exploded in such a cheer that it was a moment Lincoln would never forget. He had never felt so much pain or felt so good at the same time in his life. Everyone patted him on the back, and they all meant well, but there wasn't a spot on his body that didn't cry out with pain.

Soon the crowd dispersed and Lincoln managed to get to the steps of the barracks and sit down. He smiled to himself. His dad had never approved of fighting, but in this case he knew he'd be proud. Two men walked up to him.

"You Lieutenant Matt Lincoln?" one asked

"Yes."

"That was quite a fight you put on back there, son."

"Thanks."

The one man held out his hand. "I'm Captain Griffin Avery, and this is Captain Mike Perry."

"Nice to meet you," Lincoln replied, more interested in tending his wounds than talking to well-wishers. Avery could see that Lincoln didn't understand.

"Captain Avery, of the OSS. Hermes."

The light came on in Lincoln's eyes. "Nice to meet you, sirs. I'd salute and shake your hands, but I don't think I can lift my arm," he said with a weak smile.

"That's okay," Avery replied. "We can carry you the rest of the way."

"To where, sir?" Lincoln asked.

"We need you to take us to the villa where you've been working and to the airfield. They have a bomb capable of changing the course of the war, and a plane that's able to deliver it to American soil."

Lincoln tried to stand, but his rubbery legs were still recovering from their ordeal and didn't want to move. Avery and Perry each grabbed an arm and helped the stubborn airman to his feet. "The airfield is right below the camp. You can see the hangars and part of the runway from Stein's house. It's only a couple of miles east of here, but I don't think I can walk that far unless you two are planning on carrying me all the way there."

"You leave that up to us." Avery smiled as Perry helped carry Lincoln to the camp entrance.

"Is this our man?"

Lincoln looked up to see a colonel.

"Yes, sir. Lieutenant Matt Lincoln," Avery replied.

"A Tuskegee Airman. You boys do a great job. Well done," Adams said. Lincoln saluted as best he could, then shook the colonel's hand, his chest swelling with pride at the officer's words.

Adams continued. "Things are pretty much under control here. Most of the guards have surrendered, and those who didn't ran off into the woods. We broke into the armory, got more weapons, and we've set up patrols around the perimeter. The captain here is ready to roll, and he's going to leave one of his tanks here to watch the camp until the main body of his unit shows up. We'll take the other two tanks and about sixty well-armed men to the airfield."

"Your chariot," Avery said to Lincoln, gesturing to the Sherman tank.

Lincoln looked up at the Army captain sitting on the turret. "I've always wanted to ride on one of these things," Lincoln said.

"That's funny," Stokes said as he jumped down. "I've always wanted to fly in one of your hotrod fighters."

"It's a deal," Adams said.

Stokes grinned from ear to ear. "Okay, everyone, mount up!"

Both tanks were loaded up with fifteen men each on their backs, clinging to the tank like fleas to a dog, while the other followed behind the steel canines on foot.

FORTY-SIX

THE small advancing American tank column made good time until they reached the edge of the airfield where the Germans were waiting to mount their counterattack. Avery was leaning against the back of the turret on the lead tank with Adams, while Perry and Lincoln rode on the second tank. Those unfortunate enough not to have been able to hitch a ride walked directly behind the moving mountains, using them for cover.

The stillness of the air erupted. Every single gun from the airfield fired on the Americans. Avery saw sparks dancing like fireflies off the armor plate of the tank behind them, and three soldiers fell to the ground. Even with the roar of machine guns, he heard a sickening thud as the lifeless bodies hit the ground.

Their tank fired with a lunge. Avery half jumped, half fell off, landing face first on the ground, spread-eagle. Adams grabbed him by the arm as they dove into some nearby bushes. The two tanks fired in unison, and the concussion from their 76mm guns almost knocked them down again.

The tanks never stopped moving in their relentless push forward. The American soldiers spread out, finding cover wherever they could, and began returning fire. One by one, the German gun emplacements were destroyed by gunfire or run over by the charging beasts. Time and time again, the tanks were hit with 20mm and 37mm shells and everything in between, but their Detroit steel held.

The dreadnoughts lead the way and the soldiers followed behind, cleaning up the remaining pockets of resistance. After half an hour of intense fighting, the German defenders had either been killed, given up, or run away. Eerie silence hung over the battlefield like thick fog.

Cautiously, Avery, Perry and Adams, along with Merle and Lincoln, moved toward the end of the field and to the large hangar nestled in the side of a hill. The hangar door was open and stood like a gaping mouth. Avery crept up to the side of the hangar and peered inside.

The plane was gone and the hangar was empty.

But he noticed something.

Avery saw a dull glow, a razor-thin sliver of light, like the glow that slips out from under the crack of a bedroom door at night. This light ran the entire length of the back wall. His heart gained a little buoyancy. Avery grabbed his flashlight and shined it on the back wall. The tiny beam of light sliced through the darkness with the power of lighthouse's beam fending off the darkness to warn ships of a rocky coastline. Two massive doors made of steel were revealed: the entrance to the underground bunker.

The wall-length doors looked like gigantic vault doors of a fairytale giant's safe. Would he find Jack and the golden goose on the other side? Suddenly Avery felt a hand on his shoulder. "Congratulations," Adams said. "You did it."

"Thanks," Avery replied. "But don't congratulate me until we get in there and find the bomber still there."

"Over here!" Perry shouted. "I found another door." At the far corner of the vault doors was a small service entrance, dwarfed by its behemoth brother. With a trembling hand, Avery reached out and turned the knob. He was mildly surprised to find it unlocked.

Avery looked at his four companions, took a deep breath, then opened the door. The long tunnel he found on the other side beckoned to him like Moby Dick beckoned Ahab to his death. All thoughts of danger were forgotten as he stepped across the threshold.

They had stepped into a huge tunnel carved out of rock. The floor was smooth concrete, a gentle downward slope leading deeper and deeper into the hill. The walls and ceiling were rough; time had not been taken to finish them. Jagged peaks jutted out, showing where the rock had been assaulted with pick ax and dynamite. Two rows of lights ran down the center of the tunnel, doing a poor job of keeping the darkness at bay.

As they walked, Avery tried talking to Adams, but his words were swallowed up by the immensity of the manmade cavern.

They continued to walk in silence, descending deeper into the bowels of the earth. At last they saw a faint light. Avery's heart, along with his steps, began to pick up the pace.

Soon they emerged into a monstrous chamber. Avery stood with his mouth open like that of a small country child catching his first glimpse of a skyscraper. The main cavern towered sixty feet over their heads and was at least four times that square. For a moment, Avery envisioned himself as a character in his favorite book, *20,000 Leagues under the Sea*. Despite the size of the cavern, the air was hot and had a stale odor to it, an odor of grease and oil, cut steel, dust, dirt, and sweat.

Avery's heart froze as he spotted the *Nautilus*, or the underground equivalent of it. In the center of the cavern was an aircraft the likes of which he'd never seen. Avery stared at the plane as if he were looking at a three-headed cow.

Gaping at the plane in front of him, the realization suddenly hit him: his quest was over. They had found the plane before the Germans could launch it against America. He couldn't believe it.

He almost collapsed with joy as such a wave of relief washed over him. Taking a deep breath, he began walking around this technological wonder.

The plane was big. He guessed it at about the same size as the *Red Light Lady*, but it reminded him more of a B-29 Super Fortress than a B-17. It had a long, cylindrical fuselage and rounded nose, but that was where the similarities ended. Its most striking feature was the wings.

It looked like the engineers were drunk when they designed it and had put the wings on backwards. The wings of the jet Me 262 were slightly swept backwards and had a natural flow to them, while the wings on this big plane were swept forward, giving it an ungainly and awkward look, as if it could fly backwards.

There were no propellers. Avery knew this was the jet in the reconnaissance photos. It had two engines slung under the wings, one on each side, plus two more engines mounted to the fuselage, on either side of the cockpit. It was a dark drab green with iron crosses on the wings and sides, but no squadron markings.

"Not very pretty," Perry said, running his hands over the tail section.

Avery couldn't disagree more. It was the most beautiful sight he could ever hope to see.

A soldier appeared, dragging a short, round man in a white lab coat behind him. "Captain, I found this guy sitting in his quarters like he was waiting for us."

"Doctor Strovinski?"

"Yes, how did you know?" he asked in amazement.

"Never mind," Avery said, shaking his head. "Sorry to have spoiled your little party here, Doctor, but I guess you won't be dropping in on the Big Apple after all."

Strovinski stood with a puzzled look on his face. "Big Apple? Oh, you refer to New York City."

"Yup."

"Yes, well, I'm sorry. But General Jaeger left about forty five minutes ago."

Now it was Avery's turn to look confused. "What are you talking about? Where did General Jaeger go?"

"Why to New York of course," Strovinski said. "General Jaeger took the other plane to New York."

With the words "other plane" Avery was forever changed. In a crystallized instant, time ceased. From somewhere deep in his mind, a memory surfaced of a long-ago hour in Sunday school, where the teacher had drawn a vivid picture of the struggle between good and evil. Christ was suspended on the cross, hovering between heaven and earth, and as he inhaled his last gasp of breath in this mortal world, Satan was elated. He had accomplished his seemingly impossible mission of defeating the Son of God.

But in that terrible and horrific exhale, in that finite moment in time, Christ passed from the mortal world into His spiritual realm and assailed the gates of hell, sealing Satan's fate for all eternity. Satan went from the soaring highest of heights and plummeted to the deepest, darkest depths of despair.

He had really lost.

And so it was with the fate of Captain Griff Avery. On the inhale, he had won! But in the exhale, that split moment between the tic and tock of time's rhythm when Strovinski said "the other plane," Avery had lost.

It was as though the vast underground cavern was collapsing in on him, burying him in a grave. And it was fitting, Avery thought, that his grave be this big. It had to be this large to bury him and the huge blunder he had made. Only after several moments did his lungs overrule his mind and gasp for breath.

"What other plane?" he wanted to shout, but instead the question came out quiet and subdued, matching his state of mind.

"This plane was meant to hit London. General Jaeger took the smaller one to bomb New York."

Adams and Avery looked at each other.

"I-I didn't know," Avery stammered. "How was I supposed to know there were two planes? I didn't know!"

"Take it easy, Griff," Adams said, placing a hand on his friend's shoulder. "Nobody is blaming you. I think it's a miracle that we got this far and saved London from being bombed."

Avery didn't answer. His mind was in a stupor. Somewhere deep in his thoughts, he knew that Adams was right. It wasn't his fault, but logic didn't keep him from feeling like a failure. They had come so close. Just one hour sooner, and they could have stopped everything. One lousy hour!

The image of Anna's lifeless eyes flashed through his mind, but there was something different about the way they looked at him. They weren't blank, empty discs. They seemed to urge him on. Her eyes weren't calling out for revenge, or even justice, but were filled with compassion, urging him not to give up on the situation or himself.

"Where's Major Reinard?" he suddenly demanded, a plan formulating in his head.

"I think he went back to Gestapo headquarters," Strovinski said. "He knew you Americans were coming, and he said he had to take care of a few last minute details."

"Details, I bet! Mike, I need you to stay and take care of everything here. Nothing, I mean *nothing* leaves this base until I get back. Wes, Claubert, I need you two with me."

"Where are we going?" Adams asked.

"To Gestapo headquarters."

"Great. First we break into a German POW camp, and now we're going into Gestapo headquarters," Adams mused.

"Can I come, Captain?" Lincoln said. "I'm feeling much better now, and you might need an extra hand."

Avery thought for a moment and nodded his head. "Yeah, I think we can use you on this one."

FORTY-SEVEN

AS they emerged from the depths and stepped outside the hangar, Avery took a deep breath. The night air felt good.

"There," Avery said, pointing to a car just off to the side of the hangar. "I thought I saw a car on our way down. This will do just fine to get us into town."

"Look at this thing," Adams said, running his hand over the fenders. "This must be Jaeger's. Even Eisenhower doesn't ride in a car this nice."

"Claubert, I'll need you to drive. Do you know where Gestapo head-quarters is?" Avery asked.

Merle stiffened a little. The blood on the wall, the scratches carved on the table and the sounds, the horrible, terrible screams of people in agony. "Yes, I know how to get there," he replied softly.

It was a short drive into town, and off in the distance, they saw the glow of burning fires, a sign of the advancing American Army. On the outskirts of town, they passed a large German troop column leaving the city in hurry. The soldiers looked tired and worn out in their torn, dirty uniforms. Most looked like they hadn't had a bath in weeks. They looked more like a column of refugees than a column of soldiers. But more noticeable than all of that was the look of defeat in their eyes. It could be seen in the face of nearly every soldier they passed.

Avery couldn't help but notice how young the soldiers looked; some didn't appear to be more than fifteen or sixteen years old. Had Hitler become so desperate, or so mad, that he would allow and encourage children to fight for him? Avery shook his head as they drove past. Then it occurred to him: what if the roles were reversed, would he find farm boys walking the streets of East Brooklyn to defend it against foreign invaders? Invaders? No, we were liberators, not invaders; we didn't start this war. But would the people of Germany understand that? Would they even care? He shook his head again. Questions best discussed over a tall pint in the local pub.

The streets of the little French town were deserted except for a handful Nazi staff cars and an occasional truck carrying the last of the fleeing German troops. A few people took advantage of the breakdown in law and were looting the stores, and the Germans did nothing to stop them. They were leaving. The only stores being robbed didn't have furs or jewelry, the luxuries of life. Instead, people were breaking onto shops that had the necessities of life: food and clothing.

The Grand Touring car pulled onto the main street and up to the old courthouse, now taken over by Gestapo for their regional headquarters. Avery cringed at the sight of the huge swastika flag hanging in front of the building. It was beyond his comprehension that the day could ever come when he would see a Nazi flag like this flying on American soil. He was going to do what he could to see that day never came.

They parked the car on the deserted street in front of the building and got out. Their cover story was that they were bringing in a POW for Major Reinard to interrogate.

Avery led them up the stairs, followed by Adams and Merle who escorted Lincoln. There were no guards. When they stepped inside, the foyer was empty except for a lone staff sergeant who looked frazzled and frightened as he threw papers into a box.

Avery asked him what he was doing. The sergeant looked up in surprise and explained that he had been ordered to get the files moved before the Americans showed up. Reinard, he said, was still here, downstairs. Avery glanced at Merle who nodded his head. He knew where Reinard was. Avery turned back to the sergeant and yelled at him to get out now, that the Americans were just a few blocks away.

The sergeant looked grateful and scurried out the door, leaving his pile of papers.

"This way," Merle said as he took them through the door that lead to the basement.

The sound of their footsteps echoed in the stairwell as they descended down the cold, dark shaft. Reaching the bottom of the stairs, they peered cautiously around the corner into the main hallway, which was empty except for something very out of place: music. Avery recognized the song, "Ave Maria," by Liszt. Its haunting, rolling melody seemed to float like a ghost, as it wandered through the deserted passageways.

"He was playing music like this when I was here before," Merle said. "He interrupted my interrogation twice so he could listen to a particular piece of Brahms." Merle shook his head. "Reinard does love his music."

The four men continued warily down the hall when one of the doors opened and Reinard stepped out, his face buried in a report. He glanced up but paid no attention to any them.

"You can't bring him here, you fools," he said, walking down the hall with his back to them. "Don't you know the Americans are on the outskirts of the city and will be here within the hour?"

"We won't be staying long," Merle said.

Reinard stopped.

He glanced at Avery, Adams, Lincoln, and finally rested on Merle. Merle! His eyes flew open wide in surprise and disbelief, but he quickly recovered his composure.

"Well, my dear Claubert, what a surprise it is to see you. And you have brought guests."

Lincoln and Adams grabbed Reinard by the arms. "Where do you want him?" Adams asked.

"Here," Merle said. "Take him in here." Merle opened the door to the interrogation room that Reinard had used for him. They shoved the German down into the metal chair. Reinard looked up at Lincoln and studied his bruised and beaten face

"Who did this to you?" Reinard asked. "I admire his work."

"Admire this," Lincoln said, sending his right fist across Reinard's jaw.

Merle sat down across from Reinard in his chair, sinking down deep into the soft, supple leather, a small, satisfied smile on his face. Reinard noticed the smile.

"Does it feel good to sit there my old friend?" Reinard asked. "To sit there and know that you have the power now, that you are the one in control?" He laughed. "The position of the chairs has nothing to do with it. Whether you are on that side of the desk or on this, you are not in charge and you never will be. You may be in control of the situation for the moment, but you will never be in charge.

"You are still that frightened old man who was in this very room not so long ago. The only difference now is you believe that since you have a gun, you have the power. I do regret to disappoint you, Claubert, but you will never be anything more than a frightened old man."

"Shut up," Avery said.

For one hot second, Avery wanted to lash out and kill Reinard where he sat, bomb or no bomb, but in that second he also had a flash of insight: Reinard was right. Reinard would always have control if one reacted to him. He took a deep breath, quenched the fire of hate, and prepared to do something he should have done from the very beginning: take control of the situation and not react to it.

Avery had a plan. Something that Merle had said earlier about Reinard and his music, he only hoped he could pull it off. He walked in front of Reinard, slowly clapping, then sat on the edge of the desk. It was not the reaction Reinard had expected.

"Very good, Major, I applaud you for your deductive reasoning and if nothing else, your inventive imagination. But I'm afraid I must point out a few errors, shall we say, in your logic.

"First of all, I don't think Mr. Merle here looks frightened to me. No, I'd say he looks more pissed off than anything else. And in my experience, it's best not to make a man who's pointing a gun at me any more upset than he already is.

"We can stay here and joust with each other all night, but there's a plane headed toward my country with some god-awful bomb on it, and I want your help in stopping it."

"You don't honestly expect me to help you do you, Griff?"

"How you leave this room is entirely up to you. You can leave as a whole man, in pieces, or carried out in a box; the choice is yours."

Avery stooped over and looked Reinard in the face. "Earlier you asked Claubert if the view was different from the other side of the desk. I think you need to ask yourself that same question."

"For me, there is no difference."

"Really?" Avery moved behind the major. "Take a closer look."

Reinard sighed and looked around the room. "I see the same four walls, the same ceiling and floor, the chairs, the desk . . ."

"There." Avery stopped him. "The desk, take a look at the desk."

"I already told you that it is the same desk."

"What do you see on the top of the desk?"

Reinard sighed again. "They are some scratches. This is pointless—"

"Look at them!" Avery shouted, grabbing Reinard's hands. "You know how these claw marks got into this table top. They were made by the men you tortured. And look," he said, placing Reinard's fingers into the groves. "They're a perfect match. And when these were made, you were on the other side of the desk. *Now* do things still look the same to you?"

"Really, Griff, is all this necessary?" Reinard said coolly.

"Well, Volker, yes it is, and it's 'Captain Avery' to you." Avery nodded his head and Lincoln joined him as they strapped the major's arms down, leaving his hand dangling over the table.

"Griff, we both know that this little show isn't necessary," Reinard said. "I have studied your file, and you simply don't have what it takes for this line of work. Besides, according to the Geneva Convention, to which may I remind you, your country subscribes forbids the torturing of prisoners of war."

Avery leaned back and roared with laughter. "Yes, that would be true if you were a prisoner of war."

"What do you mean?"

Avery smiled. "I'm not here on orders," he said. "I'm AWOL. Thanks to yours and Jason's handy work, my government thinks I'm a Nazi spy and that

I killed Anna. So right now, I'm not too worried about saving my career. Torturing you would be just one more charge for the court-martial. So let's see if we can put a few new claw marks in the table tonight, shall we?"

"I haven't the information you're looking for," Reinard said. His voice sounded confident but some of the arrogance was missing. "So even if I wished to help you, I could not."

"You're right," Avery said, nodding his head in agreement. "I am just wasting my time." He took out his KA-BAR knife and stabbed it into the table right in front of Reinard. "Last chance, Volker."

"A nice show of bravado, Captain, but I can tell you nothing of value."

"Very well then, remember, you had a choice." Avery walked behind Reinard so he couldn't see him. He would have to work fast. He pried his knife out of the table, reached down and cut off a thin strip of leather hanging off his boot where he'd been hit in the heel. He rubbed it in the mud covering his boot then took the knife, pressed the point of the blade hard against the top of the cartilage, and moved the back of the blade down to the earlobe, pretending he was cutting. He was causing pain and drew some blood, but did no real damage. Avery smeared blood on the piece of leather then threw it on the table in front of Reinard.

Reinard screamed, more of out of shock than pain, staring at what he thought was a piece of his ear lying on the table. "Are you still the one in control now, Volker?" Avery said with as much sarcasm as he could muster. "That's just the tip of your ear—you should still be able to hear pretty well—but the next cut will take it off down to the skull."

Avery took the knife and snapped the leather off the table so Reinard wouldn't have a chance to look at it too closely and leaving a nice trail of blood all over the table for effect.

"But then what does this matter to a man who is serving the Fatherland? I'm sure Hitler would approve. The next instrument for surgery will be this." Avery held up a fountain pen and admired it. "I'll shove this straight into your eardrum, and that will be the end of the life of your left ear, and if I still don't get what I want, I'll do the same to your right ear. You'll be completely deaf.

"We all know that this war won't last forever, but not to worry, I'm sure a man of your many talents will be able to find meaningful work after the war. There should be lots of people willing to help a deaf, former SS major. Oh, but then you won't be able to listen to your precious music any more, will you? I know how you like to sit for hours, listening and conducting the great symphonies, arranging the music, each movement to your own discriminating taste. I guess you can still do that, only the music you will hear will be the music playing in your head, and not on the phonograph. But if Beethoven could write music when he was deaf, then I guess you can listen to it deaf."

Avery walked to the middle of the room and tipped his head to one side listening to the music. "Listen to the power of the brass section, hear how it crescendos and is accented by the pounding drums . . . now hear how the violins seem to float on the air, giving great contrast to the beginning. Beautiful, isn't it? Mendelssohn?

"I admire you, Volker: your determination and fortitude. It's not everyone who would be willing to make such a sacrifice for the Fatherland, especially at this late stage of the war. All we need now is for the fat lady to sing, as they say. Oh, but you won't be able to hear her, either, will you?"

Avery held up the pen like a trophy. "Here's to the Fatherland!" he said, then shoved Reinard's head into the blood on the table and held it down as he brought the pen in front of his face.

"Wait!" Reinard shouted. "I-I might know someone who can help."

"Sorry, not good enough. I don't have the time or the patience," Avery replied then brought the pen up behind Reinard's ear.

"Stop!"

Avery wondered how many times this room had heard that same shriek before. Reinard was sweating, his eyes wide open with fear.

"What do you want from me?" he screamed.

Avery yanked his head up and swung him around. "That plane of yours out there is heading to my country, and it's carrying a bomb. The Luftwaffe uses a series of radio transmissions to triangulate and to tell the bombers when they're over the target. Since the plane is over the Atlantic Ocean, the only way you could do this is with U-boats. I want you to contact the subs and change their transmission beam so the plane drops the bomb over the ocean."

"General Jaeger will kill me!"

"Perhaps, but you *know* I'll kill you if you don't. At least with me, you have a choice."

"If I help you, you have to promise to protect me."

Avery sat back down on the desk. "Well, if the information proves to be useful, okay. But if it isn't, then you'll be dead by morning."

Reinard relaxed. "Now if you'll release me, we can get on with this."

"Where to?"

"My office, it's just down the hall."

"Claubert," Avery said, "hand me your first aid kit please. I wouldn't want to track blood all over this beautiful floor." Merle tossed him the kit and Avery wrapped the gauze around the German's head so Reinard couldn't touch his ear and see that it really wasn't cut.

Avery released him and the group walked down the hall to Reinard's office. Opening the door and stepping into the office was like stepping into another world. Avery marveled that such a place of beauty could be tucked away in such ugliness. The walls were paneled in rich mahogany and inlaid with delicate hand carvings. A beautiful tapestry adorned the right wall, an oil painting of Hitler hung on the other, and a large Nazi flag hung behind the desk. Also on the back wall in the corner was a small, well-stocked bar.

Reinard walked into his office like it was business as usual. "Help yourself to a drink, gentleman," Reinard said as he sat down at his desk and opened the bottom right hand drawer. He reached in and pulled out an Enigma decoding machine, placed it on the top of his desk, then sat there with his hands folded.

"Captain, I have been thinking. I believe it is time to renegotiate our arrangement."

"Negotiate what? You either help us or you go deaf for the rest of your life . . . and if you keep this up, that won't be very long."

"Yes, well, it seems to me that I am your only hope in averting the devastation that is about to befall your wonderful country. If this were not so, you wouldn't have made a deal with the devil, so to speak. I think this is a situation where we can both get what we want."

"I'm listening," Avery said suspiciously.

"I'm a simple man and have so few needs. All I require is safe passage to the United States and a modest pension to see me through my old age. After all, how much are all the American lives worth that I'm about to save?"

"I don't have time for this," Avery said as he took out his knife.

"Come now, Griff, is what I'm asking for all that outrageous? You'll be a hero, not only for saving the lives of countless Americans but for bringing me in as well. I can provide detailed information on my spy ring, and I also have information that will be helpful with your war in the Pacific with the Japanese."

Avery considered what Reinard was proposing and agreed.

"What?" Adams shouted. "While you two were talking, I found six jail cells in the back that have thirty to forty prisoners in them. Most of them looked banged up, and there were a couple that I couldn't tell if they were alive or dead. You can't make a deal with this man. He needs to stand trial and pay for his crimes, not be set up in some cabin by the lake in upstate New York."

Avery turned and faced Adams. "I'm sorry, Colonel, but we don't have time to debate this. This is my mission and my decision. I don't like it any better than you do, but I need the information that Reinard has. If I have to make a deal in order to save thousands of lives, and it leaves a bad taste in your mouth, I'm sorry, but so be it!"

Avery turned back toward Reinard. "Wipe that smile off your face," he snapped. "And if you try to double cross me, I'll turn you over to the colonel here."

Reinard held up his hand. "There is no further need for threats, Griff. We shall both get what we want." He turned back to the Enigma machine and pulled out a sheet of paper that was taped to the bottom of the drawer. "I know that you and the British have long since broken the Enigma codes, so this is a code within a code that I devised between myself and my operatives.

"Griff, if you will come and stand behind me, I want you to see the code sheet when I input the information. I want you to see that there is no sleight of hand or trickery here. I am sending the transmission to Peters, because my transmitter is not powerful enough to reach the U-boats directly."

Avery moved behind Reinard to watch him work. "What are you going to tell him?"

"That there has been a change of target because of a weather front. I will send him the new coordinates. The new setting should have the pilot dropping the bomb about twenty miles off the East Coast."

Reinard sat at the desk and began entering a code into the Enigma machine as if he were writing a letter on a typewriter.

The door burst open and four armed U.S. Army soldiers rushed in, Thompson machine guns raised and ready.

"Don't anybody move!" the lieutenant shouted. "Drop all your weapons now!"

Adams hesitated for a moment, as did everyone else.

"Do it," Avery said. As they lowered their weapons, Avery looked at the officer in charge. "This isn't what it seems, Lieutenant. I'm Captain Griffin Avery of the OSS."

"Move over to the left, sir, away from the major."

"You don't understand. Major Reinard is my prisoner and we're here on the most urgent of business."

The lieutenant reached into his left inside pocket and pulled out a photograph and studied it for a moment. He looked at the photo then at Avery and then back again.

"You're under arrest, Captain Avery, for espionage, treason, and for the murder of Second Lieutenant Anna Roshinko."

"Hold on here, Lieutenant," Adams said. "There's a huge misunderstanding here, and if you would just stop for a moment and listen to what he's telling you, we can all avoid a whole lot of grief later on down the road. I'm Colonel Wesley—"

"Yes, sir," the lieutenant interrupted. "You're Colonel Wesley Adams with the 222nd Fighter Group."

Adams nodded his head.

". . . and you're under arrest, too, for treason and theft of U.S. government property."

"We haven't got time for this!" Avery shouted. He took a step forward but stopped as all four Thompsons trained on him. "Okay, Okay." Avery raised his hands and took a step back. "You don't understand, Lieutenant. At this very moment there's a German jet aircraft bound for New York and it's going to hit the city with a new type of bomb that will kill hundreds, if not thousands, of innocent people. Major Reinard was sending a message to the pilot to change his orders and drop the bomb over the ocean."

"Let's see here," the lieutenant said. "Two American officers dressed in German uniforms, in a Gestapo headquarters, in the company of an SS major . . . and you're trying to *stop* a plot to bomb New York? And I have orders to arrest you for treason? Yeah, I'm going to believe that."

"Who signed the arrest orders?" Avery demanded.

"Brigadier General Sizemore."

Avery nodded his head. "Yeah, I figured it'd be him. I'm sure Peters put the general up to it, too, filling his head full of lies and misinformation about me. Wait until I get my hands on him—"

"Hey, can I get some help here?" Lincoln said, coughing in the corner.

"Who are you?" the lieutenant asked.

"First Lieutenant Matthew Lincoln."

The lieutenant looked through his papers and was satisfied that he didn't have any orders pertaining to him. "What happened to you?"

"These guys broke in to the prison camp a few miles from here and grabbed me. When I resisted, they beat the crap out of me."

He studied Lincoln for a moment then nodded. One of the soldiers put his gun down and reached into his bag to grab the first aid kit. As soon as his hand disappeared into the pack, Lincoln sprang into action, unleashing his pile-driver on the medic. The man was out cold before his head hit the table. Lincoln grabbed the Thompson and swung it around hitting the next man in the jaw with the butt of the gun, dropping him like a ship dropping its anchor.

Adams didn't need a program to tell him what to do next. He rushed the sergeant in front of him, dropping his shoulder, and slamming into him like a linebacker going after the quarterback. Adams grabbed the man's head and brought it down hard against the top of his knee. The man let out a cry of pain then collapsed unconscious to the floor.

Avery looked at the lieutenant in front of him, then took a quick step forward. As he did, he reached out with his left hand and grabbed the barrel of the machine gun. With his right hand he grabbed the butt, right behind the trigger, and yanked. The gun twisted out of the lieutenant hands and in one smooth action flipped around and landed in Griff's waiting arms. He enjoyed the look of surprise on the face of the young lieutenant.

"Sorry, son, I hate to do this," Avery said and snapped the butt of the gun across the lieutenant's jaw, sending him to the ground with the rest of those in his command.

"Not bad," Adams said.

"Thanks," he said to Adams then turned back to Reinard. "Did you finish sending the message?"

"No."

"Well, then, get to it."

"Sorry, Griff, I'm afraid I can not do that. I have just sent an emergency message to General Jaeger, who, if you didn't know by now, is the pilot of the aircraft. I told him that the security of the mission has been compromised and to disregard any further messages." Reinard leaned back in the chair, smiling. "You really did not think I would give in that easily do you? Besides, your American Army is here, and I will soon be safe in their custody.

"So, Griff, it looks like you failed again. New York will be bombed and you have no way of stopping it. You might as well keep on that German uniform, because ours is the only country now whose army you can serve in."

Avery shook his head and drew a deep breath. He didn't think things could have gotten any worse. Yet Reinard was right; they just had. His career, his very life, was all but over. He looked at Reinard and the smugness on his face was unbearable. He had failed.

Reinard put the Enigma machine neatly back into his desk, then leaned back in his chair, clasping his hands around the back of his head, wearing a smile that would make any dentist happy. "Yes, Griff, you have something to say?"

"You know, Major, we have a saying in the States: *It ain't over until the fat lady sings.* She's up on the stage right now, warming up her vocal chords, but she hasn't started singing, which means I ain't through yet, either." Avery started to turn away then turned back to Reinard and swung his fist, hitting the German in his jaw, knocking him out of his chair and sending his sprawling across the floor. "Oh, and I already told you once: don't call me 'Griff.' It's 'Captain.'"

Avery turned towards the door shaking his hand. It hurt like hell but was well worth it. "Come on," he said

"Where we going?" Adams asked.

"Back to the base."

"Roger that."

The three men quickly changed out of the German uniforms and back into their own. Reinard had picked himself up and sat in his chair, rubbing his jaw. He still looked arrogant and smug despite his position.

"What do we do with him?" Adams asked, pointing to Reinard.

"Bring him."

The group left the plush office for the stark surroundings of the hallway and interrogation rooms. "Where did you see those other prisoners?" Avery asked.

"Over here," Adams said, taking the lead.

As they opened the last door on the left, the Americans were hit with a stench that they had never experienced before. It was very familiar to the Frenchman: the smell of the decaying flesh and of hope long dead. Breathing was difficult because the air was so stale and stagnant. Avery had to fight the urge to vomit.

The room was very large, with six jail cells. The first cell on the right had about twenty men packed in it like cattle. The men were so crammed together they looked like bushels of standing wheat, unable to sit. As they walked by, staring in horror, Avery saw several of the men standing with their eyes closed; he only hoped they were sleeping. The middle cell next to it only had three men in it, but the last cell was stuffed beyond capacity.

On the left side, the first two cells were empty but the third had ten corpses laid out like firewood. In a daze, the Americans and their French companion walked slowly through the room.

"Reinard, where are the keys?"

The Nazi major walked to the end wall and opened up the center drawer of the small desk. He grabbed a set of keys and tossed them to Avery.

"Here, free your people," Avery said as he gave the keys to Merle.

"What about him?" Adams said, pointing at Reinard.

Avery turned to his French companion.

"Claubert, were you ever in the military?" Avery asked.

"Yes, I served as a corporal in a construction battalion for two years."

"Good." Avery snapped to attention, and out of reflex, Merle stood up straighter. "As an officer in the United States Army, I am hereby giving you a battlefield commission to the rank of Second Lieutenant. Since we are in your country and you are the senior-ranking officer of that country in my presence, and since we are allies, I am turning over to you my prisoner of war.

"You are free to handle the prisoner in any manner you see fit under your command." Avery relaxed his stance a bit. "If I am not mistaken, this was once a courthouse, a place of justice. I suggest that you and your countrymen dispense some justice of your own."

"What!" Reinard shouted. "You can't do that! I have valuable information that you need."

"What information? You already said that Jaeger won't listen to any further instructions, so what's the point?"

"I have other information that you would find very useful."

"I doubt it." Avery opened the cell with the corpses inside and shoved Reinard in. "Gentlemen," he said to Lincoln and Adams, "this is now a matter for internal French security. Come on, we've got a lot to do."

"You know, Griff," Adams said as they walked out of the room, "Reinard probably does have some information you could use."

"Yeah, I know," Avery replied. "But he pissed me off one too many times."

Adams just smiled.

FORTY-EIGHT

AVERY stood on the steps outside of the city hall, drawing in a long, deep breath. The air was cool, sweet, and refreshing, a stark contrast to the dungeons below. And yet there was no mistaking the faint taste of death riding on the wind, the tang, the smell of gunpowder. Brilliant pops of light flashed around the city like so many flashbulbs at a news conference. Artillery from one side fired, soon answered in turn with a barrage from the other side. The thunder and lightning show from the dueling armies was an awesome spectacle in its stunning beauty and destructive power. Avery sighed.

They got in the car and raced back to the airfield. The road was deserted now, except for a lone rider on a bicycle wobbling down the road. As they passed, they saw the harried sergeant from Gestapo headquarters, pedaling as fast as he could. Avery smiled as they drove past. He might have been a German soldier, but inwardly Avery hoped he made it home, or at least to the American lines, and not into the hands of the Russians.

The sun had crested the horizon and was rising to reclaim the sky from a pall of dark shadows. As they drove slowly past the prison camp, raging bonfires were scattered around the compound, and singing could be heard as the prisoners celebrated their liberation. The guard towers that had once been glowing jewels in the camp's thorny crown now looked like used matches, their heads burned off with smoke drifting lazily upward.

Morning's light revealed the POW camp and exposed the carnage that had taken place on the airfield just a few short hours before. The area was strewn with broken men and machines, and blast craters covered the once-smooth ground. Some of them looked like open pit mines. The ground was covered with crisscross lines where machine-gun bullets had chewed long paths across the earth.

Avery tried not to stare at the carnage as they drove passed, but it was hard not to. Last night in the prison camp was his first real combat experience, his first taste of death. People had died next to him, but seeing the death and destruction here at the field was different. There was no darkness to cover the blood or to hide the distorted features frozen in place at the moment of death.

Even from a hundred feet away, he could still see their eyes. Some, like Anna, had blank stares. Death had come so quickly and unexpectedly they hadn't had time to react. Others had horror etched in their eyes, having suffered great pain or seeing the arrival of the Grim Reaper.

But there were also a few with an almost peaceful look about them. Quite an oddity in war, Avery thought. It was like they had seen the Pale Rider and welcomed him. No . . . they hadn't welcomed it, but weren't afraid of him. Were they the bravest? The most simple-minded? Or were they those who had faith in God and were ready, even happy, to meet their Maker? Avery sighed. He never realized that death was as complicated as life.

It was bad enough to see a whole man lying dead; it was worse still to see bits and pieces of men scattered about like discarded toys. Legs missing feet, bodies missing legs, hands without fingers. Lying next to one German soldier was an arm, separated at the shoulder. Its hand clutched at the grass like it was struggling to get back to where it belonged. Avery saw several helmets spread over the field and he fervently hoped they were empty.

Tiny wisps of smoke rose up from the charred debris, burning like incense, offering up prayers for the dead. American soldiers moved through the nightmare scene, some checking for those still clinging to life, others checking the bodies for information, and still others retrieving souvenirs. Collecting trinkets, perhaps—not so much to prove that they had beaten the Germans as to prove that they had beaten death.

Avery turned his mind away from the immediate death at the battlefield to the future death that would come if they didn't succeed with their mission.

If he didn't stop that plane within the next few hours, Reinard's prediction of thousands of deaths would come true. The Allied advance would be too little too late to change the outcome of the war if that bomb reached its destination. But try telling that to a grieving mother as she watched her baby die from radiation poisoning.

The entrance to the massive underground complex was just ahead, both the main hangar door and the large blast doors open. They drove into the hangar and straight down the long access tunnel to the main cavern. They parked the car to see Perry drop out of the bomb bay of the backward-winged bomber.

Avery sat in the car for a moment, staring at the big plane, a plan formulating at breakneck speed.

He'd had a lot of crazy ideas in his career and up until now, this mission had taken the cake. What he was thinking now would not only take the cake but the whole bakery, too.

"These jets are supposed to be faster than anything we've got, right?" Avery asked.

"Well," Adams replied, "if the one that took off is anything like the Me 262, then yes. I've seen the 262 in action, and once it gets going, there's no way to catch it."

"Nice wheels," Perry said as he came walking up. Adams just smiled.

"How's this plane, Mike? Can she fly?"

Perry shrugged his shoulders. "For as much as I know about German jet bombers, yes."

"How fast do you think it'll fly?"

"About the only dial I did recognize was the speedometer, and it pegs at one thousand kilometers per hour."

"Okay," Avery said, "since we don't have anything that will catch it, let's take one of theirs."

Adams looked at his friend. "You want to take this plane and go after the other one . . . and, what, shoot it down? You're kidding, right?"

"I'm not kidding. Why not? We can use the same radio beams to navigate that the Germans are using. And look," Avery said, walking to the back of the plane, "it's got a pair of guns in the tail. We sneak up behind it, drop down over the top and WHAM! It goes down in flames. New York is saved."

"Who's going to fly this thing?"

"Mike can. It's a bomber, and he's a bomber pilot."

"All the instruments are written in German. Can he read German?" Adams challenged.

Perry shook his head.

"I can," Avery said. "Mike can fly the plane, you can help him fly, navigate, and handle the rest of the technical stuff while I can translate the instruments and work the gun."

Adams shook his head. "I don't know, Griff, it's a million-to-one shot."

"That's right, but a million to one is still better than a million to none."

"Colonel, Captains," a shout came from behind them.

They turned to see a corporal standing in the doorway of a small office. The man reminded Avery of a walking bowling pin. He had a thin face sitting on a long neck attached to narrow shoulders. All his weight blossomed out into wide hips and thick upper legs.

"I've got something I think you might want to see, sirs."

"What do you have, Corporal?" Avery asked, finding it difficult to keep a smile off his face. He knew it was inappropriate, but after all that he'd been through, he was having a hard time of it.

"Over here, sir," the corporal said as they entered the office. "There's a chart over here on the table that's got the United States and other markings on it."

"Thank you, Corporal, that'll be all," Avery quickly dismissed him as he saw the map. As the door closed, the three officers smothered the map like maple syrup over pancakes.

"This is a navigational chart," Adams said.

"Look here." Avery pointed on the European continent. "This looks like their flight path." He traced the line over France, across the Atlantic, and stopped at New York, covered by an ominous red circle with an X through it.

"Too bad it doesn't show the subs' positions. If it did, we could send a couple of B-17s and blow them out of the water," Perry added.

"Let's see what we've got here." Avery grabbed a ruler and started measuring. "Okay, let's figure out if we even have a chance here. We take the total distance, which is approximately four thousand miles, and divide it by the cruising speed of the aircraft—which I'm going to guess to be a conservative three hundred and fifty miles per hour, since Jaeger will want to make sure he has enough fuel. So, Jaeger should be right about here." His finger landed on a spot in the Atlantic.

"The plane out there"—Avery tilted his head toward the hangar—"should go faster than normal since it's not carrying any bombs, right? So if we push it and fly at around five hundred miles per hour, we should intercept the general's plane here, about six to six and a half hours from now." He drew a circle in the middle of the Atlantic Ocean.

"Just that simple?" Adams said skeptically.

"Just that simple. You guys make these high-altitude rendezvous between bomber and fighter groups all the time." Avery could see less than convinced looks on their faces. He let out a heavy sigh then rubbed his forehead. "I know it's like looking for the proverbial needle in the haystack, but I'm not willing to let thousands of people die and the Germans get the upper hand just because it looked too hard and we didn't want to try."

Adams nodded. "I've always tried to teach my pilots to think and to fly with their heads and not to do anything stupid, not to push their luck just a little further and try to force the shot. And I've also tried to teach them that there are times, despite everything, you have to say to hell with it, and just do it."

Avery nodded and smiled. After a moment, he clapped his hands together in a show of camaraderie and turned to his nephew. "How long before we can get this thing in the air, Mike?"

"I guess it's ready to go now," Perry said. "She's all gassed and prepped for flight. If we hadn't of raided the place last night, it would have taken off this morning for a mission."

"Then it's a go," Avery said. "You two go get the plane ready, and I'll get the corporal to clear the area so we can taxi out and take off."

FORTY-NINE

AVERY rounded up the corporal, found a towing tractor, and hooked it up to the German plane. With less than two feet clearance on either side of the wings, exiting the tunnel was tedious and nerve-racking. The progress was so agonizingly slow that Colonel Adams ordered Avery to wait at the tunnel's entrance because he kept telling them to go faster.

Avery cooled his heels at the tunnel's entrance, leaning against the hangar door and smoking a cigarette. He heard the strained sound of the tractor as it struggled to bring the big plane to the surface. Slowly the big plane emerged from its dark womb like a new butterfly waiting to greet the world. Just as the nose reached the hangar doors, the sun broke out from behind a cloudbank, casting long, glowing shafts of light down onto the small valley, flashing its light across the wings. It illuminated the cockpit, filling it with light and life. A good omen, Avery hoped.

Captain Stokes' armored units had secured the POW camp. Word had spread fast of the discovery of the hidden base and the strange-looking aircraft. Four dozen soldiers milled around the runway, with more sitting on the hillside in front of Stein's house, enjoying the county-fair-like atmosphere, staring at the spectacle on the runway, wondering if anyone was really crazy enough to fly it.

"Look at that," Perry said looking out the windshield of the bomber. "We've got an audience."

"Yeah, no pressure," Adams said.

Perry sat in the pilot's seat, Adams in the copilot's, and Avery knelt behind them, a position he was getting used to.

Neither pilot moved.

"Okay, what are we waiting for?" Avery asked.

"You!" Perry replied. "I can't read German. I couldn't even guess which

254   PAUL BYERS

switches to throw to start this thing. The only things I recognize are the four throttle levers."

Avery scooted closer so he could get a better look at the instrument panel. "Okay, here are your flaps, these look like the temperature gauges, and here, I think these must be the ignition switches."

"You think?" Perry said.

"They are, really. They are." Avery tried to sound more positive than he felt.

"Okay, here goes nothing." Perry flipped the first switch and the left engine began to whine. It started out as a slow, low pitched whine but grew in intensity and became a piercing sound as the engine picked up RPMs. When the engine settled into a steady drone and they were relatively certain it wasn't going to blow up, Perry flipped the next switch, and the engine on the right wing behaved just as the first one did.

There was very little vibration coming from the two engines—a big contrast to the B-17, Avery thought. The noise was much different, too. With the B-17, he felt comfortable hearing the engines roar and vibrate. He much preferred the thunder of the Flying Fortress to the whine of these new jet engines.

With a little more confidence, Perry flipped the third switch and panic swept across everyone's face as the cockpit began to shake. Was the plane about to blow up? Had he accidentally flipped a switch that he shouldn't have?

He realized that it was only the engine mounted on the left side of the fuselage starting up. He flipped the last switch, and soon all four engines whined in unison.

Perry looked at his companions and took a deep breath. "Well, here we go." He shoved the throttles forward, the engines responding with a higher pitched whine, and the plane began to move. The awkward-looking plane picked up speed, going faster and faster down the runway. About halfway down, he pushed the four throttle handles all the way forward.

The plane surged at the extra power and left the ground.

Gently, Perry applied pressure to the controls to see how this beast handled in the air. He was surprised that anything with the wings on backwards could fly, but his astonishment soon turned to amazement at how well the plane actually handled. The controls took a lighter touch than those on the *Red Light Lady* and were more responsive.

"Find the altimeter and the speedometer," Perry said.

Avery scanned the dials. It had been much easier when they were on the ground and nothing was moving. Now every dial, gauge, and indicator light was either moving up or down or glowing.

"Here it is. We're doing about four hundred kilometers per hour."

"English, please."

"Ah, about 250 miles per hour. It's this one right here," Avery said pointing it out on the instrument panel.

"How high are we?"

Avery scanned again. "Ah, there we are, about one thousand meters . . . uh, I mean about three thousand feet."

"Already? Wow, that was fast! This ugly duckling is turning into a real swan. She's got power to burn, especially since we're empty; I'm throttling back to three-quarter power."

"I suggest you get us as high as you can, as quickly as you can," Adams said. "Anything much below thirty thousand feet and we're still vulnerable to fighter attack."

"Roger that." Perry applied full throttle again and pulled back on the stick, and they could feel the plane surge upward. "I could get used to this thing," Perry said.

"Ready to join the Luftwaffe, are you?" Adams smiled.

"Not quite, but this sure would make a great recruiting tool."

Avery looked out his window and was amazed, too, at just how fast this German bomber could climb. Suddenly he noticed three very high dots out his window. "Dots, I mean, bogies at two o'clock high!" he called.

Perry leaned over and caught a glimpse of them. "I see them, Griff. You'd better get back there and man the tail gun."

"What'll I do if they're ours?" Panic filled his voice.

"It's up to you if we shoot down our own planes in order to reach our target. I'll do my best to avoid them, but this is your mission. It's your call."

Avery nodded and started toward the tail gun. As he climbed through the empty bomb bay and made his way though the narrow fuselage, his mind raced as fast as the plane. Is this a mission to be completed at all costs? Can I shoot down and possibly kill Americans? The math said he had to, but that didn't make it any easier. He had killed Germans, but that was in battle and a necessity. Could he pull the trigger on American pilots who were just doing their jobs? He glanced at his watch, he had about two minutes to decide if he could or not.

"I got a bogey eight o'clock low, its pretty big, looks like a buff," said Lieutenant Stevens.

"Roger that, Stevens. Drop down and identify it. The lieutenant and I will provide top cover," Major Reins ordered.

Beyond Stevens' canopy, the three Mustangs flew in perfect formation, yet things were still out of place. There was a hole in the sky without Colonel Adams' plane. Stevens felt like a third wheel on a date, tagging along with Reins and Wiser without the colonel there. He was mad as hell when the colonel ordered them not to go. They were a team and it just wasn't right, but he respected the colonel and knew he must have had a good reason. Stevens pulled the stick over and sent his Mustang down like a shooting star.

"I see it, but I don't believe it!" Stevens said moments later in astonishment. "The fuselage is flying west but the wings are pointed east. The damn thing's built backward."

"That's impossible," Lieutenant Wiser added.

"And it's got no props, either . . . the damn thing's a jet! I didn't know the Krauts had a jet bomber."

"Well, they're about to have one less jet bomber. Stevens, set up your attack and take it down," Reins ordered.

"Roger that, with pleasure, sir." Stevens could see the barrels of the tail gun sticking out like the stinger on a scorpion, so he would be careful to avoid its venom. Best to aim at the right engine then rake his bullets up through the cockpit before he pulled up and out. If that didn't drive the beast to its grave, he would set up and make another run.

The German plane would go down.

Waiting for the perfect angle, Stevens pushed the nose over and started his run. How he wished the colonel could have been there to see it!

"THEY'RE Mustangs alright," Adams said. "One of them is dropping down now. Damn good angle, too. Do you have a shot at him, Griff?"

"Negative, he's too high. The gun won't swing that high and wide." Avery was both frustrated and relieved at the same time.

"Hang on back there," Perry shouted. "I'm going to try and shake this guy's first pass then shove the nose over and see if we can use some of this German speed and out run him."

Remembering what happened the last time Perry told them to hang on, Avery put his hands against the top and side of the fuselage to brace himself and mentally warned his stomach to behave. The plane lurched over on her side and Avery tumbled back to the cockpit as Perry pointed the nose almost straight down then reversed his course, flying the big plane more like a fighter than a big bomber. Avery banged his head against the side, sending up a galaxy of stars before his eyes. The quick maneuver worked, throwing the fighter pilot's timing off, zooming overhead without firing a shot.

"DAMMIT!" Stevens cursed as his intended target slipped and slid out of his gun sights. "Did you see the way that thing . . . moved?" Suddenly he had a wild and impossible thought.

"Need any help down there?" Rein taunted him. When Stevens didn't reply right away Reins called again, "Are you okay, Lieutenant?"

"No, sir. I mean, yes, sir."

Reins hesitated. "Okay, then we're coming down."

"No, wait!" Stevens almost shouted.

"No? Why not?"

"I can't tell you yet, sir; you'll think I'm nuts."

"I'm beginning to think you are already. What are you talking about, Lieutenant?"

"I can't explain it, sir. Please just trust me on this one. Please?"

Reins shook his head. "Alright, Lieutenant, this had better be good."

"Thank you, sir." Stevens let out a sigh, tuned his radio to the frequency he used when winging for Colonel Adams, then he prayed.

ADAMS watched as the American fighter pulled up and away. He couldn't see the squadron markings on the plane because it flashed by so fast, but there was something familiar about the way the pilot flew. And there were only three planes. Standard operating procedure called for a flight of at least four aircrafts. He made a decision, one he hoped wouldn't be his last.

"Captain, slow the plane down and lower the landing gear."

"Sir? We've almost got enough speed to get away."

Adams shook his head. "The other two are still high enough to drop down and catch us, and if they do, we're dead."

"Yes, sir." Reluctantly, Perry pulled back on the throttle levers and the plane began to lose speed.

STEVENS watched as the bomber slowed down and lowered its landing gear, the international signal for surrender. Stevens slowed his speed but kept a wary eye out for any trickery from the bomber. The next move was theirs.

"GRIFF! Get up here quick!" Adams shouted.

Avery banged his head again as he scrambled out of the long tail tube and back into the main fuselage. There were no stars this time, only a sore spot that he knew was soon grow into a knot. He made his way back through the belly of the metal bird as fast as he could, reaching the cockpit out of breath.

"Where's the radio in this crate?" Adams demanded.

Avery scanned the instruments again, but the panel looked bigger this time because of the urgency in the colonel's voice. "Here it is!"

"Good." Adams tuned the radio and grabbed the headset.

"This is Colonel Adams of the United States Air Force to unknown American fighters, do you copy?"

All they heard was static.

STEVENS wore a smile from ear to ear. He'd only seen a bomber maneuver like that once before, and the colonel was on that same plane last night when it took off. He didn't know how they had managed to trade their B-17 for a German jet. All he knew was that Colonel Adams was on that plane.

"Good morning, Colonel, this is Stevens."

Adams smiled. "I thought that was you. You're still not bringing your nose up quick enough after your passes."

"Yes, sir, begging the colonel's pardon, but what are you doing in that German bomber?"

"Are majors Reins and Wiser with you?"

"Yes, just a second, sir." Stevens re-tuned his radio and told the major about the colonel. Soon all radios were tuned to the tactical channel.

"Major, what are you doing out here? I thought I gave you specific orders to stay put!"

"You did, sir, but we were ordered on a fighter sweep this morning and somehow we got separated from the rest of the group. We were looking for targets of opportunity and somehow ended up out this way," Major Reins said.

"Yeah right. I ought to come over there and kick your butt," Adams replied.

"Well then, I'm glad that there's only room here in my cockpit for one, sir."

Adams smiled to himself. "Henry, we're on the most important mission of the war. We're still vulnerable in this thing for the next few minutes until we can gain altitude and speed. I need you, Luke, and Andy to give us cover until we're out of range. After that, see if you can somehow manage to find the rest of the squadron and get back home."

Lieutenant Stevens was listening along with the other pilots. What was the colonel talking about? Henry? Luke? Andy? The colonel rarely used their first names, and never once when they were in the air. What kind of mission was this, anyway? Stevens wondered. It was like he thought he wasn't coming back!

"Okay, sir," Reins replied, drawing the entire depth and meaning of the mission from just those few words. "We've still got our drop tanks, so we can go with you quite a ways."

"I'm afraid not, Henry. In ten minutes, we'll be faster and higher than you can fly. But in the meantime we'll enjoy the company of our little friends."

"Roger that, sir," Reins said with as little emotion as possible. He continued on in the most professional tone he could muster. "You heard the man, gentlemen: let's cover this thing like a glove."

"But, Colonel!" Stevens called.

"It's alright, Luke. You have your orders, son, we'll be fine," Adams replied.

There was such a strange finality in the tone of Adams's voice.

Stevens didn't know what else to say. He took the left side, Wiser on the right. Reins brought up the rear. He let out a heavy sigh. As they passed above the clouds, he couldn't help but see the shadow they cast, that their formation looked like a giant flying cross, befitting what seemed to be their commanding officer's last flight.

There was little chatter as the planes flew in formation.

Gradually, the German bomber began to pull away from her American escorts. Soon the bomber was little more than a tiny speck, flying higher and faster than the Mustangs could run, and yet they stayed. Reins didn't order them to break, and Stevens and Wiser didn't ask. They flew in silence for another half-hour, long after the plane had disappeared from sight, then reluctantly turned north, toward home.

FIFTY

FOR the next six hours, the only sounds were the high-pitched whine of the Junkers jumbo jet engines and the occasional call from Adams, giving Perry minor course corrections.

"Okay, I'm getting something on the radio directional navigation beam," Adams said. "General Jaeger should be following this exact same course as we are. The only variable now will be his altitude. I'm guessing he'll be at around forty thousand feet, and we're at forty-two. That'll put us in the best attack angle."

"How long until we intercept?" Avery asked.

"Mike's been a lead foot, and if our calculations are even close, we could run into him anytime."

"How about our fuel? Do we have enough to get back to England?"

"That's a good question," Adams said.

"That's not a good answer." Avery frowned.

"I really don't know. My best guess is that even if we find the plane where we expect too, shoot it down and turn right around, we'll still run out of fuel about two hundred miles short of jolly old England."

"Do we have a life raft?"

"Yeah, I found one in the bomb bay," Perry answered.

Adams leaned forward. "There, up ahead. Is that him?"

Avery leaned forward, straining his eyes to see what Adams was looking at. "I don't see anything."

"You'd better get back there and get ready. I'll let you know when we get close to his tail. Our plan is to go into a shallow dive and slip under, then pop up right in front of him. The element of surprise should give you a three to four second advantage to start shooting before he realizes what's happening and maneuvers. You've got plenty of ammo, so once you start shooting, don't stop until he blows up or a wing falls off. Anything less and he might be able to dive away and outrun us."

"What if I hit the bomb, will it explode?"

Adams shook his head. "No. It has to be armed before it'll explode. Now hurry up and get back there. This is going to happen a lot faster than you can imagine, so you need to be ready."

Avery nodded his head and started the long journey back to the tail gun.

After Avery left, Perry turned to Adams. "You know, he could explode the bomb if he hits it just right."

"Thanks, now I have one more thing to worry about." Both men laughed.

Avery was sitting back at the tail gun, holding the grips lightly. His pulse raced in his fingertips, and he waited. He wished he could be up front to see what was happening, but he had to be ready the instant they pulled in front of the German plane. Even though they were flying swiftly, time sure moved slowly.

With steady pace, they had crept to within a half-mile of their target and could make out details.

"Okay, Griff, get ready," Adams said. "We're about five hundred yards back and closing. This plane is weird-looking, so don't be surprised when you see it. Remember, as soon as it's in your sights, fire and keep firing until it blows up."

Even though they were at forty-two thousand feet and it was thirty degrees below zero outside, Avery was sweating. If only Reinard were here now so he could see the look on his face when he shot down Hitler's pride of the Luftwaffe.

"Okay, we're going to go under him now," Perry announced. "Steady yourselves, because we'll pull up quick to get you right in front of him."

Avery felt his stomach fall between his toes as Perry brought the plane up. As the plane came into view, he put the center of the cross hairs on the biggest part of the plane in the middle, at the cockpit. He looked right past the gun sights and into the plane. He aimed at the pilot and squeezed the trigger.

Nothing!

"It won't fire!" he shouted over the intercom.

"What do you mean it won't fire? Did you cock it?" Adams shouted back.

Cock it! *Idiot!* How could he have forgotten to do such a simple thing like cocking the gun?

Avery could see General Jaeger staring at him in disbelief out the cockpit windshield. It must have been quiet a shock for him, to think he was the only living thing in the universe at forty thousand feet, then see another plane appear right in front of him. Avery needed two more seconds before Jaeger would figure out that they were the bad guys.

Avery raised his right hand and waved to the stunned pilot. Dumfounded,

Jaeger raised his hand and waved back. As he did, Avery brought his hand down and pulled back on the receiver, cocking the machine gun.

And squeezed the trigger.

The yellow phosphorus burning on the tips of the tracer bullets stood out against the black skin of the target, making aiming a very easy business. The first few rounds seemed to bounce off the sharp slope of the nose but Jaeger, out of reflex, jerked back on the stick, exposing the underbelly of the plane. Avery watched them shred the metal skin of the plane like paper.

The German bomber tried to bank up and to the right in order to escape, but this only exposed more of the plane, giving Avery a larger target to shoot at. Smoke began pouring out of the right engine and pieces began to fall away. A stream of bullets sank into the cockpit area. Avery saw a flash, then another long trail of smoke, as the oxygen system in the cockpit caught on fire.

The fighter completed its turn and was diving away from its attacker now. The bullets seemed to be absorbed by the black aircraft as Avery concentrated his fire on the right engine. For a moment it appeared that nothing was happening, then he was rewarded with a huge billow of black smoke. He could see telltale flames coming out of the right engine. Now the engine exploded, tearing away the wing.

The black plane went into a flat spin.

Seconds later, the left half of the wing section sheared off, sending the center fuselage plummeting to the ocean like a flaming meteor.

Avery released the triggers, and the wild beast in his hands went back to sleep. He watched with little emotion as the flaming dart disappeared from the skies to be eagerly swallowed up by the vast ocean.

How curious: he had thought he would be doing cartwheels and dancing on cloud nine. Instead, he was simply relieved. From start to finish, fifteen seconds had passed. Avery's heart was pounding a mile a minute and his hands shook. He hated combat. He was in awe of the men who had to do this day after day. He would never complain about his desk job again.

"Good shooting!" Adams yelled over the intercom.

"Yeah," Perry added, "I think Billy had better watch out for his job."

"Thanks. Well, I don't think Billy has anything to worry about from me . . . besides, it was your great flying that put me so close I couldn't miss."

"Now let's see if that great flying of yours can get us home," Adams said to Perry.

"My pleasure." Perry gently banked the wings, and the big plane swung around and headed back to England.

Emotionally spent and with nothing else to do, Avery curled up behind the pilots' seats and went to sleep. He'd only been asleep for an hour when he awoke with a start, noticing the change of pitch in the whine of the engines. He'd been dreaming about Anna.

"What's wrong? Are we over England already?" he said, stretching the best he could in an airplane cockpit.

"No, but I think we're running out of fuel," Perry answered.

"How far out are we?" Avery asked, now fully awake.

Adams held up the map. "We're about three hundred miles southwest of England."

"We're losing the outboard right engine," Perry warned. "Griff, look for something that says 'fuel pump' or 'fuel exchange switch.' We've got to be able to switch fuel from the tanks, or we're not even going to make it as far as the colonel's finger on the map. I think I can keep this thing in the air with only two engines, but we've got to find the fuel switches."

Once again, Avery's eyes darted from one side of the cockpit to the other, desperately scanning the instrument panel. This time he couldn't find what he was looking for. "It's not here. There's nothing that says 'fuel' anywhere."

"Are you sure?" Adams asked.

"Yes!"

"We just lost the outboard engine," Perry said. "We're high, but not high enough to glide all the way back to England."

"Okay, if it's not on the instrument panel, it must be somewhere else," Adams said. Avery nodded and surveyed the entire cockpit.

"Hurry!" Perry said. "I'm getting a low fuel indicator light on the left inboard engine. I'm chopping the throttle back."

With a greater sense of urgency, Avery searched the entire cockpit harder than a drunk looking for his next drink. Just like that drunk, the shakes took over as he slammed his fist against the back of the seat, coming up dry. "I'm sorry, guys, but I just don't see anything that's looks even remotely connected to the fuel system."

"Okay then. I'm going to take her down while I still have power to maneuver. Colonel, break out the raft and life jackets and anything else you think we might need. And hurry. The third warning light just came on."

They scrambled for supplies on the doomed plane. "We're below ten thousand now, so you can take off your masks," Perry announced. Avery and Adams didn't notice it, but from twenty thousand feet on down they had been flying through a moderate storm. Rain pelted against the windshield like shotgun blasts and crosswinds tore at the plane.

"Get up here!" Perry shouted. "The last warning light just came on. We're going in hard." They broke through the heavy cloud cover at four thousand feet. "Hang on, this is going to be rough, fellas. There're twenty foot swells down there, and we've got a hell of a cross wind."

"What does that mean?" Avery asked.

"It means we're dead in the water ," Adams said.

Perry frowned at him then continued. "Look, see how the wind is blowing across the waves, ripping spray off the tops of each swell?"

Avery nodded.

"Ideally, you want to land against the wind. It gives you more stability, lift, and control. But in this case, we can't land with the wind because we can't land on top of the crests. We'd either plow into the front of a wave—and that'd be like running into a brick wall—or else we'd bounce off the top and come down, and the tail would catch and flip us over. We're going to have to try and land in between the troughs and hope a gust of wind doesn't catch our wings and flip us over."

"I agree with the colonel," Avery said.

"Oh, ye of little faith, we'll make it. Besides, look, it's a good sign: four red lights, just like the *Red Light Lady*." Perry smiled. Avery smiled, too. He knew that combat pilots were a superstitious lot, so he put his faith in the hands of an experienced combat pilot and his lucky feeling, because faith was all he had left.

"I'm going to set her down hard and fast, since I don't know how much fuel we have left. Griff, I want you to call out our altitude every hundred feet. Once we're down, get out as fast as you can. I don't think this thing will float for very long."

Avery glued his eyes to the altimeter. Counting the numbers down in a slow, steady rhythm, he felt like he was counting down a time bomb. At two hundred feet, Perry told them to brace themselves, and Avery turned around, sat once again on the floor again behind the pilot's seats, and grabbed on to whatever he could.

The German bomber raced above the waves that reached up to grab it. At one hundred feet, a gust of wind caught the plane under the left wing and nearly flipped it on its side.

Perry had just managed to level out when they hit the water in the deepest part of the trough. Water cascaded over the top of the fuselage, sounding like a freight train and enveloping the plane. For a moment, Avery thought they were heading straight to the bottom, but with agonizing slowness the plane pushed back the water and came back up to the surface.

"Is everyone okay?" Perry shouted.

"I'm fine," Avery said.

"Colonel, you okay?"

Adams was slow to answer. "Yeah, I'm okay," he replied holding his head. "One of my straps broke and I banged my head pretty good, but I'll be okay."

"Alright, let's get out of here," Perry ordered.

The plane was already beginning to sink by the tail as Perry yanked down on the handle of the emergency escape hatch right above the cockpit window. Twice Perry tried to get out the hatch and twice he was thrown back in the plane by the force of the wind and waves. It had only been thirty seconds since they'd crashed, and already water surged around their knees.

The plane rolled down on the backside of a swell, and Perry and Adams managed to get out and stood on top of the fuselage while Avery shoved the raft out after them. The plane rolled up the side of another swell, and Perry and Adams lost their balance and were washed off the fuselage. Avery was tossed back into the cockpit. The water was up to his waist, the sloshing waves in the cockpit making it nearly impossible to stand.

Avery felt the plane roll again as it slid down another trough, only this time it was different. The plane stayed in the bottom of the trough, too full of water to rise again. The plane wallowed for moment then started to sink.

The tail of the plane sank down, bringing the nose almost straight up. The only light filtered in through the Plexiglas nose. Avery stood on the seat with the water swirling around his neck, the ocean eager to claim the plane and its occupant.

It was impossible for him to climb out the hatch now, so his only hope would be to wait until the plane was completely underwater then swim up through the hatch. He was not a good swimmer, not even on a summer's day at the lake in just his swim trunks. Forget trying to fight a raging North Atlantic storm with heavy, waterlogged flight clothes.

Avery drew his last breath and watched the water sweep over the nose of the plane, closing like a giant eye. It grew very quiet. He aimed for the hatch then launched himself off the seat like a torpedo. He was halfway through the hatch when he was jerked to a halt. Something had grabbed his foot. In a panic he reached down and felt that his left foot had caught on one of the safety harnesses from the pilot's seat. He struggled frantically to free himself as his lungs started to burn and his eyes stung from the salt water.

The light slowly faded as he sank deeper and deeper into the Atlantic Ocean.

"WHERE'S Griff?" Perry shouted over the wind.

Adams tried to answer, but a mouthful of water choked out his reply. Adams swam toward Perry, who was struggling to inflate the raft. He grabbed the side and held on as another wave crashed over them.

"He was right behind me," Adams finally coughed out.

"I don't see him or the plane." Panic filled Perry's voice. "Where's the plane? I don't see the plane. He got out, didn't he? He had to have gotten out!"

"We need to inflate the raft!" Adams shouted above the wind, trying to distract his friend from the truth that his uncle was probably dead. "We'll look for him after we're in."

Perry followed orders. The two men struggled against an angry Mother

Nature and finally got the raft inflated. They dragged themselves in, then searched frantically for any sign of their friend, but the sea refused to cooperate. Cold and exhausted, they collapsed, leaning against the side of the raft.

"I can't believe he's gone," Perry muttered.

"Me neither."

"Can't believe who's gone?"

Both men turned to see a ghost clinging to the side of their raft.

"Are you some kind of fish?" Adams asked in amazement. "You were down there for a good two minutes! I didn't know you could hold your breath for that long."

"I can't," Avery answered with a grin. "But I am lucky." He held up one of the portable oxygen bottles that they used when moving about the plane at high altitude.

Unceremoniously, they hauled their friend aboard like an oversized flounder, and the three men huddled together to ride out the storm.

The storm raged the rest of the day, and twice their tiny vessel was flipped over by the unforgiving ocean. Upon seeing it would claim no more victims, the storm finally subsided in the early morning hours of the next day.

The sky was dull gray and the ocean was calm and serene. Avery awoke to find his companions already up.

"I feel awful," Avery said.

"You should see yourself," Adams shot back.

"Very funny. Do you have any idea where we are?"

"Somewhere between a rock and a hard place," Adams replied, but there was no humor in his response.

"What do we have for supplies?"

"Nothing," Perry answered. "Apparently the Germans don't believe in emergency equipment, and what little we had got washed overboard. We can live two weeks or more with no food, but water's a different story. Without water, our goose will be cooked in three, maybe four days at the most."

"Don't mention food," Adams said. "I'm starving."

"It's just as well, I guess," Avery said.

"How's that?" Adams asked.

"If we get rescued, I'd just stand trial for treason and murder and be executed anyway. I've got no way to prove I'm innocent."

"You OSS guys are such optimists. I trust you won't mind if I still hope to be rescued?" Adams responded.

"Sorry. Just feeling a little sorry for myself, I guess."

"Hey, look at it this way," Perry said. "You did manage to save New York, and eventually the truth will be known. Who knows, they may even name a high school after you."

"Yeah, Avery High. It kind of has a ring to it, don't you think?"

"Well, don't get too excited yet," Adams said. "But I think I see smoke on the horizon."

The three men almost tipped their little raft over again as they moved to get a better look. "It's a convoy, I think!" Perry shouted.

Avery thought for a moment. "Do you guys still have your IDs?"

They check and both men nodded.

"Okay, toss' em overboard."

"Why?" Adams asked.

"You, my friend, are a wanted man, and so am I . . . and I expect Mike here is, too. If nothing else, General Sizemore is efficient. We'll tell them that we were a long-range patrol that got disoriented in the storm and ran out of gas. Mike, you're the pilot, Wes is the copilot, and I will be the engineer/gunner. They have no reason to doubt us, so it's the perfect cover until we can get back to England."

With growing and eager anticipation, they watched the tiny dots on the horizon grow into columns of ships and become more steel than Pittsburgh could shake a stick at. But to their dismay, none stopped.

"Why aren't they stopping to help us?" Perry asked.

"It takes half a mile or better to stop one of those things, and they're not about to risk loosing a valuable cargo ship bound for England to a Wolf Pack for a couple of guys in a life raft," Avery said. "Don't worry, someone will stop." He hoped.

For the next two hours, the seemingly indifferent lumbering giants moved slowly passed them through the calm waters. Twice they had to paddle like crazy to get out of the way of oncoming ships. It was an odd feeling to see salvation so close, yet just out of reach; to look up and see crews waving and shouting good wishes, yet not have any of them stop. The convoy soon passed and they were left alone again, swirling in the dark waters churned up by the passing of three hundred ships.

"Looks like you might not get that high school named for you after all," Perry said as the last the ship disappeared over the horizon.

"Look!" Adams shouted. "A warship! A destroyer escort, I think, and she's slowing down."

"At last!" Avery said.

"It sure doesn't look very big," Perry said.

"Right now it looks like a battleship to me," Avery remarked.

"If you want to wait until something bigger comes along, we can always cast you back in the raft," Adams said with a smile.

"No, no, this will do just fine," Perry quickly replied.

A few minutes later, the ship pulled alongside and tossed the downed flyers a line. They were hauled on board like a net full of fish and reported to the captain. After several minutes of questioning, he seemed satisfied that they were who they said they were: the crew of a B-17 on a long-range patrol. Soon they were treated to a hot meal, dry clothes, and best of all, a warm bunk.

Within an hour of being rescued, all three were sound asleep.

FIFTY-ONE

PLEASANT dreams of home, loved ones, and thick juicy steaks were shattered by the klaxon calling the ship to battle stations.

Avery shot up in bed, hitting his head on the bottom of the bunk above him. He fell back down, holding his head, swearing, wishing a bigger ship had picked them up.

"What's going on?" Avery asked, grabbing a passing sailor.

"We're going to battle stations, sir. A sub just hit the convoy!"

Avery looked at his companions. "Do you believe it? What'd we do to deserve this?"

Adams smiled. "Let's get up on deck and see if there's anything we can do to help."

It was dark now, and off in the distance they could see several ships silhouetted by the glowing fire of the burning ship behind it. One of the freighters on the outside of the convoy had been torpedoed and was dead in the water. Flames leaped high into the air from the number one and number two cargo holds, and thick, black clouds surrounded the ship like a funeral shroud. The unlucky freighter was going down by its bow, pulling the stern out of the water. Avery could see the propeller still turning slowly as the ship clung hopelessly to life. The doomed ship stood on end like a ten-story skyscraper reaching up from the ocean.

It bobbed up and down for a moment like a fishing cork, then slid straight down. A terrible hiss followed as the water quenched the fires and cooled the red-hot steel. As the ship disappeared from view, Avery wondered if it had been one of the ships he'd waved at earlier in the day. He hoped the crew was all right.

Their little ship was picking up speed, preparing to charge into battle. Avery watched the crew scramble over the ship to their battle stations like a pack of kids descending upon an ice cream parlor. The *USS Larsen* was a Cannon class destroyer escort, just over three hundred feet long and weighing in at twelve hundred tons. The little warships were a stopgap measure by the Navy aimed at dealing with Admiral Doenitz's U-boats. They were quicker and cheaper to build than their full-size sisters, and they were ideal for dealing with the submarines. She mounted three three-inch guns, two in the bow and one on the stern, plus an array of anti-aircraft guns.

Her main weapon against the U-boat menace, however, was not her guns but her depth charges. The standard depth charge was twenty-eight inches long and eighteen inches in diameter, and packed a punch of three hundred pounds of TNT. In order to sink their underwater nemesis, the charge had to explode within ten yards in order to crush the submarines hull and send it on a one way trip to the bottom. The *Larsen* carried a hundred of these underwater bombs.

Up ahead they saw another flash. A second later they heard the explosion as another ship was torpedoed. The *Larsen* leaned hard to the right and increased speed again. Avery grabbed hold of the handrail to keep on his feet. For a fleeting moment, he thought the ship was going to roll over.

"They're onto something," Adams said, sensing the thrill of the hunt for their underwater prey.

The ship reached the area where they suspected the German U-boat was hiding, then slowed. The airmen heard a dull explosion from the back of the ship and turned just in time to see two geysers of water erupt. The ship had fired its first two depth charges.

The *Larsen* now steamed around in a large circle, hunting its quarry. They laid down two more patterns of depth charges, for a total of twenty, with no apparent effect.

Avery was in awe as the *Larsen* launched her barrages of underwater flak. White circles from the shock of the detonation appeared in the sea, followed by towers of water erupting seventy-five feet into the air. It was hard for him to imagine that anything could survive the destruction they were delivering.

But with no debris or oil slicks bobbing to the surface, an air of disappointment washed over the ship. The U-boat seemed to have escaped their grasp, and they turned back to rejoin the convoy.

A shout brought all attention to the stern of the ship as the bow of a submarine leaped out of the water like a trout after a summer fly.

The stern three-inch gun of the *Larsen* opened fire, but in their haste to fire the first round the shot went wide. The stern of the ship swung around so they could face their enemy. To the credit of the German gun crew, they were able to scramble on deck and man their own gun and fire a round just after the destroyer fired its second shot. The German gunnery was far more accurate, and their shell landed just astern of their adversary, showering everyone on the fantail with water.

The next volley from the *Larsen* landed only ten yards from their target, returning the favor by soaking the deck of the submarine. German marksmanship drew first blood when the next round landed just aft of the three-inch gun. The twenty-pound shell hit the *Larsen's* stern gun and ignited two of the three-inch shells waiting to be loaded. The fantail erupted in a ball of fire, destroying the gun and killing the entire gun crew. The ship shuddered from the explosion.

"This is not good," Perry said. "I don't want to go swimming again."

"Come on!" Avery shouted.

The three airmen-turned-sailors rushed to the stern of the ship to try and save their new home. The carnage on the fantail was worse than that at the prison camp. Smoke was everywhere and the heat from the rapidly spreading fire was intense. Debris, twisted pieces of burnt metal, and twisted, charred remains of bodies littered the deck.

Another German shell landed close to the stern, spraying the deck with water and shrapnel. The little destroyer escort struggled to turn, to bring her forward guns to bear, but the going was slow because the rudder had been hit with the Germans' first salvo. The submarine's captain was taking full advantage of the situation by steering the sub wide and staying on the outside of the destroyer's turn to avoid the wrath of her two forward batteries.

The Germans fired again.

This round was high and punched a hole through the smokestack, causing the ship to lose steam pressure and valuable speed.

"Mike, you and Wes grab that fire hose and keep it pointed on those depth charges. If they get too hot and explode, we're done for. I'm going to get in that 40mm tub up there and see if I can keep the Germans' heads down." Avery raced up the ladder to the platform right behind the knocked-out three-inch gun. Halfway up the ladder, Avery heard the German gun fire again and he instinctively pressed himself again the ladder. The shell landed at the base of the ladder, punched a huge hole in the deck, and ripped one side of the ladder off the bulkhead. The ladder swung to one side and Avery felt like Tarzan swinging through the jungle.

Although never all that good at the monkey bars as a kid, he now put any fifth grader to shame as he scampered up the rest of the broken ladder and threw himself on the deck, waiting for the round to explode. When he didn't disintegrate in a ball of fire, he said a prayer of thanks and scurried over to the gun tub.

Looking around, he found the ammunition canisters, ripped off the magazine tops, and loaded the twin 40mm guns. The 40mm shells were loaded into clips of four, and the magazines were hand fed into the gun from the top. He dropped in the first two clips, jumped into the seat, remembered to cock the guns this time, then took aim and squeezed the triggers.

The explosion of the gun firing was tremendous and it shook his seat. The noise was deafening. He saw a pair of earphones hanging on the side of the controls and put them on.

His first and second shots were well short of the submarine, so he walked the next few rounds in, watching the water geysers get closer and closer. As he squeezed the triggers, he was sure his next round would find its mark. But much to his disappointment, nothing happened, for he was out of ammo. Frustrated, he hopped out of the gun chair, reloaded, and started the process all over again. This time, his last shell managed to hit the stern of the sub, sending up sparks as it hit the metal deck. He ran out of ammo a second time and slammed his fist against his leg in anger; he would never hit the sub if he had to keep doing this!

Avery felt the heat from the flames that threatened to devour the ship. He glanced down and saw Adams holding the fire hose. Mike was helping him as they stood toe to toe in a Mexican standoff with the flames.

Thankfully, most of the smoke, black as the night, was carried off by the movement of the ship. Yet occasionally a gust of wind would drive it back to mingle with the twisted pieces of debris and smother the ship, almost as if in a competition with the fire to see which could consume the ship first.

Avery was just about to jump out and reload when he felt a hand on his shoulder. He looked up in surprise to see a sailor whose face said he was twenty-one or twenty-two, but whose eyes said he was a lot older.

"Don't worry, sir," he said quietly. "I'll load, you fire."

"Deal, son!"

Avery felt a new sense of power rushing through him. He fired and walked the rounds in again, this time hitting the sub on the fourth round. Now that he had the range and didn't have to worry about reloading, he concentrated on his shooting. He peppered the conning tower with several rounds, then went after the gun. He saw the shells explode and several German gunners go down. Someone had managed to get a spotlight on the U-boat, making aiming much easier. Several German sailors tried to man the gun, but with the help of his loader, he was able to either kill or keep them hiding behind the conning tower.

Avery heard two explosions in quick succession and thought the ship had been hit again. Instead, he saw two geysers of water erupt close to the bow of the submarine. The *Larsen* had finally turned far enough for the forward guns to fire. The next round from the destroyer came even closer, and the third hit the conning tower square in the middle.

German sailors poured out of hatches in the bow and stern of the boat. The submarine had been mortally wounded. He held his fire as long as the crew didn't try to move toward the gun, which none did. They were too busy abandoning ship.

The smoke was clearing now. Damage control parties took over and put the flames out that Adams and Avery's nephew had been able to keep at bay earlier. Avery saw the submarine sinking, going down by the stern. The bow pointed almost straight up like a tombstone, marking its own grave. It hung there for a moment as if held up by a rope, then the vessel slipped down and vanished beneath the surface, barely raising a wave.

Adams turned and looked up to his friend. "That's twice in as many days," he shouted.

"What is?"

"You shot down a German plane yesterday, and today you shot down a German sub."

Avery laughed and shook his head.

The next several hours were spent hauling German survivors out of the water and tending to their own wounded. What an odd thing war is, Avery thought. Only a few minutes ago he was trying to kill these men, and now he was trying to save them. As he reached down and dragged them up over the side, he couldn't help but notice how young they all looked. Were they really that young, or was he just that old? He felt that old.

Only nineteen Germans out of a crew of forty-eight made it out. They huddled together on the stern of the *Larsen*, many covered in fuel oil, some wounded, and all shivering from the cold North Atlantic and fear of the unknown.

Avery and his two friends leaned on the railing, totally exhausted. To the east, the whole horizon looked to be on fire. It was the first time he'd ever been at sea and seen the sunrise.

He thought of Anna and their first date, and of how much she loved sunrises. She would have loved this. The sky smoldered with color as the sun began creeping closer and closer to the horizon. The ocean burst into flames as the sun crested, merging her color and energy with that of the ocean, sending fingers of color racing through the water. The sun seemed to hang on the horizon for a moment, unwilling to be released by the ocean. Then she set herself free and began to rise, claiming her rightful place in the heavens.

"I miss her," Avery said quietly to Adams. Adams placed his hand on Avery's shoulder.

"Excuse me, sirs, the captain would like to see the three of you on the bridge right away."

The three turned to find a petty officer in a clean and pressed uniform standing in front of them. Avery did a double take: where had this kid been for the last three hours?

Beyond that, he wondered, why does the captain want to see us? Has he found out who we are already? Will he arrest us? He looked at Adams and saw the same concerned look on his face. With some hesitation they followed the sailor to the bridge.

"The three Army officers you requested, sir," the petty officer said, then turned and left the bridge.

The captain, a lieutenant commander, turned and looked at the three visitors aboard his ship. The commander was about the same age as Mike, Avery thought. He still had on his life jacket and a pair of large binoculars hung around his neck. His eyes were steely gray, but softened a bit as he spoke: "Gentlemen, I heard what you did today, and on behalf of myself and the crew of the USS *Larsen*, I'd like to thank you. Your actions probably saved the ship."

At those words, all three breathed a little easier.

"We were just trying to keep from having to swim again, sir," Adams replied.

"Well, be that as it may, you two with the fire hose helped keep the fires at bay until the damage control party could get there, and your shooting," he said turning to Avery, "gave us enough time to get the forward batteries trained on the sub. That was very good long-range shooting."

"I am a gunner, sir," Avery said with a small smile.

"I don't think it's ever been done before, but when we get to England, I'm going to put you Army boys in for the Navy Cross."

"That isn't necessary, sir," Avery said quickly. "We were only doing what we had to. Anyone of your crew would have done the same, if they'd been there first. Really, it isn't necessary. Speaking of England, sir?" he said quickly, trying to change the subject, "when do we get there?"

"We should be in coastal waters about this time tomorrow night and pull into harbor with the morning tide."

"Thank you, sir. And really, no medals or commendations are needed."

The captain shrugged his shoulders. "Suit yourself. Dismissed."

"Okay," Avery said once they were out on deck, "that gives us just over twenty four hours to figure out our next move."

FIFTY-TWO

JASON Peters sat nervously in the small one-room flat he'd rented under an assumed name. He'd rented it within three months of arriving in England after looking in a dozen different areas before deciding on the best location for his radio. He'd chosen it because it was situated close to the subway, the river, and a large shopping district where, if need be, he could disappear in a hurry if anyone tracked his radio signal.

He had always paid the rent two weeks in advance, and had been careful not to come there wearing his uniform. It was in a part of the city where no one noticed or cared when he came or went.

It had been several days since he'd heard anything from Reinard, and though that in itself was not that unusual, he'd heard some disturbing news about the hidden base being discovered. He drew another long drag on his cigarette, then crushed it out, having smoked nearly half a pack in the last half hour. Again he tapped his on-air code, letting Reinard know he was ready to transmit.

Then his wireless transmitter tapped a few beats, teasing him like a fisherman watching the tip of his pole bend with a nibbling fish. The boredom vanished as he sat up straight, waiting for the key to tap again. The seconds dragged on without movement, then tap . . . tap . . . tap-tap-tap-tap.

With a sense of relief, he listened as the proper counter-sign came in.

"YOUR last transmission said mission compromised, what happened?" Peters asked his contact over the radio.

"Avery stole the Ju 287 and apparently destroyed the flying wing somewhere over the Atlantic,"

"General Jaeger?"

"Dead."

"And Avery?"

"Unknown, but Zeus is dead. He was foolish enough to think he could capture me in my own headquarters."

Peters smiled. Reinard was never one to doubt himself; the man wore his arrogance like a well-tailored suit.

"Avery still a threat. I fear entire operation compromised. You are being recalled immediately. Do you have access to Avery's safe still?"

"Yes," Peters answered.

"Retrieve small red notebook if still there and contents of files marked 'Tom, Dick, and Harry.'"

"Acknowledged."

"All regular departure points suspect. Rendezvous Blue Moon Pub. Two kilometers south of Grimsby. Tomorrow night. Make contact. Sign: 'The ocean's currents look strange today.' Counter signs: 'The tides of war have washed upon the shore.' Speed is imperative."

"Acknowledged."

"Acknowledged. Over and out."

PETERS sat alone in the room, the tapping still clicking in his ear. Years of planning and hard work wasted—because a second-rate loser got lucky.

He grabbed his map and found Grimsby, which was on the coast 150 miles northeast of London. A large fishing fleet was harbored there, so a small boat going out to sea would go unnoticed by the British Navy. He would go to the office in the morning and leave for Grimsby by late afternoon, making a perfect arrival for a nighttime rendezvous with a U-boat that would take him home.

Peters returned his radio set to its hiding spot. He had always been cautious and thorough to a fault, but now there was no point. He would never be coming back.

THE next morning, he arrived at work, and all seemed normal. Perhaps Reinard had overstated or overreacted about the danger, he thought, then shook his head. Reinard might have been a lot of things, but an alarmist was not one of them. If he thought there was danger, there was danger.

No one paid attention as he slipped into Avery's office and shut the door. Peters opened the safe and searched for the red notebook Reinard had described. He found it under a stack of papers and thumbed through it. It looked like a simple address book. He doubted Avery was smart enough to have hidden codes in it, but Reinard had information he didn't. That's why he wanted it.

The other three files were also easy to find, and looking through those, he could see why the major wanted them. Combined, the files listed two dozen names of prominent resistance leaders and their string of contacts.

It was too late now to do any serious damage to the resistance movement with the lists. But there were also names of those sympathetic to the Allies living in Germany. Too late to stop the Maquis, but not too late to exact retribution.

He slipped the papers into his coat pocket, then shut and locked the safe. He went back to his desk and continued to work for another two hours, not wanting to arouse suspicion. He would take an early lunch and never come back. It would take him a good six or seven hours to get to Grismby, putting him there sometime after dark.

The new day would find him well on his way to Germany.

IT was a long drive on the winding coastal roads made longer by Peters' nerves. He just wanted the whole thing to be over with. He passed a road marker noting that Grimsby was ten kilometers ahead. He glanced at his watch; it was just past seven-thirty. A few minutes later, he spotted the Blue Moon pub off to the right side of the road.

It was an old pub and, even in the dark, he could tell that the building was beaten and weather worn. A "dive," as they would call it back in the States. It was perfect. Located by itself on the outskirts of the town, it looked the kind of place where a man could conduct business he didn't want others to know about. Peters stepped out of the car and shivered. The air had picked up a chill off the ocean, and it drilled into his clothes, driven by twenty-mile-an-hour winds.

He turned up his collar and rushed into the pub.

It was warm inside and, as he looked around, he was a little surprised at how crowded the dump was. More people meant less attention anyone would pay to a stranger. It was a typical fisherman's bar, decorated with the tools of the trade. Nets, fishing floats, and other maritime paraphernalia adorned the walls. Peters decided he would warm himself at the bar with an ale first, then start looking for his contact. His drink tasted good after his long trip, and he mused how much he would miss the taste of British beer after he was gone. He spun around on his stool and faced the room, taking another sip.

Peters had sipped away half his beer when one of the men playing darts lost and came over to the bar next to him and ordered a drink. He was dressed in a flannel shirt and had on the yellow rain slicker pants topped with a black, wool watch cap.

"Damn darts, I can't even buy a good throw tonight," the man said.

"Yes, I know what you mean."

"You play?"

"Just an occasional game here and there."

The man nodded, then ordered up a beer. They sat in silence for a few moments then he turned to Peters. "You come off the ocean today?"

Peters' ears perked up. He tried to remain calm and casual. "No, I drove in. You?"

The man nodded again. "Yeah, fishing was lousy today. It's getting so a man can't earn an honest day's wage anymore. The ocean currents looked strange today."

"I understand," Peters said. "Things are different now; the tides of war have washed upon the shore." He turned back toward the bar and took another sip.

The other man muttered, without looking at him, "Down the hallway to the left is the head. Just past that there's a door on your right, go through it. I'll be waiting for you there. Give me two minutes."

Peters didn't acknowledge or look up when the stranger left. He took a large gulp of his beer and tried to control his raging heart, pounding in his chest like a piston engine. He waited for the longest two minutes of his life, then got up and walked toward the hallway. With a trembling hand, he reached for the door handle, turned it, then slipped inside.

"I didn't get complete instructions," Peters said to the man sitting behind the desk. "All I was told to do was to contact you."

"What do you want?" the man asked.

"I need transportation."

"I do not have time for games. If you need transportation, a bus will come by in the morning," the man replied, agitated.

"I need transportation to Germany," Peters snapped.

"When?"

"Tonight."

The man laughed. "You don't want much, do you? Would you like to take a boat, or would you like to fly?"

Fly? Dear God. Now he knew where he recognized the man from: he was Avery's friend, Colonel Adams! He slowly backed toward the door.

"Relax, Peters," Adams said.

"I don't know what you're talking about!"

"What's the matter? Did you think you were the only operative Reinard and Jaeger had in England?" Adams smiled. "Yes, I know all about the secret base, the two jets, Strovinski, and the failed attempt at bombing New York. I was there when our good friend Griff stumbled upon it and ruined it all."

"Then why didn't you stop him?"

"Because I wasn't about to risk the long-terms goals of the operation for the likes of Avery. Besides, we won't have to worry about interference from him again."

"What happened?"

"He and his nephew are missing at sea," Adams said. "A little trouble during the night before we made landfall."

Peters couldn't hide the smile that covered his face. "That's one less thing to worry about. But if Avery is dead, why am I being recalled?"

"I don't know. You'll have to take that up with Reinard. It is a shame things didn't go as well at the OSS as we'd hoped. Tell me, did Avery ever suspect that you were a German agent?"

Peters smiled and shook his head. "No. I led him around the truth with a ring in his nose like a farmer leading his pet cow to be butchered. He was so trusting and naive, two things you can never be in this business. Besides, he was too busy trying to prove that his precious Anna wasn't a spy to do anything else."

"How very true. I must say that I admire what you did with Roshinko, very clever."

"It would have been perfect, killing her then him, making it look like a murder-suicide. There would have been little investigation, and I would have stepped right into his position . . . that damn V-2 hit and ruined everything."

"A pity."

"Am I flying out or taking a boat? I am anxious to get started."

"Actually, you're going by car. To the stockade."

Peters heard a familiar voice behind him and his jaw dropped to the floor to see Griff Avery standing behind him in the doorway.

"Surprise!" Avery said.

"Avery!"

"Hello, Jason. I can see from the look on your face that you're a little surprised to see me."

"I thought you were dead."

"Yes, well, the reports of my death are greatly exaggerated. In fact so were Zeus's. He's alive and well, too. You see, you're not the only one who can lead someone around the truth. You did a good job of setting me up, and I knew there was no way I could prove my innocence without your help. With a lot of persuasion, General Sizemore helped set up this elaborate little scheme in order to get you to confess. The whole time you thought you were talking to Reinard on the radio last night, you were talking to me.

"I'd like to thank you. You made a very nice confession and cleared me of espionage charges as well as of Anna's death."

"Yes, well nobody will believe you," Peters answered. "There's nobody here. It's your word against mine."

"Not quite." Avery smiled.

Adams opened the center drawer of the desk, showing Peters a tape recorder.

General Sizemore walked in with three MPs.

"I believe you know General Sizemore. Come on." Avery took a step forward.

Peters lunged and shoved him back into the general and the MPs. Before Adams could get up, Peters shoved him over in his chair then dove through the window.

The MPs caught Avery before he hit the ground and threw him back on his feet. He took three steps then dove out the window and chased Peters as Adams and the other went out the front door.

It was nearly dark, and a half-moon cast just enough light for Avery to see a shadowy figure running down the path toward the ocean.

"This way!" Avery shouted as he took off after Peters. Avery's heart hammered in rhythm with his feet as they pounded along the path.

Peters had a good fifteen-yard head start and disappeared around the corner. The hard gravel path soon turned into sand and running was difficult. Avery lost sight of Peters. He had just passed a large bush when something hit him from the side, knocking him off his feet.

"Surprise," Peters said as he swung his fist, sending a glancing blow across Avery's jaw.

Avery tried to roll with the punch but wasn't fast enough. He fell to the ground, coming away with a mouthful of sand. He tried to jump back up and connect with his own right, but it was too difficult to move fast in the sand, and he was too tired and slow to catch Peters off guard.

"What's the matter, old man?" Peters taunted. "Can't keep up?"

Peters moved a step closer and landed several quick jabs, drawing blood from Avery's mouth. Avery answered with a few jabs of his own. Only one really connected, snapping Peters' head back.

Peters sensed that his opponent was tired and moved in, throwing a flurry of punches, then moving out, using hit and run tactics to wear Avery down. Avery managed to block some of the barrage, but Peters was just too fast. Avery knew he had to get in close and use the only advantage he had: his weight. It was not an advantage he was proud of, but at the moment he was willing to use it.

He surprised Peters with his quick charge and landed a solid right to his young adversary's jaw, followed by a good left to his stomach. The pair fell backward to the ground, Avery on top of Peters. Avery sat on his chest and threw several good punches until Peters kicked his legs up, toppling Avery over into the sand.

Peters went back on the offensive and landed blow after blow to Avery's head. With each blow, he was being beaten badly and there wasn't anything he could do to stop it.

Peters stood up and gloated over his one-time boss, straddling him, holding him up by the front of his shirt. "There's no way you can beat me, old man. You couldn't beat me then, and you can't beat me now." Peter smiled, delighting in his triumph. "And by the way, I had your precious little Anna and was she ever so nice, uh huh."

Something inside of Avery snapped. In his mind's eye, he saw the blank look on her face as she lay dead on his couch. He had been only a few feet away and couldn't save her. He'd been helpless then, but not this time. Rage now replaced fatigue, and righteous vengeance replaced blood. At that moment, neither the gates of Heaven nor Hell could stand against his wrath.

With newfound strength, Avery's right fist shot up, connecting with Peters' jaw. In pain and surprise, the younger man staggered back, his arrogance carried away by the wind. Peters backed away. Avery plodded straight at his nemesis, his arms and fist moving like machines, swinging, blocking, smashing. Peters tried to come back with his own punches, but they bounced off the madman like pistol bullets off tank armor.

A mighty right hand collapsed Peters to his knees, numb and half-conscious, swaying back and forth like a blade of grass in the wind. Avery was a man possessed and he liked it. He liked the feeling of power and control. He wanted to kill Peters.

He had to kill Jaeger in the plane, and he had to kill those sailors on the sub, not because he wanted to but because he had to. Now, with Peters, he didn't have to kill him. He *wanted* to, and that scared him. He had to exorcise his demons before it was too late for him. A thought flashed to his mind: once again, the key was Anna.

He looked at Peters. "Yeah, Anna told me she was with you, once, when she first arrived—that's when she still thought you were a nice guy. She also said she was glad she didn't have her glasses on to see just how small it really was." With that, he threw the hardest uppercut he had ever thrown in his life. It lifted Peters up off his knees and laid him out in the sand like a log washed up on the beach after a storm.

Avery heard laughter and clapping from behind, and he spun around to see Adams. "How long have you been standing there?" Avery asked between gasps for breath.

"Long enough."

"Why didn't you help me?"

"I would have if you'd have needed it."

Avery collapsed to his knees. He would have smiled but it hurt too much.

FIFTY-THREE

The gavel came down with the thunder of Thor's hammer. It was over, finally over.

Captain Griffin Avery sat at the defendant's table with his head hung low. For the past week he had defended himself from a myriad of charges ranging from murder to espionage and treason, and ending with petty theft of government property.

He felt a hand on his shoulder. It was that of his co-defendant, Colonel Wesley Adams. He offered him a large smile and his hand. "Congratulations, Griff, you did it!"

Avery took his old friend's hand and smiled.

After hearing testimony and finding documents at the underground base, coupled with the confession Peters had made at the tavern, the tribunal exonerated him of all charges. Peters, on the other hand was quickly tried, found guilty, and sentenced to hang in three days. Avery speculated that Peters was rushed through the system for several reasons. One, he was guilty—it was at the end of the war, and the Army didn't want a spy trial to mar the victory over Germany; and, two, they didn't want the public to know that New York had almost been bombed.

In any case, Jason would pay for his crimes, both against his country and against him, and he would be there to watch. Claubert Merle came over and offered his congratulations, too. It was the first time the Frenchman had been out of his country.

Avery stood and began to shuffle out with the rest of the crowd, shaking hands with well wishers. Mike and the crew of the *Red Light Lady* were there along with Colonel Adams' pilots. He was even greeted by people he didn't know as they stepped outside onto the front lawn of division headquarters just outside London, which had served as the courtroom. Everyone soon broke off into their own little groups, leaving Avery standing alone.

He watched as the sun went down, turning the clouds brilliant yellows and reds and silhouetting the trees in the background. Merle walked up beside him. "This was Beka's favorite time of the day," he said. "In her uncomplicated way of looking at life, she always said that a beautiful sunset was God's way letting you know that no matter how hard the day was, something beautiful could still come from it."

Avery smiled. "Anna always liked the sunrises. She would tell me that God had painted the beautiful sky to show us that each day starts out beautiful and that it's our choice to do with it as we see fit." Avery paused for a moment, watching the clouds changing hues.

"Both are right," Avery continued. "Lets stop being so melancholy and celebrate their memories; I think they'd approve. Come on!" Avery slapped Merle on the back. "The drinks are on me!"

"And do you know what Beka would be saying right now?"

Avery shook his head.

With a serious expression on his face, the old Frenchman looked up and said, "Don't drink too much, you old fool, it always gives you gas."

Avery stared at his friend then burst into laughter. He put his arm across the man's shoulder as they walked. "Come on. Let's go make something of the day."

Author's Note:

Though Catalyst is a work of fiction, it is based on true events. All the aircraft in the book are real.

The Boeing B-17
Known as the Flying Fortress, it first flew in 1935, where a reporter, noting all the machine guns, said it looked like a flying fortress in the air. The nick name stuck. Originally designed for coastal defense, the looming war in Europe changed its role from defensive to offensive. Carrying a maximum bomb load of nearly 5 tons, with 12-13 machine guns and a staggering weight of 65,000 pounds fully loaded, it truly was a Flying Fortress.

The North American P-51 Mustang
The Mustang (front cover) was originally designed for the British before America entered the war. The Mustang was arguably the best fighter of WWII and the first long-range fighter that could cover the bomber formations all the way to Germany and back. It, as all fighters, were called "little friends" by the bombers crews and were always a welcome sight to see.

The Messerschmitt Bf 109
The Messerschmitt was first flown in 1935 and went through several variations throughout the war. With over 30,000 produced, it was the single most produced fighter in the world. The last 109 retired from the Spanish Air Force in 1967, a tribute to its design effectiveness.

The Focke Wulf Fw 190
Considered by some as the best German fighter of the war. Known as the Butcher bird, the 190 had a reputation of taking punishment as well as dishing it out, with some versions having up to 6-20 millimeter cannons. Twenty thousand were produced.

The Bombing of New York
In 1944, the Reichsluftfahrtministerium, Reich Air Ministry, issued specifications for a bomber capable of carrying an 8800-pound bomb load and reaching New York City and returning without refueling. Five German companies responded, but none met the requirements. Reimar and Walter Horten learned of the project and submitted their plans for the Amerika Bomber, designated the Ho XVIII A. Arguments with a committee of engineers from the other top German aircraft companies stalled the A model. Undeterred, the Hortens resubmitted another plan for the B model, with construction set to begin in the fall of 1945.

Horten IX (Go 229)

The Go 229 (front cover) was the brain child of Reimar and Walter Horten, pioneers of the tailless all-wing aircraft along with Jack Northup for the Americans. The Go 229 first flew in February 1945. Classified as a fighter, it had four 30mm cannons and a maximum speed of around 620 mph, with a ceiling of over 50,000 feet. The development of the 229 was actually delayed by the Amerika Bomber project.

Junkers Ju 287

The Ju 287 was perhaps the strangest and most radical design for the Germans in WWII with the wings sweeping forward instead of backward like modern-day jets. The prototype for this heavy bomber first flew in August 1944. To speed up production, the first version was a Frankenstein of aircraft with the nose wheel from a downed American B-24, the main landing gear from a Junker 388, and the rear fuselage from a Heinkel He 177. The factory was later captured by the Russians, and the second version was flown by the Russians in 1947.

The Tuskegee Airmen

The 332nd Fighter Group, 99th Squadron, were known as the Tuskegee Airmen because they were trained in Tuskegee, Alabama. They were real and were the first African-American fighter group. They could proudly boast of not having lost a single bomber under their charge to enemy fighters in over 200 combat missions, a record unmatched by any other fighter group.

JG 26 The Abbeville Boys

Jagdgeschwader (JG) 26 was a real German fighter squadron known as either "The Abbeville Boys" or the "Abbeville kids" by their American and British counterparts because of their base at Abbeville in Northern France. The official Luftwaffe name was "Jagdgeschwader Schlageter." They were known by their markings of bright yellow noses painted on during the Battle of Britain and for the gothic S painted on the left front of their aircraft.

Special Thanks to:

Chuck Conner
Lieutenant, Bombardier, 418 squadron, 100th Bomber Group and former
POW Stalag 3

Lisa Thompson
Photographer for The Grossdeutschland Division Living History Group.
Background Photo of German soldiers used for book cover.
www.grossdeutschland.com

Jan Riddling
Historian 100th Bomb Group (H)
www.100thbg.com

Andy Wenner
Graphic Designer, book cover
www.auroraartcompany.com

Mike Williams, ATC, USN (ret.)
Web page design
www.paulbyersonline.com

Video Production thanks to...
Col John Frisby, USAF (Ret.)
Craig Messerman

Pilots:
Col. J. "bombr" Frisby
Oscar "Osprey" Dillian
Carmine "Pappyb" Bassano
Ted "Tedboy" Camardo
Travis "Glickk" Stevely
Mark "wallyg" Walraven

Stan "blumax" Lull
Craig "c-flyer" Messerman
Doug "--bc--" Lord
John "breech" Smith
Andy "nookyb" Wenner
Paul "Vangrd" Byers

The pilots of the online Virtual Fourth Fighter Group
www.virtualfourthfightergroup.com

The Pilots of the Menacing Ferrets Fighter Squadron
www.menacingferrets.com

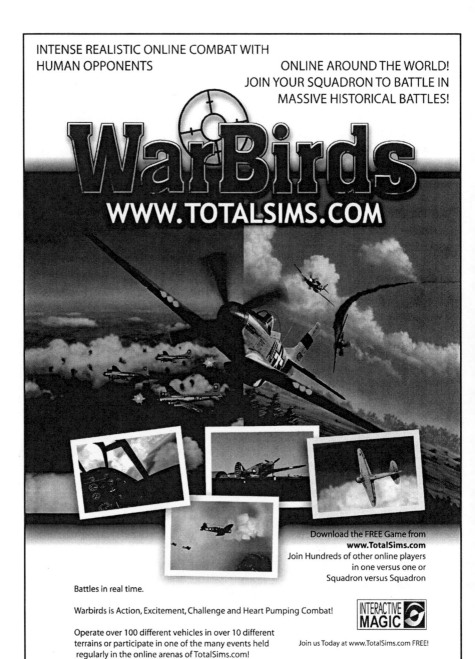

ABOUT THE AUTHOR

PAUL BYERS lives in Granite Falls, a sleepy little town north of Seattle. He's surrounded by trees, Starbucks, mountain ranges, Starbucks, Boeing and oh yeah, Starbucks. He has a lovely wife (what man in his right mind would dare say otherwise) along with his two kids at home, and his oldest son living in Portland. For two years he wrote a monthly humor column for allpets.com and started an online magazine for the squad he flies with in Warbirds, a WWII flight simulator. He enjoys reading and writing (obviously) and camping when he gets the chance.

CPSIA information can be obtained at www.ICGtesting.com
Printed in the USA
LVOW100406020412

275653LV00003B/3/P